Six-Finger

Lance Horner

Six-Fingered Stud

Pan Books London and Sydney

First published 1975 by W H Allen & Co Ltd
This edition published 1977 by Pan Books Ltd,
Cavaye Place, London SW10 9PG
© Lance Horner 1975
ISBN 0 330 25022 1
Printed in Great Britain by
Richard Clay (The Chaucer Press) Ltd, Bungay, Suffolk

I

Calico whoaed his horse to a stop under the shade of an enormous live oak whose trailing banners of tattered grey moss cast an undulating pattern of shade on the dirt road. Calico? No, he must not think of himself as Calico any more. Now that he was again ostensibly a free white man instead of a fugitive Negro slave, he must think of himself only as Tommy Verder. He must never forget that he was the same 'Tommy Verder' who had set out from New York so many dangerous months ago.

His memories of life as Tommy Verder were pleasant ones, quite unlike his tragic recollections as Calico, the slave playmate of the real Tommy Verder. The two boys apparently shared some bastard relationship, since they both had had six fingers on the right hand. Well, those days were gone forever. At least, he hoped so.

For the second time – no, the third – he was about to start a new life, thanks to Dovie. Poor Dovie! He had really hated to leave her pseudo-incestuous bed, but it was far better to have abandoned her to remain free, instead of reverting to slavery at Dove Cote plantation, where, as Dovie's 'son', he had been boss man for a few months. There had been really no alternative to leaving behind all those who knew about the telltale black spots on his otherwise white body – all his erstwhile in-laws the Ackers, all the Maxwells at Falconhurst, and yes, all those at Dove Cote where he had grown up as a slave and where he would now finish his days in slavery were he ever brought back to Alabama.

He felt something crawling under his shirt, and scratched. There must have been bedbugs in the tavern he had just left. He had slept so soundly that he had not noticed them during the night, but a few were still feeding on him this morning. He should strip off his clothes and get rid of them, but he was on the public highway and there was no privacy handy. By nightfall, he should be near New Orleans. Thank God for that! Once there he would no longer have to keep looking over his shoulder to see if, by a chance in a thousand, he was being followed. Not that there was much danger of that, he reasoned, but there was always a chance that an enraged Old Man Acker, learning of his daughter's defloration before her subsequent marriage to himself, the pseudo-Tommy Verder, might be hot on his trail. However, Missie probably had not told her father of her premarital defloration, so he wouldn't know about it, unless in time she gave birth to a black baby. For the present, he was safe on that count. Well, that had been a difficult time to live through, but he had survived it and here he was now, almost in New Orleans. Once there, he knew that neither the Ackers nor the Maxwells could find him. He was used to city ways, and there would be a thousand places to hide in New Orleans.

He did not grieve too much over the loss of Missie Acker – although she was now his wife, the fact that he was black had already cancelled their marriage – but he did grieve over the loss of his friendship with Hammond Maxwell, the only real friend he had ever had. Hammond had been a good friend to him until, along with the rest, he had discovered that he was black: those few black blotches on his body made him as black as the crudest *bozal* just out of the hold of a slave ship from Africa.

He finished his scratching – damn those filthy bedbugs anyway – and sat up straight in his saddle, the better to ease the tightness of his pantaloons around his back pocket. He took out the worn leather wallet and, glancing up and down the road to be sure that nobody was coming, opened it to count the money inside. Nearly two thousand dollars. That was certainly enough to give him a stake in New Orleans. He wouldn't arrive there penniless, and it ought to keep him until he had made the right connections and started something profitable. He had no doubts about his ability, but was undecided as to just what he would do. Would he have another stable of whores like he had had in New York? Not if he could help it. There was no great amount of money to be made by prostitution unless one had twenty or more on his string, and it would take time to acquire that many. No, there must be some other way to make big money. Just what it might be, he did not know, but something would turn up. It always had.

The soggy pone and the watered-down chicory coffee

which made up his breakfast had left him feeling hungry, but he would have to stifle his appetite until he reached another tavern or ordinary. Probably the food there would be no better – it never was – but at least he might get some ham and eggs for his midday meal. Ham and eggs were the staple diet of this part of the country. He had already sickened of them and hoped he would be able to change his menu when he got to New Orleans. He should; New Orleans was a French city, and the French were noted for their culinary art.

He stood up in his stirrups again to ease the wallet back into his pocket, carefully buttoning the protective flap. He would willingly have sat in the cool shade for an hour, but if he wanted to get to New Orleans, he could not spend the time daydreaming along the road. He pulled up on the reins, started the horse with a couple of peremptory clucks and trotted off. He even whistled a tune, timing it to the clop-clop of the horse's hooves.

It was a glorious day; the sky a deep cerulean blue with not a cloud to be seen. He had heard that New Orleans had a carnival to usher in Lent, and he hoped he would be in time for it. In his present euphoria over his escape and freedom, he would welcome a few days of carnival. It was a time when he could surely make the important connection he wanted to make – a time when everyone was gay and carefree and usually drunker than a hootie owl. And that was one thing he warned himself he must not do. He must not get drunk and perhaps it would also be better, difficult as it might be, to swear off women. The black spots on his body were far more dangerous in the South than they had ever been in New York and, he again reminded himself, it had been a combination of drunkenness and these same black spots on his body that had nearly been the cause of his death or even worse – his living out the rest of his life as a Negro slave. But damn it! that was all behind him now and he had a free road ahead.

He was now passing people on the road. They were mostly blacks, going to the cane and cotton fields. Each of them, as he passed, would look up, grin, and greet him with a 'Mornin', Masta suh'. Even the few white men whom he met doffed their hats and greeted him affably. And why not? He knew that he was young and handsome and, most important of all, white – at least as far as they could see – and he had an engaging smile along with a cheerful reply to all their greetings.

Some distance down the dusty road, he saw a carriage and horses drawn over to the side. Sensing that something was wrong, he slapped his horse's neck and spurred the animal into a gallop. When he arrived alongside the carriage, he pulled up in a cloud of dust, quieting his horse.

A woman was the only occupant of the carriage. A stalwart young Negro coachman was off the box and in the road examining one of the horse's hooves. Whenever Tommy Verder saw a woman, regardless of her age or appearance, he developed an entirely new and dashing personality. He was able to assay this woman in a glance. She was handsome, dressed in the height of fashion, and probably between thirty-five and forty. With a sweeping lift of his hat and a smile that displayed his white, even teeth, he spoke to her.

'Thomas Verder, ma'am, at your service. You seem to be in need of some assistance and I was wondering if I could be of help to you.'

Nobody could resist Tommy's smile, particularly when it was accompanied by his voice, which in all his dealings with women took on a particularly rich and vibrant timbre. The woman in the carriage smiled back at him and laid her hand, heavily encrusted with rings, on the side of the carriage. Tommy noticed the hand; it was white and well cared for, although it showed signs of age which were not apparent in the carefully powdered face. Equally important; the diamonds were costly, so she must be rich, a fact underlined by the elegant carriage and the fine pair of horses. A thought flashed through his mind. He might be able to delay his arrival in New Orleans for one night.

'I believe that one of the horses has a loose shoe. Solomon,' she pointed to the black who had the horse's hoof between his legs, 'is seeing if he can fix it,' she replied, continuing her smile.

'Then let me see if I can help him. I'm not too experienced in shoeing horses, but I've seen it done and perhaps we can repair the damage sufficiently for you to get home, provided, of course, you do not live far from here.'

Again she smiled. 'Only about half a mile. I was just returning from an overnight visit to my married daughter who lives a few miles down the road. I live at Poinciana Plantation, which is the next big house on the right. I'm Mrs Latimer.'

Tommy slid from his horse and went over to the carriage. He reached for the hand on the damask arm of the carriage and slowly lifted it to his lips, again appraising the diamonds as he did so.

'And I am Tommy Verder of Dove Cote Plantation in Alabama, on my way to New Orleans.' His kiss lingered for a moment on her hand, and he noticed that she did not withdraw it. 'I hope I may be of some slight assistance to you.'

She nodded in the direction of the coachman who was remounting the box. 'It would appear that Solomon has already solved the difficulty, but my thanks just the same.' She glanced at a tiny jewelled watch which was pinned to the lilac silk bodice of her gown. 'It is going on midday, Mr Verder. May I invite you to have a bite of lunch with me? As a matter of fact the only other place where you might eat is some ten miles down the road, and I'm certain that the food you would get there would be most unpalatable.'

Again Tommy bowed. 'Thank you, Mrs Latimer. I've been on a steady diet of ham and eggs for so long I would welcome a chance to clean up and change my clothes before I appear at your table. Would that be possible?'

'More than possible, Mr Verder, it can become an actual fact. Why don't you hitch your horse to the rear of the carriage and take the rest of your short journey to my house on the seat here beside me. If you have ridden horseback all the way from Alabama, I'm sure you must be as sickened of the horse as the beast is of you.'

'An excellent idea.' He could sense that there was more in this woman's invitation than she had implied by her lips. He led his horse around and fastened the reins to the rear spring of the carriage. Then he opened the little door in the side, took down the flight of steps that were folded inside and climbed up to sit beside her. It was a shallow landau and he had to sit with his long legs straight out in front of him. The whole interior of the carriage further proclaimed the wealth indicated by the woman's clothes and her jewellery. Here was an unexpected something that had come into his life, and he was certain that he could turn it to his advantage. He eased his body from the strained position that it was in, conscious of his soiled trousers so near the whispering lilac taffeta of her dress.

'Do put your hat back on, Mr Verder.' She smiled at him. 'The sun is hot and I would not want you to invite sunstroke. Besides, you have a pale complexion which burns easily, and a sunburn would be painful.'

'Thank you.' He replaced his hat and she adjusted the bit of black lace which served as her parasol. The coachman started the horses. With a look backward to see that his horse was following, Tommy turned his full attention to her.

'Just one thing that troubles me, Mrs Latimer, and that is what your husband is going to think when you arrive back home with a strange man beside you.'

She made a little moue of disapproval. 'I happen to be a widow, Mr Verder. My husband has been dead for several years and, now that my daughter is married, I live alone and run my own plantation with the help of my overseer. We raise cotton and, as our land is still fertile, we raise good crops.'

'You are a courageous lady to have taken over the management of a plantation.' He smiled sideways at her, noticing that her hand, which rested on her knee, was dangerously near to his trouser leg.

'I managed it for several years before my husband died. He was an invalid and, little by little, he became more and more incapacitated. I took over the reins of management, so it was no very difficult thing for me to do it all when he died. You may not believe it, but I am as versatile in getting a field ploughed and planted as I am at serving afternoon tea to my friends. It's all in getting used to it.'

'My admiration, ma'am. It isn't every woman that could do it.' He glanced at her and saw that her eyes were appraising the length of his stretched-out legs, finally coming to rest on the bulge at his crotch. They stayed there a moment and then sought his.

'It isn't every woman that is free to do what she pleases as I am.' Her hand slipped just the fraction of an inch closer to his leg. It was so near now that he could feel its warmth through the light drill of his trousers. 'Believe me, I'm no namby-pamby woman who faints at the least provocation. No, Mr Verder, I'm not. I couldn't manage a big plantation with some two hundred slaves if I were.'

He did not answer. They were turning at the gates of a long avenue of live oaks leading to an imposing house. The mansion was not quite as impressive as the Greek-revival Alabama houses which boasted porticos of classic pillars. It was more in the French colonial style – one-storied, with a wide veranda. He could see black adolescents sweeping the gravel driveway with twig brooms, and the whole appearance was one of absolute tidiness resulting from constant care.

The coachman stopped under the shelter of a covered *portecochère* and, when he had quietened the horses, he sprang from the box to open the door and assist Mrs Latimer down the tiny flight of steps. Tommy jumped down beside her and together they ascended the steps of the long gallery. The front door of the house was opened by another handsome young black in livery who bowed low to Mrs Latimer and welcomed her home with a 'Good day, Mistress ma'am. I trust yo' found Miz Eliza in good health.'

'She is fine, Pompey.'

Once inside the house, in the cool of its semi-darkness, it took Tommy a moment to adjust his eyes, but he could see shining floors, rich furniture and the gleam of gold frames around ancestral portraits.

'I'm going to give you an hour to tidy up,' she said, removing her hat and passing it with her sunshade to the servant. 'Then you will come down and we shall lunch. I must speak to the cook and let her know that I am home and that we shall be eating in the dining room rather than from the usual tray she prepares for my luncheon.'

'I hope I'm not inconveniencing you.'

'Laws no! Having a guest is always a welcome break in the monotony of my days.' Her hand touched his arm lightly. 'I just hope there'll be enough food to satisfy a big man like you.'

'I'm sure there will be.' Tommy bowed slightly. 'And I'll have your charming company along with the food.'

Again her hand touched his arm and he was aware of the warmth of it.

'You have charming manners, Mr Verder. And now I shall have Pompey take you to one of the guest rooms. He will bring plenty of hot water and towels, so do perform your ablutions and when you have finished, ring for Pompey. He will show you to the dining room where I shall be waiting for you.'

'My sincere thanks, Mrs Latimer. You do not know what a luxury it will be to feel clean again. Believe me, I shall not take too long, because I anticipate lunching with you and getting to know you better.'

She glanced at him from under her long lashes. 'You do flatter me, but I love it. I have lived here so long alone that a compliment from a man is enough to set my head a-spinning. *Au'voir*. I'll see you a little later.'

There seemed to be nothing more that Tommy could say. She made no move to depart and to cover up the momentary awkwardness of silence, he reached for her hand and conveyed it to his lips. Yes, he was right, the hand was not withdrawn immediately. He felt a fullness in his groin which he knew must be evident through the tight material of his trousers. Again he could feel her eyes appraising him. Well, he had nothing to be ashamed of, so with a confident swagger he followed Pompey down the polished floors of the hall to the guest room.

2

Tommy luxuriated in the tin tub of warm water, the scented soap and the fleecy towels which Pompey brought to him. It was the first time since he had left his wedding party at the Acker's that he had had the opportunity for a real bath. At most of the taverns where he had stopped, he had had to satisfy himself with hasty ablutions under the pump at the horse trough or a scant attempt at cleanliness with a minuscule basin of water brought to his room. Now he felt clean all over and far more respectable. He opened his saddle-bags and took out a change of small clothes, a clean shirt and a reserve pair of white pantaloons which he had been saving for New Orleans. Well, he argued with himself, if he wore them for one afternoon he would not soil them too much. They were badly creased from packing, but they were clean.

He opened a small leather case and took out his razor, shaving himself easily in the still warm water and viewing his face in a tripod shaving mirror which he could tilt to just the right angle to catch the light. The clean clothes which had been a part of his wedding finery felt good against his scrubbed skin. And when he had combed his still-damp hair he felt ready for any occasion, not the least of which would be luncheon with the – as he hoped – already infatuated Mrs Latimer.

Tommy had been born with a sixth sense about women, just as he had been born with six fingers on his right hand. He knew instinctively when he had appealed to a woman, and he also knew just what that woman desired of him. Usually, it was one thing: she wanted to go to bed with him. He had come to realize that most women he met wanted this even though they would not admit it to themselves. There was a certain electric something which passed from them to him, communicating their secret desires. And this was the wordless message he got from this erstwhile stranger – this Mrs Latimer. Perhaps her desires would never be expressed, but he knew that she wanted him. As for his wanting her – he shrugged his shoulders – one woman was about the same to him as another. To be sure, none could quite compare with his bride of a few hours, Melissa Acker. He had been really in love with her, or so he told himself. But if he couldn't have Missy Acker, who was now far beyond his reach, almost any woman would do. That she might be young and beautiful could make it more exciting, but almost any woman, unless she were old and repulsive, appealed to him. This Mrs Latimer, although older than he was, was certainly a beautiful woman, and – he remembered the diamonds on her hand – undoubtedly wealthy.

He surveyed himself in the mirror, a long pier glass, which showed him from head to foot. Despite the fact that his shirt and pantaloons were wrinkled, he was quite pleased with the result. He wished he might have been a few inches taller so that he would exceed six feet, but that couldn't be helped. He admired the way his muscular body was evidenced under the thin garments he was wearing. He was also well satisfied with his own good looks; the strength of his neck and the way his head was so powerfully supported. He admired his face, the clear whiteness of his skin and the brightness of his eyes. He smiled at himself and was proud of the sensual curve of his moist red lips. He nodded in approval at his image in the glass, then ran his comb again through his hair, setting a wave in its dampness. Yes, he was thoroughly satisfied with himself.

What a shame that when he undressed, those telltale black spots on his body branded him as a Negro, even though the rest of him was white. Well, he didn't have to show those spots to anyone, and nobody would ever again know about them. That was a promise he made to himself. Even in his most intimate moments in bed with a woman, he always made certain that the candles were blown out. Although many women had begged him to leave them lighted the better to enjoy him, he was adamant. If he could not be protected by darkness, he would always wear his shirt and long practice had made him adept at reciting many reasons why. His favourite explanation was that this particular idiosyncrasy of his enabled him to perform better as a lover. At least, he had never had any complaints about his performance. He knew that in this department he couldn't be equalled, and he had never met a woman that he could not satisfy. So, to hell with those black spots!

To be sure, the spots branded him, but, thank God, they did not detract from his appearance with his clothes on. He leaned closer to the mirror and winked at himself solemnly, as though asking confirmation. Then, he smiled and nodded to his reflection, which nodded back to assure him that he was all he thought he should be.

He wished he had brought some scent with him, but that was a luxury which he could not carry in his crowded saddlebags. He noticed, however, a bottle of Florida water on the dressing table. He broke the seal, splashed some on his hands, and rubbed his newly-shaven face with it. Now he was prepared for Mrs Latimer. Quite!

She had said to summon the butler, Pompey, when he was ready, so he looked around the room for the bell-pull which he knew must be there. He found it beside a French gilt *étagère* which contained a collection of dainty porcelain bibelots. He peered at them more closely and smiled to himself. They all sounded the same keynote and some of them were actually pornographic – dainty Dresden nymphs and fauns disporting themselves most goatlike and licentiously. Quite a collection for a widow lady! Yes, indeed, quite a collection! He wondered if they expressed some subconscious desire on her part to be pursued and raped as was surely happening to one of the little nymphs. True, he was no goat, but he imagined he could do even better than the half-goat who had the nymph clutched tightly in his embrace.

He was still smiling to himself as he pulled the bellcord. On further thought, he returned to the mirror and carefully adjusted his trousers so that the bulge in his crotch was even more apparent. He might as well leave no doubt in Mrs Latimer's mind of his capabilities. If she enjoyed the gambols of china fauns and nymphs, it was not only possible, but probable that she would enjoy the real thing far more. He thought he saw a secondary role for the young and handsome coachman, as well as the equally young and handsome butler. He nodded. Indeed, Mrs Latimer might turn out to be a woman after his own heart.

He heard steps in the hall and when he opened the door to his room, he appraised the butler with new interest. Yes, he fitted very well into the picture of a sporting bedmate for the lady of the house. He was tall, as muscular as a field hand and undoubtedly a mulatto, because his face was finely featured and his lips not too thick.

'Yo' rang, Masta suh?' The butler was properly obsequious.

'Yes, Mrs Latimer said that when I was ready, you would show me the way to the dining room.'

'This way, Masta suh.' Tommy welcomed the 'Masta suh'. It showed him that he was accepted as a white man by a black, and he knew that the eyes of a black man were far more experienced in detecting coloured blood than any white man's.

Tommy followed Pompey down the long windowless corridor with doors opening on both sides to a large and ornately furnished drawing room and through it into an equally large dining room where, at a long table set for two, Mrs Latimer was already sitting. He felt her eyes appraising him as he walked across the room and, instead of seating himself immediately at the table, he walked around it to her side and once again lifted her hand to his lips.

'This is indeed a boon to a weary traveller,' he murmured, holding her hand which she made no effort to recover. 'You will probably never know how really pleasant it is to sit at a table like this after so many hit-and-miss meals in roadside taverns. But of course, the pleasantest thing of all is the pleasure of your company.' Her hand still rested in his. 'It is not often that a mere wayfarer is given a taste of heaven.'

With seeming reluctance, she withdrew her hand slowly and waved it to indicate the seat across the polished table.

'But it is so far away, dear lady.' He drew down the corners of his mouth in mock distaste. 'A whole expanse of wood between the two of us. I shall have to shout to make you hear . . .'

'A fact which we can remedy. Pompey!' She beckoned to the butler, who had moved away. 'Please change the table setting. Mr Verder is going to sit here, just around the corner from me.' She indicated a place at the table, then looked up at Tommy and smiled. 'How thoughtful of you, Mr Verder. It is really not necessary that we be so formal, is it?'

'And doesn't that apply to our names as well.' His smile was infectious. 'Everyone calls me Tommy and I scarcely know whom you are addressing when you say "Mr Verder". Couldn't it just be Tommy?'

'It can and it will. But you must reciprocate by calling me Helen.'

'Thank you, Helen. See, it is already much easier and pleasanter than Mrs Latimer.' He leaned back to let Pompey place a cup of bouillon before him. He tasted it with the silver spoon and found it delicious. He wondered if his hostess had a male cook, too, and if so, if he would be as young and handsome as her butler and coachman.

The meal progressed. Pompey deftly removed plates and substituted clean ones. There followed a slice of fish, delicately

16

poached in wine, a thin slice of veal with a sauce of tomatoes and onions, a ragout of beef, a salad of crisp greens and, to top it all off, a moulded pudding which Mrs Latimer served herself.

'I was determined that you would not have ham and eggs again.' She passed him the dish of pudding which she had served. 'You see I remember.'

He tasted the pudding before he answered her. 'The only difficulty, Helen, is that you are going to spoil me for the time when I must go back to ham and eggs.' He felt a slight pressure against his knee. It was immediately removed, and it had been so fleeting that he did not know whether he imagined it or not; but when he put his hand down under the table, it encountered hers. He looked at her and she seemed to nod at him. It was an almost imperceptible movement of her head, but it implied a tacit understanding between them. Her nod to Pompey was certain and emphatic.

'Thank you, Pompey,' she said. 'Now, if you will bring cigars and a light for Mr Verder, you may be excused. You can clear away after Mr Verder has finished smoking.' She straightened up, freed her hand from his grasp, waited until Pompey had brought a silver-mounted mahogany box, and opened it to release the delicate odour of fine Havana cigars. Tommy selected one, clipped it and accepted a light from a candle burning in a silver candlestick which the butler held for him. With a discreet bow to Mrs Latimer, Pompey disappeared behind a green-baize door and Tommy was alone with his hostess.

As soon as the door had closed, Mrs Latimer put her finger to her lips, tiptoed over to the door, and quietly opened it. Seeing nobody, she smiled and returned to the table. 'Servants,' she said, 'have a way of eavesdropping, and I wanted to be sure that there was nobody there.' She sat down once more while Tommy drew the aromatic smoke into his lungs and expelled it in floating blue rings. Once more her hand sought his lap. He squeezed it, daring to move it a bit higher on his thigh. She did not take it away.

'You must think me a very forward person, Tommy.' She blushed as she apologized. 'But sometimes something happens between two persons which immediately sweeps away all hesitation and formalities. You see, I wanted you from the very moment you stopped your horse to rescue a lady in distress. We have no time for long and wordy discussions, so I have come directly to the point. I want you. Do you want me?'

Without answering her, he moved her hand farther along his thigh until it encountered a throbbing hardness.

'Isn't that your answer?' he whispered.

His hand was searching for her warm flesh under the multitude of petticoats and the whalebone stiffness of the hoop skirt she was wearing. He finally encountered the moist warmth he sought, and his fingers moved in a rhythmical caress which caused her to gasp and edge her chair closer to his. His lips found hers, and his tongue darted between her teeth to explore the smooth, warm depths of her mouth.

Now her hand on his thigh became more active, struggling with buttons and frantically undoing them. After a moment, it was his turn to gasp and push her hand away.

'You are flirting with danger,' he murmured in her ear.

'But it is a danger which I do not fear,' she replied.

'But which I do,' he answered. 'It is something which will be all the more pleasant if it is delayed a bit.'

'You mean . . .?'

'I do not consider New Orleans so pressing but that I could remain overnight. Surely, that would be better than some half-consummated affair here at your table.'

She withdrew her hand and freed herself from his fingers.

'Then you do not have to jump on your horse and leave immediately after our luncheon together?'

He shook his head and kissed her again. Slowly, they stood up while he rebuttoned his trousers and came close to her.

'There are some things,' he promised her, 'that are better at night when all your house has retired and there is no danger of any of the servants popping in.'

She waited until he had done kissing her.

'Pompey will not come back until I ring for him.'

'But for all you know he may be listening on the other side of the door. One needs to be free from all fears to enjoy love to the utmost.'

'Then you will stay?'

'If I am asked.'

'And oh, I do ask you. Will you stay, Tommy?'

'I'll stay.'

'You'll not regret it.'

She became limp in his arms while he counted the diamonds on the hand resting on his shoulder.

'And I'm sure you won't either.' He countered her promise with one of his own, then left her standing alone while he stepped to the wall and pulled the bell-cord.

Linking his arm in hers, he slowly left the dining room. They went out into a small, leafy patio where the vines sheltered them from the sun and a little fountain splashed with a lilting rhythm into a turquoise pool.

'And now that I am to be here all day and all night,' he finally said, 'why don't you have your horse saddled, and mine, too? We will ride and look over your plantation and spend the whole afternoon in anticipation of what lies before us tonight. Maybe we can find a shady spot under some tree where we can lie in the grass and explore each other a little further. Our final discovery of each other, however, must wait until tonight. Believe me, it will be more enjoyable.'

'Is that what you would like to do?' She clung to him. 'The curtains in my room could be pulled, and we could enjoy ourselves this afternoon there.'

'But after an afternoon of anticipation, we shall enjoy the night even more. If we did as you suggested, tonight would be only an anticlimax. Let us get the full joy of each other then and not now.'

'Can I wait?' She pulled him closer.

'We can both wait,' he answered, 'because we have so much to look forward to.'

'I already know what I have to look forward to.' She gave him a little pat.

'Perhaps you'll have more to anticipate than you realize now.' He grinned at her. 'Now, go and change into your riding clothes, and I shall be waiting for you here.'

She was loath to let him go, but he gave her a gentle shove. 'Remember, you'll be glad you did.' He smiled down at her.

In a moment she was gone, and he sat down on a wrought-iron chair to enjoy the rest of his cigar. It had been easier than he thought it would be. It had not been necessary for him to make any of the advances. She had done it all. Perhaps he should spend more than one night with her. No, one would be enough, and it should provide some reward for him, in addition to pleasure – while his little job would not be too difficult – she was an attractive woman and he knew full well that he could satisfy her. He felt that somehow this chance encounter was going to stand him in good stead. He could not realize then that Helen Latimer was going to be the key that would unlock doors which would otherwise have been shut for him.

He flicked the ash from his cigar which he then stamped out on the floor tiles. At least, he would not have to perform in daylight. But then, he wondered, thinking of the strength and good looks of Pompey the butler and Solomon the coachman, would she mind so terribly if she discovered that he was a Negro? Probably not, but it was better to stay on the safe side. After a ride around the plantation, after dinner, and after a time spent in the cool of the evening on the balcony, she would be all the more willing, provided, of course, he could hold her off that long. He was confident he could. Women always did what he wanted, and this woman was no exception.

Good God! Was he glad he was Tommy Verder, and not Calico! Life was good and had all the prospects of getting much better.

3

A faint light in the eastern sky had awakened Tommy, and he became slowly aware of his surroundings. He tried to extricate himself from the tight embrace of Helen's arms. She too awakened and drowsily pulled him closer to her, but he demurred and gently removed her hand.

'It is nearly daylight,' he whispered, 'and it's far better for us both that I be found sleeping in my own bed and you in yours when your Pompey arrives with his morning tray of coffee. I'm leaving you now, my dear, and it will give us both time for forty winks before the household day begins.'

She clung to him, hoping to arouse him again despite his resistance, but he gently pushed her away. He stood up and his feet groped over the floor for the clothes he had thrown off so hurriedly the night before. He donned his shirt and trousers, but found some difficulty in buttoning them. Then, with his underclothing, socks and boots in one hand, he leaned down to implant a swift kiss on Helen's cheek. Quietly, he tiptoed across the floor, opened the door slowly so that the hinges would not creak, and crept down the hall to his own room. Once there, he heaved a sigh of relief, took off his trousers, and sought a chamber pot which he needed badly. He welcomed the comfort of his bed but did not immediately go to sleep. He had so much to think about.

It had been, he congratulated himself, a successful night. He had thoroughly enjoyed it, and he knew that Helen had enjoyed it equally, if not more. He was a consummate actor – he knew that – but last night he had not had to resort entirely to acting. He had not had a woman for a long time, and Helen's perfumed body had responded to every nuance of love-making which he inaugurated. She had been insatiable, but so had he. He had matched her hungry summons not once, or twice, but at least three times, if he remembered correctly. And she was obviously ready for more when he had left that morning.

But, enough was enough! He always liked to leave his women wanting more. It made them more amenable afterwards. All in all, as he remembered it, yesterday had been a pleasant day which had led up to an eventful night. They had gone riding in the afternoon, found the shady spot which he had suggested and rested on a smooth bed of leaves under the huge live oak. Here they had tantalized each other almost beyond the limits of his endurance, but he had been adamant that they must leave the dénouement until night. So they had torn themselves away from each other, sought their horses again and rode back to the big house. Here each had had a short nap alone – she would have had it otherwise, but he was stubborn – and then dinner together by candlelight and a long evening on the cool gallery, where they had talked of many things – her husband, her life in New Orleans before she had been married, and his life in New York, embellished with much fiction of his own invention.

He had told her that he was leaving his mother's plantation to go to the city. He was not, he said, cut out for plantation life as it lacked the excitement of a day-by-day changing scene of life in a city. He was bored with a plantation full of blacks, and he longed for company. She admitted that it had been difficult for her, too, to adjust to the isolation of plantation life, but now she was accustomed to it and did not want to return to the city. Tommy wondered if her handsome butler and coachman had anything to do with her being reconciled to rustic living. Probably so.

Then, when they had watched the moon come up with its silver light casting black shadows under the trees, they had entered the house. She would have lighted a candle, but he persuaded her not to, and they made their way down the long hall to her room, clasped in a tight embrace. Once inside, she would have again lighted a candle, but he did not give her an opportunity. His hands were stripping her bare. He then shed his own – all but the protective shirt.

The rest of the night was exactly like so many other nights that he had spent in so many other beds. It had been pleasant and he had enjoyed it, but now that it was over, he wanted to sleep and forget all about it. Despite the great mental activity of plotting a golden future, it was not long before he was snoring.

When a knock on his door awoke him a few hours later, the sun was streaming through the jalousies. He clutched at his body to reassure himself that he was wearing his shirt before he gave permission to enter. It was Pompey, as he had suspected, bearing a silver tray with a pot of coffee and the information that Mrs Latimer would be awaiting him at breakfast in half an hour. He gulped down a cup of coffee and had barely enough time to wash his face and dress before presenting himself, radiant and glowing, before his hostess.

She was seated at the table behind a large silver coffee urn, and, when she looked up at him and smiled, he noticed the sooty circles under her eyes. Well, it had been a strenuous night, but he considered the circles under his own eyes as a badge of courage and a reward for meritorious service and all-night endurance.

'Tommy, dear,' she greeted him, 'I imagine that you are ravenous this morning.'

'Ravenous indeed,' he answered, looking around the room to make sure that Pompey was not there before he kissed her lightly on the cheek. 'And you?'

'Equally so, although I doubt if I shall be able to eat anything.'

'And why not?' he asked.

'Because something tells me that you are about to leave me today.'

'That I must.' His half smile implied that he regretted his departure as much as she. 'I should not have delayed here overnight, but it was such a strong temptation I could not resist it.'

'Why must you hurry to New Orleans, my dear? Surely you could spend a week or two here.'

He shook his head. 'I must go, dear lady. I have so much to accomplish that I feel I must start at once. You see, I have got to find a place for myself in the city. I have no friends there, and I do not know what I am going to do when I get there. The small amount of money which I have with me will not last an eternity. I am entirely at sea, and the sooner I can find a safe harbour, the better I am going to feel.'

She turned the spigot on the coffee urn, refilled his cup, and passed it to him. 'Black as usual?' she asked.

Tommy nodded. Pompey came through the green-baize door with a covered silver serving dish. He helped Mrs Latimer to scrambled eggs, then served Tommy. While Pompey was fussing around, Tommy could communicate with his hostess only by meaningful glances and little smiles. Pompey went out for a platter of bacon, then once again for hot biscuits, honey, and butter. During this time, there was no chance to talk, but Tommy was sure that Pompey was looking at him with a baleful eye. Undoubtedly, Tommy thought, the man was jealous of him. He certainly must have realized all that had gone on during the night despite their efforts to hide it. Tommy was glad he was leaving. He would not put it past

Pompey to put arsenic in his coffee should he remain. He looked capable of it.

Finally, however, the butler could find no further excuse to linger in the dining room. Whether or not he was eavesdropping behind the door, Tommy could not tell. Mrs Latimer had not taken the precaution this morning of checking his whereabouts.

'I'm desolated that you cannot stay.' She buttered a hot biscuit and spooned honey on it.

'And so am I. I can think of nothing more delightful than being here with you, but you can understand why I feel I must go. I have to establish a place for myself in the city.'

She nodded halfheartedly.

'Perhaps I can help you in some small way,' she volunteered.

It was just what he had been waiting for. He wondered what form her assistance might take. Was she going to offer him money? He hardly thought so, but, if she did, he would willingly take it. He wondered for a fleeting second just how much she valued his stud services for a night. Highly enough, he hoped, to show true appreciation. But even if she didn't pay him, he would don a role of gentility and say nothing, although he did feel that some recompense was due him.

'How?' he asked, and then added, 'dear lady.'

'I have friends in New Orleans. As you know, I used to live there before I married Mr Latimer. I was thinking of giving you a letter of introduction to someone who is very important in New Orleans. It might open a door that you could not possibly enter otherwise.'

Inwardly he considered a mere letter pretty poor payment for his services of last night, but he smiled back at her as though she had given him one of those rings sparkling on her fingers.

'You think a letter might be of use to me?'

'The letter I propose would surely be. I'm certain you would not quibble about what it might represent?'

'Then, dear lady, I shall accept it most gratefully. I'm sure any friend of yours would be most worthwhile and most helpful, too. May I ask to whom the letter would be addressed?'

24

'To Captain Dominique You,' she answered and then, noting the blank look on his face, she added, 'Do you know who Dominique You is?'

He shook his head, woefully ignorant.

'You have heard of Jean LaFitte?'

Again he shook his head.

'Then you are entirely unacquainted with New Orleans and the people who matter there.'

'Perhaps you can enlighten me.'

'It's a long story.' She poured him another cup of coffee. 'So long, in fact, that I hardly know where to begin.' She hesitated a moment and then talked as he finished his breakfast.

She began by telling him about the brothers LaFitte, Jean and Pierre, who not only owned a blacksmith shop on the little street which was named St Philip and which ran alongside the cathedral, but also owned a large store on Royal Street where they sold New Orleans' finest merchandise.

There were those, she said, who regarded Jean LaFitte as merely a pirate, but this, she assured him, was not entirely true. Yes, to be sure, he was a pirate of sorts, but he operated legally under letters of marque from the Republic of Cartagena and that allowed him to prey on all Spanish ships. To be sure, he did not take them to Cartagena to claim them as prizes. That was too far away, so he brought them to Barataria, near the mouth of the Mississippi.

Of course, she admitted, sometimes he mistook a French or English ship for a Spanish vessel and captured those as well, but it hardly mattered to him; he was not too particular. These ships, too, were brought to Grand Isle, which was located on Barataria Bay some sixty miles south of New Orleans. Here he maintained a settlement which was the home port of the privateers, and it is here that he had his base of operations. He had changed it from an unlawful community of pirates to a respectable community (if such a community could be said to be respectable). In fact, the leading merchants of New Orleans were accustomed to going there to buy merchandise and were treated with respect and all considerations of safety.

Now, the merchandise of slave ships, profitable though it

was, represented only a small part of his business. Since Congress passed the law that no more slaves were to be imported into the United States, LaFitte had branched out, so that at present, he was doing a big business selling contraband Negro slaves which had been confiscated from slavers plying the route from Africa to Havana. The plantations of the south were avid for slaves, and they didn't care where they got them. It was impossible to supply the market, and LaFitte was making more money selling slaves than he had ever made trading in the fine laces, satins and other European goods which he had brought from Barataria to his shop on Royal Street. He maintained huge barracoons at Barataria, but the finer slaves were brought to New Orleans to be sold through his blacksmith shop. Fine specimens, even though they were rough *bozals* straight from Africa, were bringing around eight hundred dollars each.

Without exception – she emphasized the point by bringing down her dainty fist forcefully on the table – Jean LaFitte was just about the most important personage in New Orleans. He was openly accepted there, if not socially, at least among the leading businessmen of the city. Yes, she knew him well, but she didn't know him as well as she did his principal lieutenant, Captain Dominique You, and it was to this Captain You that she was giving Tommy a letter of introduction. You was a good friend of hers, and if she asked him to pay particular attention to Tommy, she was certain he would.

After hearing this, Tommy changed his mind about the letter. Perhaps this introduction would be even better than one of her rings. He would sell the ring, spend the money, and have nothing left to show for it. But if this Dominique You was as important a person as she said he was, and if the brothers LaFitte were the ruling men of New Orleans, undoubtedly the letter would prove more valuable than some paltry diamond ring.

He questioned her. 'Do you think there might be a place for me in their organization?'

She nodded. 'I'm sure they would be glad to have your services. You're a most delightful person, Tommy, and I would be only too happy if you were to stay here with me for a while. I think I know you pretty well, even after this short acquaintance. You see, I know men. You are, I am afraid, somewhat of a rogue. No, no. I do not mean that in a disparaging way, but you'll do anything to get ahead in this world, and I'm sure you would have no conscientious qualms about working with the LaFittes. Would you?'

He smiled back at her and nodded in agreement.

'Then let me ring for paper and ink, and I'll write the letter.' She pulled the bell-cord, and when Pompey appeared, she instructed him to bring her writing case. When he returned with the leather box, she spread out the silver inkhorn and quills on the table.

Tommy watched and listened to the quill scratch across the sheet of fine note paper. He wondered just what she was saying, but he was satisfied that she would say only good about him. When she had finished, she shook sand over the paper, read it over, and passed it to him. A smile crossed his face as he read it. He was more than satisfied.

> M. Dominique You
> c/o. M. Jean LaFitte
> The Blacksmith Shop
> St Philip St
> New Orleans

Dear Friend Dominique,

The bearer of this letter, Thomas Verder Esq, is a very good friend of mine and he is coming to New Orleans to seek his fortune. It occurred to me that you might have a place for him in your organization.

I am sure you will be delighted with him and I know that he will be a good man for you. Anything that you can do for him will be appreciated by your old friend,

Helen Latimer

... who sends you her best wishes and hopes that you are in good health and enjoying yourself.

When Tommy handed the letter back, she folded the sheet of paper and sealed it with a blob of red wax, into which she pressed a gold seal bearing her initials. She stood up from the table. He followed suit and came over to stand beside her.

'This,' she said as she handed him the letter, 'is something I am only too happy to do for you, as you have made me so very happy. But there is something more – something more per-

27

sonal – that I would like to do for you.' She reached into the bodice of her dress and fumbled for a moment until her fingers drew out a fine gold chain, at the end of which hung a cross of intricate workmanship set with small diamonds. She unclasped the chain and cross and handed them to him.

It was still warm from her body.

'Please accept this as a talisman from me. Wear it always, Tommy, and it will remind you of me and perhaps it will bring you the good luck it has brought me. Don't part with it ever. May I put it around your neck?'

He bowed his head, and she took the chain from his palm and circled his neck with it. Then she unbuttoned his collar and tucked the charm under his shirt. He could feel the warmth of it against his skin. He could also feel her hand creeping down over his chest, seeking and tweaking his nipples.

'How can I thank you?' he mumbled, seeking her lips.

Her fingers slowly undid the buttons of his shirt and then, when they met the obstruction of his heavy belt, they undid the brass buckle, and crept still lower. He pushed himself into her clutching hand, thrilling as it clasped him tightly and moved slowly and rhythmically.

'You don't know?'

He shook his head.

'I can tell you, but I hoped you might guess!'

'How?' he repeated.

'Delay your departure by one hour. We'll go to my room. Agreed?'

He kissed her. 'It is small payment for all you have done for me.'

'I disagree.' She smiled up at him. 'I would consider it an extravagant payment.' Without releasing him, she started to take a step, but he did not follow.

'Let's not waste any time.' Her voice trembled.

'But, dear heart,' he demurred, 'something inside of me makes it impossible to do what you want in the light of day.'

She put the fingers of her free hand against his lips to silence him.

'Remember what I told you yesterday. The curtains in my

room can be drawn. They are so heavy that no light can enter.'

He swept her up in his arms and carried her through the door. 'Just one hour?' he asked.

'Just one,' she answered, 'then you must be on your way. Don't stay any longer or I could never let you go.'

He carried her down the hall, kicked open the door of her room with one foot, and lowered her to the still-unmade bed. Going to the window, he pulled the cord and the heavy draperies closed. It was as dark as night in the room, and he shed his clothes in a heap on the floor. As he bent over her, the little cross dangled in her face and she kissed it.

'See,' she whispered, 'it always brings me good luck.'

'And me too.' His weight pressed against her.

4

Tommy had found it more difficult to leave Helen than he had imagined. Although she had asked for only one hour, their enjoyment carried them well beyond two. After his second climax, he was exhausted. He would willingly have napped for the third hour, but he was anxious to be on his way. He knew that at the end of another hour the whole performance would start over again, and by that time he would not have the strength to quit the house. So he had dressed himself reluctantly, opened the draperies wide to let in the sunshine, kissed her as she lay sleeping among the sweaty sheets, and went to his room to gather his saddle-bags. Going out to the barn, he found his horse had already been saddled. He rode past the front gallery, where they had sat the night before, half expecting to see her waving to him. She was not there. He turned his horse down the long avenue of trees to the main road.

Instead of focusing on the day ahead, which he hoped would be his last on the road, his thoughts turned back to the woman he had just left. Although surrounded by all the accoutrements of respectability, she was not inherently what her Southern peers would call a respectable woman. In fact, according to his experience, she knew all the tricks of a trained harlot, and he wondered where she might have learned them. Surely no woman, reared in the respectability which her surroundings called for, could have been such an avid and tempestuous bedmate. Usually, he had been able to satisfy, and that thoroughly, any woman he had been with, but, he had to admit to himself, this woman was more adept than any professional, and more demanding than a sex-starved amateur. Surely she had not learned her technique from satisfying an invalid husband. But then, he considered, perhaps her husband had not always been an invalid, and he might have demanded such erotic dexterity in their love-making. On the other hand, perhaps her very avidity had made him the invalid that he became. He had heard of such things happening.

He wondered if she practised all her tricks on her handsome butler and equally handsome coachman. It was well that she had two of them, for certainly no one man could stand a nightly diet of her insatiable vagaries. Well, she would not be able to sap *his* manhood, and as delightful as might have been the prospect of staying with her – at least until the novelty had worn off – he was glad he was on his way.

Perhaps her talisman would bring him good luck. He transferred the reins from his right hand to his left and unbuttoned his shirt to pull out the cross. It was a beautiful thing, he had to admit, although he would have been happier had the diamonds been larger. Still he would never go broke as long as he had it. It must be worth around a thousand dollars; not bad for a night's willing labour. Not bad at all!

His way led through flat and uninteresting country, and the sun beat down upon him unmercifully. He was glad he had eaten a substantial breakfast because as noon approached he was getting hungry, yet saw no signs of any tavern. When he passed a fairly substantial house with a well sweep in the front yard, he stopped to ask for a drink of water. The woman of the house smiled at him while two small children tugged at her skirts. She accompanied him to the well and drew up a dripping bucket of water for him. It was cool and quenched his thirst. Afterwards, he elicited the information from her that there was a tavern a few miles down the road.

On arrival, he ordered feed for his horse and went into the slatternly public room where he had a hearty bowl of soup, thick with tomatoes and okra. It was surprisingly good, so good, in fact, that he had his bowl refilled before starting on his way again.

A few miles down the road he noticed a large body of water on his right which, a passer-by told him, was Lake Ponchartrain. The city of New Orleans, the traveller informed him, was just beyond.

He arrived in the city late in the afternoon when merchants were putting up the iron shutters on their shop fronts. After several stops to inquire about rates, he finally found a small hotel on Bourbon Street where he could stable his horse and get a room for himself at a reasonable price. For another dollar, he could get three meals a day. It was a fairly decent room, he discovered after the proprietor had taken him up and raised the jalousies to let in the light. The thing Tommy liked most about it was a door opening on a balcony furnished with chairs and flowering plants.

Before the man left, Tommy ordered a bath. When an attractive looking coloured boy came in with a tin tub and buckets of water, Tommy asked him if there was a tailor's shop nearby. The boy, who seemed alert and intelligent, nodded in assent but informed him that, if he needed clothes, it would take at least two weeks to have them made. There was no place, he assured Tommy, where he might find new, ready-made clothes.

'If'n yo' a-needin' things in a hurry, Masta suh,' he said, passing water from the cans into the tub, 'whyn't yo' go to Congo Square? It mostly for de black people, but they have second-hand clothes which sometimes might' good. If'n yo' asks my masta, he 'low me to go with yo' 'n' show yo' de way. Reckon yo' never find it yo'self. Kin I help yo' wash?'

Tommy denied the second request but promised that he would avail himself of the first. The boy told him he had only to ask for Ramon and Mr deVeau would fetch him. So when Tommy had finished washing off the dirt of the road and put his travel-stained clothes back on, he went down to arrange with the proprietor for the boy to accompany him. The fee for this, he was told, would be two bits, and Tommy changed one

31

of his dollar bills. The man then rang the bell on his desk for Ramon.

The boy and Tommy set out together. Tommy was enthralled with the narrow streets and the iron lacework balconies of New Orleans which was quite different from any city he had ever seen. As they walked along the narrow sidewalks – Ramon informed him they were called *banquettes* here – he could often catch a glimpse of tropical greenery through the doorways they passed. Tommy wondered what further delights might be hidden from the eyes of passers-by.

It was quite a long walk to Congo Square. It was nearly dark when they got there, but the square was illuminated by torches outside the temporary booths which had been erected around it. Several minutes elapsed before Tommy realized that he was the only white person there. The square was teeming with blacks, walking up and down the *banquettes*, eating and drinking at the stands, gossiping in small groups or examining the merchandise for sale in the stalls.

'Thinkin' mayhap yo' a-goin' to find somethin' here.' Ramon stopped before a stand displaying various articles of clothing and presided over by a wizened black man with white kinky wool for hair. 'Ol' Père Antoine, he gits the best clothes in all N'Orleans. He a-makin' the rounds o' all the rich folkses every mornin'.'

He nodded to the old man and then presented Tommy.

'This yere young masta, he a-lookin' for something special in the way of clotheses. He a-wantin' only the best. Ain' a-lookin' for no cheap nigger trogs.'

The man came out from behind his kiosk and measured Tommy with his eyes, smiling and nodding his head in approval.

'Mighty fine lookin' young gentleman. Yas suh! He shore is one handsome man. Got somethin' jes' for yo', Masta suh. Jes' got it this mornin'. Belongin' to young Masta Trouville, it did. He got hisself killed in a duel yesterday mornin' so I right on hand to git his clothes. His folks a'sayin' it ain' bin worn never.'

He disappeared inside the stall and came forth with a bundle carefully wrapped in an old sheet. His gnarled black fingers undid the cloth to disclose a suit of bottle-green broadcloth which he held up proudly for Tommy's inspection. It appeared, as the old man said, to be brand-new. While he held it, Tommy fingered the sleek broadcloth and caressed the satin lining. It was a far more wonderful suit than he had ever possessed, and he hoped that it would fit him. It appeared that it would as Père Antoine held it up, measuring the shoulders, but Tommy wanted to be sure. Where could he try it on? That was easy, the old man informed him. He had only to slip behind the kiosk where it was dark, take off his old clothes and try on the new ones.

How much would it cost if it did fit and Tommy decided to buy it? The old man scratched his white wool with a bony finger and hesitatingly quoted a price of $25. Tommy shook his head in denial. He was certain that this was not the final price and that old Père Antoine was merely starting high so that he could come down if necessary.

So Tommy passed the coat back to Père Antoine. It was roughly shoved back into his hands with an offer to sell for $20. Once again Tommy shook his head and made a counter-offer of $10, which nearly drove the old man to tears. He stroked the material, explaining the high quality of the cloth and the excellence of the tailoring, then finally came down two dollars. But the bargaining continued until a price of $15 was reached. Tommy agreed to take the suit if it fitted.

Following Père Antoine's gesturing hand, he stepped behind the booth, accompanied by Ramon. Stripping off his white trousers and jacket, he handed them to Ramon to hold while he struggled to get into the fashionably skin-tight pantaloons, made to hug the legs so snug that a strap under the shoes was necessary to keep them down. With Ramon's help, Tommy squirmed into them, smoothing the cloth like a sausage skin around his legs. He found all the necessary buttons and had only to suck in his stomach a little to fasten them. Ramon rubbed his fingers over Tommy's legs and exclaimed at the perfect fit. He passed Tommy his boots and promised to spit and polish them next morning. The coat strained against Tommy's broad shoulders, but it fitted well, and the sleeves were just the right length. Remembering to take his wallet from the trousers which Ramon was holding, he stepped out in front of the kiosk in the glare of the torch while Père

Antoine held up a shard of mirror for him to see. Both Ramon and Père Antoine were unanimous over the fact that the suit fitted perfectly, and Père Antoine bobbed his head up and down on his pipestem neck as much as to say that he knew all along it would just fit Tommy.

'Yo' a-goin' to need a weskit,' he informed Tommy, and it was true because the short-waisted coat with long tails called for a waistcoat. Tommy waited while Père Antoine rummaged through a pile of clothes on the floor of the booth which was nothing more than trampled earth. He finally unearthed a brocade waistcoat and brushed off the dust with a stubby whiskbroom. It was of pale apple-green brocade with filigreed gold-and-amber buttons, but when Tommy removed his coat and tried it on, it was somewhat too large – a condition which the old man remedied by pinning in the back so that it fitted snugly. He then threaded a long needle with coarse white thread and stitched up the back. Now it fitted perfectly.

His boots were new and with Ramon's offer to polish them, they would serve. He did need a decent white shirt, however, with a fashionable high collar which came up under his ears, along with a stock to go with it. Père Antoine was unable to supply either of these, but he asked Tommy to wait while he slipped into the neighbouring booth. He was back in a moment with a freshly laundered shirt of white lawn and a black satin stock. He measured Tommy's broad neck with a greasy tape-measure and then measured the neckband, grunting his satisfaction when he found that the shirt would fit.

He made a neat parcel of Tommy's old clothes and the several pairs of silk socks which Tommy had chosen, wrapped them in a smoothed-out newspaper, and tied them with a knotted length of twine, handing them to Ramon. Tommy carefully counted the bills from his wallet and passed them to Père Antoine.

While waiting, Tommy had noticed a shirt of lavender silk which was supported on a stick at the side of the booth and called Ramon's attention to it.

'How'd you like to have a new shirt, boy?'

'That one?' Ramon pointed to the lavender silk, his eyes popping out of his head. 'If'n that the one yo' means, ain' never had nothin' so elegant like'n that in my whole life.'

'Then it's yours if it will fit you.' Tommy motioned to Père Antoine to take it down, and Ramon quickly stripped off the soiled and sweaty tow linen shirt he was wearing. His fingers lingered for a moment on the softness of the silk and tweaked at the pearl buttons. He slipped it on over his bare milk-chocolate skin. It was too big for him, and he had to turn up the cuffs, but he assured Tommy that it didn't matter. It was something so far superior to anything he had ever owned that he would have worn it even if it fitted him like a tent. Père Antoine made a bundle of Ramon's soiled shirt, and they were finally ready to leave.

They paused in the square to drink a cup of coffee from the hands of an enormous coloured woman who had a pot boiling over a fire of twigs at a tiny wayside stand. The coffee was hot and black and bitter with chicory. Tommy followed Ramon's example of sweetening it liberally with brown sugar which the woman passed in a stoneware jar. When Ramon discreetly retreated a few feet behind Tommy to drink his coffee, Tommy made a mental note: the boy was well trained.

He appraised the lad. Ramon was somewhere between eighteen and twenty, not overly tall, with strong muscular shoulders that Tommy had observed while he was trying on the shirt. He was good-looking with an intelligent face, somewhat more Latin than negroid. He had wide-set brown eyes, a straight nose with small nostrils, and his lips were thin and not blubbery. From what Tommy already knew of the boy, he was intelligent.

Any young man of Tommy's pretensions should have a black boy to attend him, and this might be the right boy. It would be much easier if he could buy him directly, rather than go to some vendue house and bid for someone with unknown qualities. All the fingering in the world could give no more than an idea of a slave's physique; no amount of fingering could determine his disposition or character.

He was reluctant to spend the money necessary to buy a slave, for there was the subsequent expense of feeding and housing him, but his fictitious status demanded one. He thought with regret of the many servants at Dove Cote whom he could once have had for the asking, but it was far too late now. The faithful Colt would have been just the ticket, but

35

just wishing would not magically transport Colt from far-off Dove Cote Plantation. However, Tommy Verder without a black servant would be just another young man in the big city, but with a boy attendant on him, particularly a fine-looking boy like Ramon, he would instantly acquire prestige. He was tempted; if Ramon was for sale, he'd make an offer for him.

It was late when they returned to the hotel from Congo Square, but Mr deVeau was still sitting behind the desk in the minuscule lobby. He bowed to Tommy when he came in and signalled to Ramon to leave by the door that led to the servants' quarters.

'Thank you for loaning me your boy.' Tommy was anxious to start a conversation with the man.

'Might's well be doin' that as sittin' on his ass all day long. He's a right smart boy, he is.' DeVeau seemed equally anxious to talk; he was probably bored to death sitting alone behind the desk all day. 'He been with us some spell. As a matter of fact, he was birthed right here 'n' been with me always. His dam died a spell back, and I been thinkin' o' sellin' him 'cause ain' rightly got much use for him round here, but it hard to part with a boy what was borned here.'

Tommy walked over and sat down on the counter, dangling one tightly-encased trouser leg.

'Thinking of selling him, were you?'

DeVeau nodded.

'How much you planning to ask for him?'

The man got up from his chair and came around to the front of the counter where he could face Tommy.

'He a likely buck; strong and ain' got nary an imperfection on him. Biddable too. Comes from good stock, he does. His dam, she purentee Fanti 'n' his sire a Cuban free mulatto which I hired to stud her, so the boy he ain' all black. Sire a damned good-looking man.' He suddenly looked up at Tommy. 'How come yo' askin' me all these questions. Yo' thinkin' mayhap yo' want to buy him?'

'Mayhap.' Tommy nodded. 'Just a passing fancy, that's all. I like the boy, and he certainly was a help to me. Seems bright and intelligent.'

'Shore is. Jes' got one bad fault. That boy shore is wench

36

crazy. Jes' let a wench pass by in the street 'n' he a-poppin' the buttons right off'n his pants.'

Tommy grinned. 'Well, that's only natural for a young buck like him. I like a boy with spirit, I do. Tell me, how much you asking for him?'

DeVeau hesitated a long moment, watching Tommy's foot as it moved back and forth. 'Likely young bucks like'n him a-bringin' round $800 at vendue these days.'

Tommy shook his head. 'That's too much for him. He's not big enough nor strong enough to be a field hand, and he's not light enough nor pretty enough for a house servant. If he was about six inches taller and about thirty pounds heavier, he might fetch that much, but as he is, I doubt if you'd get more than six hundred for him on the vendue table, and then there'd be your commission to pay.'

'He's a right likely boy.' DeVeau was loath to give up his slave's good points.

'Let's say he's a fair specimen. He ain't no fancy, but I've sort of taken a notion to him. Don't want to get me some ornery boy that's hard to get along with, and this boy of yours seems biddable. Tell you what. I'll offer you $500 spot cash and, as long as I stay here, which may be for some time, he can continue on working for you.'

DeVeau thought for some moments, stroking his chin as he considered Tommy's offer.

'How about five-fifty?'

Tommy shook his head. 'Five hundred cash, take it or leave it.'

Again deVeau was silent for some time, and Tommy could almost hear him thinking.

'Might just take yo' up on it. Been thinkin' o' gettin' shet o' him 'cause they ain' much here what he can do. Got us enough help 'n' he sometimes underfoot.'

'Then call him in here.'

'What for?' DeVeau looked at Tommy with surprise.

'Don't want to buy any buck less'n I go over him and finger him. He appears all right, but want to see him with pants down.'

'Tol' yo' he right sound.'

37

'Prefer to finger him myself, and, besides, I'd like to know how the boy would like me for a new master.'

DeVeau grunted in disgust. 'Don' make him no neverminds if'n he do o' if'n he don'. He up for sale; he a-goin' to git solt 'n' that's that. All foolishness.'

'But that's the way I do business.' Tommy nodded his head vigorously to emphasize his point. 'Finger him first and then ask him.'

'Better step back with me.' DeVeau indicated the door. 'Cain' have yo' a-fingerin' no nekked buck here in the lobby. Got us some women folks a-stayin' here, 'n' don' want them to see it. Come this way.'

Tommy followed him through the door into a dark open courtyard and across it, cautiously picking his way over rubble until they came to another building on the far side. Inside, a tallow dip burned in an iron candlestick, showing the meagre furnishings of the room. The boy Ramon sat on one of the chairs, an arrangement of string between his fingers as he studied the next move in the intricate cat's cradle which was occupying him.

'This man here a-thinkin' o' buyin' yo', Ramon,' deVeau said.

Tommy saw a smile spread across the boy's face. 'How'd you like me for a new master?' he asked.

'Shore like it fine, Masta suh, if'n Masta deVeau he kin spare me.'

'Masta Tommy, if'n yo' a-goin' to belong to me.'

'Yas suh, Masta Tommy suh, shore like to be yore boy, though Masta deVeau he a right fine masta.'

'Then come over here beside me and strip off your trogs.'

The boy took a nimble step and stood beside Tommy. At another nod of Tommy's head, he carefully undid the pearl buttons of the silk shirt, took it off and hung it on a chair. He hesitated a moment, a question in his eyes before he undid the buttons of his pants. Tommy's nod was encouraging, and he let the pants slide to the floor, standing naked before Tommy.

It was really a waste of time to examine the boy, as Tommy could see that he was physically perfect, but nevertheless he let his hands wander over the smooth satin of the boy's skin. Then he bade him kneel so that he could spread his buttocks.

At a prod from Tommy, he stood up and faced him. Tommy ran his hand over the hardness of the boy's belly and down into the wiry hair of his genitals. Then cupping his genitals in one hand, he pulled the foreskin back and examined the purple glands. He was surprised at the almost immediate erection which took place.

'Quick on the trigger, ain't you, Ramon?'

Ramon grinned self-consciously.

Tommy expressed surprise at the smallness of the boy's genitals.

'Ain' never going to make much of a breeder,' Tommy said to deVeau. 'He's pretty small.'

'Yo' a-buyin' him for a breeder?' deVeau asked.

Tommy shook his head. 'Funny though that he ain't hung heavier.'

'Sometimes I think that all poppycock 'bout all niggers a-bein' hung heavy. They jes' like white folks, they are. Some hung heavy 'n' some not. This one jes' ain'.'

Tommy nodded in agreement, thinking as he did so that he was among the favoured ones. He told Ramon to put his clothes back on.

'Plannin' on buyin' you, I am, Ramon.'

'That shore fine, Masta Tommy, suh.'

'You'll continue to work here for a while, but remember, when I want you, you're to come when I call you.'

'Shore will jump to it, Masta Tommy suh.'

'And another thing, I want that you should make yourself a pallet in front of my door and sleep on it.'

'Kin do, Masta Tommy suh.'

Tommy and deVeau passed out of the room and across the courtyard. Once again in the lobby, the man sat down behind the counter and wrote out a bill of sale for Tommy, and Tommy reached for his wallet and carefully counted out five hundred dollars in bills. He handed them to deVeau, took the bill of sale in exchange and bade him good night.

Slowly he climbed the stairs to his room, candle in hand. Ramon was already before his door, spreading a torn blanket on the floor.

'You're my boy now, Ramon.' Tommy produced his key and unlocked the door.

'Shore am glad to be, Masta Tommy suh. Likes yo' a lot, I do. Sick o' staying here. Bin here all my life 'n' want to go places.'

Tommy smiled at him. 'God alone knows where we're going, boy. Let's hope it will be to a lot of good places.'

'Shore do hope so, Masta Tommy suh.' He waited until Tommy opened the door. 'Bed myself right down here, Masta suh. Ain' no boogers nor hants a-goin' to git in.'

'Watch out, Ramon. I'll see you in the morning. Remember, you're my boy now.'

'Ain' fergettin'. Thank yo' for the shirt. Bestest shirt I ever had in my life.'

Tommy smiled and closed the door behind him. He stood for a moment in the room, candle in hand before he walked over and placed it on the stand beside his bed. Well, he had five hundred dollars less than before, but he had bought a fine young buck who, he was sure, was worth more than five hundred. It was like having money in the bank. Ramon would be a good investment, and he could always sell him if he had to. Maybe he should have hinted to Mrs Latimer that he would rather have had a black boy than the trinket she had given him. He pulled out the cross and looked at it, letting the flame of the candle send the diamonds into sparkles of iridescence. No, the diamonds in the cross were worth more than Ramon. And he always had the cross in reserve.

He'd made a good investment. Of that he was sure. Ramon was as good as cash any time. Besides, he couldn't cut any figure in New Orleans without a black boy. He'd have to get some new clothes for him though. Couldn't have him around in linen tow pants. Well there was always Congo Square and Père Antoine. He'd make another trip there so Ramon would be a credit to him.

All in all, it had been quite a day. Here he was safely in New Orleans where neither Acker nor Hammond Maxwell would be able to find him. He'd already fitted himself out with a decent suit of clothes, and he had a good-looking servant to follow him around. Not bad for one day – not bad at all for the illegitimate offspring of a quadroon wench and a passing stranger who had six fingers on his right hand.

5

Anxious as he was to present his letter of introduction to Captain Dominique You (and he reminded himself how very fortunate he was to have even this feeble connection in a strange and friendless city), Tommy decided he would first take a day off to get acquainted with New Orleans. He had seen only a sample the night before on the way to Congo Square, but what little he had seen had intrigued him. He stretched out his legs in the comfortable bed and was tempted to turn over and go back to sleep but regretfully decided against it. Inspired by his awakening sensuality as he got out of bed, he wished for a moment that he were back with Helen Latimer. Man! What a woman she was! But when he saw what merely thinking about her was doing to him, he forced her image from his thoughts, donned his shirt and under-drawers, and unlocked the door. He half expected to see Ramon curled up on his torn blanket, but both were gone.

Back in his room he discovered a dangling wire with a white porcelain knob on the end, pulled it and listened to a faint jangle down in the courtyard. While waiting, he slipped on his old trousers and stepped out onto the balcony, parting the growing plants to peer down into the street. Already the streets were awake with a languid activity far different from the bustle of New York. A Negro walked by, his person bristling with brushes, with a clutch of brooms over his shoulders, sleepily calling out his wares. He was followed by an immense black woman in starched white with red bandanna tied in a perky bow on her head. She had a tray suspended by a strap around her neck and was calling out 'pralines', what-ever they might be, probably the waferlike confections in her tray. A well-dressed man walked by with a somewhat faster step as though he had some important business in mind, and an attractive young lady, frothy in blue silk and lace, accom-panied by a stern elderly woman all dressed in rusty black. Her chaperon, he supposed. He hoped that every attractive young woman was not so attended, but he reminded himself of the French and Spanish background of the city and feared that this might be the general custom. However, in a city this size there must be many houses of prostitution, and he would inquire of Ramon who seemed to know everything. Just now, after thinking of Helen Latimer he felt in need of a woman, although he disliked having to spend his own money for such a service. Even when his prime equipment found no paying customer, there was always plenty of volunteer talent about. All of which reminded him of Helen Latimer again, and in his present condition he cursed himself for having left her so soon.

A rap on the door took his mind off his present exigency, and he left the balcony to open the door. Instead of Ramon, it was a most attractive mulatto wench, slender yet curvacious, with a piquant heart-shaped face around which clustered ringlets of dark brown hair.

'Yo' a'ringin' for me, Masta suh?' She eyed him up and down quickly, then smiled at him provocatively. 'I'se Zelda 'n' what can I do for yo', suh?'

He wanted to tell her that there were a number of things which she could do, but hesitated because he did not know in what capacity she was there to serve. By her smile and her glance from under long lashes, however, he suspected she would not be averse to helping him in any way.

'No.' He hated to let her go, but it seemed better not to become embroiled in something which might cause trouble. He would ask Ramon about her status in the household before he started anything, but he was glad that someone attractive was close at hand, should she be available.

'No, Zelda.' He smiled at her. 'Nothing you can do for me right now except to see if you can find Ramon and send him up here.'

'So.' She appraised him again with a little cluck of approbation as she allowed her glance to sweep down over his body, then lifted her eyes and looked at him directly. 'Ramon he shore a lucky boy to get himself such a fine new masta like'n yo'. Wishin' yo'd have bought me instead. Kin serve yo' better'n Ramon 'cause he jest a boy, less'n yo' the kind what likes boys best.'

'No, it's not that, Zelda, and I imagine you could serve me in many ways better than he could.' Tommy grinned back at her. 'But it wouldn't look too good to have you following me up and down the streets. Have to have a boy for that.'

'But a boy he no good at nights 'n' yo' say yo' ain' one of those men what's a-likin' boys better'n gals.'

'I'm not – most certainly not – but now, Zelda, if you'll send Ramon to me, I'll appreciate it. Perhaps we can arrange something for some night. Yes?'

'Shore kin if'n yo' ask Mr deVeau. He don' like me a-messin' round with the guests less'n he know.'

'Then I'll ask him.' Tommy could hear running footsteps on the stairs, and Ramon's head appeared.

'Yo', Zelda, what yo' all a-doin' here a-sweet-talkin' my masta Tommy?' he demanded between gasps for breath. 'Whyn't yo' a-tellin' me his bell's a-ringin'? He my masta 'n' I don' want no wench like'n yo' a-foolin' round with him. He quality, my masta is 'n' if'n he wants hisself a gal he kin go to Madame Alix's 'n' pay her five silver dollars for one 'n' I don' want no wench like'n yo' what spreads her legs for any man what pays Masta deVeau two bits a-foolin' around with him.'

'Whoa there, boy,' Tommy grabbed him by the shirt collar and swung him around. 'Can't have you talking like that to this pretty little Zelda. Could be that I'm needing her some-time, and, if so, two bits is a right likely sum to pay. Now you come in my room. Things for you to do, but, first of all, I want you to fetch me a pitcher of hot water. Got to shave and you've got to learn how to do it for me. It's going to be your first lesson, so get back here, and, as for you, Zelda, come in my room for a minute. We've got a little business to attend to also.'

She waited until Ramon left and then sidled in the door beside him. He closed the door and locked it. Slowly he approached her and lifted her face to his and kissed her, feeling the warm wetness of her tongue penetrating between his teeth. Her hand slipped to his crotch, and he helped her un-button his trousers while she exclaimed in surprise and ecstasy.

'We haven't got time this morning,' he whispered hoarsely. 'Ramon will be back in a minute.'

'Won' take me no whole minute,' she said, sinking to her knees before him, her arms clutching his thighs.

He felt the warmth of her body and the pressure of her breasts against his legs, and he retreated a step to make sure that he had turned the key in the lock. Her arms tightened around his body, drawing him closer to her. Her mouth was warm and wet and sweet and, before he knew it, his body arched in spasm. He clung to her, as the weakness of his knees endangered his footing. He went limp all over, then straightened up and pushed away her still questing lips while he rearranged his trousers. When he could get his breath, he felt in his pocket and found two bits which he gave to her. With a faltering step, he went to unlock the door. Ramon was standing in the doorway.

'How she do, Masta Tommy suh?' Ramon stood aside while Zelda slithered through the doorway.

'Fine.' Tommy had scarcely regained his breath.

'She do it for everyone else, but she won' do it for me, even if'n I offers her money. She a-sayin' I'm too young 'n' too little, but I'm a-tellin' her that I'm mighty potent, I am.'

'Well, let's forget about it. You talk too much, Ramon. Too damned much. Better learn to keep quiet, or I'll take a strap to you. Now I'm going to teach you to shave me, and if you give me a single nick I'm going to have you whipped, so you'd better pay attention and be careful.'

Tommy showed Ramon how to prepare a lather, then sat down in a chair and taught him how to put a towel around his neck and spread the lather on his face. Then he pointed to the leather case that held his razors and had Ramon select the one with the ivory handle. Tommy told him where to find the strop and showed him how to strop the razor and apply it to his face.

Ramon's hands trembled ever so slightly, but he was all care while he proceeded to shave Tommy according to his master's instructions. Although unused to such work, he did it deftly and quickly and did not even nick the skin. Tommy had feared he would emerge a mass of bloody cuts. When he was finished, Ramon admitted that he had to shave himself occasionally and was not a tyro.

His face now smooth and glowing, Tommy showed him how to help him dress, although he warned him, without giving any explanation, that he was never to remove his shirt. So, according to Tommy's instructions, Ramon removed the soiled white pants and the drawers. Then, according to

Tommy's instructions, Ramon held the pair of clean linen drawers while Tommy slipped them on. The boy unbuttoned them, then eased on the sausage-tight pair of new trousers.

'You're a-needin' galluses,' Ramon informed him. 'Kin git those thout'n goin' to Congo Square for 'em.'

'And handkerchiefs too,' Tommy mentioned. 'Reckon I'll go out later, after I've had my breakfast and see what we can find.' He regarded Ramon quizzically. 'You're a boy who seems to know everything. Reckon working around a hotel has taught you a lot. Tell me. Where does a man go in this town if he wants to get laid?'

'Laid, Masta Tommy, suh? Don' rightly know what yo' means by gettin' laid.'

'Where does a man find a woman in this town? I need one. Haven't had one in a long time.'

'Yo' jest had Zelda, Masta Tommy suh.'

'That doesn't count. I want a woman.'

'Yo' mean a whore – someone yo' pays?'

Tommy nodded his head vigorously and winked at Ramon. 'Exactly.'

Ramon grinned back at him. 'Well, they's a lot of 'em right here in N'Orleans. First off, they's the cribs, but they not too good. They not for a gentleman like'n yo'.' I go there when I kin save up 'nuff money. Fo' bits it is 'cause them two-bit whores ain' so good.' He sighed, 'Ain' had 'nuff money to go there for a long time.'

'And would you like to go?'

'Jes' a-rarin' to go, Masta Tommy suh, but only got me three bits. Bin tempted to take a two-bit hussy tho', I a needin' it so bad.'

'So outside of the cribs, what would you recommend for me?'

Ramon scratched his head. 'Reckon yo' a-wantin' the best.'

Tommy nodded again. 'Best ain't none too good for me.'

'Well, then, that's Madame Alix's place. She got a whore house tho' she ain' a-callin' it that. She a-callin' it the Academy o' Music, tho' the kind o' music they make ain' like any yo' ever heard afore. All the young bloods 'n' a lot o' older men go there. Right fancy place it is, Masta Tommy suh, 'n' right costive it is too. She got white gals in there 'n' some

45

octoroon gals too for them that fancies 'em. Heard tell she a-puttin' on a show if'n a man got 'nuff money to pay for it. They a-sayin' she got a nigger boy there by the name o' Drum what puts on a show with the coloured gals 'n' it costs twenty-five dollars just to watch it. Shore do wish I could get me a job like'n that, but reckon I'm too picayune. They a'sayin' that Drum he the heaviest hung nigger in the world. Shore do wish I could be like'n that Drum – or yo', Masta Tommy suh.'

'Guess that's something you can't do anything about, boy.' Tommy motioned for Ramon to hand him his stock, which Tommy tied himself and then pointed to his boots which Ramon eased on, not forgetting to put the strap of the pantaloons under the heel. Then he held Tommy's coat for him and stood back to admire his master.

'Yo' shore looks scrumptious, Masta Tommy suh. I do declare yo're downright handsome.'

'Need a new hat, I do.' Tommy had in mind a wide-brimmed Panama hat such as he had seen the men wearing.

'Kin show yo' where to get it. Yo' a-wantin' that I bring yore breakfast up here to yore room 'n' then yo' won't have to go down to the dinin' room?'

'A good idea. Do I have any choice for breakfast?'

'Yo' gits ham 'n' eggs 'n' grits 'n' hot bread 'n' coffee. Everyone here gits the same. Kin put a li'l table out on the balcony for yo'. Be right back.'

Tommy went out on the balcony and once again became engrossed with the teeming life of the street below while he waited for Ramon to bring up his breakfast. His short encounter with Zelda had been interesting, but it had been over almost before it had begun and had not satisfied him. Perhaps he would try this famous house of Madame Alix's which Ramon had mentioned. At least he would have Ramon point it out to him so he'd know where it was. Poor Ramon! Tommy felt sorry for him. He was a likeable boy, and it was a shame that he had been so woefully short-changed when the genitalia were given out. Well, everyone could not be as generously endowed as Tommy himself, he mused. He was grateful; it had stood him in good stead all his life.

He heard the door of the room open, and Ramon entered with a big tray covered with a napkin. He set up a small table on the balcony, placed the tray on it and removed the napkin. Tommy sniffed eagerly at the savoury aroma. It looked and tasted delicious. No more wayside taverns for him from now on. He guessed that there must be something in this tradition of French cooking because the ham was delicately pink and tender, the eggs white and golden with a crisp brown border, the bread hot and oozing butter and the coffee savoury with chicory. When he had finished, Ramon took the tray. Tommy went inside to comb his hair. He decided to go bare-headed until he could buy a hat, as the one he had worn on the road was soiled and the band sweat-stained. He went downstairs to the lobby where he found Ramon waiting for him. After bidding Mr deVeau a good morning, they went out together into the street.

Ramon took him to a shop on Bourbon Street where he found a hat to his liking. No wonder the men here wore straw hats – they were so much lighter and cooler than a heavy beaver.

After leisurely wandering about the streets for a while and looking at the displays of various things in the windows, Tommy sat for a while on a bench in the park in front of the cathedral. The sight of this imposing edifice brought to mind Mrs Latimer's instructions as to how to find Dominique You. She had said to go to the blacksmith's shop of the Brothers LaFitte near the cathedral. It seemed that Ramon knew where it was, and, although Tommy did not intend to present his letter that day, he wanted to see the shop. Ramon took him past there, but they did not stop.

When Tommy asked Ramon if he had heard of Captain Dominique You, Ramon looked at him wide-eyed. He told Tommy that after the Brothers LaFitte, You was probably the most important personage in New Orleans and that he was now engaged in building a house especially for the Emperor Napoleon whom he and the Brothers LaFitte planned to rescue from some island where the English had imprisoned him. Ramon seemed to know about almost everything of interest that was happening in the city.

Tommy stopped at a sidewalk café for lunch while Ramon ate in the alley at the back of the kitchen. As the afternoon wore on, and it seemed as if they had covered most of the city

47

by foot, Ramon suddenly took an abrupt turn and led Tommy down a narrow street.

'This here's Dumaine Street,' Ramon explained.

'Dumaine Street?' Tommy looked at him blankly.

'Yes suh, Masta Tommy suh, this here's where Madame Alix have her whore house. See, it that one.' Ramon pointed to a well-kept house with several delightful girls sitting on one of the balconies, abloom with potted plants. They walked slowly by, oblivious of the smiles and welcoming gestures of the young and exceedingly pretty girls. Tommy took a note of the doorway so that he could find his own way here in case he wanted to go alone.

In contrast, later that afternoon, Ramon asked Tommy how he would like to see the cribs. Tommy had never before seen cut-rate commercial sex in a southern city. He expressed interest. Whereupon Ramon took him through a series of narrow streets to an even narrower alley paralleling the river with long rows of one-storey buildings, each with a narrow doorway and one iron-barred window.

It was a sordid street. The gutters beside the narrow *banquettes* were filled with dirt and offal, and the street itself a dusty stretch of hard-packed earth, scarcely wide enough for a chaise to pass through. As it was not yet dark, there was not much activity on the street – just a few men, both white and coloured, peering at the prostitutes, one of whom sat behind each window. Some women wore bedraggled finery, and others had nothing on but carelessly draped robes which they opened to display their fading charms. One side of the street, Ramon informed him, was for blacks and the other for whites. As far as Tommy could see, the black girls were younger and far more attractive than their white sisters who were, all in all, a pretty tired and shopworn lot.

Ramon's whole manner had changed from the moment he entered the street. He was now bubbling with animation, fairly dancing along as he pointed out the occupants of the cribs. He admired them all, particularly the white ones which were forbidden to him. Several times, he stopped to wave at the occupants on the coloured side, explaining to Tommy that he patronized them in the past.

The women were too sordid for Tommy's taste, but their squalid appearance did not disturb Ramon. They might have all been beauties as far as he was concerned, for he gazed upon them with admiration and desire. After they had gone through the street once on the white side, he begged Tommy to repeat the trip again on the coloured side. Here he pointed out those he had been with, extolling their virtues to Tommy.

Tommy stood Ramon's slavering admiration as long as he could.

'How'd you like one of those women this afternoon?' he asked, knowing full well what the reply would be.

'Like it fine, Masta Tommy suh, but ain' got me no money with me.' He pointed to a girl in one of the cribs. ''N' if'n I did have, I'd take that one. Ain' never bin with her, and they a'sayin' that she shore somethin' special. Shore been a-hankerin' to try her out.'

Tommy looked in the direction of Ramon's pointing finger. The girl, seen through the iron bars, was younger and more attractive than her sisters. Moreover, she looked clean. Her *peignoir* of flimsy pink silk boasted an edging of tattered marabou, and, when she caught Tommy and Ramon staring at her, she stood up, opening the gown to display a lithe young body. Cupping her breasts in her hands, she beckoned with her head.

'You like her?' Tommy asked.

'Shore do, Masta Tommy suh. Yo' a-likin' her too?'

Tommy shook his head. 'She's pretty for a coloured wench, and she's far above the rest on the street, but I've no taste for this sort of a place.' He hesitated a moment. 'I'll wait outside.' Then he had a second thought. 'Remember what you told me about that boy Drum who works for Madame Alix?'

'The one what puts on the shows for her? 'Member a-tellin' yo' that he mighty heavy hung.'

'Not particularly. I'm thinking about the show he puts on. Was just wondering how you'd like to put on a show for me if I paid for the girl. I could go in and sit on the foot of the bed and watch you. It would be something for me. I think I'd like to see you a-humping.'

'Don' know if'n I could do anythin' with yo' a-watchin'.'

'But you say this Drum does. Guess you could do anything he can. Looks to me as though you're ready right now.' He looked down at Ramon.

'Gotta see what the gal a-sayin'. Mayhap she not a-wantin' a white man a-lookin' on.'

'Then go in and ask her.'

Through the open barred window, he could see Ramon talking to the girl who at first seemed highly indignant but became more interested as Ramon continued to cajole her.

'What did she say?' Tommy asked. He hoped he might receive some vicarious pleasure in watching Ramon perform.

'She a-sayin' that even if'n she is a whore, she's a decent girl. She ain' puttin' on no show for anyone less'n she gits paid double. She a-wantin' a whole dollar to let me pester her whilst yo' a-lookin' on 'n' she say no funny business like'n yo' done with Zelda this mornin'; jes' straight pesterin' tha's all.'

A dollar seemed reasonable enough, so Tommy pushed Ramon ahead of him into the single room. The girl, somewhat overawed by Tommy's presence, closed the door and drew the curtains at the window. The room was in semi-darkness, but Tommy could still see.

'White masta a-goin' to give me a dollar?' she asked.

Tommy produced the dollar and handed it to her, whereupon she let the flimsy robe slip from her shoulders and stood naked before Ramon. Her two well-rounded breasts with their dark, reddish-brown nipples seemed almost too heavy for her slender body. She crossed the room to where Ramon was standing and slowly started to undress him. She paused after removing each garment to let her hands slide over the newly exposed part of his body. Tommy noticed that now that Ramon was aroused he was not as puny as he had first imagined. He stood rampant under the gliding caresses of the girl. At length when she had stripped him of all his clothes, she eased herself onto the bed, patting a place beside her for Tommy. Ramon knelt on the bed, spreading her legs apart, and without any preliminaries entered her.

It was the shortest performance that Tommy had ever seen. No sooner had Ramon entered the girl than a spasm shook his body, and he fell inert across her. He lay there for a few moments, gasping for breath and then gathered himself together and stood up. His erection had gone, and he looked apologetically at Tommy.

'Jes' couldn't hold it in, Masta Tommy suh. No sooner I gits in her 'n' I explodes.'

'Well, it wasn't much of a show.' Tommy had to admit. 'Think I could have done better myself. Maybe some day I'll show you just how it should be done.' The girl stood up, and he smiled at her. She came closer to fondle him.

'Now if'n the pretty white masta like to show this worthless nigger boy jes' how a girl should be pestered, ain' a-goin' to be no extra charge. Uh-uh, shore like to have yo' pester me, Masta suh. Ain' never had no white man, 'n' like to see how it is.'

Her stroking hands tempted Tommy. Reluctantly he pushed her away. If she persisted he would have to have her willy-nilly, and he had no desire to follow Ramon.

'Not today, Missy.' The utterance of that word brought rushing memories of Missy Acker. Suddenly the whole scene became distasteful to him – the panting, open-mouthed girl, her seeking hands, the muskiness of her body – and he could not wait to leave the sordid surroundings. Rather than offend the girl, he took another two bits from his pocket and gave it to her. While she was thanking him, he pushed open the door, signalled Ramon to follow and walked out into the street. He ignored the other denizens who were trying to attract his attention.

Ramon hurried to catch up.

'Whereat we a-goin' now, Masta Tommy suh?'

'Back to the hotel.' Tommy was curt with him. 'Take the shortest way there.'

His thoughts were muddled as he hurried towards the hotel, but not his feelings. The brief contact with Zelda had not satisfied him. Seeing Ramon and the girl, even for the few seconds that they had been together, had aroused him. Then there was the sudden and exciting memory of Missy Acker. Had he really loved her? It must be possible because he could not get her off his mind. Whatever it was, there was only one thing that could calm his restless nerves now. He wanted a woman; he needed one; he must have one!

When he reached the hotel, he dismissed Ramon, saying that

51

he would ring for him if he wanted him. He stopped at the desk and spoke to Mr deVeau.

'You have a wench named Zelda?'

'Shore do, Mista Verder.'

'I can use her. Send her up to my room at once.'

'But, Mista Verda...'

'No *but's*, sir. I'll pay the regular charge or more if you desire. I know she's available. Ramon told me so. Just hurry.'

'Yes suh, Mister Verder. Know how yo' feels. Gets to the point sometimes when a man cain' hold it no longer. Zelda she be right up 'n' ain' a-goin' to charge yo' more'n two bits.'

Tommy reached into his pocket and threw the money on the desk. Before Mr deVeau had a chance to thank him, he was on his way to his room. This time, he was certain, Zelda would earn her money.

6

Tommy allowed two lazy days to pass in desultory sightseeing before he could bring himself to present his letter to Dominique You. As long as he held the letter with its potential of employment, he felt almost secure, but he dreaded meeting You only to be told there was no opening for him in the LaFitte organization. After all, why should an important man like Captain You take an interest in Tommy merely because of a letter from a woman who, for all Tommy knew, he might well have forgotten? Except, Tommy reasoned, that Helen Latimer would be difficult to forget, especially if You had known her as intimately as Tommy had.

On the morning of the third day, he decided to take the bull by the horns. He took particular pains to have Ramon dress him in his new clothes. He also had Ramon don his new outfit so that when they left the hotel, they could be mistaken for a prosperous young planter in fine clothes and Panama hat, followed by his fittingly attired servant.

By now the narrow streets and the overhanging iron balconies were so familiar to Tommy that he wasted no further time admiring them. When they reached the small green park in front of the cathedral, they halted. They had walked slowly to avoid dampening the armpits of their coats with dark crescents of sweat. Nearby, Tommy knew, was the famous blacksmith's shop of the LaFitte brothers. He stopped for a moment to adjust his clothing, tighten the black satin stock around his neck, and permit Ramon to wipe his shoes and brush the dust from his trousers. Then glancing around to see if anyone was watching, he straightened Ramon's clothing so that the boy would reflect the status of his master.

It was only a few steps to narrow St Philip Street, and the smithy was not difficult to find. The wide double doors were open and in the semi-darkness of the shop, the wheezing bellows stirred the fires in the forge to spring angrily to life, painting the interior with rhythmic flashes of red and orange. They could hear the resonant clang of iron against iron and smell the acrid odour of scorched horses' hooves. They sensed the subdued hum of conversation from the small group of men sitting on the *banquette* in front of the door; the men all looked up as Tommy and Ramon approached. None of them rose, but they regarded the two with undisguised interest as they entered the gloomy interior of the shop.

When his eyes became accustomed to the darkness of the smithy after the bright sunlight of the street, Tommy noticed a formidable-looking man standing at the anvil, his hammer ringing against the horseshoe he was shaping. Tommy advanced a few steps while the man put down his hammer, and with a pair of long tongs, embedded the horseshoe in the coals. He pumped the bellows until the horseshoe became red and malleable. He then transferred it to the anvil again and delivered a few more hammer blows. Then he plunged it into a tub of water, listened with some satisfaction to the prolonged sizzling, and finally recognized Tommy's presence.

He was a short, stocky man, with powerful bulging biceps under the rolled-up sleeves of his rough blue cotton shirt. He regarded Tommy warily, but looked him directly in the eye. Even in the obscurity of the shop, Tommy could see that his eyes were a light, clear blue. Tommy was immediately attracted to the man.

'Pierre LaFitte, at your service, M'sieur.' The man's lazy drawl and slight accent showed only slight interest in his caller. 'What can I do for you?'

'Mr LaFitte?' Tommy was surprised that this man he had heard so much about, the brother of the great Jean LaFitte, should be engaged in physical labour. 'Allow me to introduce myself. I am Thomas Verder of New York. I am most happy to make your acquaintance. I have here—' he produced the letter from an inside coat pocket – 'a letter to Captain Dominique You. It is a letter of introduction, and I was told to present it to him here.'

'Ah, the good *Capitaine*.' LaFitte hesitated a moment. 'Was the name Verder, M'sieur?'

Tommy nodded.

'Then, M'sieur Verder, had you been here but ten minutes earlier, you would have found my friend Dominique You sitting right here in that chair.' He pointed to the only arm-chair in the doorway. 'But, alas, he has left.'

'It is a matter of much regret to me,' Tommy replied, 'as I was most anxious to have him read this letter.'

'Ah, but it is not an occasion for any great degree of despair, M'sieur.' LaFitte shrugged his shoulders and smiled. 'You see, I know where the good *Capitaine* You was going, and I also know that he will be pleased to see you because a letter introducing a stranger is always welcome. Dominique just left for the house of Madame Alix in Dumaine Street. He is to have his *petit déjeuner* with her, and I know that he would be only glad to have you interrupt his visit, especially with a letter.'

'If you thought I would not cause any inconvenience ... Naturally I would not want to bother Captain You.'

LaFitte smiled again. He was, Tommy thought, a truly engaging person.

'The good Dominique is an old friend of Madame Alix. He occasionally patronizes her house as a customer, but even more often he goes there merely to visit with his *bonne amie*, Madame Alix. Between the two of them they know enough scandal to overthrow the whole city, and each one is avid to

54

hear some juicy titbit from the other. No, you will most certainly not cause any inconvenience, and, as a newcomer, both Madame Alix and Dominique will be happy to lay eyes on you.' LaFitte picked up the horseshoe he had been making, looked at it intently and turned it over in his hands before placing it back in the coals.

Tommy realized that he had been politely dismissed, but it had been so tactfully done that he felt nothing but friendship for the man. This was indeed a city of courtesy and good manners. He took his leave of LaFitte, walked out of the shop into the bright sunshine, passed the curious stares of those about the door, summoned Ramon and walked up the street.

It was only a short distance to the cunningly misnamed Academy of Music, and he asked Ramon to take short-cuts. He did hesitate to break in on You's tête-à-tête with the famous (or possibly infamous) Madame Alix, but, on the other hand, he was delighted that his first visit to her house was on business affairs rather than pleasure. Being officially introduced to the place as a person disinterested in Madame's wares was much better than knocking at her door some evening as a stranger come to see and sample her merchandise. In the very near future, however, he would indeed be a patron of hers, and, now that he thought about it, the sooner the better. He had already been too long without having a woman ...

With Ramon following him, Tommy turned the corner into Dumaine Street and had no difficulty finding the door of Madame Alix's house. It was a most formidable door of oaken planks studded with iron spikes, and its very grimness seemed to accentuate the promised delights available within. A chain with a metal knob dangled on the outside. Tommy had been hoping that some of Madame Alix's beauties might adorn the balconies above; he was disappointed. It was too early, he told himself, for any such teasing display. Perhaps later in the afternoon when offices closed, and men had the leisure to stroll down the street with lecherous eye for the lovelies above ...

He pulled the chain, listening to the high-pitched jangle of a bell in the interior courtyard. Moments later he heard the rasping of bolts being withdrawn, and the door was opened by an outstandingly handsome young black. Tommy considered him quite the finest looking Negro lad he had ever seen, surpassing in physique even Colt, the Falconhurst Fancy who was almost the ruination of Dovie of Dove Cote, Tommy's putative 'mother'.

'Good mornin', Masta suh.' The fellow was soft spoken and polite. 'Kin I do somethin' for yo'?'

'You must be Drum. I've already heard about you from my boy here.' He gestured over his shoulder to Ramon behind him.

'Yes suh, I'm Drum.'

'The one who puts on the famous shows?'

'Yes suh. We calls 'em *mêlées*.'

'I understand you are to be congratulated on your performances. Perhaps I'll see one sometime. But for the moment, will you kindly convey my good wishes to your mistress and tell her that I come here from Mr LaFitte who sent me to see Captain You.'

The boy Drum bowed and flourished his hand in a welcoming gesture. 'Yes suh, Masta suh, will you kindly come inside and I'll tell Madame Alix. Captain You is with her.'

Tommy stepped through the grim doorway into a courtyard lined with balconies surrounding a compact and verdant garden where broad banana fronds cast fringed dark shadows in the sun-splattered interior. Drum motioned him to a seat on a marble bench, then skipped lightly up a flight of stairs to the first balcony. He rapped softly on a door opening on the court. At a word presumably from inside, he opened the door only to reappear a moment later and trip down the stairs.

'Captain You and Madame Alix mighty happy to see yo', Masta suh.' He beamed at Tommy. 'Yore nigger boy kin wait for yo' out'n back with me, but yo' tells him to keep his eyes on the ground. He ain' supposed to look up at the girls ifn' they walk along the balcony. They's for white men only 'n' cain' have no nigger a-eyin' 'em. Specially now 'cause sometimes they ain' all dressed at this time o' day.'

Tommy told Ramon to accompany Drum and to follow Drum's instructions and keep his eyes on the ground. He knew, of course, that Ramon would do no such thing, but at least he had been so instructed. He knew that Ramon would be wise enough not to be caught staring open-mouthed at the girls. If he did steal a look, he was only doing what came naturally.

He followed Drum up the stairs, noting as he did so how the thin pantaloons shaped themselves to the powerful muscles of the boy's legs and how the tow linen of his shirt stretched across his massive shoulders. This young black was indeed a handsome man, and Tommy wondered where the lady of the house might have bought him. Seeing Drum in the flesh, Tommy could understand how his mistress could easily charge a high price for one of her spectaculars. Surely he would be exciting to watch, provided his partners were equally good-looking. Of course, the partners would be black, but Tommy supposed that any black girls *chez* Madame Alix would be super-superior.

Tommy followed Drum along the balcony until he rapped at the same door. A voice inside asked him to enter. The first thing that caught his eye in the gaudy, over-furnished room was the figure of a woman of uncertain age on an elaborately carved and gilded chaise longue. She was so painted and bedizened that Tommy wouldn't even hazard a guess. Nor could he judge her age from her hair which had been dyed a bold and brassy yellow. Her ample figure was tightly corseted, and she was dressed in a froth of laces and satin. Jewels sparkled at her throat, her wrists, in her ears and on her hands. She looked a question at Tommy and then answered the question herself by pointing to the occupant of a chair with one hand and, at the same time, patting a chair near her for Tommy's occupancy.

'Captain Dominique You,' she said. Her words were slightly accented, but her lovely voice was so low and controlled that the accent made it even more enchanting. The cultured voice issuing from the wrinkled harridan surprised Tommy. Even with her brassy appearance, and, in spite of her profession, he recognized that she must, at one time in her life, have been a lady of some quality.

Dominique You half rose from his chair and nodded his head perfunctorily at Tommy. 'I'm Dominique You,' he said.

The size and corpulence of the man, his round red face and his deep-set almost black eyes, combined with the fringe of white hair, gave him a forbidding appearance.

'And I am Thomas Verder,' Tommy answered. 'I have a letter for you, and although I much dislike breaking up your tête-à-tête with Madame, I would much appreciate it if you would read it.'

Her stays creaked as Madame Alix reached over and tapped Tommy lightly on the wrist with her fan.

'Tut, tut, young man.' She smiled at him, and he could see that like most women, she was already intrigued by him. 'Nothing could interrupt our tête-à-tête. We have already ruined quite half the reputations in New Orleans, and now we shall have a new subject to talk about after you leave. Yourself! And that, I am sure is going to make a most interesting bit of conversation, *n'est-ce-pas*?'

'I hope it will be entertaining even though you do not know me.' Tommy smiled his most engaging smile at her.

'Who needs to know you?' She opened her fan with a click of the ribs and fanned herself vigorously for a moment. 'You are young and you are extremely handsome and that is your *carte blanche* to any situation. In addition, I would not be a bit surprised but what you are an unprincipled rogue. Otherwise why should you have a letter for Dominique You who is the veritable prince of rogues, aren't you, Dominique, *mon ami*?'

'I like to think so, my dear Alix, but each day I am getting older, and the profession of rogue is only for younger men like our friend here. However, my dear' – he nodded to Alix – 'with your permission we shall see what this young man's letter contains.'

'I'm even more curious than you, so hurry, Dominique. I can scarce contain myself. We shall have so much to talk about after M'sieur Verder has gone.'

While You was breaking the seals on the letter, Madame Alix again pointed her fan to the armchair near her chaise longue. Tommy distrusted the spindly gilt legs, but the chair held his weight when he sat down. Captain You flipped open the silver-handled lorgnette which he wore on a black ribbon around his neck, adjusted the paper at arm's length and read the letter. When he had finished, he dropped it in his lap and winked at Alix.

'You'll be surprised when I tell you who wrote this letter,' he remarked. 'From someone we both know very well.'

'*Hélas!* You have piqued my curiosity. Don't keep me in

suspense any longer. Tell me. From whom?'

You delayed a moment in answering her, a knowing smile on his lips. Finally he spoke: 'From Helen.'

'You mean . . .?'

'I do. From Helen Gordon.'

'Who married the rich Mr Latimer and is now a widow. Damn! She must have led him a merry way to the grave. Well, well, from Helen Latimer.'

'The same, my dear.'

'And what does my dear Helen want?' She wagged an admonitory finger. 'Don't tell me, I already know. She has taken a fancy to this young man – Helen always did like handsome young men – and she wants you to help him. Right?'

'Quite right. How did you know?'

'Because I know Helen. Any handsome man would interest her and this one particularly.'

'Yes?' You raised his eyebrows.

'Oh, for heaven's sake, Dominique, you never notice things the way I do but when M'sieur Verder walked across the floor, I knew immediately that he would satisfy any woman.'

Tommy looked from one to the other. He wanted to hear more about Helen Latimer but felt it would not be in good taste to ask.

'And how is my dear Helen?' Madame Alix asked Tommy.

'In the best of health when I saw her a week or so ago.'

'And a widow if I am not mistaken?' You asked.

'A very rich widow I am sure.' Madame Alix smiled. 'And so, Dominique, what are you going to do for Helen's protégé who is here with us now?'

'I think possibly we could use him.'

'Not possibly – probably or rather certainly. I told you he was a rogue, and that is the kind of man you are looking for in your business. Yes?'

'Yes, most assuredly.'

'I shall be happy if I can be of any service to you.' Tommy broke into their conversation.

'Don't be too happy, young man,' Alix warned him.

'Anything to do with the LaFittes may well cost you your neck, especially if you are connected with Dominique. But then, we are all no better than we should be.'

Captain You heaved himself up from his chair and took a couple of steps to stand before Tommy.

'Report to me at the blacksmith's shop tomorrow morning at ten. We'll try to find something for you to do to keep you out of mischief.'

'Better say to keep him *in* mischief,' Alix interrupted. 'And speaking of mischief' – she smiled archly – 'I think we should do something to celebrate this young man's entry into your business.'

'A glass of champagne?' You suggested.

'Tut, tut, Dominique. What does a young man want with a glass of champagne except perhaps to quench his thirst? I ask you, Dominique, what did you think about when you were Mr Verder's age? Certainly not champagne. *Jamais!* You had other more important things on your mind.'

'Such as?'

'Women, if I remember correctly, and I most certainly do.'

'Madame is a wise woman.' Tommy smiled at her.

'After the years I have spent in this business one has to be wise, particularly in knowing men. Right at this moment I'm wishing I were as young as you are, Mr Verder.' Instead of tapping him with her fan, she let her fingers rest on his arm. He could not help noticing that her diamonds were much larger than Helen Latimer's.

She sighed. 'But I am not as young as I would like to be, so I must find a worthy substitute for myself. Dominique, ring the bell for Drum.'

Once again Tommy listened to the distant jangling of a bell. After a moment, running steps sounded on the stairs, then a knock on the door. At Madame Alix's word, the door opened and Drum stood framed there.

'You rang, Madame?'

'Of course I did.' She could be petulant, Tommy noted.

'Drum boy, go to the top floor and tell Chloe I want to see her here.' She waved him out of the door.

'Chloe?' Dominique asked, breaking the silence. 'Perhaps our young friend does not care for coloured girls.'

Alix sat bolt upright on the chaise. 'Any man would appreciate Chloe. Despite a touch of the tar brush, she is the loveliest girl I have ever had, except perhaps Helen Latimer.'

Tommy smiled to himself. So he had not been wrong. The elegant Mrs Latimer had indeed been a professional and right here in Madame Alix's house. He knew it; she was too far practised in ways to please a man to be only an amateur. Now he was already anticipating this unknown Chloe. He could feel the incipient swelling in his groin at the very thought of her, stranger though she might be.

'I yield to Madame's choice.' He spread his hands palms up. 'I am sure she knows.'

'You can be damned glad you didn't add "after years of experience". I would have resented that.' She turned towards the door, listening to the soft tapping. 'Here she is now.'

The door opened slowly and Tommy sucked in his breath. Never before had he seen such a beautiful girl. She was the colour of a tea rose with a vibrant pink showing through the pale ivory of her skin. Her long dark hair was gathered in a clasp at the nape of her neck and fell nearly to the floor behind her. Her eyes, deep and luminous like the eyes of a sacrificial virgin at the ancient Egyptian corn festival, peered out from under long lashes, first at Madame Alix, then briefly at Dominique, and finally at Tommy where they lingered. Her red lips parted in a half smile, showing perfect teeth.

'Chloe,' said Madame Alix, who was all charm, 'we have here a Mr Tommy who is going into business with Dominique You. We felt that a celebration should be forthcoming to mark the occasion, and I know of nobody with whom Mr Tommy could celebrate better than yourself. Do you think you could help him celebrate?'

Again Chloe looked at Tommy and her admiration for him was apparent in the little in-drawing of breath that she made. The tip of her coral tongue circled her lips.

'Most certainly, Madame.' She hesitated a moment and then added: 'Between Mr Tommy and myself we shall be able to make fireworks. Skyrockets and Roman candles will be set off to celebrate.'

'Don't be so damned poetic, *ma chérie*. We'll take the fireworks for granted. And now if you will conduct Mr Tommy upstairs to your room ...'

'With pleasure, Madame.'

Tommy was so enraptured with Chloe that he had scarcely

paid attention to Madame Alix. Compared to Chloe, Missie Acker was a washed-out second-rater. He finally came back to earth and added his own, 'With pleasure.'

Together they walked out of the room.

Madame Alix waited for the door to close, then smiled at You.

'You have a new recruit,' she said. 'And if I am not mistaken, this young cockalorum will prove valuable to you.'

'I would have said that myself, my dear, but now that I know you approve of him, I am doubly sure. Yes, he will prove valuable.'

'And,' she added, 'I am sure that tomorrow morning Chloe will brag that he is a man among men. *Hélas, mon ami*, there are many times when one wishes one were younger, but never in my life have I wished it more than I do now.'

'But you . . .'

'Hush, *mon ami*. Let us observe. Let us both tiptoe quietly upstairs to the linen closet on the floor above. Perhaps you do not know, but there is a peephole there which looks into Chloe's room. I have charged as much as fifty dollars for a man to stand at that peephole, but for once I shall be magnanimous and charge you nothing at all, provided . . .'

'What?'

'You will give me equal time at peeping as you preempt for yourself.'

7

Tommy left Madame Alix's Academy of Music walking in a world of his own. The overhanging balconies, the glimpses of verdant courtyards, the people passing in the hot street had no existence for him. Within his new horizon there was only the exciting memory of Chloe's lips, the perfumed softness of her hair, the tea-rose smoothness of her accommodating body. He had never been happier in his life.

The unforgettable image of unbelievably beautiful Chloe

had completely displaced Melissa Acker. Could he ever have been really in love with Missy? No, he decided as he strode back to his hotel with a sweating Ramon panting to keep up, Missy must have been a passing fancy. Her shining prettiness would have surely faded as the years progressed, and she would have become a stout second edition of her mother with all the cloying cuteness inappropriate to her age. He was lucky – even though the drunken carelessness that revealed his Negro blood almost cost him his life – that his marriage to Missy was invalidated. Otherwise he might never have met Chloe who was now the most important thing that had ever happened to him.

His experience with Chloe had been pure unalloyed rapture. He did not know, of course, that he had also been performing for the delight of Madame Alix and Dominique You, who sought vicariously to recapture their youth. Even if he had suspected that there were eyes beyond the wall, he had been so completely absorbed by Chloe that it would probably have made no difference.

When Tommy reached the hotel, deVeau was sitting behind the desk, yawning as he again offered Zelda to him. However, Tommy was so completely satiated that he desired nothing more than to wash the sweetness from his body and relax alone with his thoughts of Chloe. After sending Ramon to fetch hot water, he dismissed the boy for the day, stripped off his clothes, bathed himself with a soapy rag, and collapsed on the bed, luxuriating in his physical exhaustion and his vivid recall of the one perfect woman he had ever had. Yes, he continued to assure himself, he had finally encountered complete feminine perfection.

Although he thought himself both physically and mentally exhausted, he found that his thoughts of Chloe were beginning to arouse him again. As the mental images persisted, he became so rampant that he would even have welcomed Zelda to his arms just to find physical release. He was far too tired, however, to get up and ring the bell to summon her. There was an easier way, and he resorted to it. When release came, he relaxed, at last able to leave his mind a blank. Sleep was his answer because he needed to renew his strength and clear his thoughts before his appointment with You in the morning.

Ignoring the sun that was still shining through the jalousies, he turned over on his side and within moments was dead to the world.

He was awakened once during the night by hunger; he had nothing to eat since breakfast. He struggled from bed and groped his way to the door to find Ramon curled up on the blanket outside. He woke the boy and dispatched him to the kitchen to forage for food. Ramon returned with a cup of warmed-over coffee and two stale croissants which Tommy ate. Back in bed, he slept until the morning sun, streaming across the sheets, awakened him.

His first thoughts on awakening were of Chloe. He remembered how she had insisted on his removing his shirt and how piqued she had been when he had refused. He could not know that both Madame Alix and Captain You had puzzled over his curious behaviour, but accepted his explanation to Chloe that it was an idiosyncrasy affecting his virility. Yes, Madame Alix assured You, some men had strange quirks; she had known those who could perform only with their shoes on; some who could not remove any clothes, and others with even weirder wonts. One man she had known was impotent unless he wore a coon-skin cap. Another had to don women's pantalets ...

Reluctantly Tommy got out of bed and summoned Ramon, who stared in amazement at the state of his master's anatomy until a soft cuff on the ears reminded him to start helping Tommy dress. Ramon then ran to the kitchen to order a huge breakfast. Tommy realized reluctantly that man cannot live on love alone – that bread is also necessary. And when the bread is served toasted, with ham and eggs and grits along with a pot of steaming coffee, the whole world seems brighter.

On this day, Tommy decided to leave Ramon at the hotel while he visited the LaFitte blacksmith's shop. He knew the way now, and it was only a short walk. Moreover, he had already established his status as a slave-owner, so Ramon would only be in the way. He walked slowly on the shady side to avoid arriving bathed in perspiration.

Dominique You was awaiting him in an armchair on the *banquette* before the smithy. Sitting beside him was a man who bore such a striking resemblance to the humble black-smith he had met the previous day that Tommy was sure he must be Jean, the more famous of the LaFitte brothers. Captain You lifted himself ponderously a few inches above the seat of his chair and made the presentation, explaining that this was the young man who had come with a letter of introduction from Helen Latimer.

LaFitte smiled in recognition of her name, rose from his chair, made a sweeping old-world bow and welcomed Tommy with outstretched hand.

'My friend Dominique tells me that you would like to join our organization,' he said. His smile showed a row of perfect white teeth, contrasting with the deep mahogany tan of his face.

Tommy returned the bow with equal courtesy and extended his own hand. LaFitte grasped it with fingers like steel clamps. Tommy winced inwardly but did not betray his feelings. This was evidently a test; LaFitte seemed satisfied.

'Indeed I would, sir,' Tommy answered. 'I've been in New Orleans only a few days, coming here as a perfect stranger. But since I have arrived I have heard nothing but praise for you and your brother, as well as for Captain You. It seems that I could not have come to finer people. I am eternally grateful to Mrs Latimer.'

LaFitte smiled. 'The fair Helen is a good friend, but there are some who might counsel you against joining our organization. Believe me, we are not all that popular in New Orleans. Some even call us pirates, but I can assure you we are not pirates. We operate legitimately under letters of marque from the Republic of Cartagena. Our business here at the smithy is legitimate. Otherwise why would my brother wear himself out daily shoeing horses? And our store on Royal Street is patronized by the finest and most respectable women in New Orleans. As to our base of operations in Barataria . . .' LaFitte did not finish the sentence, but added as an afterthought: 'You will find out about that later.'

He paused to stare thoughtfully at Tommy. Then: 'Our business has recently taken a new turn which may not be to your liking. The silks and laces, the brocades and gewgaws at our shop on Royal Street are all profitable. But we are engaged in a far more productive business at present. I'll be the first to admit that it is not entirely legitimate, but it is infinitely more profitable.'

'May I ask what it is?' Tommy interrupted, sensing that LaFitte wanted the question.

'Indeed you may,' Dominique You answered, 'seeing as how we have both decided that we want you in this business – provided, of course, you are willing.'

'I shall answer in one word.' LaFitte smiled at Tommy. 'And that word is – slaves. Yes, black men and women, but, more particularly, black men. That is the great demand today, Tommy. No longer can we import slaves into the United States legally, and yet the demand for them is greater than ever. Fine *bozals* just off the ship from Africa will bring $800 or more, and the market is ever expanding. Negroes are sold on sight. Plantation owners can't get enough slaves.'

Tommy thought of the Maxwells and their great slave-breeding operation at Falconhurst. He asked: 'Why can't the market be supplied with slaves bred locally? I had a friend who kept a stud book, raised his stock carefully and made a fortune.'

Both LaFitte and You shook their heads. 'It will be a long time before that sort of breeding will catch up with the expanding market. Some few places in the south are already breeding slaves, true, but their output is only a drop in the bucket,' LaFitte said. 'Figure this: it takes about eighteen years for a slave to develop fully. We can't wait that long. Perhaps in another twenty years the supply problem will be solved, but the demand for slaves is today.'

'So where are you going to get them?' Tommy asked.

'There is only one place,' You answered. 'Cuba. Or more specifically the city of Havana.'

'It is the only legitimate slave market left today,' LaFitte added. 'Spain has not outlawed slavery.'

'And Havana is only a short sail from here,' You continued. 'We bring the slaves here from Cuba. In Cuba, a likely *bozal* just off the ship from Africa sells for around $300. Here we sell him for $800 or more and there are no questions asked.'

'You smuggle them in?' Tommy looked from LaFitte to You and back again, finally looking at LaFitte for an answer.

'It is not a word we like.' LaFitte shrugged his shoulders. 'But, alas, we have to accept it. We bring them here to meet the demand which is mounting every day. There's not a plantation owner in the country who doesn't bless us. We are really helping the prosperity of the nation because slaves are needed to produce more cotton and cane. The more we raise the richer the country gets, and after all, isn't national prosperity everyone's business?'

Tommy nodded. If smuggling was the only way to get needed slaves into the country, who could do it more efficiently than the LaFittes, Captain You and company, and get away with it as practically legal? Men who walked the streets of New Orleans with the prestige and respectable reputation of the LaFittes were no furtive smugglers. They were businessmen, and he would be proud to be associated with them.

The two men were staring at him intently, waiting for him to speak.

'Then, gentlemen,' Tommy said, smiling as though agreeing to a proposition which had not yet been offered, 'what is it that I can do for you? Is there a way that I can be of service to your organization? If so, please tell me.'

You heaved himself out of his chair and waved his hand at Tommy to remain seated. He entered the wide door of the blacksmith's shop and reappeared in a few moments, followed by a huge black whose velvety skin glistened in the sun from a liberal application of oil. A fine specimen of manhood – tall, muscular, and well featured – he was naked except for the leg irons on his ankles.

'This is what we mean.' You had the man stand before Tommy on the *banquette*. 'You can help us round up more stock like this. Our business in slaves is growing so rapidly that we need more men to help us. We need men to go to Havana and bring these critters here. We need men to take care of them, we need men to contact our customers, we need help in every direction. And good men are hard to find.'

Tommy took his eyes reluctantly from the black and looked from You to LaFitte. His mind was already made up. First, he was offered entry into a lucrative profession which, if not entirely legal, was at least tolerated. Second, he liked both Jean LaFitte and Dominique You personally. They were his kind of men. He belonged with them.

'I'm flattered, indeed, gentlemen, that you should consider me good enough to join your organization. After all, you know very little about me except for a letter of introduction from a mutual friend. But be that as it may. If you offer me a job, I'll attend to it to the best of my ability, and I promise to give you one hundred cents worth of labour for every dollar you pay me. Frankly, gentlemen, do you want me?'

You nodded in silent approval. LaFitte answered Tommy. 'We do. It will take a little time before you are valuable to us, for you have a lot to learn. Later we shall discuss final monetary arrangements, but for the present we'll pay you ten gold dollars a week and food and lodging. Ultimately we will offer you a share in our profits, but meanwhile accept ten dollars a week while we are training you.'

'Agreed.' Tommy shook hands in turn with both LaFitte and You.

'We have a schooner leaving tomorrow evening for our base in Barataria about sixty miles below the city. We would like to have you aboard and prepared to spend some considerable time with us there. It is there you can become acquainted with the way we do business.'

'Agreed,' Tommy repeated.

LaFitte led the big black into the shop, his leg chain clanking on the *banquette,* and Tommy was left alone with Dominique You.

'So enjoy yourself, lad. You've all of today and tomorrow until sundown to do exactly as you please. You're going to find plenty of work to do at Barataria. It won't be laborious, I assure you, but you will need time to learn the ropes. However, you will find many ways to enjoy yourself. Our little settlement is by no means spartan. There will be plenty to entertain you.'

'Thank you, Captain You. May I ask if there are women there?'

'Women a plenty, young cockerel. I cannot guarantee any rare hot-house blooms like Alix's Chloe, but you'll find plenty of serviceable wenches. Women seem to play an important part in your life, yes? It was a woman's letter which introduced you to us, and yesterday my good friend Madame Alix entertained you with one of her loveliest young women. Tell me, how did you like Chloe?'

'Quite the loveliest experience of my whole life, Captain

You. I've thought about little else since I was with her.'

'You'll have more to think about from now on.' You winked at him. 'There'll be plenty of time for the women, too. But' – he hesitated for a moment – 'tell me one thing, young cockerel...'

'Yes?' Tommy looked at him expectantly.

'Do you always perform with your shirt on?'

'You mean...?'

'Don't get excited. News travels fast in an establishment like Madame Alix's. You had scarcely left the house before Chloe started raving about you. She was eminently satisfied with you and wanted everyone to know it, but she did have one tiny fault to find with you.'

'The shirt, you mean?' Tommy laughed.

You nodded in assent, joining Tommy's laughter.

'Well, put it down as an idiosyncrasy, Captain You. I cannot really explain it except to say that I am more comfortable that way. In fact, otherwise I can do nothing.'

You laughed long and boisterously. 'Well, young cock, if a shirt helps you, by all means wear it. And now, I suppose you are headed back to your hotel.'

Tommy smiled. 'Eventually, sir, that is where I shall be going. But for the present I think I shall walk down Dumaine Street and pull the chain in front of a particular door. Then when the young fellow they call Drum answers it, I shall ask for the services of Chloe, and, if she is not otherwise engaged, I'll be spending some time with her.'

'Then good luck to you and have a pleasant time.'

'That I shall, Captain You, even though I continue to wear my shirt.'

You gave him a little push. 'Get on with you, boy. Enjoy yourself. I envy you.'

LaFitte appeared in the doorway and crossed the *banquette* to shake hands with Tommy.

'Be here tomorrow afternoon about five,' LaFitte advised.

'You can count on it,' Tommy answered.

8

Next morning, Tommy dragged his feet reluctantly through the sunshine of Dumaine Street. Several times he had to step into the gutter to avoid being splashed by black women who were scrubbing down steps and sidewalks in front of houses. The women always looked up at him with engaging smiles that displayed rows of gleaming white teeth. To their murmured 'Good morning, Masta suh,' he responded only with a wan smile, for he was still remembering his tearful farewell to Chloe. She had clung to him, loath to let him go, her hands vainly trying to seduce him into another hour's stay with her. But he was truly spent, and, much as he might wish it, was physically unable to respond to her caresses. He had left her weeping and felt like weeping himself as he descended the stairs from her upper room to the first-floor gallery.

He had to pass Madame Alix's door and was surprised to see it open. She called out to invite him in for a tête-à-tête over a cup of chocolàte, confessing that she had had Drum leave her door open, as she wanted a word with Tommy before he left. He was glad, for he would certainly have tried to see her before sailing.

She had been all smiles as she sat upright against a hillock of small lacy pillows on her huge bed. After motioning him to sit in the chair beside her, she rang for Drum and ordered chocolate and brioches for Tommy. 'Just can't have an important guest of mine leaving on an empty stomach,' she had informed him, patting his hand, then letting her fingers slip down to rest on his leg.

Tommy counted the little breakfast as charged against the fifty dollars he had handed over to her the night before. Not that he regretted the money – not a single copper penny of it – but he had other ideas in his head while he sat beside the wrinkled harridan whom he recognized as having once been an extremely handsome woman. He hoped that her talon-like fingers on his leg would not start moving. To forestall any provocative fondling he picked up the hand and kissed it, placing it back gently on the satin sheets. It was a matter of business that he wanted to discuss with her, and he could not allow his thoughts to be diverted. Besides, if he had not been able to respond to Chloe earlier, he certainly could not react to this old woman.

Yes, his business had to do with Chloe. He wanted her for himself alone. Would Madame, when he had accumulated sufficient money, sell Chloe to him?

She delayed answering for several moments while she sipped her chocolate and crumbled a brioche into tiny balls. It would take a lot of money to buy Chloe, she finally said. Why buy her? He could enjoy her here whenever he wanted, and, if his taste leaned towards tea-rose octoroons, she would find one for him, one that she could guarantee to be a virgin. But he shook his head. It was Chloe alone he wanted. He knew she might be expensive, for she was no ordinary octoroon, but a very beautiful and accomplished one. Still, he was quite unprepared for the figure of $5,000 which Madame quoted. He wondered if he had allowed Madame's fingers to inch their way to his crotch, where they had most certainly been headed, if her price would have been a little lower ...

Yes, $5,000 was a lot of money, said Madame Alix, but not an unusual price to ask for an octoroon. The young bloods of the town often paid that much for one at the Octoroon Ball and then set her up in a little house on Rampart Street. This would be little enough for Tommy to pay for her if and when he had accumulated his pile, as he surely would.

So, he had left Madame Alix a little frustrated, true, but with her solemn promise not to dispose of Chloe to any other person. She would reserve her for him. Then, as though she sensed the intensity of his desire for Chloe, she added a kindly word of encouragement. If he were successful with the LaFitte organization, as she was sure he would be, she said, it would not take him long to accumulate such a sum. 'Something tells me, young man, that you usually get what you aim for. True?'

'Not always, Madame.' He shook his head.

'But there is one thing of which I am sure.' She smiled up at him, and, despite her lack of paint, powder and rouge, she had a charming face. 'You usually get any woman you want, don't you?'

His compressed lips smiled back at her as though they

shared a secret – which they did, although he did not know it.

'And, I'll venture to say you have never disappointed a woman yet.' She wagged a forefinger at him.

'Never, Madame,' he admitted somewhat proudly.

'Now get on with you. Dominique tells me you are going to Barataria, and I don't want you to be late.'

He squeezed her hand, then impulsively reached over to kiss her on the cheek. He walked out the door without turning back to look at her. At least he had her solemn promise not to sell Chloe to anyone else. Well, if his job under the LaFittes went the way he hoped, it would not take him too long to accumulate the money. True, any time at all would be too long, but he had to take Madame's word, and leave Chloe behind for the present. He walked along the gallery, down the flight of stairs and into the courtyard where Drum was waiting to let him out.

His footsteps dragged automatically. His mind was still in the scented room where he had, at least for a few hours, owned his Chloe. What an artist she was! He mentally reviewed all the women he had ever known. Only one, Helen Latimer, had approached Chloe, but then, Helen Latimer was an older woman, quite old enough to be Chloe's mother, but all her sophisticated tricks in bed could not outweigh Chloe's youth and beauty.

It hurt him deeply to leave Chloe, knowing that other men would lie with her as intimately as he had, and that she would fondle them as professionally and perhaps as lovingly as she had fondled him. No, that could not be quite true! There had been more to her embraces than mere commercial pantomime. He was certain that she cared as much for him as he did for her, yet what could she do about it? Or what could he? Five thousand dollars! Indeed she was worth it, but would he ever really have that amount of money to buy her, even though he told himself he would? All the more reason then to take advantage of his present opportunity. The ten dollars a week would not go on forever. He must work hard to begin to share soon in the profits LaFitte had promised. Hurry the day when he could place the money in Madame Alix's hand and lead Chloe away so that she would belong to nobody but himself forever and ever!

Ramon was in the tiny lobby of the hotel when Tommy entered, and he gestured him to follow. Maybe, he thought, Ramon had been a foolish investment. He was just that many dollars further away from buying Chloe. But even if he had not purchased Ramon, he would not have enough to buy Chloe, so why torture his mind? He must concentrate on the great opportunity for gain ahead of him. Here he was only a few days in New Orleans, and he had already been accepted by the LaFittes. Chloe would have to wait. His immediate purpose was to succeed in this chance that Helen Latimer had provided. His thoughts turned again to Helen. Should he have stayed longer at her plantation? She had been infatuated with him, he mused, as his fingers instinctively sought the diamond cross at his neck.

But enough of these thoughts of females! Women had always been his greatest source of trouble, although they were also his greatest source of pleasure. What a mess he had gotten himself into over Missie Acker! Forget them all – forget Missie Acker, Helen Latimer, and even Chloe – at least for the time being. Concentrate on the job he had to do for the La-Fittes. Even if he had not yet found one, there must be other women whose lips were as beguiling as Chloe's, whose skin was as petal-soft, and whose murmurs in his ear as passionate as hers. And yet – he allowed himself one fleeting second of doubt – if there were, he had never found them. He tried to convince himself if such a woman existed, perhaps she would not be a professional whore in Madame Alix's Academy of Music. So forget Chloe. Concentrate on the business at hand! Be practical, Tommy!

He needed a valise. He couldn't travel with his saddle-bags now that he had accumulated more clothing, so he sent Ramon out with instructions to buy one for less than the five dollars he gave him.

When Ramon had closed the door behind him, Tommy sat down on the edge of the bed. He must think clearly, but he still had trouble getting Chloe and her embraces out of his mind. After all his experiences with women, was he going to let an octoroon whore get the better of him? Not by a damned sight! He managed to smile to himself. If Chloe was an octoroon whore, then what was he but an octoroon whore-master? Was he forgetting that his most vital job, a matter of life and death, was to keep the world from unmasking him as the slave Calico? As a first step, he must forge papers that would ensure his freedom from Dovie. Dovie would not object, were she to find out, and they would provide him with at least some protection. He went downstairs to the desk where deVeau was sitting behind the zinc counter.

Putting on his most amiable smile, Tommy asked to borrow a sheet of white foolscap, with a quill and some ink. For a tip of five cents, deVeau produced from under the counter a sheet of plain white paper, then passed Tommy an inkhorn and quill. Thanking deVeau, Tommy took these up to his room and sat down at the table, staring into space. Suddenly inspired, he dipped the quill in ink and wrote slowly in as perfect an imitation of a feminine hand as he was able:

Brownsville, Alabama

Know all men by these presents:
That I, Dovie Verder of Dove Cote Plantation, have granted complete and absolute freedom to my natural son and slave, Calico, who is henceforth to be known as Thomas Verder and I hereby acknowledge him as the rightful heir to Dove Cote and The Patch Plantations.
(Signed) Dovie Verder

Witnessed by
Ephraim Glover, Justice of the Peace
(Signed) Ephraim Glover

It was masterfully executed, he thought, even if it was not legal. He had been able to change his handwriting so that Dovie's letters were round and flowing, while the forged script of the imaginary Glover was cramped and crabbed. If worst came to worst, he could at least present this document and stay clear of the auction block. It was worth a try, anyway. Never again would he be a slave. He would die first.

As the horrid images of the slave cabins at Falconhurst and Dove Cote crossed his mind, he tried to reassure himself of his freedom by standing up and looking in the mirror over the chest of drawers. No, there was nothing in the face looking back at him that would betray his secret. It was, he felt sure, far too handsome a face to cause doubts in anybody's mind. His skin was white and clear; his hair light brown and wavy but not too wavy, at least not kinky. Perhaps his nostrils were just a shade too wide, but they added to his good looks by making his face more sensuous. His lips were curved and full and moist looking, but not in the least negroid. Damn it, if it were not for those telltale black spots on his back and belly, he would never have to be afraid. So he would not be afraid. He would put his own blackness from his mind. He looked in the mirror and was again inspired by his own image. Men liked him and so, damn it, did women. What had he ever to worry about? He smiled cockily at his reflection in the mirror. Nothing at all – at least for the present.

He opened the door at Ramon's knock. The boy carried a large valise, which he proudly presented to his master, along with two dollars. It was not a very prepossessing piece of luggage, made of cardboard with a shiny brown finish that proclaimed its cheapness, but it would have to do. Tommy hated any sign of poverty, but he was in a hurry and couldn't be bothered with trifles. The valise would serve.

A glance at his watch showed him that it was already time for lunch, and he was hungry after the meagre breakfast at Madame Alix's. He sent Ramon running to the kitchen for whatever was on the table d'hôte for the day, advising him to bring his own lunch along, and so it happened that for the first time in his life, Ramon sat at table and ate with a supposed white man.

After lunch they transferred the contents of the saddle-bags to the valise. The saddle-bags reminded Tommy of his horse, which, in the flurry of excitement, he had forgotten. He certainly wasn't going to need a horse at Barataria, so he dashed out to the stable to try to sell the beast. He was lucky to make a fairly good deal with the owner of the stable. Should he need a horse on his return to New Orleans, he could get one through the good graces of Pierre LaFitte.

Once back to his room, he sent Ramon for hot bath water, banished the boy and scrubbed his body clean of the lingering odour of Chloe's perfume. When he had finished, he recalled the banished Ramon and ordered him to scrub himself with the secondhand soapy water. Then, sniffing Ramon to see that he had no musk, he dressed himself in his best clothes with a change of linen.

By the time they were both dressed, an hour remained before they were to report to LaFitte. Tommy considered using the spare time to return to Madame Alix's for another glimpse of Chloe, but he realized that another farewell would obliterate all sense of time. So he restlessly paced his room, stepping out on the balcony from time to time to watch the traffic below. Ages later, the hands on his watch finally showed a quarter past four, and he went downstairs, followed by Ramon with the valise. After settling his account, they left together for LaFitte's.

The carriage standing before LaFitte's shop looked familiar to him as he strode along the *banquette*, and, as he drew nearer, he recognized the handsome coachman. At that moment, the last thing in the world he wanted was to see Helen Latimer, but if he was to keep his appointment, there was no escape. He could see the frills of her lilac gown behind You's crossed legs. Well, he assured himself, he was enough of an actor to take the situation in stride. A moment later he greeted Helen even more effusively than he thought possible – and realized, moreover, that it was not all acting. Helen Latimer was a most attractive woman for her age, and, despite his initial aversion to her unexpected presence, he was really glad to see her.

He threw her a kiss while darting a sidelong glance of recognition at You. He held her hand longer than the prescribed moment, remembering how eagerly this same hand had so recently explored his body.

'Madame Latimer,' he said, expressing the proper astonishment at seeing her. 'You are quite the last person I expected to see here, but nothing, absolutely nothing, could have been a pleasanter surprise.'

She smiled at him, her eyes travelling up to his, but lingering an overlong moment on the bulge in his trousers. 'It seems,' she said, 'that I have come just in time to see you. I arrived in New Orleans last evening, and somehow I felt compelled to see my good friend Captain You, as much for his own genial company as to find some news of you. He tells me that you are now a part of his organization and that you are leaving for Barataria this afternoon.'

'Quite so,' Tommy included You in his smile. 'And now I sail with regrets, for I shall be leaving you behind.'

'Yes?' Her one word was a question. 'Perhaps you had better tell him, Dominique.'

'As if I could tell him as charmingly as you,' the old gallant simpered.

'But he is going to think it odd of me if I tell him.'

'How could I?' Tommy could be as gallant as You.

'Then I shall.' She clicked her fan open, her eyes lingering for a moment on the painted cupids before she looked at him. 'I too am going to Barataria. My main reason for coming to New Orleans was to find some suitable damask for new curtains in my drawing room, and Dominique has just been telling me that there was a new shipment at Barataria which has not yet been brought to Royal Street. He suggested that I make the short trip to pick it out myself and I agreed even before I knew that you were going to be on the same boat. Alas, you probably will not believe me! You will think me a most conniving baggage, but it is, I assure you, only a coincidence and not something prearranged.'

'I would be most flattered if it had been.' Tommy picked up her hand and squeezed it. 'I can think of no more delightful way to enter my new profession than in your company.'

'But remember,' You interposed, 'this is not a time for gallantry, even for a pretty lady. You have work to do at Barataria, so don't let Madame Helen distract you.'

'Bah, Dominique!' She laid a reassuring hand on his arm. 'I can only stay there a few days – I've many things to take care of back at the plantation – so I cannot divert him either too much or too long.'

'And I, Captain You,' Tommy spoke up, 'have always had the happy facility of not allowing any woman, regardless of how attractive she is (and surely nobody could be more attractive than *la belle Hélène*) to distract me from my work. I can easily divide my life into two separate worlds – the days for my work and the evenings for Madame Latimer during her short stay at Barataria. Yes?' He smiled at You.

'Then do just that,' You nodded. 'And perhaps having

Helen around will take away any feeling of strangeness you might have there. She will help bridge the gap.' He smiled benignly on them both. 'And now if you will excuse me, I must leave you alone. I have to talk to our good Pierre.'

Helen was silent for a moment, listening to his ponderous footsteps as he crossed the *banquette* and disappeared into the darkness of the smithy. She stood facing Tommy, her hands on her hips, almost defiant.

'I hope you didn't for a moment believe all that drivel about new draperies in my drawing room. Nonsense! You probably don't remember, but they are practically brand new. I came to New Orleans for only one reason – to be with you, Tommy. I have thought about nothing else since you left. That one night with you was only enough to make me crave more. I called on my old friend Madame Alix last evening. She said you were to leave this afternoon, so I came over here and wangled permission from Dominique to go with you. See.' She pointed to the carriage. 'My bags are all packed. I have only to have them set down on the *banquette*, dismiss my coachman, send him home, and go off with you. The few days I have to spend with you, I intend to enjoy to the utmost. Dominique has offered me the guest house, and, if you stay with me, there will be no questions asked. Barataria is not New Orleans. There nobody knows or cares if you spend the nights with me.'

'Least of all myself,' Tommy answered. 'I can think of no happier introduction to my new life than having you beside me.'

'Nor I,' she answered, 'but first you must forgive me for being a conniving woman.'

'I forgive you.' He picked up her hand and kissed it again. 'And perhaps I can prove my forgiveness to you the first night we are together.' He almost believed it. She certainly was an attractive woman and a joy to bed with. Nevertheless he found his thoughts going back to Dumaine Street to linger for one nostalgic moment on his Chloe. How wonderful it all would have been if Chloe could trade places with Helen. Impossible, of course. Helen was a free woman and Chloe a slave he could possess exclusively only if he had five thousand dollars. Well, perhaps Helen could help him there. He mentally assayed the rings on her fingers. Yes, perhaps she could.

9

The pale disc of the rising sun struggled through the mists that shrouded the delta to make silvery patterns on the scrubbed decks of the trim little schooner. The swift ship had carried Tommy and Helen Latimer down the broad sweeps of the Mississippi and through the tortuous short-cuts of creeks and bayous that led to LaFitte's settlement of Barataria, south of New Orleans. Tommy tried to stifle his yawn with his hand; he had passed a sleepless night, an exciting one, but somehow lacking the thrilling enchantment of the previous night with Chloe.

Both he and Helen had been received on board by a solicitous captain who had evidently been well briefed on his passengers, for he addressed Tommy as 'Mister Verder' and was obsequiously deferential to Mrs Latimer, whom he seemed to know. He had shown them to two diminutive cabins and on the floor of one of them had provided a shake-down for Ramon.

Tommy and Helen had remained on deck when they sailed, watching the ever-shifting movement of the port of New Orleans. Tommy was astounded by its magnitude. The shipping seemed busier even than New York. As far as he could see up and down the river, a forest of masts stood silhouetted against the sky. Hundreds of ships were tied up at the levees and as the LaFitte craft sailed down the river, Tommy could see the multicoloured flags of many nations at many sterns. The levees themselves teemed with life. Long lines of black stevedores carted produce to and from the ships. They sweated under cotton bales bound for the spinning and weaving mills of Old England and New England. They laboured under beams of mahogany and rare hard woods from the islands of the Caribbean, under burlap bags of coffee from Brazil, crates of porcelain from China, and machinery from the northern states. They also unloaded velvets from Lyons, furniture from Paris and all the myriad things demanded by a thriving city like New Orleans and the big houses of its inland plantations.

Tommy and Helen were quite content to stand there,

scarcely talking, hands clasped, enjoying the nearness of each other's presence. From time to time, she would free her hand from his, sliding her fingers down over the tight fabric of his pantaloons until he could stand it no longer. Whispering to her that it would be advisable to wait at least until after dark, he would remove her hand. She suggested that although her tiny cabin was piled high with luggage, the narrow bunk would be plenty wide enough for both of them for such an occasion, as two would take up no more room than one.

In a few hours, experiment proved her to be right. After a bite of supper in the captain's cramped quarters, they again stood for a while at the rail watching the rare lights on the bank reflected from the blackness of the river. When Helen's tantalizing hand and avid mouth had raised Tommy's inner climate to a fever pitch of desire, they went below.

Stopping at his cabin to shed his clothing (except his perennial shirt), Tommy found Ramon asleep on his blanket spread on the deck. Stepping around him, he opened the door a crack, made sure the coast was clear, then tip-toed down the passageway to rap lightly at Helen's cabin. The door opened instantly.

In the dark he could feel the softness of her naked body. The aura of her perfume enveloped him as she pressed her breasts against him. His arms encircled her, and he lifted her from the deck. She swung open her thighs and straddled his hips. He staggered a few steps across the cabin. His knees struck the edge of the bunk and they fell together. The narrowness of the bunk was no problem...

It was nearly daylight when he stole back to his own cabin. Exhausted, he fell asleep immediately. He had scarcely closed his eyes, it seemed to him, before there was a knock on his door and a voice pierced his half-consciousness, calling:

'Wake up, Masta suh. We 'rivin in 'bout an hour. Cap'n has coffee waitin', Masta suh, 'n' yo' tell that boy o' yourn he kin have coffee with the crew.'

Reluctantly he dressed himself, still groggy, still exhausted. He always marvelled at how his women could drain the last ounce of strength from him and still be eager for more.

He joined Helen again on deck where they watched the sun breaking through the clouds until it shone with hot tropical splendour. The stream had widened into a body of water that was, Helen told him, Barataria Bay. Yes, she admitted, she had been here several times before. In fact, she owned, she had once had a lover here. For all she knew, he was still here, but she was no longer interested in him. He might present a little problem, she said, but certainly not an insurmountable one. Whatever claim any other man might have to being her lover in the past, the present belonged to Tommy. Absolutely nobody could compare with Tommy.

'And while I'm letting down my hair about the past, Tommy dear,' she said and turned her head so that Tommy could not see her eyes, 'I have a confession to make. It is something that you will find out sooner or later, and I'd rather have you hear it from me than from someone else. I hope it will not change your feelings towards me. I realize that they are not very deep, but inconsequential as they are, I treasure them.'

'No, Helen, I'm sure my feelings towards you will not change, and they might not be quite as inconsequential as you think. Surely you must realize that what happened last night was not merely an act. I could not have enjoyed it as much as I did were I pretending, and, after all, why should I pretend?' He lifted her chin so that she would look at him, but she pushed his hand away and pressed her face against his chest.

'You know me only as Mrs Latimer, the owner of a plantation and a most respectable woman, yes?'

'Agreed.' He laughed at her unwillingness to face him. 'As Mrs Latimer, yes, but let me say one thing, my dear Helen. I would hardly call you a respectable woman, at least in bed. So-called respectable women endure contact with a man rather than enjoy it. They lie still, grit their teeth, and let a man take his pleasure, but all the while they are praying that it will soon be over. As for you—'

'Don't tell me. I don't want to be respectable if it means lying like a log of wood. I like men, and I think a woman can get as much pleasure out of sex as a man. I've known men before, but, oh, Tommy, I've never known a man who satisfies me the way you do.'

'That's gratifying. I seem to have what it takes to satisfy any woman. I've never had any complaints. But perhaps you have not had many men in your life.'

'Not many? You'd be surprised. I've had all kinds and all ages – from virginal schoolboys to doddering old men – more than enough to know that nobody can compare with you.'

'Then I'm unique?' He felt a glow of pride to think that this woman thought him so wonderful.

'Unique? Indeed you are, darling. Physically you are a phenomenon, but you are more than that. You are an ideal lover. You make love not only for your own pleasure but for the pleasure of your partner, and that is indeed unique. Most men do not care how a woman feels. They lunge, plunge and gasp. Bam! Bam! Thank you, ma'am! Then it's all over, with no thought of the woman's feelings or needs.'

'My pleasure is always heightened if the woman is enjoying herself too.'

'And for that I am grateful. But I am getting away from what I started to tell you – my confession, as it were. This is going to be difficult, so I might as well put it briefly and very bluntly. I was once one of the girls at Madame Alix's house.'

This time he succeeded in lifting her face to his. His forefinger gently brushed the tears from her cheek. 'Is that your terrible confession, my dear? What of it? It's nothing.'

'Nothing that I was a whore, sleeping with all kinds of men just for money?'

'I'm sure you gave each his money's worth, from the schoolboy virgin you initiated into the wonders of sex, to the old men you comforted.'

She nodded silently.

'Did I ever tell you that I preferred a woman who had never yet known a man?' He continued to stroke her damp cheek. 'As a matter of fact, I don't like virgins and never have. Passion is a highly developed emotion, and a woman, as well as a man, must have some experience in developing it. Where, my dear, could a woman get better experience than in Madame Alix's house where she may learn so many different ways to please a man? I never mentioned it to you, but I could see that you were well trained. A man can tell. So believe me, I'm all the more grateful for it. And now I, too, must make a little confession.'

'What? Don't tell me that you have been a gigolo!'

'Hardly.' He laughed. 'But I have a confession to make nevertheless. You see, I am madly in love with one of the girls at Madame Alix's house. Does that seem strange to you?'

'It only makes me feel miserable because I love you too much. Yes, absolutely miserable, but I shouldn't complain. I knew I couldn't hold you, Tommy. There is far too much difference in our ages. A woman of my years can hope for only so much from a younger man. Sooner or later he is bound to drift away. That is why I have pursued you so relentlessly. I must hurry to get all you can give me while I am still reasonably attractive. My mirror tells me I won't be able to hide the rush of time much longer.'

'Does it make any difference?'

'More than you could imagine. But I must know who this girl is. Yes, I am jealous, more jealous of her than I can tell you, but I'll not do anything to stand in your way. Will you tell me, Tommy? I know all the girls at Madame Alix's, you could have fallen in love with almost any one of them. Which one is it, my dear? Tell me.'

'But why? It will only make you more unhappy.'

'Yes, I know it will. But tell me, and I promise you I won't do anything to spoil your romance. You see, I love you enough to want you to be happy too.'

Tommy was silent for a moment. He looked towards the shore, watching the distant blur as it materialized into buildings. Finally he spoke. The mere mention of her name would, he knew, be gratifying. He had said 'Chloe' so many times in his thoughts that it would be a relief to pronounce it aloud.

'It's Chloe. I know she is not white, but she is supremely beautiful and I love her.'

'Chloe?' She pulled away from him abruptly and stared at him in shocked amazement. 'It can't be Chloe! It mustn't be!'

'But it is,' he insisted.

'Have you any idea who Chloe is?' She put both hands on his shoulders, and he could feel her fingers trembling.

'I know nothing about her except that I spent the night with her. I too am not inexperienced, Helen, and I have known many women: but Chloe, despite her coloured blood, is the most exquisitely satisfying woman I have ever held in my arms.'

She still clung to him. Her face had grown suddenly haggard, as though she had aged ten years in ten seconds. Her voice was nearly inaudible as she said:

'Why shouldn't she be satisfying to you? Chloe is my daughter.'

Tommy recoiled as if he had been slapped. His mouth went dry. He swallowed several times before he could speak.

'Helen, you're joking. How could Chloe be your daughter? She is coloured and you are white.'

'Yes, I'm white. But you are overlooking one important factor.'

'I am? What?'

'Her father. He was not white. Her father was René Jiminez. He's been dead for years, but even today if someone in New Orleans wants to make a favourable comparison of a good-looking man he will say "as handsome as René Jiminez". He was a quadro but by far the handsomest man in New Orleans. He was not a slave; he was a free man of colour from Cuba, and he was connected with Dominique You. As a man of colour, he was not permitted entrée to Madame Alix's. I had seen him frequently on the streets, and the first time I saw him I was intrigued. Then I met him through Dominique You. It was a case of love at first sight. He loved me as much as I loved him. I looked at him, and he looked at me, and we both knew it. Nothing else mattered to me – it made no difference that he was a man of colour. I was so completely enamoured of him that I was willing to throw everything away for him. And I did.'

'You left Madame's house?' Tommy was still so shaken that he could hardly speak, but when part of his numbed mind was able to think about Chloe, he could see her resemblance to the woman standing beside him.

'René bought my way out, and I went to live with him. He was not a poor man, and we rented an apartment together. Of course, we could not marry because of his colour, although I wanted that more than anything. Then Chloe was born. Somehow having a baby seemed to come between us. He worshipped the child, and I was jealous of her. I couldn't share him even with my own daughter. Whenever I looked at her, I couldn't help feeling that she was not my daughter but his – because she and her father were coloured, while I was white.

'René and I were together for three years when I lost him. I have always been grateful that he died and did not go off with another woman. He was on one of LaFitte's ships which ran into a hurricane off the Tortugas. He was swept overboard and lost at sea. I inherited quite a sum of money from him, enough for me to live on comfortably, but I had Chloe on my hands. Although she was nearly white, I could not acknowledge her as my daughter. Nor did I want to. She was a constant reminder of the fact that she was still living and her father whom I adored was dead.'

'Poor Chloe,' he sighed. 'No wonder she needed love. She'd never had any.'

'Yes, I can even feel sorry for her now. Strangely enough, I do not hate her, even knowing that she has your love.'

'So, tell me, what became of Chloe?'

'Madame Alix came to my rescue. We had always been friends since I left her. She arranged for Chloe to be adopted by an octoroon woman over on Rampart Street. I had to promise that I would never see her again. Well, you know what those octoroon women train a girl for – to please a man, nothing more or less. She did not make her debut at the Octoroon Ball; instead Madame Alix took her into her house when she was sixteen. She had been well trained for her profession and, as you know, she is lovely to look at.'

'The loveliest person I have ever seen, but then, Helen, I never saw you at her age.'

'Thank you, Tommy.' She managed a wan smile. 'So that's my rather sordid biography – a whore, mistress to a coloured man, and mother of an illegitimate child who is coloured. Not a very pretty story, but at least I've told the truth, and I feel better.'

'And is that the end of it?' he asked.

'The end to the sordidness. After René's death, I went to live in the American part of the city, divorcing myself from the French Quarter. It was there that I met Mr Latimer and married him. He was a wealthy man and a lot older than I. I tried to be a good wife to him, but I never loved him.'

He placed a protective arm over her shoulders and drew her close to him.

'This has been a great shock to me, knowing that you are Chloe's mother.'

'To me, too, especially as you are in love with her. But, Tommy, stay in love with her. Grant me these few days with you. Then I'll drop out of your life forever.'

'How can you?' He shook his head as if to clarify the tangle of ideas. 'If I marry Chloe, you'll be my mother-in-law.'

'You can't marry Chloe.' It was Helen's turn to shake her head. 'She's coloured, and you know there can be no marriage between black and white. However,' she added, 'there are other ways to set up housekeeping besides marriage, my dear.'

The matter seemed settled for Helen, and she snuggled against Tommy's chest.

But the revelation that Helen was Chloe's mother had so shocked Tommy that he seemed sunk in a deep stupor. He put one arm around Helen automatically without being really aware of her presence.

*

As the LaFitte schooner threaded its way among the small islands that dotted the expanse of Barataria Bay, Helen pointed out to Tommy the geography of his future home. The two larger islands that separated the bay from the Gulf of Mexico – Grand Isle and Grand Terre – provided good anchorage for LaFitte's armada of corsairs safe from the prying eyes of revenue cutters. Grand Terre, which lay straight ahead, was actually the capital of Barataria. As they drew nearer, the settlement appeared to be a small town of substantial wooden houses clustered about a three-storey red-brick mansion like a brood of chicks about a mother hen. The tree-lined streets were well kept and prosperous-looking. Massive warehouses lined the waterfront. A sleek three-masted sailing ship gave an impression of speed even while tied up to the pier.

Helen pointed and Tommy's eyes followed the direction of her finger.

'That's Jean LaFitte's house.' She indicated the big brick house. 'The smaller ones surrounding it belong to his men,' she said. 'Each man has his own house with a servant to take care of it, male or female depending on his preference. Some are neat and immaculately clean, others are slovenly, just like the owner ... Those warehouses are for the storage of goods before they are taken to New Orleans, but there' – and she pointed to an immense log stockade – 'is probably the most important place in Barataria today. That is where they keep the slaves before they are sold or taken to New Orleans.' Again, she pointed to the big house. 'I wonder if you will be living there.'

He shrugged his shoulders. 'Hardly. Why should M'sieur LaFitte honour a ten-dollar-a-week apprentice with accommodation in his own house?'

'Ten dollars a week? Is that all Jean offered you?'

'With promises of more later if I'm a success at learning the business.'

'But you said you were going to buy Chloe. She is technically not a slave, but Madame Alix customarily expects payment from any man who takes a girl from her house. The usual price is $5,000. That's what René paid for me. I don't know how much money you have, but at ten a week it will take a long time to meet her terms.'

'I have hopes,' he answered.

'Maybe I can help you. I might persuade Madame to lower her price.'

'I would certainly appreciate it.'

While they had been talking, the schooner was being manoeuvred up to the pier. Ropes were thrown and caught, and she was quickly warped in. When the gangplank was lowered, the captain came up to them.

'May I escort you ashore, Madam?' His bow was punctilious. 'I have a letter here that says you are to be given one of the guest houses. I'd be happy to take you there myself, although I do believe there is a carriage awaiting you.'

'It can't be for me,' she replied. 'M'sieur Jean did not know I was coming.'

'I'm sure he did.' The Captain took her hand to assist her to the gangplank. 'You see we have a very fast messenger service between here and New Orleans, and undoubtedly the messenger arrived before we did.'

'And that he certainly did, my dear Helen.' A man bounded across the gangplank and took her in his arms. 'I have been waiting an hour here so that I could be the first to greet you.' He kissed her on the cheek and took her hand to lead her ashore, but she hesitated.

'I must introduce you to Mr Verder who made the trip down with me.' She turned to Tommy. 'Mr Verder, may I present Monsieur René Beluche, one of Jean LaFitte's principal lieutenants.'

Tommy's hand was clasped by Beluche, a big, handsome man dressed in a scarlet broadcloth coat and tight-fitting white trousers. Tommy judged the man to be about Helen's age; there were flecks of white in his jet-black hair.

'Oh yes, I heard about this young fellow. Have your bags taken ashore, lad. Then report to M'sieur Jean at the big house. Come, Helen, we have a lot to talk about. It's been so long since I saw you.' He leaned down and kissed her again. Helping her into the carriage, he jumped in after her and flicked his whip.

Tommy watched them go. Helen turned and waved at him – languidly, he thought. So René Beluche was her lover here, and Tommy had one of LaFitte's lieutenants for a rival. Already things were becoming complicated. He must be careful not to make an enemy before he had made a friend here. One thing was certain; he would not tread on Beluche's toes. No woman was worth it. He'd stick to business and let Beluche take care of Helen. He certainly looked capable. Whistling to Ramon to follow him, he started up the shady street towards the big house. Another new life was beginning, and he hoped that it would be a tranquil one. He wanted it so much to be that, perhaps luck would be with him.

IO

With a sweating Ramon following him, toting the big valise and mumbling complaints under his breath, Tommy started out on foot for the Big House looming grandly at the end of the street. He passed the small houses he had seen from the schooner, each flush with the beaten path that served as sidewalk. He had an occasional glimpse of gardens in the back. As Helen had said: some were carefully tended and neatly painted with flowering window boxes; others were shabby in the extreme.

A man sprawled in the doorway of one house that Tommy passed. He was sound asleep and naked, his torso covered with golden hairs which caught the glint of the sun. He slept so soundly that the swarm of flies crawling over his body did not disturb him. His mouth was open, mucus ran from his nose, and he snored raucously. He was a disgusting sight, but his indifferent nakedness brought one fact home to Tommy; this was a man's town; here men did as they wanted.

A slatternly wench, also naked, leered at him from an open window, her plump breasts hanging over the sill, her body marked with purplish bruises, her head a tangle of matted curls. She smiled a provocative greeting at him and he smiled back at her, stopping for the moment to remove his hat and wipe his forehead with an already sopping handkerchief.

'Ay, qué hombre!' She hailed him, closing one eye with a suggestive wink. 'And hung like a stud horse if I'm not mistaken. You're new around here, verdad? Ain't seen you before, 'cause if I had I'd remember it. A handsome young man is hard to come by here. Mostly old bastards who've been to sea so long they don't appreciate what a woman's got between her legs.'

He could not but grin back at her audacity, and this seemed to encourage her. The corner of his eye could see poor Ramon wetting his lips with his tongue and staring at the brown, rose-tipped breasts of the girl.

'Why don't you come in? Venga! That goddamned Pieter, he's passed out. It's the bastard's day off, and he's been drunk since last night. Ain't no chance of his coming to, and, even if he does, he's a puny varmint. Been needing me a man all night, and, try as I can, I can't get him up. Like playing with a dishrag it is. Won't take you a minute, man.' She stood up, fingering herself lasciviously. 'Go around to the back door so's you won't disturb the damned Dutchman.'

He replaced his hat and grinned back at her, shaking his head. 'Thanks for the invitation, lovey, but can't do it even if I wanted to. Just can't at the moment. Got to see M'sieur LaFitte at the Big House.'

'Then come back when you gits finished with him. Just can't wait to git my hands on you.'

'Perhaps.' He doffed his hat and motioned to the staring, open-mouthed Ramon to come along.

'She shore is a forward wench.' Ramon was wishing she had asked him in.

'Shut your mouth, boy. She's no wench; she's a white woman.'

'But she's a whore, Masta Tommy suh.'

'But a white whore, so mind your manners, especially down here. We don't want to get into trouble.'

'No suh, Masta Tommy suh. This yere's a funny place. Ain' never seen anything like it before. Naked men a-sleepin' practically on the street 'n' a woman standing nekkid at the window. Funny place.' He picked up the valise to follow Tommy.

Tommy wondered if the whole village of Grand Terre would be like this. Then he told himself that the women who came here were probably as tough as their sisters in Tchoupitoulas Street, where Ramon had taken him to see the cribs. What other type of women would be attracted by these rough men, gathered from the four corners of the earth and who were actually pirates, no matter what LaFitte called them? Still, he mused, the girl at the window had been young and might even be pretty if she washed off the grime and combed her hair. At any rate, there apparently would be no dearth of women here. He had been propositioned five minutes after landing.

He arrived at the wide, brass-studded door of the Big House, sweating profusely and out of breath. He banged the heavy brass knocker and the door was opened for him. When Ramon was sent around to the rear of the house with the valise, Tommy entered and took the chair which a grave-faced old Negro indicated. It was a relief to sit down under the cooling draught of an immense ceiling fan which was operated by a nude black boy in the corner. The boy lay on his back and slowly moved one leg, activating a rope attached to his ankle and the fan. At the same time, oblivious of Tommy's presence, he was vigorously manipulating an erection which seemed too large for his skinny body.

'M'sieur Jean, he a-spectin' yo', Masta suh.' The old man bowed and started to leave when he caught sight of the boy in the corner. 'Yo', Sammy, yo' stop a-doing' that o' I a-goin' to lambaste yo' proper.' He turned to apologize to Tommy, muttering something about how shameless the younger generation was, before shuffling out of the room in his worn carpet slippers. The boy in the corner raised himself on one elbow, looked at Tommy indifferently, then lay down and began again.

Tommy ignored him. He looked around the immense room at the costly Persian carpets on the floor, the carved and gilded armchairs, the pendant crystal chandeliers and the broad steps of the staircase which led to the second floor. He had never been in Europe, but he had heard about the palace of the Sun King at Versailles which had been gutted by the revolutionists and he imagined it must have been something like this. Certainly, it was far more elegant than either Dove Cote or Falconhurst. And yet when he looked at it closely, he could see that there was a thick coating of dust on the polished tables, wine stains on the damask of the upholstered chairs and cobwebs greying the lustre of the chandeliers. Again, he realized that this was a man's place – this house and all of Barataria. Well, he was a man himself. He didn't mind.

It was, however, surprising to come upon so much elegance at the end of nowhere. Certainly, the dark little smithy in New Orleans had not prepared him for it, nor the squalor of some of the houses he had passed since he landed. He did not have long to wait until the old coloured man came back. The boy in the corner had finished his finger exercises and was dabbing at his stomach with a dirty rag. Tommy feared the boy might be punished, but the old man did not look at him. Instead he beckoned for Tommy to come with him, and although acting as Tommy's guide, managed to stay a step behind him.

They passed through tall double doors into a fantastic oriental drawing room whose elaborate *chinoiserie* he imagined had once been on some clipper en route from Canton to England. The old man, scuffling ahead of him opened a green baize door into a smaller room where, behind a broad mahogany desk, Jean LaFitte sat, his curly black hair moving in the breeze from another ceiling fan operated by another naked black boy in a corner. LaFitte did not rise to greet Tommy, but extended a cordial hand across the desk and gestured to a carved, gilded Empire chair. Tommy stared at the huge initial 'N' on the back.

LaFitte's quick eyes detected Tommy's interest in the big initial. 'Yes,' he said, nodding in the direction of the chair, 'it belonged to Napoleon. He is a man I admire. It's no secret, so I might as well tell you that we have plans to rescue Napoleon from St Helena. We have built a house for him in New Orleans, and Dominique You is going to bring him back here in the schooner *Seraphine* which we have just purchased. The *Seraphine* is said to be the fastest ship on the seas today. Perhaps I'll be sending you along with Dominique when the time comes.'

'That would be an adventure, believe me, sir.' Tommy was emboldened by LaFitte's smile of welcome. 'But first I've got to prove myself to you. You don't know much about me yet, but I hope you will soon discover that I am here to serve you in any way possible and to the best of my abilities.' He hoped his words were not too stilted and formal; he was just trying to make a good impression.

LaFitte compressed his lips and studied Tommy under veiled eyelids, appraising him. 'Naturally we're going to give you a workout down here – that's why we brought you here. We need men who can take responsibility and men who are equipped to meet and deal with the public. For that we are looking for educated men, businessmen, respectable-looking men, men who are the peers of plantation owners we sell to. I've got hundreds of good men here – men who'd go to hell and back for me – but I'll have to admit that most of them are riff-raff, the sweepings of the docks from London to Tangiers. They're the finest men in the world aboard a ship but no good in dealing with a stiff-necked plantation owner. I've got my brother and Dominique You in New Orleans and I've got René Beluche here, but I need more men of their calibre. Our business is expanding, and we four can't handle it alone. That's why I'm hoping that you will work out.' He stopped to pour two glasses of sherry from a decanter on his desk and offered one to Tommy.

'I'll do my best, M'sieur LaFitte.' Somehow sitting here in Napoleon's armchair across the desk from this purposeful man, Tommy felt more self-confident than he had ever felt before. He sipped the topaz wine, letting its taste travel slowly over his palate and generate a warm, comforting glow in his stomach.

'Well, there's a lot to learn. Tell me, Verder – hell, I can't call you Verder – what's your other name? Thomas isn't it?'

'But most people call me Tommy.'

'Then Tommy it is. Tell me, what do you know about niggers?'

'A little but not too much.' Tommy wondered just how he should answer LaFitte's question. 'My mother has a couple of large plantations in Alabama. She is starting to breed slaves there, and I've had a little experience with blood lines. I've helped her pick out dams and sires which should result in good stock.' It was on the tip of his tongue to tell LaFitte that he had once been a good friend of Hammond Maxwell's and had stayed at Falconhurst Plantation, which LaFitte surely knew by reputation. He decided, however, to keep his one-time friendship with Hammond a secret.

'So *Madame votre mère* has joined the ranks of those who will be competing with us in another ten or fifteen years. She isn't the only one; there's another Alabama plantation doing the same thing. Raising dammed fine niggers, I'm told, but just at present *we* have the market. For every slave bred in this country, we can supply ten, even a hundred fine specimens direct from Africa.

'What I want of you, young fellow, is to learn to judge nigger flesh. That's going to be your job here. I'm not going to waste you on the fol-de-rols and the foo-fa-rahs that we have

93

for the trade in Royal Street. I can't see you measuring off yards of velvet and picking out buttons to match some society lady's frock. I want you to become an expert judge of blacks, and I'm going to place you in the hands of René Beluche who is the best judge of niggers here or anywhere else. You'll work with René. I hope the two of you will get along well together.'

Beluche! Helen's former lover and already Tommy's potential enemy. Well, to hell with Helen! This was more important than a night's sweating in bed. 'I've already met him,' Tommy volunteered. 'He was at the pier to meet Mrs Latimer.'

'Who also sponsored you? Right?'

Tommy nodded.

'Poor René's had a hankering after that woman for a long time,' LaFitte winked a knowing eye at Tommy. 'It's strange too because René's never taken up with a woman here for long.'

Tommy swallowed hard. Here was a complication which he had been dreading. Not that he minded giving up his nights with Helen. It was a question of whether or not she was going to be difficult about it. He was afraid she might be.

'René's a hot-tempered man. Pay no attention to him if he flies off the handle. He'll get over it and try to be a better friend to you than he was before. But don't rile him. Like all of us, he's led a hard life, and he's in the habit of commanding men.' LaFitte half rose from his desk as though to terminate the conversation. Again he shook Tommy's hand while his other hand pulled vigorously at a bell-cord beside his desk.

'First of all, you've got to get settled in. I've allotted you a house, but it will probably have to be cleaned out. I know you brought a servant with you, but would you like another servant to keep your house and get your meals?'

'That would be fine, sir. I'm afraid Ramon has not much experience in cooking and cleaning . . .' He cut his sentence short when a tall rather handsome mulatto man entered the room. He was immaculately dressed in the height of fashion. His long hair was oiled and fell to his shoulders. He wore a long-tailed coat of wine-coloured broadcloth, and his white trousers were strapped under varnished boots. He stood at the

94

door, his eyes on LaFitte, but Tommy was sure he had not escaped the man's peripheral vision.

'Lionel,' LaFitte addressed the fellow, 'this is Thomas Verder whom I spoke to you about. Mr Verder is going to be with us here at Grand Terre for a spell. Will you take him to the house you allotted him? Then he wants a woman to keep house for him. See if you can find him something, or better still let him pick out a woman. Get her to clean up for him. Issue her chits so she can lay in supplies from the store. Then take him to Mr Beluche. He'll either be at the compound or in his own house, and, if he's not, he'll be at the guest house where Madame Latimer is staying.'

'Yes, sir.' The mulatto bowed, then finally looked at Tommy. 'Welcome to Barataria and Grand Terre, Mr Verder.'

For the first time LaFitte stood up, walked around the corner of the desk and put an arm over Tommy's shoulder. 'Get settled and rested up today, Tommy. Your duties won't start until tomorrow morning. In the meantime, get acquainted with the place and make yourself at home.'

'That I shall, sir, and thank you.' He started for the door, then turned, 'A favour, M'sieur LaFitte.'

'Granted if possible.'

'Would you mind if I took some of this man's time to guide me around and give me the lay of the land?'

'By all means. Use him as long as you want.'

'Then thank you, sir, and *au revoir*.'

'*Au'voir*. We'll be seeing a lot of each other from now on.'

'I hope so, and thank you again, sir.' Tommy preceded the servant (or so he thought he was) through the rooms to the entrance hall. Out of curiosity he glanced at the boy in the corner whose leg was still waving to power the fan. His hands were still and the pearly beads glistening on the black of his stomach testified to the successful culmination of his renewed efforts. Lionel opened the big door for Tommy, and they passed out into the heat and the sun.

The mulatto followed a step behind him as they walked down the same street. Tommy noticed that the Dutchman was still asleep in his doorway, but there was no trace of his slatternly woman. Probably she had inveigled someone else into the house and was entertaining him while the man continued to sleep off his drunken stupor.

The street ended at the waterfront, where Lionel told Tommy to turn right. They walked along another street which lacked the welcome shade of the live oaks. Here the houses were spaced a little farther apart. After only a short walk they came to a house built of wood. It was a little sprucer than the others, with the distinction of a little veranda and a few blooming shrubs in front. Several tall palms grew in the rear.

Lionel signalled for him to turn in, then with a word of apology went before him and unlocked the door. 'Better keep your door locked when you are away,' he warned. 'Not that I think any of the men in the settlement would steal from you, but I'm not so sure about the women. They come and they go and most of them are a pretty bad lot, if you'll pardon my saying so, sir.'

Something about the fellow's precise speech and clipped vowels interested Tommy. He spoke with a decided English accent, far different from the slurred vowels and shortened words of the gombo-speaking Negro. 'Where do you come from, Lionel?' Tommy asked.

'From Barbados, sir.'

Tommy wondered if he was a slave or free man but immediately dismissed the question as of no consequence. Sooner or later he would learn all these things.

The snug little house was hot and stuffy inside. The smell of meals long since cooked and eaten vanished when Lionel opened the casement windows and a cool breeze blew in from the bay. A knock on the door brought Lionel to open it, and Ramon was there with the valise. The naked teenager who had guided him spun around on his white-bottomed feet and ran back up the street.

Tommy sat down in a Windsor chair by the door, wiping his face as he took stock of his new abode. The fair-sized room had windows front and back to allow cross-ventilation. A small fireplace bisected one wall, with dirty brass firedogs standing among old ashes and refuse. An elaborate but badly tarnished silver candelabrum occupied a table in the centre of the floor. Small tables with silver candlesticks stood beside each chair. One large winged chair with red damask upholstery, frayed and torn, looked comfortable enough, to serve him as a haven of rest after a hard day's work. The floor was of wide boards, stained and spotted with candle grease, but there was a fine although much soiled Turkey carpet on the floor. When he had caught his breath, Lionel saw him through one of the two doors leading from the room.

Tommy admired a huge four-poster bed, hung with embroidered curtains of Chinese silk. He felt the mattress and found it soft and comfortable. A walnut armoire which was certainly too big for Tommy's modest wardrobe stood against one wall. A mahogany chest of drawers against the other, a tripod shaving mirror, and a straight-backed chair completed the furnishings. Heavy red serge curtains billowed inwards when Lionel opened the windows to the welcome breeze.

Tommy called Ramon in to unpack the valises and put the clothes away. He then followed Lionel back into the living room and through the other door into the kitchen where a big fireplace yawned blackly in one wall, flanked by a hanging assortment of pots and kettles. Spotting a bunk with frowsy blankets and a soiled pillow in one corner, Tommy called Ramon from the bedroom. 'You'll sleep here,' he said.

'You can draw supplies from the commissary,' Lionel explained, 'and the well is but a few steps away. Several trips a day to the well by your boy or other servant should keep you supplied. And, by the way—' he looked quizzically at Tommy – 'do you prefer a boy or a girl for housekeeper? You can be perfectly frank about it – such things do not matter here. Many of the men have been to sea for so long that they have lost their taste for women and prefer a boy both for housekeeping and for bedding, but let me warn you: the boys here are as bad as the women, perhaps even more flighty and undependable.'

'I've never lost my taste for women,' Tommy laughed, 'never, Lionel. So I'd prefer a woman for housekeeping and most certainly for bedding. I'd like someone who knows how to cook and can keep a place clean; someone to wash and starch my shirts, and, if she is not too damnably ugly, someone to bed with if the urge comes over me.'

Lionel paced the floor from one end of the room to the other, chin down, concentrating.

'Now that is going to be a rather difficult combination to find.' He pursed his lips. 'We've got a lot of women here as I told you, but they're a pretty worthless lot. I could get you a fine cook and housekeeper in old Mother Christmas, but you wouldn't bed her if she were the last woman on earth. And, I could find you a nice bed companion in a little Spanish girl who isn't attached at present and who, they say, is hotter than a charcoal brazier – but I'm sure she couldn't even make you coffee for breakfast.' He thought for another moment, then, suddenly inspired, snapped his fingers. 'I've got it! The right solution for you if you don't insist on the woman being a raving beauty. We've got a girl here called Gretchen, either German or Dutch. I don't know which. She's as plain as a board wall, but she's clean and men whom she has been with report that she is a good cook.'

'Clean and neat and a good cook! That part sounds interesting at least.'

'And like all plain girls—' Lionel winked wisely – 'she'd appreciate a lover. She was shacked up before with old man Trudeau who died. He was too old to do anything for her.'

'You mean she's never had a real man?'

Lionel looked at him appraisingly. 'Well, maybe not like you, but I can assure you she's had plenty. She wouldn't be here if she hadn't. But as far as I know she's never lived with one permanently. She stayed longest with a Barbary Coast sailor – a little squirt that stood about five feet high. He went to sea and then she went with Trudeau. But I'll swear to one thing. She kept her men clean, well fed and happy.'

'Then bring her around.'

'May I suggest, sir, that when I take you around the settlement you stop in at the women's house and do your own picking? She'll be there, but it's best you make your own choice. Some other girl might appeal to you. But another word of warning; you'll be begged and importuned by all the girls there because everyone wants a steady man. But there's not a one of the sluts I would recommend except Gretchen.'

Tommy followed Lionel out of the kitchen into the living room and saw Ramon standing there. Noticing a broom beside the wall, he thrust it into the boy's hand, told him to get busy, sweep out as much of the dirt as he could and get the house as livable as possible. He and Lionel would return later with a woman who would do the cooking for them. Lionel told him to go to the kitchen door of the Big House at lunchtime and he would be fed. When they left, Ramon was raising more dust with his broom than he swept out.

The village proved quite a bit larger than Tommy had envisaged it from the deck of the schooner that morning. He was surprised when Lionel informed him that there were between four and five hundred men in the town, probably an equal number of women, and some fifty or so young boys in their teens. Lionel was sort of a general factotum. He had been born a slave in Barbados, he informed Tommy, but had been captured by the LaFittes while on a journey to Trinidad. Now he did not know whether he was a slave or not. Because he had been fairly well educated in Barbados, he had become Jean LaFitte's right-hand man and enjoyed a position of prestige over the internal and domestic workings of the settlement. René Beluche, as LaFitte's lieutenant in the settlement, made executive decisions and ran the business of the place under LaFitte's supervision.

In his walk around the town, Lionel showed Tommy the general store where groceries and provisions were issued on presentation of a chit; the small red-brick building that served as a calaboose where drunken and obstreperous men – and sometimes women – were confined on occasion; the promenade where the unattached women and boys strolled in the evening; the storehouses for goods en route to Royal Street; and, last of all, the stockade. Lionel told him he was not permitted to enter the slave enclosure, as this was under Beluche's supervision. They dallied outside for a moment and Tommy could hear the mournful sound of the plaintive songs of the homesick Africans within, longing for the homeland from which they had been torn.

Finally after an hour or so of strolling around and having Lionel point out the places of interest, Tommy found himself in front of a substantially larger house than all the rest. This, Lionel explained to him, was where an unattached woman stayed until claimed by some man who wanted a change in his housekeeping arrangements or who, like Tommy, was new in the settlement and anxious for a woman. With a renewed warning about what was likely to ensue, Lionel ushered him in through the open front door into a large room. No sooner had he stepped over the threshold than Tommy was the centre of a mass of grasping women whose howls and screams brought others running from different parts of the house. They overwhelmed him in such numbers that he feared they would pull his clothes off. Some of them were certainly trying. Avid hands were seeking his crotch, and no sooner had one succeeded in touching his fly then it was yanked away by another. Hot lips were pressed against him, naked breasts dangled before him and feminine flesh pressed against him. In the general hubbub, he could distinguish only a few individual cries.

'I'm Elisa. Try me, man.'

'Pay no attention to the bitch. It's me, Marietta, that you want.'

'She's got the pox; she's a regular fire ship.'

'No, no, me, señor. I'm clean and I can do things in bed that no other woman can.'

'Quiet, all of you!' Lionel shouted. Reluctantly the female tide ebbed from Tommy and retreated to the other side of the room where they continued to exhibit their charms from a distance. 'Now line up, all you sluts, and come over here one by one so that this man can look you over and make a choice. He's looking for a housekeeper, not a two-bit whore, so behave yourselves.'

Tommy had never seen such a motley group of women and girls. They ranged in age from about fifteen years to a couple of wrinkled old harridans who apparently realized that no amount of paint or powder could hide their ugliness. The women were clad in everything from plain cotton shifts to the rags and tatters of finery, but the lace on the elaborate ball gowns was torn, the embroidery unravelled, and most dresses were dirty and grease-stained. Hopefully, they passed before him one by one. Several were young and pretty enough for his consideration, but each time he hesitated, Lionel shook his head.

'She's a wanton hussy; stabbed her last man.'

'You don't want her. They say she's fine in bed, but she stays there all day.'

'Not that one; she's only interested in other girls.'

'They say this one's poxed; better stay away from her.'

'Wait.'

And wait Tommy did until Lionel presented a girl with obvious pride.

'This is Gretchen. I talked to you about her.'

Tommy looked her over and indeed she presented a far different appearance than the others. To begin with she was plain but not ugly, and her cleanliness shone out in those tawdry surroundings like a ray of sunlight on a dark, dreary day. Her round face was scrubbed clean and radiated health. She wore no trace of the heavy *maquillage* that some of the others wore. Large, cornflower-blue eyes, free from sooty mascara, gazed back at him over rose-pink cheeks. Her nose was short and uptilted, but her lips were full and red. When she smiled back at him, her teeth were white and even. Her pale blonde hair was parted in the middle and combed back tight. By the size of the chignon in the back, Tommy judged her hair might fall below her waist when loosened. She was a tall girl – a Teutonic Juno – with swelling breasts and ample hips. In contrast to the others, her starched blue and white cotton dress was clean. Her bare legs were milk white, her calves well rounded.

He continued to stare at her, and, in contrast to the voluptuous leers of the other girls, she returned his glance shyly. But despite her prim smile he could somehow sense that she wanted him to choose her. He made up his mind. Perhaps her decorous lips did not promise as much as the tongue-circling invitations of the others, but her big breasts and ample rump promised other delights.

'Would you like to keep house for me, Gretchen?' He smiled at her, hoping that his invitation would be accepted willingly.

'If you wish, Mein Herr.' He could detect no particular urgency in her words, yet he thought he could see desire in her eyes.

'Do *you* wish it, Gretchen?' He wanted her to come voluntarily, not because she felt she was forced.

She hesitated a minute before replying. 'It would be nice to have a house of my own again. Being here with all these females is no life for a woman.'

'Granted you would like a house of your own. How about me? Do you like me?' He still wanted her to commit herself.

'Indeed, Mein Herr. You are young and handsome and what woman would not like to serve you?'

'Can you cook well?'

'Indeed I can. My mother taught me back in the old country. Also I can wash and iron and keep you and your house clean. I can do anything you want me to do. I can serve you well.'

'Then have Lionel tell you where my house is. Do you think you could get it cleaned up a little and have supper waiting for me? My boy Ramon is there, and he will help you to get water and do the heavy work for you.'

'Ya.' Her smile broadened and she beamed at him. 'I shall be most happy to serve you, Mein Herr. I'm sure every woman envies me the chance. I'll have a clean house and a meal waiting for you.'

'I'll give her a chit, and she can take it to the store and draw provisions.' Lionel, too, seemed pleased that Tommy had accepted her. 'It's the third house around the corner on River Street,' he instructed Gretchen, 'and Mr Verder will be back later in the afternoon.'

Lionel turned to go and once more the girls pounced on Tommy. He managed to fight them off, but in trying to adjust his clothes, he noticed that three buttons were missing from his fly. He pulled up his trousers as best he could do to hide the loss and followed Lionel out the door. Poor Gretchen might have been far down the list of Tommy's choices had it not been for Lionel, but with all her plainness, she was undoubtedly the best of the lot. She was clean and wholesome-looking, despite the life she had lived in Barataria, and that was saying a lot for character. Gretchen was going to suit him well, and, he smiled to himself, that big bosom and those fantastic hips would be as good as a feather-bed on chilly nights – if it ever did get chilly here.

Lionel was waiting for him outside the house. There was, he informed Tommy, only one more place to go. He would take

him to the office of Mr René Beluche where he would leave
him.

Beluche! Helen's old lover. Tommy dreaded the encounter,
but he made up his mind not to let Helen interfere. Helen was
just another woman – Beluche was his whole career. He wasn't
going to antagonize this man who was practically all powerful
here merely because Helen had a yen for him. No, sir. It
wasn't worth it. He could satisfy himself just as much with
Gretchen's big bosom as he could with Helen's tantalizing
gyrations. Women here were a dime a dozen, and if he didn't
like Gretchen he could stroll out on the evening promenade and
pick up a dozen if he wished. But, he promised himself, there
was one thing he would not do – he would not antagonize
Beluche. There was too much at stake – far too much.

II

Lionel left Tommy at the massive gates of the slaves barracoon, telling him to be sure to signal him if he needed anything in the way of domestic stores or if he had complaints
about Gretchen. At the gateway, Tommy's way was barred by
a grizzled man gripping a musket in both hands. Tommy
explained to the scar-faced one with a black patch over one eye
that he was here to see Mr Beluche on orders of Jean LaFitte.
The fellow scrutinized him carefully, scratched his head in
somewhat idiotic perplexity, then dug in his pocket and produced a soiled scrap of paper. He squinted his good eye at the
writing before he asked if he might be facing a certain Thomas
Verder. Upon Tommy's assent, the man grudgingly lowered
his musket, opened a small door in the big gate and beckoned
to Tommy to come through.

Inside Tommy could see hundreds of blacks in the blazing
sunshine of the large corral. Some were aimlessly milling
around; some were hunkering in the shade of the stockade,
talking and gesticulating. Other lonely souls were stretched

out flat on the ground, oblivious of the heat and strong sun. In the centre of the corral, a tall black was beating his chest and crying out the same unintelligible phrase over and over again. However, all was not complete despair, for Tommy could see a big buck vigorously and unashamedly sodomizing a slim youth who was stretched out on the ground. The boy's legs were entwined around the big fellow while he screamed encouragement to his ravisher.

An acrid stink of sweat, offal and excrement assailed Tommy's nostrils and for a moment the stench was so bad Tommy thought he would lose the meagre breakfast he had eaten aboard hours ago. With difficulty, he gulped down the acrid bile in his throat and stumbled along behind the man to the small house that stood against the stockade near the gate. The man bawled his name through an open window and a moment later the door was opened and Beluche stood on the threshold, a smile on his face and his hand outstretched in welcome.

The putrid stink still permeated the little house (which Tommy rightfully assumed was Beluche's office) despite the ubiquitous small boy in a corner whose rope propelled the sweep of the big ceiling fan. Although it did not dispel the terrible stench, the fan at least made it more bearable. Tommy's stomach settled down, and he was able to return Beluche's hospitality with a wan smile instead of a torrent of vomit as he had feared. He was, however, glad to reach the safety of the chair to which Beluche had gestured. As he sank into it, he realized that he must be pale. He felt as though all the blood in his body had drained into his stomach and congealed into a hard lump. He was happy to see Beluche lean over the desk and nod his head to indicate his understanding of the situation.

'This unholy stink get you, Verder?' His voice was kindly solicitous. 'It's pretty awful when it first hits you: enough to make a strong man puke, but believe me, your nose soon gets accustomed to it, and, after a while you don't even notice it. I know because it stopped affecting me a long time ago. When we first took up slavery for a business I thought I'd vomit every five minutes and sometimes I did. Here, have a glass of wine.' He poured a glass of deep ruby port for Tommy, who sipped it slowly. Tommy wondered how it would sit in his stomach what with no lunch and the glass of sherry he had drunk at LaFitte's.

'You see, Verder—' Beluche also poured a glass for himself and sipped it – 'I was expecting you about this time so I delayed my lunch until you arrived. If the nigger stench hasn't taken away your appetite, we'll eat here at my desk. I usually do because it saves me time.' He jangled a bell on his desk. A knock on the door followed and a stark naked Negro giant entered. He deposited two linen-covered trays on Beluche's desk. With a deft movement of his wrist, he whipped off both napkins and Tommy saw delicious cold plates for two. Now that he had quite recovered from his nausea, he felt he could do justice to his lunch.

Beluche poured a cup of hot tea from the teapot on his tray into a delicate eggshell-thin Chinese cup and handed it to Tommy, assuring him that the hot tea would certainly settle his stomach. It did and Tommy joined Beluche in eating. He realized now that although the stench might have precipitated his queasy feeling, it was really an empty stomach which had caused it.

Beluche was a congenial host, attentive, courteous and with a personality which invited intimacy. True, Tommy felt that while there might soon be trouble between them over Helen Latimer, he would be forced to yield to the other man's charm and good manners. Here was a man whom he would like to count as a friend; he would be quite willing to forgo a few nights with Helen for this man's good will. As the brief glimpse of him that morning at the pier had hinted, Beluche was indeed a handsome, virile man, exuding masculinity from every pore. Although he was only of average height, his sturdy build and powerful shoulders made him seem taller than he actually was. His short hair was silvered at the temples and curled close to his head in tight ringlets. It seemed to have a vitality of its own, drawn from the man's vigorous body. He was clean shaven but a blue shadow still lingered along his square determined jaw. The diagonal scar across one cheek seemed to give him a devil-may-care expression. The dark brown eyes, deep set under his overhanging brows, were kindly and belied the otherwise dogged, almost savage face. Tommy had a feeling that the kindness of these eyes could change in a second to steely hatred. He shuddered to think what Beluche might be as an enemy.

Beluche wore no coat and suggested that Tommy take off his own and be comfortable. Tommy stood up to doff the heavy broadcloth and caught Beluche's eye staring at his gaping fly. Embarrassed, he apologized for the missing buttons, explaining what had happened at the women's house. His recital was so dramatic that Beluche started laughing, agreeing with Tommy that the women of Barataria were a carnivorous breed who would stop at nothing. Tommy sat down. He liked the man.

'We'll talk business while we eat.' Beluche was still chuckling over Tommy's mishap. 'If you don't mind we shall kill two birds with one stone.' Beluche poised a forkful of food before his mouth and waited for Tommy's nod of approval before he continued.

Slaving, he informed Tommy, was a comparatively new venture for the LaFitte organization. Previously, when vessels from Africa had been permitted to unload their black cargoes directly on the levees of New Orleans, there had been no reason for the LaFittes to enter into the traffic of black flesh. But now that Congress had outlawed the legitimate importation of slaves from Africa, new ways had to be found to supply the plantations' insatiable demand for more and more Negroes.

Fortunately there was still Spain. Yes, Spanish traffic in slaves was still legal for Spanish ships. It had not been outlawed by the Spanish government because more and more slaves were required to work the cane plantations of Cuba, Santo Domingo, and Puerto Rico. A slave's life in the cane fields was a short one – eight years at the most, Beluche asserted – so there was a constant demand for slaves in the islands. Spain, as always, was hungry for gold, and she would not kill the goose that lay the golden egg. Cutting off the needed supply of black labour to her island plantations would mean just that. So, what was the answer? Beluche asked.

Tommy had it on the tip of his tongue to say 'piracy' but he decided not to risk offending Beluche.

Well, they had ways of solving the problem, Beluche answered his own question. First, operating under letters of marque issued by the Republic of Cartagena (at that time a small independent nation at war with Spain), they could legitimately capture a Spanish blackbirder or a slaver flying any flag because any slaver except a Spaniard was operating illegitimately. Instead of bringing the captured slaver to Cartagena, however, they took it and its living cargo to Barataria where the cargo was confiscated. When the slaves were sold in New Orleans, they would bring a huge profit. There was, of course, another way to cash in. Did Tommy know what that was?

Tommy shook his head, not wanting to interrupt Beluche.

Beluche nodded portentously. If the demand exceeded the supply of captured slaves, the LaFittes could always go to Havana, buy slaves and smuggle them into the country at Barataria. A likely young buck bought for about $300 in Havana would bring about $800 in New Orleans. Although the profit was limited to about $500, in some ways this method paid off better than piracy. A trader buying in Havana could choose only the best, the strongest and the handsomest of the *bozals* that had come from Africa legitimately. A captured shipload of slaves, however, would include the sickly, the unsightly, the weak and the crippled. Some of the slaves would not be worth selling and had to be disposed of. When Tommy ventured to ask how, Beluche compressed his lips in a tight line and answered only one word: 'Shot.'

He added that it was a toss-up which method was the better – consequently they used both. The market in Havana was a steady one, whereas they could never foresee with any certainty when they might capture another blackbirder. Therefore, by combing both sources, they were always sure of their barracoons being full, always ready to meet the demands of plantation owners.

But, the source of supply, although an important factor, was not the only thing Tommy would have to learn about the slave business. Slaves had to be graded, for quality was as important as quantity. Each one of the African blacks must be examined thoroughly before he could be graded and that in itself required a lot of training. Beluche did most of this work now, but he needed an assistant badly.

Slaves, he explained, at least male slaves – and that was about ninety per cent of their business today – were graded as Fancy, Prime, First, Second and Third Class. They received few Fancies from Africa. Today the trend in Fancies was for extremely handsome octoroons, quadroons or even mulattos. Usually some admixture of white blood was necessary for a slave to qualify as a Fancy. However, on rare occasions, a pure black could qualify. He must be of perfect physique, tall, handsome and commanding. These rare specimens brought unusually high prices either for plantation pets or for breeding.

The prime class comprised fine, strong, well-built and good-looking African Negroes. One requisite for this class was the size of a man's sexual endowments because slave buyers had a silly superstition that the larger a slave's penis and the heavier his testicles, the better breeder he would turn out to be. This, Beluche admitted – strictly *entre nous* – was a fallacy. The quality of a man's sperm did not depend on the size of his organ, but who was Beluche to disillusion the purchaser? If that was what the buyers wanted that was what he would sell them, and fortunately most Africans were sufficiently well endowed so there was not much difficulty in this area. Those in the prime class were rarely sold as field Negroes but as studs on the big plantations anticipating the day when they could grow their own slaves.

First class betokened good field workers, strong and healthy but not necessarily good looking. Second class, of course, were a poorer grade, healthy but perhaps not as rugged physically, and of course, third class blacks were from the bottom of the barrel but not the scrapings. The old and infirm, the sickly and the weak were disposed of as Beluche had previously mentioned. It cost too much to keep unsaleable slaves. It was cheaper to get rid of them.

Yes, these were all things that Tommy must learn and it would take time. When he started to make decisions on his own, the wrong decision could cost the firm hundreds of dollars in profits. Conversely, if he classified a first class as prime, he would lose the respect and confidence of his customer.

Tommy sighed. There was more to this slave business than

he had reckoned. However, he had a yardstick to go by. He remembered Dovie, his fictitious mother, telling him that Colt was a Fancy. Colt certainly was a handsome-looking nigger. He could use his memory of Colt for judging but he imagined there would be few who could ever compare with Colt, although he did not have a drop of white blood in him. At least Tommy knew something about niggers. He had been with Hammond Maxwell long enough to pick up a few pointers, in addition to having Colt to go by . . .

Carried away by his own thoughts, he had not been paying attention to Beluche, who was still talking on the same subject – slaves. After all, why shouldn't he be? Slaves were his business and were going to be Tommy's so the more he learned about them the better. He stopped daydreaming to listen fully to Beluche.

So, Beluche was saying, the most important thing for Tommy now was to learn all he could about niggers. It was a big subject – something to which some men had devoted their entire lives – and it wouldn't be easy because every nigger was different from every other nigger. Slaves were Beluche's business, and they were going to be Tommy's so the more and the quicker he learned the better. Yes? Tommy was willing to agree with him. At the back of his mind was the thought that he himself was technically a Negro on the run, and he wondered idly that if Beluche were grading him, how he would be rated. An extra special Fancy, he decided.

They ate for a few moments in silence. Suddenly Beluche put down his fork with such force that it clattered against his plate. He looked across the table at Tommy. For some reason, Tommy sensed that the man was nervous. Beluche coughed, patted his mouth with his napkin, took another sip of wine and then stared again. His mouth opened as though he wished to say something but could not find either the words or the nerve to say it. Finally, like a man taking courage from necessity, he smiled almost apologetically at Tommy and asked: 'You are a very good friend of Madame Latimer's?'

To see so strong and purposeful a man suddenly become so humbly hesitant surprised Tommy. This was not the man who had been speaking about the LaFitte adventures and the thriving business in slaves.

'It was she who introduced me to Dominique You,' Tommy answered. 'She has been a good friend to me.'

'And to me too.' Beluche nodded. 'She is the only woman I have ever cared for. I have known her since she was the most beautiful girl in the establishment which Madame Alix runs in New Orleans. Did you know that she had once been there?'

'So she confessed to me, and I must admit it did not alter my regard for her.'

'No, it made her a more interesting person; perhaps that is why she is the only woman who has ever really satisfied me.' Beluche took a drink of his wine, drained the glass and twirled the thin stem between his fingers. He seemed to want to say more but was tongue tied.

Tommy worried over the trend of the conversation. He wanted to break the awkward silence. Unable to think of a new twist, he said nothing. Determined to give Beluche no cause to dislike him, he realized he must skirt dangerous territory. Luckily he occupied the least involved corner of a confused emotional triangle. Helen desired him; Beluche desired Helen; but he himself didn't really care. He appreciated all that Helen had done for him, and he certainly owed her a debt of gratitude. But as long as he could not have Chloe, he was quite willing to go home and bed himself with the mountainous Gretchen, provided she would have him.

But Beluche persisted. 'You have made love to Helen? No, don't answer me, lad, I know that you have. You're a damned attractive fellow, and I know Helen even though I do not know you. I don't blame you if you have. Any man would enjoy her. But . . .' He seemed at a loss just how to proceed.

'Set your mind at rest, Mr Beluche.' Tommy had made up his mind to be frank with this man who seemed to be floundering in a morass of indecision. 'As far as I am concerned, I willingly relinquish all claims to Mrs Latimer while she is here. Her short friendship with me is as nothing compared to yours. I would not in any way come between you.'

For the first time Beluche smiled. 'Ah, my friend, but that is exactly what I want you to do. Exactly! But I have not been able to put it into words because I have been too embarrassed. Now you have said it for me.'

'You mean . . .?' A faint glimmer of what Beluche was

driving at had suddenly dawned upon Tommy. He did not know whether or not he had guessed rightly. It would be better not to commit himself; let Beluche make the proposition if one were to be made.

'I mean this, Tommy.' Beluche stretched his hand across the table and laid it on Tommy's wrist. 'We can both enjoy Helen – with her permission and approval.'

'Both of us?' Tommy was still not quite sure what Beluche meant, but he was determined to find out. He had feared incurring Beluche's anger and enmity, but if what he sensed were true, he wouldn't have to fight a duel (which he undoubtedly would lose) with Beluche; instead he would be cementing their friendship even more firmly.

'Yes, *un ménage à trois*. The three of us together. I can think of nothing more exciting. Absolutely nothing! You see, Tommy, as you are going to learn sooner or later, this little settlement of Grand Terre is a strange place. All of us here have spent most of our lives at sea. So ... what is the result? We enjoy our matings in different forms. We have expanded our horizons, so to speak. We have found more to enjoy than the simple coupling of man and woman. We enjoy variety. Why do you think we have a big selection of boys here? Because they add to our variety and enjoyment. As for me, I enjoy everything, yes, everything.'

Tommy regarded Beluche's hand on his wrist. The slight pressure of Beluche's fingers did not exactly displease him: on the other hand, it did not excite him. In that simple gesture and the quasi-confession it symbolized, he saw an opportunity to ingratiate himself with this man. How better, or for that matter, how more easily could he consolidate his position here? Beluche's idea was not his first choice, but it might add a fillip to his enjoyment. He remembered similar scenes back in New York, particularly the night he and his whore of the moment had invited an English sailor home with them. So, why not, exactly why not?

Slowly he placed his hand over Beluche's.

'Something tells me, Mr Beluche ...'

'René, please.'

'Something tells me, René, that you have hit upon an excellent idea. It will be an interesting and a new experience for me.' Let Beluche think that he had never done anything of this kind before. 'Such things can be interesting *à deux*, but *à trois*...' He snapped the fingers of his other hand. 'Three together ought to be a hell of a lot more interesting than just two. Right? So, I am overjoyed at your proposition. We'll show the fair Helen something tonight that she'll never be able to forget.'

'Nor shall I.' Beluche stood up and clasped Tommy's hand. 'You know, Tommy, you're a handsome devil.'

'Thank you, René.' Tommy grasped Beluche's hand. 'You're pretty darned handsome too. But alas!' – He drew down the corners of his mouth in a mock grimace – 'First I have a weird confession to make to you. Helen already knows about it and bears with me, but I had better explain it to you. For some reason, I can't accomplish a goddamned thing when I am absolutely naked. It's some strange quirk in my mind, I suppose. I just have to wear a shirt or I stay as limp as a damp rope end. Will you mind?'

'Mind?' Beluche pumped Tommy's hand. 'Why should I? I once knew a fellow who could do nothing unless he wore hobnailed boots. Damned tough on the mattress it was and not too easy on the girl, but that's the way it was. We all have some strange little quirks when it comes to the old-fashioned joys of fornication. Well, I've told you mine and you've told me yours, so we are even. We'll say no more about it and I'll pick you up at your house at eight.'

'At eight it is, René, and I hope to hell that the woman I engaged today will have some hot water waiting for me so I can take a bath.'

'Which floozie did you take?' Beluche relinquished Tommy's hand.

'A Dutchie by the name of Gretchen.'

Beluche laughed – a loud resounding laugh – and clapped Tommy on the back. 'I know her. You certainly picked a good one. She'll not only have a bath ready for you, boy, but she'll scrub you clean herself. She's a good girl, if I do say so, compared to most of the sluts we have around here.' He walked towards the door. 'And now, Tommy, seeing that we have settled both business and pleasure, I suggest that you hurry back to your house and spend the afternoon getting settled in.

We'll have our first lesson in judging black meat tomorrow. Come along and I'll daresay that, even in this short time, you'll find the stench not as unbearable as it was at first.'

Tommy sniffed. Strangely enough, the stink did not bother him any more. He congratulated himself on how well this important interview had come off. Beluche was no longer the formidable employer nor the grim rival he had feared. Instead they were companions and after tonight they would be even more than that. He sniffed.

'You know, René, I can't smell a damned thing.'

Beluche held the door open wide for him. 'Thanks a lot, Tommy, I'll not forget it. I've more to look forward to tonight than I've had in a long time. You've done me a great favour.'

'And who knows?' Tommy gave him a reassuring grin. 'Perhaps tonight I'll do you an even bigger one. You may be surprised.'

'I like surprises,' Beluche answered.

Arm in arm, they sauntered out to the big gate.

Tommy was so pleased with himself that he was not even aware of the irony of the situation: Calico, the fugitive slave, was about to learn the fine points of the slave trade!

12

Tommy sauntered slowly back to his own house, congratulating himself over and over again on the successful and most unexpected outcome of his interview with René Beluche. Lady Luck was certainly with him. How could he ever doubt it? He had been providentially delivered from the *débâcle* of his marriage with Missy Acker. True, his well-guarded secret that he was not white but coloured had been discovered, but he had nevertheless escaped from the wrath of old man Acker, from the fury of his one-time friend Hammond Maxwell, and from the blood lust of all the rest who would have enthusiastically tortured him to death. Thanks to Dovie.

Poor Dovie! Although she was no relative of his, he could not help but think of her as his mother – incestuously, for her relationship with him had surely been far from maternal. She had done as much for him as any mother. She had saved his life, and he owed her a debt of gratitude. Yet, even in his gratitude, he was glad that he would never have to sleep with her again. Dovie and Dove Cote; Hammond and Falconhurst; Missy Acker and his marriage were all behind him, thank God! Now he could look forward to the future – a future which hopefully held Chloe and success in his new venture with the LaFittes.

Chloe! It was strange to think that Helen Latimer really was her mother. Well, he should have guessed it because no two women were more alike than Helen and her daughter Chloe. True, Chloe had youth and a freshness which had not yet been dimmed by Madame Alix's whorehouse, but then, Helen had beauty too, even though it was more mature than Chloe's. Good God! Helen must have been a real beauty in her day. Thinking about Helen, he found himself anticipating the night ahead of him which he was going to spend not only with Helen but also with René Beluche. Instead of dreading it, he found himself titillated in anticipation. He really liked René.

He supposed René wanted more than anything else to sit and watch him and Helen frolic together. René was probably a *voyeur*, but if he wanted to enter into the *mêlée*, so much the better. Tommy really didn't mind. He was experienced and broad-minded enough so that anything new and different was worth anticipating. What was it Beluche had said? *We enjoy our matings in different forms.* Well, when he came to think about it, so did he. Perhaps that was why he was so attracted to both Chloe and Helen. Not only were they mother and daughter – a new experience – but they too enjoyed variety in love-making. They were both more exciting than poor Dovie who had known and practised only the old tiresome papa-mama techniques. He should have educated her; she would have been an apt pupil.

The sun was high and the heat had increased when Tommy stopped in the welcome shade of a massive live oak. He removed his heavy broadcloth coat to let the breeze dry his shirt which was already plastered to his skin. He felt better without his coat, but little rivers of sweat rolled down his legs and his groin itched. As there was nobody around, he felt free to scratch himself. But what did a little heat amount to? He was going to enjoy it here at Grand Terre; of that he was certain. He had a house of his own, and now, for the moment, he could let the images of Helen, Chloe and Dovie slip from his mind and concentrate on his new housekeeper, Gretchen.

She was certainly not the type of woman he would have picked out had he plenty to choose from. He had never favoured stout women, but somehow she seemed to fit into the picture. It would be interesting to investigate her possibilities. She might possibly be satisfying when he had an opportunity to explore her. The more he thought about her, the more exciting the prospect became, and he experienced a moment of regret. He almost wished he was not going with Helen and René tonight. He wanted something new and novel, but hell, what was he thinking about? It would be new and novel with Helen and René, and afterwards Gretchen would still be there. He even considered dallying with Gretchen this afternoon but decided he'd better conserve his energies to satisfy Helen and René. He was certain that he could. He'd never failed yet.

At least he would not have to fight a duel – which he was bound to lose – with René. And he was not going to be kicked out of Barataria because René was jealous of him and Helen. He blew a kiss to Lady Luck. Here he was, free, white – well, almost white – and twenty-one. The whole world was his succulent oyster, just waiting to be opened, and there was a damned good chance that his particular oyster would have a pearl in it.

When he arrived at his own little house, he found it a hive of bustling activity. Gretchen, her skirts looped up around her plump, milk-white hips, and her sleeves rolled up over her brawny arms, was directing Ramon. Ramon had stripped off all his clothes except his white cotton underpants and was kneeling on the floor in a froth of soap suds. Neither had heard him open the door, and he stood for a moment listening to Gretchen berate Ramon in language that would shame a sailor.

'You goddamned worthless chunk of black meat! You lazy,

shiftless brat of Satan! Put some elbow grease into that scrubbing or I'll wallop you again, and this time it won't be with a wet rag; it'll be with the flat of my hand. I'll lay you flat on your black ass.'

'Please, Gretchen,' Ramon whined, the sweat running down his face.

'Don't you Gretchen me, you black son-of-a-bitch. Remember who you are, nothing but a worthless slave. Remember when you speak to me again, it's "*Miss* Gretchen" – or I'll clout you.'

'I'm a-goin' to tell my Masta Tommy on you,' Ramon's high-pitched whine continued. 'He don' want me a-doin' work like'n this. Masta Tommy's good 'n' kind, he is, 'n' he don' mean for his body servant to be a-scrubbin' dirty ol' floors.'

Tommy laughed to himself. 'But he does want a good clean house, Ramon.' He entered the room, stepping carefully so he would not slip on the soapy floor. 'You do as Miss Gretchen tells you. And show respect to her. Remember, she's a white woman.'

'Oh, Herr Verder!' Gretchen retreated a step and made an awkward little curtsy. 'Wasn't expecting you home so soon. Haven't got this pig-sty cleaned out yet and never will if I can't get some work out of this shiftless nigger.'

'Keep him at it, Gretchen, and you, Ramon, mind what she tells you. She's the overseer here in the house, and if you don't mind her, I'll whip you myself and send you up in the next shipment to New Orleans to be sold as a field hand.'

Ramon started to bawl, his tears mingling with the sweat on his cheeks. 'Don' do it, Masta Tommy suh. Don' sell yore Ramon. Ramon loves his matsa 'n' always will. Yo' knows I do, Masta Tommy suh.'

'Then get to work and prove it to me. What can I do to help, Gretchen?'

'Nothing, sir. Your bedroom is all cleaned and ready. Had a hard time scrounging fresh sheets, but I managed to steal some. The kitchen is still filthy, but I'm leaving that till last. Will you eat supper here, sir?'

Tommy nodded.

'It'll be ready for you. I don't know what it will be yet, but

116

you can it eat.' She looked at him, studying his face carefully. 'Herr Verder, you look peaked.'

'It's been a busy day, Gretchen. I'm tuckered out.'

'You should rest. Your bed is waiting.'

Suddenly he realized that he was not only tired but completely exhausted. He had little sleep the night before, and he had arisen early. No wonder he was exhausted.

'Think I shall, Gretchen. I'm dog-tired.'

She came over to him, taking him by the arm and gently guiding him across the wet floor to the bedroom. She opened the door and gave him a gentle push. He could see the bed, freshly made with unwrinkled sheets, the pillows plumped up and covered with white pillow cases. She ducked past him and lowered the jalousies at the window, shutting out the glare of the sun, and then turned down the bed.

'I'll bring you some coffee, sir, and then your nigger boy and I will work quietly. Here.' She came close to him, reached up and untied his cravat. He stood still while she stripped him of his sweaty clothes, stopping her only when she started to take off his shirt. He took the few steps to the bed and sank down upon it. She came over to stand beside him, her eyes lingering to admire his half-bared torso, then gently pulled the sheet up over him. He reached up a languid hand to fondle one of her breasts. He could feel the hardness of her nipples through the thin cotton of her dress.

'Would you like I should sleep with you and clean the house later?' She smiled at him.

'No, Gretchen. Go ahead with your cleaning. I'll sleep alone. Wake me when supper is ready, and I'll take a bath and dress. I've got to be ready by eight. Mr Beluche is going to call for me.'

'No need for you to dress for dinner, Herr Verder. I'll bring it in here on a tray and then I'll have hot water ready for your bath.'

'Thank you, Gretchen. I have a feeling we are going to get along well together.' Already he was so sleepy that he could scarcely keep his eyes open. She tiptoed out of the room. When she returned with his coffee, he was sleeping so soundly she didn't wake him. She put the coffee down on the table beside the bed, walked softly across the floor and closed the bedroom door so that Ramon could not see. Then she tiptoed back to the bed and looked down at Tommy's sleeping form. She admired his face and the sturdy outlines of his chest, disclosed by the unbuttoned shirt. With a backward glance to ascertain that the bedroom door was still closed, she slipped her hand under the sheet. Her fingers sought and found and marvelled. Ach, but she was a lucky girl! Regretfully, she withdrew her hand, walked out and closed the door behind her.

*

The next morning early, Tommy and René Beluche closed the door of Helen's house behind them and confronted each other for a brief moment on her doorstep. In the bright sunshine of the morning, their experiences of the night before seemed overly fantastic. Like a couple of truant schoolboys, they winked solemnly at each other and grinned sheepishly, as much as to say, 'What's done is done and we'll forget about it.' They strolled along the dusty *banquette* towards the stockade.

It had been a night of wild and frenzied bliss, and both were thoroughly satisfied, satiated and emotionally exhausted. There were episodes which Tommy tried hard to remember and others which he tried equally hard to forget. But it was over, and he knew that he was closer to Beluche than even he wanted to admit. Their steps lagged, and Tommy looked forward to the short respite they would have in René's office while they waited for their coffee to be prepared.

Neither discussed the events of the previous night, for their memories of any particular episode were vague. The writhing tangle of arms, legs and bodies in every conceivable position was now, in the bright light of morning, difficult to separate in recollection. Better by far not to try. Better to keep silence, to drink some strong coffee and to forget the night in the hard work of the day ahead.

When they had finished the hot coffee and the croissants which had seemingly come from nowhere in the hands of Beluche's black servant, René yawned, stretched and managed to get to his feet while he offered a helping hand to Tommy.

'Getting too old for that sort of thing,' he admitted.

'I'll never be the man you are,' Tommy put an arm around

his shoulders. 'And now, what about my starting to learn something about our stock in trade?'

'Good idea.' Beluche walked across the room and opened the door. He waited for Tommy to precede him into the courtyard with its shifting pattern of black humanity.

Against one of the outer walls, not far from the little house that was Beluche's office, an open lean-to with supports of barked tree trunks and roof of palm thatch gave a welcome spot of shade. Under it were two rudely made armchairs which faced a circular, raised platform about a foot high and some three feet in diameter. The same naked black buck who had served their breakfast was standing beside the chairs, awaiting their arrival.

It was a relief to get in the shade and sit down. Beluche beckoned to the black, and when he stood before them, he made a quasi-introduction of Tommy.

'Tommy, this is Mosho, and he knows quite a lot about niggers himself. He ought to, because according to his story, he's the son of some tin-pot sultan in Africa who was a big slave dealer there. He's a good boy, Mosho is, and you'll find him willing and helpful. He'll do anything you ask.' He looked up at the black and gestured towards Tommy. 'Mosho, this is Master Verder, who has come here to be my assistant. You'll treat him the same as you treat me, and you will help him in any way possible.'

Mosho showed a smile of white teeth and knelt before Tommy. He lifted Tommy's hand and placed it on his head, then stood up, awaiting his orders.

'All right, Mosho, let's get to work. Bring us a man.'

As Mosho turned to leave them, Beluche explained to Tommy. 'None of the men you see in the coral has been inspected or graded. You see – here' he pointed to a collection of thonged wooden discs on the ground beside the chairs – 'our method of grading.' He picked up a random handful and dangled them before Tommy. 'After a man has been examined, we put one of these around his neck. Blue is for Fancies, red for first class, white for second class, and yellow for third. If I consider a man to be absolutely worthless, he gets a black disc which means he will be disposed of. Once graded, the men are taken to separate barracoons for a course of special diets, exercise and grooming. Naturally the Fancies and the first class men get special attention so their barracks are somewhat better than the others. You'll see all this later.'

Tommy's eyes scanned the pile of tokens. He noticed that the red and white discs were considerably larger than the other colours. He was about to ask about this, but Beluche jogged his arm and pointed to Mosho who was leading a black across the enclosure. The slave was little more than a boy – an adolescent youth of about sixteen – and it was apparent that he was frightened. He walked with faltering steps, and when Mosho had pushed the boy up onto the little platform, Tommy could see that he was trembling the muscles of his body contracting spasmodically.

'Damn you, Mosho.' René was irritated. 'You made a poor choice for our first man.' Beluche appraised the boy with his eyes. 'It's difficult to categorize these younger boys. Damned poor market for them. They're not much good as field hands, and they don't bring a very high price. Of course, they're a good investment because they'll reach their prime in a few years, but they must be fed in the meantime. Now, you watch and I'll give you an idea how to proceed. I'll tell Mosho to bring a grown man next.'

To overcome the boy's nervousness, Beluche walked over to the platform where the boy was standing. He laid a gentle hand on one of the boy's arms, stroking it and making reassuring although unintelligible sounds. In a few moments the boy had quietened down and looked at Beluche with bovine eyes wide open. Beluche continued to croon more words of reassurance and although the lad did not understand the words, he could gather from Beluche's tone of voice that he had nothing to fear. With his free hand Beluche reached into his pocket for a lozenge that he tried to pop into the boy's mouth. The boy clamped his teeth tightly.

'It's nothing but a horehound drop,' Beluche explained to Tommy, 'but he's afraid it might be poison.' He laughed, put the lozenge in his mouth and sucked on it, then took it out and placed it in the boy's mouth. The lad sucked on it, liked the taste and grinned his thanks to Beluche. 'It's wonderful how a bit of sweet will calm them down. Usually I have lemon drops which they like better. Trouble is that most of these fellows have been badly treated on board the slavers, and they distrust all white men.'

The boy had now relaxed and his smile broadened. In answer, Beluche patted him on the back and watched him suck with relish on his horehound drop.

'Come nearer, Tommy.' Tommy came over and stood beside the boy, who glanced up at him, fear born anew in his eyes.

'Pet him a little. Let him know you are not going to hurt him. Lacking words, the only language we have with these fellows is physical. They all understand gentleness.'

Tommy let his hands glide over the boy's smooth skin and spoke to him. 'What is your name, boy?' he asked.

Mosho poured out a brief, unintelligible torrent, whereupon the boy brightened and answered.

'Ibrahim,' he said.

'He a Moor,' Mosho explained. 'That boy, he black but he a Moor.'

Beluche nodded knowingly and resumed petting the boy. 'Now if Mosho's right, and he probably is, I think we've got something pretty good here. Could be either Mandingo or Hausa, as they are both Muslims, like many other smaller tribes in North Africa. We don't get many of them, but they make the best house servants. So let's get to work on Ibrahim. Notice how I go about it.'

His practised hands glided over the muscles of Ibrahim's chest, seeming to assay their depth and strength merely by passing his fingertips over the smooth skin. 'This boy'll never be big and brawny,' he explained. 'He'll be slender, but I'll guarantee one thing: he'll be strong. His muscles will never bulge, but they'll be of whipcord strength. It's hard to explain how I know them, but you'll get the feel of it some day.'

The practised fingers left the boy's chest and examined his arms. René nodded in confirmation of his words. When he had finished with the boy's arms and back, his thumbs prodded deeply into his abdomen. The boy flinched but did not cry out in pain.

'Best way to find out if his guts are all right. If he'd yelped out from pain at my prodding, I'd know something was wrong with him.'

René hitched his chair closer to the platform and carefully

examined the boy's legs, picking up each foot and tweaking the toes.

'I'd say he meets all requirements. He needs some good food and more exercise which we'll give him.'

'Is that all?' Tommy was surprised that the examination had taken so little time. This was going to be easy.

'Well, that's enough for his body,' René answered. 'Seems to be in good condition, and remember this one thing; for a man to be in as good condition as this after all the mental and physical hardships he has gone through betokens a good strong body and a well-balanced mentality. The only fault I have to find with him is that he's a bit thin, but as I said before, we'll condition him before we offer him for sale. What's your opinion of him so far Tommy?'

'Seems like a well-set-up boy. Ought to develop into something pretty good in a few years.'

'Exactly. Now I'll go a little further.' He ran his fingers through the boy's hair which fell to the nape of his neck in dark curls. 'Got real hair, this one has,' Beluche remarked. 'That shows he's got some Moorish blood in him. A real nigger's hair is either kinky or peppercorned.' He lifted the boy's chin in his hands and examined the face. 'Good-looking kid, too, don't you think?'

Tommy studied the boy's face. Although his skin was dark, it was not the prune black of central Africa, rather a rich tobacco brown. He had heavily lashed, almond-shaped eyes of so dark a brown that they seemed black. His lips were well shaped and not overly full. His teeth were white and even. When Beluche opened the boy's mouth and ran his fingers over the teeth, he nodded to Tommy and insisted that he do likewise. Tommy did and found the teeth all intact.

'Now, we'll proceed further.' Beluche returned to his chair and motioned to the boy to come over and stand before him. 'Every slave sold today,' he explained to Tommy, 'must be a potential breeder. There's no way we can guarantee that a fellow is not sterile, but we can find out a few things about him. Now watch!'

His fingers reached up and gently squeezed the boy's testicles. 'Always be sure that a boy has two balls. Occasionally you'll find only one, which means that the other has never descended. Once in a great while, we find one with no balls at all. Sometimes we get eunuchs with none. It's something you have to check whether you like it or not. Eunuchs are saleable for house servants, but a fellow with only one testicle is graded in third class. Chances are he won't be able to breed.'

His fingers encircled the prominent penis. 'This boy's been circumcised.' He called Tommy's attention to the absence of a foreskin. 'All the followers of Islam are circumcised, but that is no guarantee that the boy has Moorish blood because some other tribes also circumcise. Some of them do a most barbaric job. However, the majority of the blacks have a long foreskin, and you must always be sure that you can pull it back. Otherwise we have to snip off the end before a man is sold.'

Beluche's fingers tightened and slowly caressed the boy's penis until it rose in his hand, stiff and straight, standing out from the boy's body.

'Fairly well hung, too, for a kid of his size, and it will probably grow a little in the next couple of years. He's not unusual but passable. I don't know why it is, but most buyers today want a fellow to be enormous. It really doesn't signify a thing, and sometimes these big-cocked guys aren't as good at breeding as the smaller ones, but I say, if that's what the buyer wants, that's what we'll give him and charge him for.' He continued to stroke the boy.

'Mayhap you won't particularly enjoy this part of our examination, but it's more or less necessary.' He looked across the boy's erection at Tommy. 'Yes, it's important. It's the best way to judge a man's sexuality. Not quite so important on a boy of this age as on a man who's going to be bought for a breeder.'

The back-and-forth motion of his hand increased, and he gripped even harder. 'Normally he should spurt off in about two or three minutes, but, of course, you must realize that conditions are not normal for him, and it might take a little longer.' The boy's muscles were becoming tense. He closed his eyes, his back arched, and he was gasping for breath. Beluche's hand moved even faster. 'See, I told you so.' He held up his other hand to catch the boy's ejaculation. He rubbed some between his thumb and forefinger and nodded with satisfaction. 'It must have the right viscosity. Thin and watery semen is not a good sign, but notice how thick and creamy his is. It's a pretty good indication that the boy's fertile.'

Tommy gingerly touched the warm fluid in Beluche's hand. He too tried it between his thumb and forefinger, sensing its thickness and richness. 'Have to try this on myself some day.' He winked at Beluche, then wiped his fingers on his handkerchief.

'No need to worry about yours, Tommy.' Beluche cleaned his fingers on the boy's back. 'After last night, I'd be willing to grade you in the very top bracket as a breeder.'

'Guess you're right. Say, do you have to do this to every slave you examine? Damned messy, ain't it?'

'You'll get used to it, just as your nose gets accustomed to the stench here. It's all in a day's work. We're almost finished with this lad now.'

Beluche turned the boy around. His hand on the nape of the boy's neck bent him over. He spread the boy's buttocks and inserted a finger in his anus. 'No piles,' he announced, 'clean as a whistle.' He picked up a stick from the ground and flung it as far out into the courtyard as he could. He motioned to the boy to run and fetch it. Ibrahim loped off like a gazelle, swooped up the stick and brought it back, handing it to Beluche.

'That's finished,' Beluche nodded. 'Now I've already made up my mind. I'd be interested to find out what you think, Tommy.'

Tommy considered the boy before him. It was going to be difficult to grade him. Had he been an ordinary *bozal*, he would be either a first, second or third class field hand, but the boy was too young to fit into any of these categories. He might grow up into a Fancy, and then again, he might not. He evidently had a good disposition because he had bounded off after the stick willingly, and now that he was no longer frightened, he had an appealing smile.

'It's a hard decision to make,' he replied, still studying the boy.

'Granted.' Beluche nodded in agreement. 'Hardly fair to you that your first one had to be like this. But go ahead, give me your candid opinion. We'll see if it agrees with mine.'

'He's certainly no field hand – at least not yet.'

'True.'

'But given a few more years, I'd put him down as first class.'

'Possibly.' Beluche was evidently not going to help Tommy with his decision.

Tommy continued to study the boy who was now so much at ease that he grinned, showing his perfect white teeth.

'Well, I'll tell you what,' Tommy said portentously. 'If I didn't already have a servant, I'd be willing to buy this boy. It would be fun to train him and teach him to speak English. I'd say that he's a far better boy than the one I already have. If I were looking to purchase him, I'd start at about $300 and be willing to go up to $500 for him. That's a high price for a young lad.'

'It would be,' Beluche agreed.

'So in my opinion that would make him a Fancy. Right?'

Beluche negated Tommy's remark with a shake of his head.

'No, he's not quite a Fancy, Tommy.' Beluche rummaged through the heap of discs on the ground and picked out a red one which he hung around the boy's neck. 'Almost, I agree, but not quite. In a few more years he might well be. He'll be strong, but he will never have heavy muscles. He's more suited to be a house servant than he is to be a field hand, but he's not sufficiently handsome, not sufficiently well hung to be a Fancy. Still, he's got excellent blood because these black Arabs are rare, so I'm going to grade him as first class. And, by the way, your estimate of the price he should bring is just about correct.'

'Sorry to be wrong on my first test.'

'Pshaw! Think nothing of it. It's difficult to put these young lads in their right class – difficult even for me. But, remember, you weren't far from right. Some would make a Fancy out of him, but I don't think he quite comes up to it. First class? How's that?'

'Reckon you've got to be right.'

'So we'll feed him up. We'll give him some oil for his body to make his skin shine. We'll put him through a series of exercises, and we'll purge him because he's probably constipated. If he brings $500 I'll present you with a bottle of my best Napoleon brandy for your good judgment. Now, Mosho, bring the next man.'

All that morning Tommy watched Beluche as he judged man after man. There was not another who would qualify for Fancy among the lot, although Tommy saw plenty of first class red discs passed out. The majority, however, were white ones with only a few yellow. The one solitary black disc went to a man whose leg had been broken on the voyage and never set. He was a pitiful sight, limping on makeshift crutches and still in great pain. Beluche took one look at him and gave him a reassuring pat on the back as Mosho led him away without even a cursory examination. No sooner had he disappeared from the corral than Tommy heard the sound of a shot.

Beluche shook his head sadly. 'That's the end of the poor devil. Sometimes I feel like God – dispensing life or death – but it's better to put the poor bastard out of his suffering.'

They quit work at noon and repaired to Beluche's office for a bite of lunch. After they had finished Beluche yawned and stretched his arms.

'It's the custom around here to rest until midafternoon. It's too hot to work in the middle of the day. Better go home, strip, and stretch out on the bed. Man, you had a hard night and a little rest will perk you up. Come back about four o'clock, and we'll work until dusk, and,' he wagged an admonitory finger at Tommy, 'leave that Dutch wench alone this afternoon. You'll need a couple of hours of good sleep to recover from last night.'

'One hour will do it.' Tommy laughed. He had had a busy morning, but he had enjoyed it. He was beginning to learn about blacks, and he enjoyed it. True, his judgment had not coincided with Beluche's in every case, but he had made sufficient right guesses so that he knew he would soon become proficient. Damn, it was going to be an interesting job! He even found it somewhat titillating to manipulate the blacks, but he would have preferred examining females to males.

'Do you ever get any women, René?' he asked as they neared the gates.

'Damned few, Tommy. The demand today is for males, and it's more difficult for the slavers to transport females. We do

126

have a few women in another compound. Some day soon we'll go over there. But you'll find damned few virgins if that's what you're looking for.'

'I don't give a damn about virgins, especially black ones, but it will be interesting,' Tommy laughed.

'Granted, it's a change of pace, but don't go home and dream about them. They're not so much-a-much.'

'At least they're females.'

'They're that. Now off with you and get your rest. Be back at four and we'll go on. Hope you're going to like your work.'

'It's fine, René. I can see I've a lot to learn.'

'You'll learn. *Au revoir*. See you at four.'

'Until four.'

Tommy analysed his feelings and found that he was extremely happy. He was going to amount to something in the LaFitte organization. He and Lady Luck would see to it that he did.

He was half tempted to take his siesta at Helen's house, but he knew that he'd get no rest there. Better to do as Beluche had told him. But first he would wash his hands and get the smell off them. He was sleepy – he had to admit it. If Gretchen wanted to stretch out on the bed beside him, that would be all right, too. He could stand a little pink and white skin after all this black. It would be a change.

He whistled as he took the path from the barracoon to his own house.

13

Tommy's presentiment that he would be happy at Grand Terre came true beyond his most fantastic dreams. He had never been happier in his whole life, not even in those few halcyon days preceding his marriage to Missy Acker when he lived in a roseate anticipation of bedding her. He liked his work here. What could be more interesting than working with

127

human beings? Well, perhaps not exactly; niggers may not be human, but at least they had human form, and judging them made him feel entirely white. He enjoyed working with René Beluche – certainly he could never have found a more congenial colleague or more dedicated teacher. It was nice, too, having a home of his own, and he was increasingly thankful that he had picked Gretchen to keep his house for him. His house and his clothes were immaculate, she ruled Ramon with a rod of iron, and she was a good cook. She provided a variety of tempting menus from the rather limited stock of meats and groceries available at the company store. Also of considerable importance, she was an agreeable (if rather unimaginative) bed companion. For her, the height of passion was to lie flat on her back and passively let Tommy mount her. He decided that teaching the placid Gretchen more complex and enjoyable techniques would be too much effort.

Gretchen did, however, satisfy his needs at night, and he was fully absorbed by his job with René by day. After a few months of René's expert tutelage, he realized he had become a good – if not expert – judge of black flesh. Just when he would be ready to congratulate himself that he really had nothing further to learn, something unexpected would come up which would confound all his experience. A tall, muscular specimen would turn out to have yaws and instead of being in first class, as Tommy would have graded him, he would be demoted to a poor third. Well, that would be something to look for in the future. Again, a rather short, thick-set young fellow with a face like an African ape which Tommy would have consigned to third class would prove to be the strongest man René had ever examined, and his extraordinary musculature would put him in first class. One slender, wispy fellow with an engaging face, but with no pretensions to muscular strength, would turn out to have super-Herculean genitalia which caused René to gasp and summon Jean LaFitte himself to see and marvel. Consequently, this black Priapus was enthusiastically graded by René as a Fancy when Tommy would have put him in third class. Frankly, Tommy thought, compared to his own equipment, he saw nothing unusual about the lad, certainly nothing enough to rate him Fancy.

These differences in judgment did, however, prove one

thing – a cursory examination would never scientifically place a slave into the proper category. There were subtle ramifications which could be learned only through experience.

But, Tommy was learning, and perhaps most important of all, René, his teacher, was his good friend. When he passed René's house on his way to the barracoons in the morning, Tommy would stop to pick up his friend, and the two of them would walk on together in the shade of the live oaks. At René's office, they would remove their coats. Tommy, by this time, had discarded his heavy broadcloth for a wardrobe of cooler white cotton drill which Gretchen kept spotless. They would sip their chicory-flavoured coffee and eat the croissants which, Tommy discovered, Mosho brought down from Jean LaFitte's own kitchen, wrapped in a napkin to keep them warm.

This was a pleasant time for both of them, a time for desultory gossip and the minor doings of Barataria, but rarely for business. On this particular morning, however, René gestured towards the corral and asked Tommy if he had noticed any change.

Tommy put down his coffee cup, walked to the window, and raised the jalousies to peer into the courtyard. Yes, now that René had called his attention to it, he did notice something different. For the first time since he had been at Barataria, the big enclosure was almost quiet. Instead of the teeming mass of black humanity, and the constant wailing and keening, there were now only a few men walking back and forth and conversing in small groups.

'Damn it!' Tommy let the jalousies fall with a clatter. 'It sure as hell looks like we're running out of business. Can't be more than fifty or sixty men out there. Does that mean our job is finished?'

'Hardly.' Beluche brushed a fly from his forehead and waited for it to light on his desk before he swatted it. 'We have calls here for more and more slaves, and we've got to find some way to supply them. Masfero's Exchange in New Orleans has placed an order for a hundred first class blacks, acting as agent for one of the big plantations up river. Then, there's to be a big auction at the Hotel St Louis in about a month and that's one of the best ways to get rid of any Fancies we might have. We also have orders from a number of private parties for up to

129

twenty second class men for work in the cane fields.'

Tommy jerked his thumb towards the nearly empty barracoon. 'None of which we can supply?'

'All of which we've *got* to supply or go out of business. Do you realize we haven't brought in a single slaver for over two months?'

It was true. The LaFittes had been notoriously unsuccessful in taking any rich prizes of late. To be sure, another slaver may be captured tomorrow, but it could be three months. Nobody could prophesy. Word by fast ship reported that several 'blackbirders' had sailed from ports on the west coast of Africa. None had been captured yet, but, as René had said, they had business commitments. Blacks smuggled through Barataria met the most urgent demands of the ever-growing slave business, and the southern states, as far north as Virginia, looked to the LaFittes for help.

Tommy spread his hands palms up in a gesture of helplessness and waited for the omniscient René to answer.

'All of which means that we've got to get over to Havana and see if we can round up some three hundred good *bozals* to tide us over. Of course, the day after we get them here, one of our own ships will come in with a goodly supply. That's always the case, but since we can't depend on it – we must get into action soon.'

While René was talking, Tommy allowed his mind to engage in voluptuous fantasy. Havana! All the fantastic stories that he had heard about that fabulous city across the Gulf of Mexico surged through his memory. Havana – the metropolis of Spain in the new world; the fabled city of adventure and excitement; the home of dark-eyed señoritas who spoke a language of their own with their painted ivory fans; the city of proud *caballeros* who, because they were born in Cuba and could call themselves *cubanos*, considered themselves better than any Spaniard. *Ay, la Habana, la perla de las Indias!* He regretfully roused himself from his dream of a voluptuous Cuban beauty in silk-fringed embroidered shawl leaning over the balcony, beckoning him with a fan that echoed the invitation in her dark eyes.

'Did I hear you say *we've* got to get over to Havana?' The Cuban beauty lingered on the periphery of his thoughts.

'You may have, Tommy lad, but I didn't mean it in exactly that way. I can't get away from this damned place as much as I would like to. A couple of weeks in Havana would be much to my liking – a taste of living again after this god-forsaken ass-hole of civilization. But I can't do it. The day after I left, a ship would probably come in. Then begins the rush, rush, rush to get every nigger on it graded in a matter of hours and packed off to New Orleans. No, Tommy lad, I can't go, but I'm sure as hell looking at somebody who can.'

'Who, me?' Tommy realized it was a useless question, because there was nobody else in the office.

'Yes, you! And why not?'

'But you know I haven't enough savvy about blacks to rely on my own judgment.' Tommy was sincere. He truly did not feel that he was qualified.

'Well, I think you're qualified, but even more important, so does Jean LaFitte.'

'You mean ...?'

'I mean that you're sailing this afternoon on the barque *Sainte Claire*, which is the only ship we have in port at the moment. You're going to Havana and you're going to buy three hundred of the best African *bozals* you can get. If you can't get *bozals* right off the ship, see what you can get through private sales. There's a bastard of slave dealer there called Emilio Hernandez who has good specimens sometimes, although I'd rather deal with the devil himself than to deal with him. Also –' he peered intently at Tommy – 'we could use a couple of Fancy octoroon wenches if you can find some good ones cheap in Havana. Old man Gaspard Cosette in New Orleans is pissing his breeches to slip it into something new and warm, and he'll pay through the nose for it, so we can't let him down. There used to be a queer bird named Solano who specialized in female Fancies. Try him if he's still in business.'

'Now there's where you can trust me, René. If anyone can find that class of merchandise, I can. You can trust my judgment on wenches. Those I pick out will be the best. Of course,' he winked at René, 'I just might have to try them out first to be sure that M'sieur Cosette will be satisfied.'

'I've no doubt about your qualifications to judge the wenches. The time will come for doing that, but now, get yourself over to your house and alert that Dutch wench, Gretchen. Tell her she's got to have all your white suits and shirts ready to go on board at four this afternoon. Just how in hell you're going to get three hundred slaves back on the *Sainte Claire*, God alone knows. A hundred would jam the vessel, but that's one of those impossible problems that you'll get used to solving when you've been with Jean LaFitte a few years. He always asks the impossible and then expects to have it done day before yesterday. Presto! You'll have to be a magician to get them here, but you'll do it somehow – if you have to tow them on a line behind the ship.'

'I'll put corks in their asses and float them across.'

'I don't care how you do it, as long as you bring them here. Now get started. Better take your boy Ramon along. While you're getting ready, I'll have drafts prepared for our Havana bankers. Jean will be at the dock to give you instructions.'

'Aye, aye, sir.'

'Why be so damned nautical?'

'Well, you're a captain, aren't you?'

'Once I was. Now I'm nothing but a jacker-off of niggers.'

'And what am I?'

'With a little more experience, you'll work up to the same goddam thing.' Beluche smiled wanly at Tommy. 'But we come in handy at times, and this is one of them.'

Tommy was at the door, but René reached out a hand and restrained him.

'Going to miss you, kid. It'll be dull eating breakfast alone.'

'Same here, René. But I'll be back and we can start over.'

'*Vaya con dios*. It's an old Spanish expression which means, "go with God". Drop in here about an hour before sailing time and I'll brief you.'

'And we'll say good-bye then.'

Tommy was excited as he made his way home. To be trusted with such an important mission after so short a time with the LaFittes meant that they already had confidence in him. Well, he'd show them he was worthy of their trust. He'd even cut out women while he was in Havana and stick to his work. Yes, by God, he'd do exactly that. To hell with the señoritas and their languid fans! They'd be like all women

132

anyway, first making a big fuss over him and then, after a little huffing and puffing and one final shove on his part, he'd be gasping for breath, and it would be all over just like it had been a thousand times before. So to hell with it! He would be representing the LaFitte organization, and he'd conduct himself accordingly. By God he would!

He arrived home to find Gretchen hanging washing on the back yard lines. His white shirts, trousers, jackets and small clothes were flapping in the hot breeze. She might have had a presentiment of his leaving, for every article of clothing both he and Ramon owned (except those he was wearing) was on the clothesline.

Through the open window he called to her. 'Good thing you started early. I'm going to need those clothes today, *liebchen*. Where's Ramon?'

'Gone down to the store to get some flour. I need some to make dumplings to go with the beef stew I'm cooking for supper.'

'Won't be needing any supper today, Gretchen. I'm sailing at four along with Ramon. We've got to hurry to get everything ready. I'm leaving for Havana.'

'Havana?' As far as Gretchen was concerned this might be the other end of the world.

'Yes, Ramon and I are leaving on the *Sainte Claire*, so we'll have to get busy. Here's Ramon now.' The door opened and Ramon came in.

'Drop the bundle in the kitchen,' Tommy yelled at Ramon. 'We're leaving, you and I, so stir your stumps and get busy. Get the clothes in off the line as soon as they're dry so Gretchen can iron them. Get the valises down and start packing.'

The little house suddenly became a hive of activity. Gretchen started up the fire to heat the irons, and, although the clothes were damp, she said she could iron them even better. Ramon got out his shoes (he had been going barefoot since his arrival at Barataria) and his master's boots and polished them until he could see his reflection. He got out Tommy's cravats, steamed the creases out and had Gretchen press them. When she had finished ironing, Gretchen darned socks and mended underclothes. Tommy supervised the packing of his own valise and told Ramon what to take in his bundle. They were all so engrossed with getting ready for the trip that they completely forgot about lunch.

By two in the afternoon, all was in readiness and Tommy had Gretchen heat the iron cauldron full of water and bring in the big wooden washtub. This she filled with hot water, diluting it with cold until her finger informed her it was the right temperature. When it was ready she offered as usual to wash Tommy's back, and as always he refused, although he would have liked the feel of her strong, soapy hands on his skin. When the bedroom door had closed behind her, he scrubbed his body with perfumed soap (pirated from some Spanish ship) and donned a clean undershirt. It was only then that he called Gretchen to help him dress.

He was surprised, when she entered, to see tears glistening on her cheeks. She closed the door and stood against it, staring at him for a moment, then started to sob.

'You're leaving, Mr Tommy, oh, you're leaving! You're taking Ramon with you and I'm going to be left alone here. Or must I go back to the women's house? Oh, Mr Tommy, let me live here while you're gone. Please. I'd rather cut my wrists and bleed to death than go back with those *verdammte* women. And ... I don't want to serve any other master but you. Oh, Mr Tommy, I know I shouldn't say it, but I'm in love with you. You're so beautiful, Mr Tommy, no woman could help but being in love with you. Please, sir, please, don't send me back.'

She stumbled across the floor to kneel before him, clasping his legs with her hands and burying her sleek blonde head against him. She seemed to find comfort in the damp warmth of his body.

The pressure of her face against him stirred familiar feelings within him, and he felt himself rising and swelling. His hands sought her head and gently turned it up so that he could look at her face. With the corner of his shirtsleeve, he wiped the tears from her cheeks and smiled at her.

'Of course, *liebchen*, I'm not sending you back to the women's house. Don't worry, Gretchen, I'm not taking any chances on losing you and having to put up with one of those harridans when I get back. No indeed, Gretchen. I'll be seeing M'sieur LaFitte at the dock before I sail, and I'm sure that I can arrange with him for you to remain. I won't be gone very long anyway.'

The warmth of her head pressed against his nakedness, and the smooth silkiness of her hair in his hand excited him even more. Now he was throbbing, rampant with desire. Her arms, entwined about his legs drew him closer to her. He felt her hand first stroking the soft inside of his thigh, then reaching up to cup him, her fingers gently kneading. Her other hand seized the turgidity of his maleness, grasped tightly and stroked, gently at first, and then rapidly. He sucked in his breath as he felt the wetness of her lips enclosing him and her tongue making vibrant little caresses against him. It was something she had never offered before and something which, no matter how he had desired it, he had never demanded of her. He sensed that she was overstepping the limits of her own self-imposed proprieties, and he welcomed her sudden expansiveness. He suspected that this was a new experience for her, that it was the ultimate expression of her love for him.

He felt the hot fluid rising within him, and he pushed her head away, but it was only for an instant. Sensing the approach of his climax, she avidly sought him out again. Her lips closed around him . . .

His hand plucked the hairpins from her hair, and her tresses fell to the floor in a cascade of silken gold. He ran his fingers through it. Although this was by no means a novel experience to him, it took on a whole strange newness, for he was sharing her sense of initiation . . .

She coughed and again he moved her head away, but she brushed aside his restraining hand and continued her ministrations with renewed vigour. Suddenly the muscles in his groin twisted into knots of exquisite pleasure. Although for the instant his whole world revolved around the continuation of her sensuous caresses, some primeval subconscious force urged him to try to resist her. His strength had left him, however, and willy-nilly he submitted to her mastery over his manhood. Yet this was what he wanted – desperately.

He arched his back, pushing himself farther into her. She felt his imminent release and clasped him tighter, her lips forming an inescapable clamp upon him. Then it happened. For one brief second which stretched into light years of sublime ecstasy the glory was indescribable. He soared on dragonfly wings into an empyrean of kaleidoscopic colours until he sensed that it was no longer possible for him to stand such exquisite torture, and he floated back to earth, gasping for breath. He pushed away her reluctant mouth which had come to seem a part of him. He leaned against her for support, then tottered to the bed and collapsed upon it.

'Thank you, Gretchen,' he mumbled.

'I shall miss you, Mr Verder.' She already seemed to envisage the long nights alone without him.

'But I'll be back. I promise you that.'

'Hurry back, Tommy.' It was the first time she had ever used his first name.

With her help he dressed. Then, while Ramon waited with the valise and bundles, he was ready to go. He gathered her in his arms and kissed her lightly on the lips – those lips which only a few moments ago had pleasured him so. In a way, he hated to leave her, but she was already behind him. Havana was ahead of him now. Havana! The name alone thrilled him. Somehow there was a world of promise in those alluring syllables.

14

The long monotonous days at sea were a salutary tonic for Tommy. The hot sun, the gentle salt breezes, the timelessness of being out of the world and suspended between the mundane responsibilities of two ports, produced utter relaxation. Gone was the tension of his daily routine of fingering and assaying blacks. Furthermore, sleeping alone and doing absolutely nothing except eat soothed Tommy's nerves, erased from his face the lines of fatigue and dissipation, and gave him a physical buoyancy he had not known in years.

There were no women aboard the *Sainte Claire*. The first night he missed the warm, comfortable plumpness of Gretchen beside him. Frustrated by his erotic thoughts, he tossed and turned in the narrow confines of his bunk, unable to sleep. But with the dawn creeping over the sea, he finally sought his own release and dozed off.

When he awoke to the full blaze of the sun, he was thankful for once in his life that there was no damp female flesh beside him. Strangely enough, this feeling continued throughout the rest of the voyage. Although he knew he could never savour it as a steady diet, he enjoyed the unfamiliar sense of freedom. He knew it wouldn't last, but he could tolerate it for a few days. Celibacy was all right as a novelty but not as a way of life. Not by a damned sight!

So now, reinvigorated by his abstinence and his regime of sun, sky and rest, he stood at the prow of the ship, scanning the dim strip of land that appeared on the horizon. That blur against the clear sapphire of the sea, the captain had said, was Cuba. The very thought made his pulse quicken. Cuba – where he was to represent the LaFittes; Cuba where he would have almost unlimited funds to purchase slaves for his organization and live like a lord while doing it; Cuba where he planned to make up for his monklike continence; Cuba where a whole new world of prestige and importance opened up for him. He had only one regret: that Chloe could not be with him to realize what an important personage he was becoming.

Gradually the dark blur on the horizon turned green, spotted with tiny, sun-washed flecks of whiteness which he imagined were houses. Then, as he came nearer, the greenness dissolved into fields of waving cane and tall royal palms. The blue water dissolved into white spume against a rocky shore or crept in lazy laciness up sandy beaches. Nearing the shore, he saw he had guessed correctly that the white cubes were houses, red roofed and sparkling in the sunshine. The moving dots along the dirt roads, materialized as ox-carts, laden high with green stalks which he rightly assumed to be sugarcane. Cuba, as he had heard, was already one of the world's greatest producers of sugar – one reason why the country had become such an avid market for slaves. The cane fields had a cruel appetite for men's lives. Slaves did not live long in the excruciatingly hard labour of the sugar plantations.

As the ship progressed along the coast, the big farms gave

way to a long row of trim, grey fortifications cresting the high hill which rose abruptly from the water. Nearby an immense fire basket stood high on wave-dashed rocks. It was obviously a beacon that burned only at night; there were still glowing coals in the huge iron basket. The ship which had until now been coasting along the shore, suddenly tacked and headed for the beacon. But as they came nearer, Tommy could see that the beacon marked the entrance to an anchorage. He concluded that this must be the famed Morro Castle which guarded Havana harbour. Across from the Morro on the other shore of the narrow harbour entrance, he discerned other forts. Havana, as he could see, was well guarded. No craft could survive between the crossfire of the opposite fortifications.

The land was now so close on both sides as they sailed through that he felt he could almost stretch out his hands and touch the guarding forts on either shore. He could not decide at first which side afforded the best views – both were fascinating – but finally chose the starboard because it presented a panorama of the city of Havana itself – truly a metropolis, one of the great cities of the western hemisphere. For a moment, he was stunned by the spectacle stretched before him – a froth of buildings in white and pastel colours, relieved by the darker grey of weathered masonry and the feathery green of palm fronds. The water on both sides of the ship was alive with small boats paddled by vociferous vendors of various tempting fruits – bananas, oranges and many which Tommy did not know the names of.

The *Sainte Claire* hove to, awaiting a longboat manned by sailors who pulled vigorously on the long sweeps. When they neared the barque, one of the men caught a line thrown to him and made it fast to the stern of the longboat. Then the straining muscles of the Cubans towed the *Sainte Claire* against a long pier extending out into the water. At the end of the wharf was a huge timber 'X' used for unloading ships. This derrick-like contraption, Tommy was to learn later, gave the pier its name: 'La Machina'.

A chorus of curses in English and Spanish, shouted from ship to longboat and from boat to pier, got the larger vessel secured to the pier with hawsers that would have held a ship twice its size. Then came the moment for which Tommy had been waiting: the lowering of the heavy gangplank from ship to pier. No longer were they a tiny nonentity, a speck on the boundless sea; they were now connected to the land, secure and safe. He had enjoyed the voyage, but he was glad to be back on familiar ground.

He wanted to run across the gangplank and plant his feet firmly on the pier, but a brisk officer, backed up by two rather ragged-looking soldiers, barred the way. The captain, however, now that the work of berthing the ship had been accomplished, came to the gangplank and spoke to the officer in a mixture of Spanish and English. The officer did not deign to answer him but merely pointed to a white-uniformed official sauntering along the pier, followed by an equally smart-looking mulatto carrying a small bag. The two men came aboard, greeted the captain effusively, and disappeared with him into the cabin. They reappeared a few moments later, the assistant now loaded down with bundles and packages. The boss man was introduced by the captain as the port's chief customs officer, and he bowed low while shaking Tommy's hand. In precise and stilted English, he welcomed Tommy to Havana. The man's schoolboy English made Tommy aware of the difficulty he might anticipate in trying to barter for slaves in an unfamiliar language. Somehow, somewhere he must find a competent interpreter, one who was not only accurate but loyal.

Although not dressed to go ashore – he wore only denim trousers and an old shirt – the excitement of his first arrival in a foreign port intrigued him to such an extent that he bounded down the gangplank. Not only was he happy to get his feet on solid ground again but he was thrilled by the strangeness of this new world. The sun beat down with an incandescent brilliance and a tropical heat he had never encountered before. His shirt was already plastered to his back, his hair was damp, and his trousers clung to him like wet skin. He promised himself only a quick walk to the end of the pier and back, but he was so intrigued by everything he saw that his quick walk became a journey.

The long stretch of the pier was littered with crates and boxes and piles of strange-looking fruits awaiting shipment. Black stevedores, naked to the waist, their oily skins glistening with sweat, formed an endless chain, passing boxes from swaying arms to swaying arms. A continuous, low-pitched chant gave their movements a precise rhythm. Tommy passed a stall where a toothless old crone was paring oranges, the white peel falling to her feet in an unbroken ribbon. While peeling, she too kept up a similar monotonous chant, doubtless a sales pitch for her wares. At another rude kiosk, shaded from the sun by a meagre thatching of palm fronds, a man was squeezing fruit juice into fly-studded glass jars. Another man, sitting behind a row of small cups on a rickety table, fanned a copper charcoal brazier which supported a steaming coffee pot. The air was raucous with a pulsating din in which the quick fluid syllables of Spanish dominated, sometimes low and sibilant, sometimes loud and bombilating.

A brazen slut, her thin blouse pulled low on one shoulder, barely concealing her breasts, sidled over to him. Her words – low, inviting and sensual – were incomprehensible, but he had no difficulty understanding the obscene gesture of her hands. Under the heavy coating of rice powder she was still young and good-looking. Her rounded hips and heavy breasts tempted him, but he shooed her away with emphatic signs. Thereupon she erupted a torrent of words which, although he could not understand them, seemed to be profane reflections on his manhood.

He came to the street and watched the continuous stream of traffic for a moment, then reluctantly retraced his steps down the long pier back to the ship. Before crossing the gangplank he hesitated for a moment to relish the flavour of the exotic scene. Once back in familiar surroundings, he almost resented their very familiarity. Impatient to be a part of the colour and vibrant activity of the city, he hurried below decks to dress. Without the cooling breeze of the ship under sail, his cabin was stifling hot, and the sweat channelled down poor Ramon's naked back as he struggled to repack the valises.

'We're here, Ramon!' Tommy picked up a boot from the floor and flung it at the perspiring black. 'Come, boy, stir your stumps. Let's escape this floating hellhole and get ourselves settled. There must be a cooler place somewhere in the city. Hurry, get me a bucket of fresh water so I may get myself a bit cleaner before I put on other clothes. I smell like an unwashed whore, and I'm an abomination even to myself. After I finish, you'd better scrub yourself because I can smell your stench even over my own. Be sure to get fresh water. I don't want the stickiness of salt to be mixed with my own.'

'Shore glad we're here, Masta Tommy suh. Don' like no boats 'n' no water neither. What yo' say this place called? Havana? Hotter'n hell in here, ain' it?'

'Then hurry!' Tommy searched through the bags that Ramon had already packed until he found a freshly laundered suit of white drill, a clean shirt and small clothes, then stripped off his damp attire (all but his shirt) and stood seeking whatever stray breeze might wander in while he waited. In a few moments, Ramon returned bringing a brimming sailcloth bucket in one hand and a large palm leaf fan in the other. 'I fans yo', Masta Tommy suh, whilst yo' gits cleaned up . . .' He looked at his master, half expecting a reciprocal offer.

'If you think I'm going to stand around fanning you, you black son-of-a-bitch, you're wrong. Now, hoist your ass out on deck while I wash.' When Ramon had closed the door, he soaped a washcloth to a good lather and scrubbed himself all over. He rinsed himself off and diligently applied the towel, but he felt as wet as ever when he had finished.

Ramon returned and bathed while Tommy dressed. As Tommy's fresh clothes seemed nearly as wet as those he had taken off, he tried a liberal application of eau de cologne to overcome any residual body stench. However, he was sure nothing could cloak Ramon's; the exertion of fanning his master while dressing had made the boy quite as sweaty and musky as before.

'Mayhap after we get out in the air we'll cool off a little.' Tommy spoke more to himself than to Ramon. While Ramon strapped the valises, Tommy reached under the bunk for an oversize leather wallet which he opened to choose two envelopes. Then he closed the case. From one addressed envelope, he removed a quantity of Spanish gold and silver coins which he pocketed. The other envelope was addressed but unsealed. Tommy studied it for a moment. The address intrigued him:

Señor Don Cipriano Olivarez,
San Felipe 128,
La Habana, Cuba.

This gentleman, so LaFitte had informed him before sailing, was his confidential agent in Havana, a powerful man with his fingers in many pies, and especially those backed by the corrupt Spanish government of Cuba. Tommy had only to present this letter and anything he needed would be immediately forthcoming. Never before had he possessed such an open-sesame to wealth and authority. He did not forget that it all started with the letter of introduction to the LaFittes from Helen.

Without Helen's letter he would probably have ended up as a pimp or a paid stud in some New Orleans whorehouse, getting a percentage from the men he brought in and earning some small handouts of cash from the women whose husbands were neglecting them. Helen's letter had saved him from that. Perhaps this letter would be equally effective. He certainly hoped so. Beyond Helen's letter he had to prove himself *to* the LaFittes; beyond this new letter he would have to prove himself *for* them. Both tasks were equally important for his own future. He had accomplished the first; now let him bring off the second. Olivarez? He wondered what the man would be like. Well, he'd hope for the best. Surely with the LaFittes behind him, he was halfway home.

The two other letters still in the wallet he knew to be addressed to two banks in Havana, giving him almost unlimited credit for the purchase of the blacks he had been sent to get. There was also a third letter addressed to a certain Señor Hernandez who, he understood, was the leading slave dealer in the city. He would not yet need these letters, as he was going first to Olivarez. Again he wondered what the man would be like. Perhaps through him he would be able to meet some companionable people in Havana. He hoped so. He had no desire to lead a solitary existence in this city which seemed to be bubbling over with life and animation.

With Ramon struggling with the valises and complaining under his breath about their weight, they stepped ashore. The pier was still bustling with activity. As they made their slow progress down it, dodging the stevedores and the itinerant merchants, Tommy felt a tugging at his coat tails. The tugger was a lad whose dark curls and spontaneous smile encouraged him to slow his footsteps.

The boy, who looked to be around thirteen or fourteen, might have been handsome under the accumulated grime covering his eager face. His ragged shirt scarcely covered his shoulders, and his pants, equally ragged and full of holes, left no doubt as to his sex. But his smile was so engaging and his manner so ingratiating that Tommy stopped.

'You American?' the boy asked.

Tommy nodded.

'I Vincente.' The boy grinned up at him. 'I speak American. *Si, Señor*, I clean your shoes.' He pointed to Tommy's dusty shoes and then to the box slung over his shoulder by a leather strap. 'They need it. Important *caballero* like you don't want no dust on his shoes. For just one centavo I make them look like new.'

Tommy stared first at his shoes and then at the boy's upturned face. Indeed, his shoes were a bit dusty, and he would talk to Ramon about it later. Meanwhile it would certainly do no harm to have them shined.

'I've no copper centavo with me. Only silver.'

'I get change for you. I not run away, señor. I am honest. They call me Honest Vincente, that's what. I'm a good boy, *verdad*?'

'You look like an imp of Satan to me. But get to work. Can we find a shady place?'

'I wipe off your man's shoes too,' Vincente pointed to Ramon's boots. 'Maybe not make so much shine as yours, for he is nothing but a black, but serving fine master like you, he must look good too. I think he very lazy to let fine *caballero* go out with dusty shoes.' He scanned the pier and pointed to a spot of shade in the lee of a pile of packing cases. The three of them walked over to it.

Tommy put his foot on the box while the boy produced black liquid and a brush and set to work. He applied the polish, brushed heartily, then spat copiously on Tommy's shoes and polished again. 'Spit makes good shine,' he said.

Tommy drew the letter from his pocket. 'You speak English well, boy. Where did you learn it?'

'From American sailors.'

'Then perhaps you can tell me if there is a street called San Felipe?'

143

'*Sí, señor*, but *muy lejos* – long distance from here. Too far for walk. When I finish your shoes and wipe off your man's, I fetch *volanta* so you can ride there. That will be another copper centavo, sir, for my services.'

He gave a final flip of the rag to Tommy's shoes. Never before, Tommy had to admit, had they looked so brilliantly clean. When he had finished with Tommy, he perfunctorily wiped the dust from Ramon's shoes. After Tommy had passed him the piece of silver, he darted among the crowd to the man who was selling coffee and returned quickly with the change which he carefully counted into Tommy's hand. Then, shaking his head wisely, he pointed to Ramon and the valises.

'Tell him go back to ship with valises and wait for you. A *volanta* will not hold us and valises too. You come back for him later. I go with you so driver don't cheat you. I also bring you back. I better go speak Spanish for you.' Tommy agreed to send Ramon back to the ship, and followed his new guide to the end of the pier. Here they waited until a conveyance such as Tommy had never seen before came along. It was a mule-drawn vehicle with two unusually high wheels and a hood of battered canvas.

'What number on San Felipe do you go, señor?'

'128.'

'The house of Don Cipriano Olivarez, yes?'

'Yes.'

'*Muy importante, este caballero.*' The name of Olivarez impressed the boy. '*Muy importante.* But, *señor, un momento, por favor.*' Vincente beckoned a grimy finger to Tommy. 'I say something to you in *confianza.*'

Tommy leaned over, the better to hear the boy's words.

'You like to fucky-fuck, sucky-suck, señor?' Vincente made an obscene gesture, closing the fingers of his left hand around the forefinger of his right and moving them suggestively while his tongue made slurping sounds against his lips.

Tommy laughed at the boy's earnest impertinence. 'Who doesn't, Vincente?'

'Then, señor, you are lucky man. I have for you my sister. She is young, señor, only fifteen and most beautiful. Ay, so beautiful! *Qué linda!* Clean too, señor.' He inserted his finger in his mouth and sucked on it avidly, his eyes rolling in

144

ecstasy. 'Ay, what she won't do for you, señor, my sister Perla. She can do everything and she is the best. She's a nice girl, not really a *puta* yet.' He smiled up at Tommy. 'You want? What is an hour?'

Tommy shook his head. Yes, he did want – God knows how much he wanted – but he had promised himself (and even now he regretted the promise) that this time business would come before pleasure. He remembered the long nights at sea with his feet braced against the bottom of the bunk. An hour! No, for once he would discipline himself. 'Perhaps later, Vincente.'

'Then, señor, I go with you and wait while you are in the house of Don Cipriano. Without me, who knows how much this son-of-a-bitch driver of broken-down mules will charge? I protect you, señor, because you do not speak the Spanish. I wait for you outside Don Cipriano's, then I will help you find a hotel. Indeed, señor, in Havana you are safe in Vincente's hands.'

'But . . .'

'No but, señor. These damned *cubanos*, they skin your eyes and sell the hide if I do not watch over you. You need me, señor. I sit beside driver and point out beautiful sights of Havana.'

Tommy did not protest. He did need somebody who could speak English, and the boy certainly could. Furthermore, there was no point of Ramon going. Moreover, he had to admit, the boy appealed to him. His very brassiness was charming. He was indeed an engaging brat. There was also the promise of his sister, whatever she might be like, and if she were only fifteen, she couldn't be too bad. He told Ramon to take the bags back to the ship and wait for him.

He got into the queer-looking vehicle that Vincente had hailed.

15

Once he had managed to clamber over the high wheels and settle himself inside on the worn cushions, Tommy found the well-sprung *volanta* quite comfortable. The hood sheltered him from the sun, but left Vincente, who had climbed up beside the driver, quite exposed. Vincente, however, born to the heat of the tropical sun, did not seem to mind. Thanks to his voluble guide, Tommy's first journey through Havana was an education. He was surprised by the industrious bustle of the town; it seemed as though every inhabitant – at least, every male, from ragged urchins to well-dressed businessmen – was out in the narrow streets, crowding the minuscule sidewalks, dashing to avoid the heavy traffic or stopping to embrace each other with Latin effusion. Each man or boy seemed to have a determined air of knowing just where he was going, but was in no hurry to get there, aware of the dire effect of heat and haste when combined against man in the tropics.

Most conspicuous, however, was the almost complete absence of women on the streets. Always on the lookout for a pretty face, a well-outlined bosom or a pair of shapely ankles, Tommy noticed – subconsciously at first – that there seemed to be none in Havana. The occasional few that he did see when he became aware of their scarcity were always in pairs. These pairs consisted invariably of a younger, well-dressed woman accompanied by an elderly female, usually clad in rusty black, in contrast to the brilliance of her younger companion's costume. How strange! And yet, there must be as many women as men in Havana. Where were they?

His curiosity, compounded by his desire to see a pretty face, prompted him to ask Vincente. Were all the women in Havana hidden behind the iron-grilled balconies, and if so, why?

Vincente appeared much surprised by the query. What was so unusual about that? Condescendingly, as though the answer to a rather stupid question should be self-evident, Vincente informed him that no woman ever appeared alone on the streets of Havana except for some emergency, and even then, she never went alone, but always in the company of a *dueña*, an older woman whose presence would frighten off any male daring to accost her. A respectable lady seldom left her home, except to visit her friends. If she needed new shoes, jewels, or material for a dress, a note sent to a merchant would bring a representative of the shop to her home – usually an elderly woman. If she did go without her *dueña*, her social position would be jeopardized.

Of course, there were women who appeared on the streets alone, usually in the evening, but these were the *putas* – the whores – and even these were far from the best class of whores. Every self-respecting whore (and it was a profession considered respectable by its practitioners) either had an *alcahuete* – a pimp who drummed up business and brought it home to her – or else was in a respectable whorehouse.

For instance, Vincente explained, there was his sister. She was a respectable whore who depended on Vincente for her clients, and the only time she ever went out on the street was for a short trip to the *especiería* on the corner to get black beans, rice, or other groceries for their supper.

Once started on the subject of his sister Perla, Vincente began to expatiate to his captive audience on her charms and the many ways she had of pleasing a man. Yes, she was well versed in the *manera francesa* – he again put a grimy thumb in his mouth to demonstrate. She was, Vincente admitted, a *puta* without rival. Why shouldn't she be? He had taught her all she knew, and young as he was, there was no better teacher in all Havana. She was not old enough – she was only fifteen – to have a professional pimp, but he considered himself far better than a professional. He also allowed her to keep most of her money for herself, so he was cheaper for her in the end.

Eventually, in a couple of years, Perla hoped to go to the Casa de Josefina, which, Vincente told Tommy, was the best whorehouse in all Havana. But it was difficult for a girl to get in there. If by chance, the *Señor Americano* might not care for his sister Perla, Vincente would willingly take him to the Casa de Josefina. There was a blonde Spanish girl there whom every man in Havana wanted, but in Vincente's opinion, she did not compare with his sister. *Ay*, what beautiful hair, what soft skin, what dazzling eyes and what accomplishments! Let *el señor Americano* just try her, and if he was not entirely satisfied, there would be no charge. But of course, and Vincente turned to stare momentarily at Tommy, if by chance the señor did not care for women, there was always Vincente. Yes, he himself was most certainly available.

Tommy laughed in his face and assured him that he was not in the least interested in boys. However, he would consider his sister and, most probably, the Casa de Josefina, but later, much later. Just now, he was interested in business. He knew as he spoke that he was lying to himself. Just now, more than anything else, he wanted either Vincente's sister or the blonde girl at the House of Josefina. Damn! After those nights at sea with nothing but his hand for company, he would have settled for the old woman selling oranges on the pier. If he could only release himself, he felt he could concentrate better while talking with Don Cipriano. But no! He had promised himself that business would come first on this trip, and Vincente's Perla would be waiting when he got through. At least, with Vincente acting as Tommy's guide, he would not be able to drum up much business for her . . .

They had left the narrow crowded streets behind them, and swung onto a wide boulevard of trees and stately homes. This avenue, according to Vincente, was called El Prado, and led straight to the sea from the small park in front of the Tacon Opera House. According to Vincente, Don Cipriano's house was not far away in this new and prosperous part of the city. Vincente knew the house, and there would be no difficulty in finding it. As Vincente turned to speak to the driver, Tommy found himself staring at the way the black hair curled around the boy's neck. Good God! Was he so hard up he was even looking at a boy with strange desire? Nonsense! But he sincerely hoped Vincente's sister was equally attractive.

Following Vincente's gesturing arm, the driver turned into a narrower side street, peering intently at the numbers on the houses.

'No need to stare like a starving sparrow looking for a horse turd,' the boy said in Spanish. 'It's Don Cipriano's house he wants, and I know where it is. Even you should know that.'

'*Sí, sí,* but I know only the number. Why didn't you tell me it was Don Cipriano's house?'

'Because I did not know you were so stupid,' the boy replied. 'Had I known it, I would not have engaged your broken-down dung cart for the *americano ilustre*.' Vincente pointed down the street to an imposing house of brilliant white stone. 'There it is.'

The house before which they had stopped was an ornate fanciful pile of white masonry. Tommy could see bronze gates leading to immense double doors of carved mahogany. Had it not been for Vincente, who clambered down before him, he would not have known how to gain entrance, but Vincente had spotted a bell-pull. He yanked at it and waited beside Tommy for the doors to open.

'I tell driver to wait, señor, and I wait with him because without me you can't get another *volanta* here. Even if you can, can you tell driver to return to La Machina wharf for your man and your bags? And when Don Cipriano does not offer you hospitality because Cubans do not take strangers into their homes, I be glad to take you to a good hotel, señor, and see that you are comfortably settled.'

Tommy nodded in agreement. The big mahogany doors opened and a black servant whose immaculately white clothes made him seem even blacker came down the steps to open the gates.

'Mr Thomas Verder,' Tommy spoke to the black, 'to see Mr Olivarez.'

'*El ilustre señor Don Tomás Verder, quiere ver al Don Cipriano,*' Vincente translated as the black stared dumbly at Tommy. 'Let him in and don't keep him waiting out here in the hot sun, you ignorant black *hijo de puta*. Otherwise, your master will send you to the public whips and you'll not sit on your ass for a week.'

The black answered sharply in Spanish to Vincente, and motioned to Tommy to enter. He turned for a moment as though to reassure himself of Vincente's white-toothed grin and then ascended the steps. Somehow, he was loath to leave the boy who had so providentially befriended him. Although he had no doubt that Don Cipriano could speak English, he was grateful for this ragged street boy's service so far. Had he been cleaner and better dressed, Tommy might have insisted that he come in with him. He might need an interpreter.

'Be sure to wait for me,' he called out as he stepped inside the closing doors.

'*Seguramente, señor*, if I have to wait all night.'

The dim coolness of the house was a welcome relief after the heat of the bright sun outside. Tommy noted the high ceilings, the cool, uncarpeted tile floors and the stiff formalities of the rooms, with their absence of draperies and upholstered furniture. He followed the servant into an immense front room, where many cane-seated rocking chairs were aligned in four rigid rows, facing the centre of the room. There stood the life-sized figure of a nearly-nude female, obviously intended to attract the eyes of all those sitting in the chairs. The servant indicated a chair for Tommy and mumbled something in Spanish as he left the room. Almost at once, a tiny black boy dressed in white glided into the room on bare feet, took his seat in a corner and started pulling on a long cord. A big fan suspended from the ceiling swung into slow motion. Tommy could detect a slight stirring of air.

Alone in this stately house, except for the black boy who stared at him, Tommy had a curious feeling of utter loneliness. He was tempted to go to the window and call for Vincente. There was something eerie here in this strange dim interior with the ghostly white figure of the marble woman staring him in the face. The sensuous curve of her full breasts under the thin marble veil made him think again of Vincente and the promise of his sister. It was something to anticipate. What was this mysterious feeling of kinship for an unknown girl and for the brother who pimped for her? How strangely and precipitously people came into his life, even when he was not looking for them. A chance encounter with a street urchin had already developed into friendship.

The silence was broken by the sound of leather heels on the marble stairs in the hall. Good! He would no longer be alone in this mausoleum with its funereal statue. He stood up as a man entered the room, an elderly man with snow-white hair, whose eyes were brightly alert and whose step light and springy as he advanced across the floor, his right hand extended.

150

'*Señor Verder. El que viene de mi buen amigo, Jean La-Fitte! Hemos recibido su carta. Que lástima que mi hermano no está aquí. El habla inglés, pero yo...*' He spread his open hands, palms up, in a gesture of helplessness. '*Pero, quisáz usted habla español, señor?*'

'Not a word.' Tommy had caught the word *inglés* and he shook his head in negation as he grasped the other man's hand. Aware that he would not be understood, he withdrew the letter from his pocket and handed it to Don Cipriano. He did not know if it was written in Spanish or English.

The old man bowed graciously as he accepted it and then after opening it and scanning the page, he handed it back to Tommy. It was written in English.

'*Es en inglés,*' Don Cipriano said.

Tommy smiled fatuously at the man. They were at an impasse. He could say nothing and neither could Don Cipriano. They were unable to communicate. Suddenly he thought of a possible solution – young Vincente. But Vincente with all his filth? Could he even suggest to the immaculate Don Cipriano that he allow this street Arab with his torn clothes, his unwashed body and his tousled curls to step inside the threshold of the polished mahogany doors? Impossible! And yet, it would be a solution. Although he realized that the words would be unintelligible, he murmured a 'With your permission' and walked over to the tall windows whose *persianas* were tightly closed to keep out the light. He examined them for a moment, conscious that Don Cipriano was watching him, then turned and faced the older man and, after pointing to the blinds, put his palms together slowly, then spread his hands.

Don Cipriano gave him a searching look, probably wondering if this personable young man, this agent of the powerful LaFittes could possibly be in his right mind. Suddenly comprehending that Tommy desired the blinds open, he crossed the room and pulled a cord at one side of the window. The blinds opened, letting barred streaks of sunshine into the room. Tommy peered out. The horse and carriage were waiting in the street and, seated on the curb nearby, was Vincente.

Tommy pointed out the window to the boy. 'He,' he spoke loudly and slowly, as if speaking to a deaf person. 'He speak English. English.' Suddenly he remembered the little paper-backed dictionary which LaFitte had given him, saying it might come in handy. Certainly it would never come in handier, and he reached in his pocket for it. He flipped hurriedly through the pages. '*Hablar inglés y español.*' He had to look up every word and pronounce it haltingly. 'But he is *sucio, muy, muy sucio. Desear el,*' again he searched the pages for the right words, '*entrar su casa?*'

Don Cipriano had evidently understood, because he smiled at Tommy and let forth a spate of Spanish which terminated in his crossing the room to pull a bell-cord. Tommy could hear the faint jangling of a bell and in a few seconds the same manservant entered the room to be greeted by another spate of Spanish. The man quickened his steps to the front door and called out.

'*Tu, muchacho, ven aqui.*'

Tommy heard the bronze gates open and close and the voice of Vincente in the vestibule. The servant seemed to be chiding him. There were steps in the hall and the servant entered, pushing Vincente ahead of him. Vincente advanced, first cast an appraising glance at the statue, then made a courtly bow, the effect of which was somewhat marred by his shoeshine box hanging from his shoulder.

'Don Cipriano.'

The old man looked aghast at the boy. 'Vincente!' He stared at him for a moment, then loosed another flood of Spanish. At the conclusion, he turned towards Tommy, shrugged his shoulders, pointed to Vincente and then to Tommy. It was a signal for Vincente to speak.

'Don Cipriano,' Vincente bowed slightly, as though to some august personage, 'wishes me to say to you that although I have been a frequent visitor to the house, this is the first time I have ever been permitted to come in the front door. You see, I have known Don Cipriano all my life. He has given me permission to say to you that he is my father, although I am a bastard. So, I am allowed to come here once a month to the back door and this Juan, who is Don Cipriano's servant, hands me an envelope which contains four silver pesos. It is for my sister and myself for, although my sister Perla is not Don Cipriano's daughter, he nevertheless helps her too, because she is the daughter of my mother, whom Don Cipriano loved at one time.'

'*Un de mis bastardos.*' Don Cipriano smiled almost paternally at Vincente and then rather shamefacedly at Tommy.

The word was close enough to the English equivalent that Tommy needed no translation. Already he knew two Spanish words. *Sucio* meant dirty and *bastardo* meant bastard. Rather a good combination, he thought: *sucio bastardo*, dirty bastard. At least it was a good beginning.

Don Cipriano spoke again to Vincente, who turned to Tommy.

'Don Cipriano says that I am a rascal, which is not true. He also says that my sister is a whore, which is indeed true. But' – Vincente flashed a most engaging smile at both Tommy and his father – 'he also says that I have enough of his blood in my veins to make me sufficiently trustworthy to be a good interpreter for both of us. Do you wish me, señor? If so, I shall serve you most faithfully, and also Don Cipriano, because he is my father and I honour him.'

'Then first read this letter to him.' Tommy handed him the sheet of neat copperplate writing.

'Alas, señor, I do not read.'

'Then I shall read it for you in English and you can translate it for your father.' He unfolded the letter and proceeded to read it slowly, stopping at the end of each sentence so that Vincente could translate it into Spanish. Don Cipriano listened attentively.

Esteemed friend Don Cipriano:

I hope on receipt of this letter that it will find you and your brother Don Eugenio in good health, as indeed I am through the grace of God.

This will serve to introduce Mr Thomas Verder, who is to act as our agent in Havana with your kind help and assistance. We are in urgent need of some 300 fine strong male slaves, which Mr Verder will purchase in Havana, with possibly a dozen extra fancy female slaves, if such are on the market.

We have warranted letters of credit for Mr Verder at both the Banco Real de España and the Bank of Barcelona.

Anything you can do to help Mr Verder will be sincerely appreciated.

Your good friend

Jean LaFitte

Through Vincente, Don Cipriano remarked that it would indeed be a pleasure to serve the Señor Thomas Verder, and anything he could do to expedite matters would most certainly be his pleasure. As a matter of fact, a ship had arrived in Havana only yesterday – a Portuguese ship – with, he understood, about a hundred good males. It had previously stopped in Port au Prince and possibly the best had been unloaded there, but he would send messengers and arrange for Don Tomás to see them at the barracoons of Emelio Hernandez, which were across the bay in Regla. And there were other sources. As to the Fancies which Señor LaFitte had mentioned, those would be at Solano's. Policarpo Solano was the leading slave merchant in Havana for that type of thing. He would dispatch another messenger at once. Furthermore, if Don Tomás wished him to handle the letters of credit with the banks, he would be happy to do so.

Tommy thanked him and then waited until Vincente could translate Don Cipriano's next words.

Don Cipriano regretted, so Vincente said (and had already foretold) that he could not offer him the hospitality of his home while he was in Havana, as he and his brother were both bachelors and lived very simply. And, speaking of his brother, Don Eugenio would be back in Havana tomorrow and he spoke excellent English.

Tommy thanked him and asked if he would be willing to recommend a hotel.

Yes, indeed, he could. The Hotel de Paris was conveniently located on the Prado and was new enough to be comfortable. Also, he had heard that they had a master chef there and the cuisine was highly recommended. He would send a messenger there to reserve a room for Tommy.

'Make it a suite of two rooms,' Tommy answered. 'I have a servant with me, and, although I have not quite made up my mind, I believe, with your permission, señor, I shall retain this young Vincente with me as an interpreter, after cleaning him up a bit. Without an interpreter, I shall be helpless in Havana.'

Vincente grinned with joy as he translated to Don Cipriano and waited for the other's reply.

'He says I must first clean myself up.' Vincente shrugged his shoulders. 'And he will give me money to buy some new clothes which I must promise to keep clean. But that will not be difficult if I do not shine shoes any more.'

Tommy could sense that the interview was over. With a low bow to Don Cipriano and an extended hand, he turned to leave. Vincente followed him. Don Cipriano lifted a retarding finger. He jingled some coins in his pocket and gave them to Vincente. Then, with more formal adieus, they left, escorted to the door not by the manservant but by Don Cipriano himself, his arm around Tommy's shoulder. Once out in the sunshine, they entered the *volanta*.

'To La Machina, Don Tomás, to collect your man and your baggage and then to the Hotel de Paris.'

'Hell no, boy.' Tommy slapped him on the back. 'I've been looking at the tits on that marble statue so long, I've got such a hard-on I had to keep my hand in my pocket to try and hide it. Let's stop at your house and see if your sister is busy. For once, pleasure comes before business.'

'You'll not be disappointed, Don Tomás.' The boy glanced at Tommy's crotch. 'My sister will be very happy.'

16

The house in which Vincente lived was deep in the maze of crooked old streets which had not changed since the time Havana was a walled city. Although these streets grudgingly allowed the passage of a slow-moving ox-cart or a horse-drawn dray, they were little more than alleyways, so narrow that a pedestrian meeting traffic had either to duck into a doorway or flatten himself against a wall. Their very narrowness almost blotted out the sun, but the fact that they were originally built this way for that very purpose never occurred to Tommy. As he penetrated farther and farther into this rabbit warren he became more and more apprehensive.

Yes, here he was totally dependent upon this teenage boy whom he had met only by chance. Unable to speak the language, it was only through Vincente that he could make himself understood. Now he was being led into an area where any of the drinkers in the tiny *bodegas* and coffee shops, any of the men lounging at street corners and in open doorways might well be assassins of the first order. Certainly most of them looked the part. They were mostly young, suavely handsome in a rather oily way and in all colours from white through *café-au-lait* to brown and ebony black. There seemed to be little colour distinction here in Cuba. Blacks and whites mixed much more freely than in New Orleans. They all looked as though they would gladly slit his gullet for a tenth of the gold he carried in his pocket.

Another worry: Vincente's sister might well prove to be entirely fictitious – a decoy to lure him into an escape-proof trap. Furthermore, this seemingly friendly boy knew he was unarmed. His only weapon was a clasp knife and what good would that do if several of these bravos ganged up on him? Any two or three of them could easily overpower him.

Yet, as he looked at Vincente sitting up beside the driver and the boy turned to grin at him, he lost some of his fright. Vincente made another obscene gesture of his hands and said 'pronto'. Tommy hoped the word meant 'soon'. Surely, if the boy really was Don Cipriano's bastard, and expecting more money for serving as an interpreter for Tommy, he would not kill the goose that was about to lay a golden egg. Common sense and what logic he could muster told Tommy that his fears were groundless, yet he wished momentarily that he were back on the ship with Ramon. It would seem good to see a familiar face, even Ramon's black one.

A few blocks farther and Vincente ordered the driver to stop before what Tommy was sure was the most disreputable house on the most disreputable of all the streets they had traversed. Moreover they had stopped at the centre of the most disreputable crowd he had yet seen – young bravos, gaunt scarecrows of old beggar women, old men with the look of evil etched on their faces, and a screaming swarm of urchins. With Vincente's help, he alighted before a large arch opening in the grey and mildewed wall surmounted by rusty, iron-railed balconies. More men lounged in the doorway and cast side-long glances at them as they entered; one called Vincente by name. Once inside the inner patio they dodged naked children playing among heaps of offal, the ribs of old furniture, and a conglomeration of dirty papers, broken boxes and the litter of hundreds of families who had lived there before. One of the children ran up and spoke to Vincente, reeling off sentences of rapid Spanish in which Tommy was able to catch the one word *Americano*.

This inside courtyard was lined with iron railings on all four sides on each of its three stories. A bedlam of shouts and curses echoed off the walls as the slatterns hanging over the railings called to the children below and yelled to each other. Vincente beckoned to Tommy to follow him and started up a flight of worn stone steps situated just inside at the left of the arched opening. Tommy followed, now more apprehensive than ever. He wished that he had thought of bringing a pistol with him, but of course, when he had left the *Sainte Claire* he had not foreseen an expedition like this.

They ascended the two flights of broken, cracked and dirty steps to the accompaniment of various jeers, catcalls and invitations of the women. When Tommy distinguished the words *Americano, puta* and *Perla* as well as an occasional *Vincente*, he reasoned that his errand to the house was by no means unknown. Therefore he decided that there really must be a Perla, that she must be a whore and that indeed Vincente must be her pimp. Well, that was a situation much easier to handle than a gang of cutthroats lurking somewhere to jump him. Perhaps, after all, he had nothing to fear. He hoped not, for despite his anxiety he was determined to bed this unknown Perla. Never in his life had he needed a woman so much. He had been continent much too long.

Once on the third floor, Vincente beckoned Tommy to follow him along the gallery. They ran a gauntlet of women of all ages, several of whom offered themselves brazenly to Tommy. One reached with her sweaty hand for the growing

157

bulge at his crotch, and another loosening her bodice to reveal her over-plump breasts. Although he could not understand their words, their gestures and catcalls plainly expressed the opinion that the unknown Perla was about to draw a prize. Probably, he thought, he was the only well-dressed *Americano* ever to enter this den of thieves and prostitutes.

Vincente pushed through the brawling crowd of women, opening a way for Tommy to follow him. He scanned the women crowded about them, seeking his sister. When he failed to see her, he pushed Tommy ahead and knocked on a battered door.

'Are you busy?' he asked in Spanish.

'No,' came the answer through the door. At least here was one word that Tommy could understand. Whereupon Vincente opened the door and they stepped inside. Vincente closed the door and shoved home a big bolt to secure it. Tommy took a deep breath. There were no men in the room.

Thank God!

It was not an overly large room but Tommy was glad to see that it appeared reasonably clean. At least the old tiles, cracked plaster and unpainted wood were neat. A double bed covered with a clean white sheet stood in one corner. A smoke-blackened hole in the masonry counter which ran along one side apparently served as a charcoal stove. The only other furniture beside the bed was a plain deal table with one leg mended, a straight-backed chair and a box which also served as a chair. A big window with unglazed French doors faced the street, and beyond this he could see the scaling iron of a balcony. One corner of the room was curtained off with a tattered piece of flowered cotton, now an overall grey from many washings. That was all except for a meagre collection of feminine garments which hung from nails over the bed. Perla, if there was such a person, was not visible.

'Where's this sister you have been talking so much about?' Tommy scanned the empty room. 'Have you been deceiving me?'

Vincente's thumb jerked in the direction of the screened-off corner. '*Un momento,*' he said, a look of anticipatory pride on his face.

And it was only a moment before the curtain was lifted and a girl emerged. She was unabashedly naked. Tommy was cognizant of the fact that Vincente was a handsome boy under his grime, but he was quite unprepared for the beauty and delicacy of the girl who stood before him. She was, as Vincente had said, about sixteen and her short life as a prostitute had not yet robbed her of her virginal look. Somehow the innocent appearance of childhood, that youthful bloom of springtime and chastity, had endured. She was a trifle taller than Vincente with a heart-shaped face framed by long dark curls. Her eyes were a disturbing grey-green which seemed unusual with her tea-rose skin and black hair. These eyes stared at him from under long sooty lashes with a wide-eyed expression of youthful anticipation. Her breasts, not yet fully formed, were beautiful in their youthful plumpness. The rosy points of her nipples were hard and upstanding. Her waist was slender; he felt he could almost encompass it with both hands but her hips swelled in a provocative curve. A small patch of black hair punctuated the rose and white complexion of her body and Tommy guessed from the beads of moisture on it and the freshly towelled glow of her skin that she had just finished bathing. She wore no powder or makeup. She needed no heavy *maquillage* to be beautiful.

'My sister Perla,' Vincente whispered. Then, changing into Spanish, he spoke to her. 'A rich American; see that you treat him right. He is a friend of Don Cipriano's.'

Her little bare feet made no noise as she stepped closer to Tommy. Smiling up at him, she raised her arms and clasped her hands like a garland behind the nape of his neck. For a long moment her eyes appraised his rugged handsomeness. He was so different from the rough sailors and the Cuban street rowdies which Vincente was wont to bring her. He smiled down at her and felt a tightening in his crotch. She was aware of it and moved away from him, so that she could see what she felt. Then she pressed her body against him, slowly undulating her hips. Her lips, moist, pink and rose-petal soft, touched his. He returned her kiss, thrilling to the soft, warm, wet and tender tip of her tongue which entered between his teeth.

'*Ay, tan joven y tan guapo!*' She turned and smiled her appreciation to Vincente who stood stolidly looking on.

159

'Are you going to get to hell out of here, Vincente?' Tommy was impatient with the loitering boy.

'I'll not leave you, Señor Tommy, but neither will I be any trouble. See.' He lifted the curtain to disclose a pallet on the floor alongside a washbasin and damp towels. 'I shall clean myself up a little and take a little nap perhaps too. It's better that I stay because if you need anything I'll be here to talk with my sister and tell her in Spanish what you want.'

'A *dueña*, huh?'

'But alas, a blind one, Señor Tommy.'

'But not deaf?'

'What can you say to my sister that she will understand?'

'Nothing,' Tommy shook his head, 'but at times when his blood runs hot, a man speaks out whether or not a girl understands.' He shrugged his shoulders. 'And girls and beds have a way of squeaking.'

'. . . which I have listened to many times before. Go ahead! Nothing will disturb me. If either girl or bed is squeaking, it will mean you are enjoying more.' He ducked into the corner and pulled down the curtains. 'Now, you see I have disappeared.'

'And if you peek out, I'll have your father cut your allowance,' Tommy admonished him. But, he had to admit that he felt better with someone near at hand who spoke his own language.

'I'll be asleep, señor, I was up this morning before dawn.'

'So be it,' Tommy dismissed Vincente from his thoughts and turned his attention to Perla.

She stood before him, smiling, not at all self-conscious over her nudity. He drew in a long breath and expelled it through half-pursed lips. Good God! She was so young and so damned beautiful! Adolescent though she was, her body held great promise. Her skin was a shade lighter in colour than her brother's. Her youthful rosiness shone through the faint tinge of olive. True, her breasts were immature, but perfectly rounded with an aureole of sepia surrounding the taut pink nipples. His eyes strayed to the patch of dark fur between her legs and his fingers itched to touch that triangle of sable.

Now her tiny hands busied themselves with his cravat which they loosened and draped over the back of the one chair. His white coat followed. She spread his damp shirt over the box, smoothing out the wrinkles. She tried to pull the knitted silk undershirt over his head but he stopped her by shaking his head and moving her hands to his groin where his pulsating hardness was all too apparent. Her fingers stroked and caressed him through the cloth, then rose to struggle impatiently with the big brass buckle of his belt. His fingers stopped fondling her breasts long enough to help her. She unbuttoned his straining fly, stripped down his trousers and his underpants, and stared in wonder and delight when his rigid maleness, freed from its prison of cloth, popped out in all its magnificence.

'*Ay, qué magnifico! Pero tengo miedo que está demasiado grande para mi.*'

'She says she's afraid you are too big for her,' Vincente called from behind the curtains. 'But don't worry, she'll manage.'

Her hands left him reluctantly while she pulled off his boots and stripped off the socks, waiting while he stepped out of his trousers and underpants. Then, with these folded and deposited on the chair, she knelt before him, her hands stroking and caressing him while he teetered on his feet, holding her head between his trembling hands while her wet mouth and her darting tongue conspired to thrill him to the utmost. Marvellous though she was, he stopped her, determined to delay the denouement as long as possible.

He pulled her up to him, his mouth seeking hers, and then curtailing this pleasure too, he picked her up in his arms – she seemed light and fragile – and carried her to the bed where he lowered her to her back. He let his eyes dwell on her a moment before he lay beside her. Now it was his turn to seek out the secret parts of her body, letting his mouth taste the moist freshness of her. Although her squirming and gasping for breath might appear highly professional, he was convinced that her actions were entirely unfeigned. He had had too much experience with women not to recognize the real thing.

For long moments they played with each other – that little game in which strangers in love explore each other's bodies – seeking and discovering all previously hidden treasures. Their fingers and lips heightened their passion until she extricated herself from under him, turned him gently onto his back. Mounting him, she lowered herself astride him, raising and lowering herself rhythmically upon his rigidity.

As he felt the hot liquid building up within him, he was unable to take more of her tantalizing. He overturned her and spreadeagled her on the bed, holding her shoulders with both hands while he mounted her in turn.

Her legs clasped themselves around him. Forgetting everything but the desperate urgency to fulfil his own great need, he plunged into her and although she cried out, he knew that his brutality was more satisfying to her than gentleness. Then in a cataclysm which started in his toes and rushed like red hot lava to his loins, he exploded within her. Panting for breath, he fell inert on the mattress beside her.

Her hand reached down to fondle his increasing limpness, trying to resuscitate him until he pushed her away. He turned his head slightly and saw Vincente, the curtain raised with one hand while the other pumped himself vigorously. Then the boy too reached a climax and the curtain fell again. Finally there was no sound in the room but their breathing, mingled with the daytime noises of the street below. Tommy rested beside the girl, listening to the splashing of water in the curtained-off alcove. Just as his eyes were closing in a sleep of exhaustion, he heard sounds of activity in the curtained alcove, and out walked Vincente – a changed boy.

Yes, it was Vincente, but he was clean – so clean that he seemed to sparkle all over. He *did* possess a clean shirt because he had it on and although the white pantaloons were darned and patched, they also were clean. He even sported a pair of rope-soled *alpargatas* on his feet. He was indeed a different boy, as handsome in his way as his sister Perla was beautiful.

'Forgive me, Señor Tommy. I promised not to watch you but I got so hot I had to. So you have enjoyed Perla? I know you did. Didn't I promise you? You would not have believed me if I had told you she was the best fuck in all Havana but now you will. Ay, Vincente never lies, never.'

He spoke to his sister in rapid Spanish and she nodded.

'And she agrees, too, that it was the best she ever had although she says you did hurt her. She says, judging from you, that Americans are better than Cubans. Cubans – Wham! They push a girl down on the bed, spread her legs, stick it in and it's all over. They have no patience. Get it in and get it off. That's all they ever think about.'

Tommy sat up on the bed and grinned at Vincente over Perla's body glistening with sweat. It was impossible to be angry with the boy for spying, yet he wanted the last word. 'And you enjoyed it too, didn't you? I saw you banging away like a stallion on a mare.'

Vincente grinned sheepishly. 'That's how I get my kicks, watching Perla perform when there is nothing else to do. *Si señor*. Each time she takes a man to her room I watch and then sometimes when the man is gone, she lets me get in bed with her. She says these damned *Cubanos* never give her time to get satisfied herself so I have to help her along. I teach her too. All she knows is what I've taught her and I've been a good master, no?'

'You seem to be pretty good at everything.'

'Ah, señor, but you did not try me. You would have much better time if I been in the bed with you too. But *Americanos* think only a woman can please. What about a girl and a boy too?' He rolled his eyes. 'That señor is real *éxtasia*!' He shook his head vehemently to give accent to the spoken words. Then, turning on Perla, he cursed her in Spanish for not getting up to wash Tommy and help him to dress.

She climbed out of bed, poured water from a pitcher onto a clean rag and went over Tommy's body with it, washing him carefully. Then she poured a few drops of eau de cologne onto the palm of her hand and wiped his face.

'It is almost time for our *almuerzo*, and you must be hungry, Señor Tommy.' Vincente was impatient. 'You've been working hard. Come, you and I will eat at El Paraíso – such *langosta*, such Morro crabs, such shrimps.' Vincente waited while Perla helped Tommy on with his clothes. They were dry now and although he would have preferred a bath, he knew that the only water in the apartment was that in which both Perla and Vincente had already bathed. He would have to be satisfied with Perla's cat-licking.

When they were ready to leave, Tommy took out one of the smallest gold pieces from his pocket and gave it to Perla but

Vincente snatched it from Perla's hand and gave it back to Tommy.

'There is no charge for you today, señor. None at all. Perla enjoyed it, I enjoyed it, and I'm sure you enjoyed it, so why should we charge you? Just say I work for you from now on for four silver pesos a week, with my food and room in your hotel extra.'

'So, you have already made up your mind, have you? You've even settled on your own salary. But, young fellow, if you work for me, who's going to pimp for Perla?'

'I'll ask Jorge, a friend. No friend really. A damned mean bastard. He'd slit his grandmother's throat for a copper. A real *ladrón*, that Jorge. He'll keep Perla flat on her back and get his own free.' Vincente hesitated a moment. 'Remember, he spoke to us on the street?'

Tommy vaguely remembered one of the toughs in the doorway speaking as he eyed him. 'Was he one of those hanging around the door?' He sat down so Perla could ease his boots on. She had not dressed and her small breasts jiggling with her movements, gave him a renewed urge, but he stifled it.

'Si, Señor Tommy, one with long pointed *patillas* on his cheeks. Because he's so handsome and so well hung he thinks he shouldn't pay a whore but she should pay him instead.' He leaned over Perla 'Don't give him too much, Perla, even if he is pimping for you.'

'I'll not,' she answered, 'but you keep in touch with me. It's going to be strange around here without my *hermanito*.'

'I'll see you every day because I'm sure my boss will want to come here every day. But now we must go. We must eat, we must go back to the ship and get his baggage and his stupid black boy, find a room at the Hotel de Paris for all of us, so we'll be busy the rest of the day.'

Tommy was surprised at the crowd which had collected around Vincente's door when they went out. He heard the murmurs of both men and women.

'*Ay, qué guapo!* How good looking he is.'

'He's an American.'

'And rich. They say he's worth millions.'

'So young and so handsome. I'd share my bed any night with him.'

164

'And what a man! Look at his crotch.'

'Ay, poor Perla will walk spraddle legged for the next week.'

All this conversation was going on among the excited Cubans who had collected around Vincente's door. Vincente signalled to the same suavely handsome fellow who had spoken to him previously, and took him aside to talk. Their conversation concluded with a nodding of heads. He returned to Tommy and escorted him down the stairs which he noticed had been swept since he went up them. When they were out in the street, Vincente suggested that they walk, as it was only a short distance, so they started off towards the restaurant which Vincente said was at the head of La Machina wharf.

'Are you hungry, *amigo mio*?' Vincente asked. It was *amigo* now and not *señor*, Tommy noticed. Well, why not? He did feel a sort of friendship for this boy.

'Starving, *amigo mio*,' Tommy answered.

'Then, señor, if we are friends, will you tell me something?'

'If I can,' Tommy answered.

'Then why is it that when you took your clothes off to go to bed with Perla, you did not remove your undershirt? It is strange that a man in this weather should wear an undershirt, and stranger still that he should not take it off when he is fucking. Why, *amigo mio*?'

'There's only one word that will answer your question and that's a word you'll not understand. It's an idiosyncrasy of mine, that's all.'

Vincente pondered a moment. 'Ah, we have the same word in Spanish. *Idiosincrasia*. Now I think I know what you mean. You don't enjoy it unless you wear your shirt. Just like a friend of mine has to look at a woman's shoe *cuando se goza* – when he plays with himself. Right?'

'Right!'

Tommy wondered briefly why he still clung to his secret fiction here in this strange country where there seemed to be no colour line – except that he still awoke at night in a cold sweat, remembering his narrow escape in Alabama. No, whether in Cuba or New Orleans or Barataria it was still better that Calico the bright-skinned slave should remain buried.

17

The rooms reserved for Tommy at the Hotel de Paris were far more luxurious and comfortable than he had anticipated. In the large, high-ceilinged bedroom with two tall French windows opening on balconies facing the Prado, there were plenty of cane-seated mahogany rocking chairs and a ponderous mahogany wardrobe with immense mirrored double doors. The enormous double bed was shrouded with a white mosquito netting that gave it the appearance of a full-rigged ship under sail. Off the bedroom was a dressing room where he had a cot placed for Vincente. He had another cot placed for Ramon in the bathroom with its big high-backed tin tub.

On another floor there was a servants' dining room where Ramon could eat with other black servants. Vincente, being white, would either eat from trays sent up to the room or occasionally with Tommy in the elaborate hotel dining room whose big windows opened wide on the street. The food at the hotel was good – Cuban cuisine prepared by a French chef – which made every meal a delightful experience.

That first morning at the hotel a messenger arrived from Don Cipriano to say that his brother, who spoke English, had returned and would call at eleven to pay his respects to Señor Verder. Fortunately Vincente was there to interpret. Tommy wondered what he would do without Vincente. He was amazed that ignorance of a language could be such a handicap.

Promptly at eleven, Don Cipriano's brother arrived, a rather pompous version of the elder Olivarez. Through Vincente again, the brother informed Tommy that his name was Don Angel and that he was ready to serve Tommy in any way possible. To be sure, Don Angel could speak a few words of halting English but scarcely enough to carry on a conversation, which made Tommy all the more grateful for Vincente.

In his slow and stilted English, Don Angel informed Tommy that if convenient, he would return after lunch and, even though it would be siesta time in Havana, he would go with Tommy to the barracoons of Señor Hernandez across the

166

harbour in Regla. A new shipment of slaves had just arrived a day or so earlier from Africa. Hernandez was about to auction the men off singly but if he had a chance to sell a large parcel at once, he might dispense with the auction. Moreover, he informed Tommy, they would probably cost less when bought by the hundred. Fortunately for Tommy, Don Angel said, slave prices were down a bit, as several slavers had arrived within the past month and more were expected soon.

So, Don Angel said, he would return home for lunch; no, it was gracious for Tommy to invite him for *almuerzo* at the hotel but he did have some business to attend to at home. He would be back promptly at two o'clock *al punto*. Would that be satisfactory? Tommy assured him it would be, and that he would be waiting. To kill time, Tommy had Vincente take him to the Mercado, that vast sprawling jungle of a market where everything from a freshly killed chicken to a vest of Lyons velvet could be bought. The clothes on Vincente's back were evidently the only ones that he possessed other than the disreputable rags he wore as a shoeshine boy, and Tommy wanted him to look respectable when accompanying him on business missions. He preferred bilingual Vincente to Ramon. He knew that Ramon resented this. Rivalry between Ramon and Vincente had already developed after only one day. Arguments as to who should wait on him were usually won by Vincente who was far more aggressive than the lazy Ramon. It had been Vincente who had helped him dress that morning; Vincente who had first used his bath water after he had finished; Vincente who had buttered his hot croissants for breakfast; and Vincente who would have chewed them for him had that been possible.

It was Vincente too, when their shopping errand had been explained to him, who led Tommy to an obscure stall in the Mercado where there were Cuban shirts for sale – something called *guyaberas*, really more jacket than shirt – embellished with a multitude of fancy tucks and four capacious pockets. Tommy had noticed many men wearing them in lieu of a jacket and they certainly appeared cooler and more comfortable. While buying several for Vincente, he laid in a stock for himself and a few for Ramon. Then there were new white-drill trousers to buy for Vincente as well as a pair of shoes. Shoes for Vincente! He had shined so many pairs for so many other people and now at last he had a pair for himself. They were, he confessed to Tommy, among the things in life he had most wanted.

By the time they had returned to the hotel and Tommy had changed his shirt and Vincente had donned his new clothes, marvelling again that he should own a pair of shoes, it was time for lunch. The two of them ate in the lower dining room to allow Vincente an opportunity to show off his new finery. Tommy marvelled at the boy's impeccable table manners – until he discovered that Vincente was watching him to copy his every movement. Smart lad! Nobody would ever guess that only yesterday he was shining shoes on the pier.

Don Angel arrived while they were still eating and drank a cup of coffee with them. He invited them to share his carriage to ride to the harbour. Again Vincente occupied the seat beside the driver and Don Angel, having run out of his meagre stock of English, sat silently with Tommy. Once at the waterfront, Don Angel dickered with a boatman to take them to the little town of Regla across the harbour. The trip took only a few minutes.

If Havana was a thriving, bustling metropolis, Regla in comparison was a sleepy little Cuban town which seemed centuries removed from Havana's cosmopolitanism. There were no carriages waiting here, so Don Angel hired a lumbering ox-cart with seats of the hardest planks Tommy had ever sat on. The cart bumped them through the cobbled streets of the town to the outskirts where a palisade of logs marked the barracoons.

Once inside the guarded gateway, Don Angel introduced him to Señor Hernandez who, he said, owned the barracoons and was one of the leading slave dealers in the area. Hernandez was one of the least likely persons Tommy would ever have envisaged as being in charge of a slave barracoon. He was a man of indeterminate age with sparse white hair and steely blue eyes that squinted through a pair of square brass-rimmed spectacles. His high-pitched voice matched his body – weak and quavering. He walked with some difficulty with the aid of a thick mahogany cane. After their introduction he invited Tommy and the others into his office which was almost a duplicate of Tommy's own office in Barataria. Even the rank all-pervading odour of the barracoons was the same, making Tommy feel quite at home.

Yes, Hernandez agreed to Tommy's question translated by Vincente, he had just received a shipment of slaves from Africa – a whole shipload. They were of good quality, he assured Tommy, mostly Fantis from the Gold Coast, plus some Kromantis and others, but all good men. Unfortunately he had not had time to condition them but they were all fine specimens, quite the best he had received for a long time. He again apologized to Tommy for their present poor condition after the long voyage, but said they would present a much different appearance in a few days, with rest and good food. He had, he explained through Vincente, intended to have an auction when the men had been reconditioned, but of course if Señor Verder wished to see them in their present state, he would be happy to show them. As to how many he had, Hernandez said there were about 250 in this shipment but he had another fifty or so from local sources for sale. Señor Verder was welcome to look at them also. Would he like to see them now or wait until early the next morning? The next morning, Hernandez said, would be far more satisfactory as he could get things lined up and the men would be more presentable after a hearty breakfast and a liberal rubbing with palm oil.

Tommy agreed to wait. He realized that he had to make himself known to the banks before he could enter into any negotiations, but he did ask Hernandez if he might take a casual look at the men before he left. Hernandez was willing and after a glass of sherry, they went out into the hot sunlight to see the slaves.

A wide thatched roof surmounted the four walls of the interior compound within the palisades, and most of the men were sitting on the ground in its shade, or lolling on the plank beds which rose in three tiers under the shelter. Tommy quickly saw that most of the men were thin and emaciated, listless, and apparently mentally depressed. There were no smiling faces and few of them even bothered to look up as he passed. They had survived the long cramped voyage from Africa, but now they did not know what ordeals lay ahead.

169

However, he noted that most of them, despite their dispirited appearance, had strong, muscular frames. When they were rested and fattened up a little, they would be prime specimens. He spotted several who might be more than prime, almost fancies. He could probably fill his whole quota right here with the exception of those few female Fancies which LaFitte wanted and for which he would have to go to – Solano's was it?

Also, he reminded himself, he must stock his own ship with food and water for these men, and again he wondered just how he was going to accommodate them all on his small craft. But it was a short voyage and they would have to put up with a few hardships. Once in Barataria they could be fattened up, exercised and fully conditioned.

He took his leave from Hernandez, promising to return early next morning. When they returned to Havana, he told the younger Olivarez brother that there was no need to rouse himself so early to accompany him, as he had Vincente to act as an interpreter. Don Angel seemed most grateful but assured Tommy that he would be at his service at any time.

When they returned to the hotel, Vincente informed him that the hour of the siesta was over, and the banks would be open. As neither of Tommy's banks was far from the hotel they could walk there easily giving Tommy his first real taste, apart from his quick trip to the Mercado that morning, of walking the streets of Havana.

He found the city increasingly fascinating, despite the absence of women. He loitered in several shops, buying a high tortoiseshell comb for Gretchen, and an elaborately-embroidered and intricately-fringed Spanish shawl as a present for Perla, whom he planned to visit again that evening. When he informed Vincente of his desire to see Perla again, Vincente begged his leave to run home after they had made contact with the banks. He promised Tommy it would take less than an hour for him to make sure that Jorge would leave Perla's time open. When they had finished their business at the banks, where the LaFitte name earned Tommy a most cordial reception, Vincente left.

Tommy remembered the turnings they had made and found his way back to the hotel easily. He stopped at the same shop

170

where he had bought the comb and the shawl to purchase a pair of long jet earrings which he had seen and which he would add to the gift of the shawl to Perla. Then, remembering Chloe – had she ever been far from his thoughts? – he bought another pair of earrings, these set with pearls and tiny diamonds. The thought of Chloe brought Helen to mind and he purchased a heavy gold bracelet engraved with '*Recuerdo de la Habana*'.

But, although he remembered Chloe with love and Helen with affection and gratitude, his immediate and mundane thoughts were with Perla and his anticipated visit this night. Chloe was far away, Perla was near. He hoped that Jorge had not been overly assiduous in bringing her too many customers. She must not be too tired to entertain him as excitingly as the night before. She was a hot little bitch. Damn! He wished he had gone with Vincente now. It would be a long wait until tonight. True, the longer he waited, the better it would be, but he wished to hell it could be *now*.

When he returned to the hotel, the jalousies had been drawn and it was dimly cool inside. Not having eaten anything since his early breakfast, he was hungry. It was now long past lunchtime and the dining room was closed, but he sent Ramon downstairs to see if he could get a sandwich and a cup of coffee. Ramon had already eaten and sped off on Tommy's errand. When he returned with the food, he stood before Tommy while he was eating, shifting his weight from one foot to another, obviously wanting to speak and yet not daring. Finally he could stand it no longer.

'Kin I ask yo' somethin', Masta Tommy suh?' He twisted his hands and spoke haltingly.

'Now what's bothering you?' Tommy was tired and a bit irritable. The siesta hour, he had decided, was a good idea and the white sheets of the bed were most inviting. Now that he had satisfied his hunger, he wanted only to strip off his sweaty clothes and stretch out for a long nap.

'Ain' nothin' a-botherin' me, Masta Tommy suh, but why cain't I go out with yo' no more? Yo' takes that Vinthentay everywhere yo' goes'n I stays here. Ain' nothin' to do, ain' no work to do, ain' nobody to talk with. It a-gittin' mighty lonesomelike a-settin' here all day a-waitin' for yo' to come home.'

171

Tommy looked at Ramon, actually seeing him for the first time in days. His own irritability disappeared and he tried to picture himself in Ramon's place. He had forbidden the lad to leave the hotel for fear he might get lost and, knowing no Spanish, be unable to return. Now Tommy was going out again this evening with Vincente and Ramon would again be abandoned. Tommy was suddenly in a mood to be generous. After all, Ramon was a man like himself and, black or not, he had the same needs.

Still chewing on the last mouthful of his sandwich, he smiled. He had no complaints against this boy; Ramon had always served him with loyalty, even affection. Since they had landed in Havana, Tommy had been so busy he had quite forgotten about him. It had been Vincente whom he had depended upon. Now he felt sorry for Ramon.

'Tell me something, boy. How long since you've been laid?'

'Good Lord, Masta Tommy suh, it been so long I plumb forgotten. Musta been that little yellow wench what lives in the house of M'sieur Delacroix out near the barracoons. It all of a month ago, Masta Tommy suh. She mighty pretty but . . .'

'A month, huh? That's a mighty long time, Ramon.'

'Shore is. Like'n yo' knows, Masta Tommy suh, my pecker it ain' such a big one but it shore git lonely. Reckon as to how it makes no neverminds how big it is, needs wenchin' jes' the same. Shore a-wishin' I like yo', Masta Tommy suh. Then I don' find it such a hard time to git me a wench. If'n I like yo', once she has it she wants it again.'

'Ain't many like me, Ramon. Sure was born lucky. Don' know just where a black boy like you a-going to get himself a piece of tail down here but I'll wager Vincente knows. Tell you what. You can go out with us tonight and while I'm getting mine from Vincente's sister, I'll see to it that he takes you somewhere and lets you get rid of your load. How's that? Better than sitting around here all alone huh?'

Ramon fell on his knees before his master and took his hand, covering it with kisses. 'Yo're jes' the best masta in all the world, Masta Tommy suh. How yo' know that's what I bin wantin' most of all. Yo're good, Masta Tommy suh, 'n' I promise yo' I'll always be good. Loves yo', Masta Tommy, 'deed I do. Loves yo' 'nuff to die for yo'.'

Tommy patted his head. 'Nobody's dying, Ramon, but I sure know that a boy like you gets horny and needs a piece once in a while. Now that that's settled, relax. I'm going to lie down for a while. When I wake up, you scuttle around and see if you can find me some hot water for a bath. Then we'll dress up – you can use one of your new shirts – and Vincente will be back and take us wherever we're going. How's that?'

With Ramon's help, Tommy peeled off his clothes and sought the comfort of his bed. He was asleep almost as soon as he hit the mattress and slept soundly for hours, awakened only by Vincente's return just as the sunlit strips on the floor were fading out and dusk descending. He would willingly have slept all night had he not been itching for Perla. Vincente informed him that he had arranged for Perla to be free after eight o'clock although he had quite an argument with Jorge who had scheduled several patrons for her. Cancel them, Vincente had ordered. Perla was *his* sister and Tommy was a rich American, able to pay more than all the paltry silver pieces the Cubans could cough up between them. Yes, Vincente had winked at Tommy, he had told Jorge how very rich and important Tommy was and that had ended the argument.

Vincente promised that while Tommy was with Perla he would take Ramon to a girl he knew. Of course, Ramon could not expect anything very luxurious, and he might have to wait in line for two or three who would be ahead of him but, although the girl was black, she was young and not too bad looking and she charged only fifty centavos. Cheap, yes, but he had heard she was good; that's why she always had so many customers. He would wait until Ramon had finished, which never took very long with this girl. Then they would come back and collect Tommy but, he assured Tommy, he was not to hurry. They would wait for him.

Once everything was settled, Tommy bathed and dressed in one of his new Cuban shirts. He then had a meal for himself and Vincente sent up to his room; Ramon ate in the servants' quarters. After that he sat out on the balcony watching the life of Havana flow past until it was time to go. Vincente didn't see the need for a conveyance, saying that he knew short-cuts which could take them to Perla's house in no time and it was foolish to spend money on a carriage for that short distance. It was cool now, the sun had gone down, and they would not mind walking.

Although it was not far, Tommy felt uneasy walking through the almost deserted streets. He wished that he had left some of his money at the hotel. The alleyways that Vincente led them through were altogether too dark and frightening. Almost before he knew it, however, he recognized the crumbling façade of Vincente's house and then once again he was in the room with Perla. Fortunately this time he was alone, for Vincente and Ramon had departed on their errand.

Perla was entranced to see him again and even more entranced with her gifts. She draped the shawl around her nude body, looking at herself in the small mirror. She said that it was something she had always wanted but never hoped to have, and the earrings – she hung them in her ears to show Tommy their lustrous effect – were something that would make every woman in the house jealous. Nobody had a pair half as beautiful. She kissed him and swiftly stripped off his clothes when she realized he had not understood a word she had said.

Her gratitude extended to her love-making which was even more ardent than it was the night before. At least it seemed so, for this time, he had insisted that she blow out the candles, and in the all-enveloping darkness Tommy even shed his shirt. The voluptuous satisfaction of Perla's body against his own without intervening fabric between them was an unusual and ecstatic experience. She was not satisfied with one exhausting climax but resuscitated him until he became rampant again. Doubtless she would have tried to revive him a third time, had there not been a discreet knock on the door and Vincente's voice asking him if he were ready. He was not to hurry, Vincente assured him; he and Ramon would wait out on the balcony. Tommy was fully satiated for one evening, however, and he submitted to Perla's efforts to clean him and help him dress. When he opened the door, Vincente and Ramon were waiting for him, Ramon with a wide grin on his face.

'Jes' wonderful, Masta Tommy suh. Wonderful! That Cuban gal she much better'n any New Orleans whore. Thank yo', Masta Tommy suh. Cain' never forget that little girl; cain' never.'

Once again, Vincente insisted it would be easier to walk than ride, so they started off through the maze of narrow streets. They had scarcely left the house when Jorge, who Tommy recognized by his long, pointed sideburns, accosted them. Tommy and Ramon waited against a wall while Vincente carried on a long and heated conversation with Jorge. Tommy could tell that both were angry by the tone of their conversation and their belligerent gestures. Vincente's eyes blazed with anger but he was no angrier than the powerful Jorge who would have struck Vincente had not Tommy intervened. Jorge turned to curse Tommy but as Tommy could not understand, he about-faced and pushed Vincente ahead of him, leaving Jorge to shout at their backs until they turned the corner.

Yes, Vincente informed him when his anger had cooled enough for him to speak coherently, Jorge was damned mad at him. Jorge had lined up two customers for Perla at the time Vincente had come back with Tommy. Cancelling their date had not only put him in a bad light with his clients but had lost him money. However, Vincente insisted, he was not afraid of the bastard. Jorge may be bigger and stronger but his knife was no longer than Vincente's and his skill at using it no greater. Just let him start something; Vincente would carve his initials deep on Jorge's belly. He'd be damned if he'd give him any money for Tommy's visit to Perla. Perla was his sister and if Tommy wanted her, to hell with Jorge and the Cuban bastards he had lined up for her! He didn't need Jorge's help. Perla was acquiring an enviable reputation and soon she wouldn't need anyone to pimp for her, not even Vincente. So, he promised Tommy, as long as he was in Havana, he could have her whenever he wanted and to hell with Jorge – *hijo de puta* that he was.

They turned off the narrow street into an even narrower alley where they had to walk single file, Vincente first, then Tommy, with Ramon in the rear. It was so dark in the alley that Tommy could barely see the blur of Vincente's white shirt ahead of him. There was no moon. Even one of the typical Havana lamp-posts with its guttering candle might have done a little to dissipate the darkness of the deserted lane.

They were well into the alley when Tommy heard a noise behind him. He turned quickly, in time to see the dark figure of a man briefly silhouetted against the stars. He saw the man leap down from the roof to a high wall and then plummet to the ground and charge towards him. Tommy ducked. The man slipped and fell, only to pick himself up like a cat and lunge again at Tommy. Vincente came running to the rescue but Tommy had already engaged the assailant.

The big, muscular thug seemed charged with superhuman strength. For a few moments the two men struggled in the darkness. There was no sound but the scuffling of feet and hoarse panting as they gasped for air.

Suddenly the ruffian got one hand on Tommy's throat and tightened his grasp. Tommy tried to pry away the fingers – in vain. He choked. The grip tightened. Tommy remembered the tricks of street fighting he had learned while pimping at Five Points in New York. He thrust a knuckle into his antagonist's eye. The man grunted but hung on. Tommy's windpipe was burning. He tried to suck in an ounce of air. He was growing faint.

All at once the grip slackened. Tommy dimly saw Ramon grapple the attacker from the flank, pulling desperately on one arm while banging him on the side of the head. Simultaneously Vincente grabbed the man from behind.

The thug disposed of Vincente with a backward mule kick. Then he squirmed in Tommy's bearlike grasp until he faced Ramon. There was a shriek – then an eloquent silence. Ramon slid slowly to the ground. The assailant fled with Vincente in pursuit.

Vincente caught the toe of one boot as the ruffian reached the top of an adjoining wall. The other boot swung out to strike Vincente in the face. He fell backward as the unknown one vanished over the wall.

Tommy was now on his knees beside Ramon. As he tried to lift the boy, his hands felt the warm stickiness of blood.

'He's hurt, Vincente. He's bleeding.' Tommy could scarcely speak.

'We'll carry him to the corner.'

Vincente lifted his feet while Tommy picked up his shoulders. They carried him to the end of the alley and stretched him on the narrow sidewalk in a patch of candlelight flickering through a window of the corner *bodega*.

Tommy knelt again beside Ramon. He winced at the sight of the bright red blood against the darkness of Ramon's skin. Ramon's throat had been gashed open. He was no longer breathing.

In a matter of seconds a small crowd had gathered around them and Tommy could hear Vincente explaining to the men what had happened. A man fetched a candle from the *bodega* and knelt beside Tommy. The blood was barely oozing from the gaping wound in Ramon's throat. The man placed his hand over Ramon's heart, and shook his head. Ramon was dead.

Tommy realized with a start that Ramon had given up his own life to save him. Yes, he had carried out the promise he had made to Tommy at the hotel – that he would die for him.

Vincente was still vociferously trying to explain what had happened when a uniformed policeman arrived. Then Vincente began his story anew. He and the rich American señor, and the señor's black man were on their way back to the Hotel de Paris when they were set upon in the alley by an unknown man. No, Vincente did not know who it was, but the American – he pointed to Tommy – carried a large sum of money on him. Where had they been? To visit Vincente's sister. They were returning to the hotel. There were more questions in excitedly high-pitched Spanish and Tommy stood in a daze, listening to the ebb and flow of language about him, none of which he could understand. He went into the *bodega*, pointed to a bottle and made the motions of drinking. The proprietor poured him a glass of fiery brandy which Tommy downed in one gulp. The warmth of the brandy in his stomach steadied him. At least he could think a little straighter.

They waited for an hour until a horse-drawn dray came to pick up Ramon's body. Tommy inquired of Vincente where they would be taking Ramon and Vincente replied that there was a public cemetery for slaves. All he would have to pay was for digging the grave. Nothing more? No, Vincente assured him, that was all. Slaves were not buried in a box nor did they have any funeral service. A hole was dug, the body put in the ground and that was that.

Tommy demurred. Ramon had saved his life and he could not bear to think of his poor body unprotected in the earth. Could he not have a decent burial? This Vincente told him, after arguing with the policeman, would be impossible. Slaves could not be interred in the hallowed ground of a cemetery. However, he could arrange for a wooden box for Ramon. Would that be satisfactory? Yes, Tommy supposed so. It could be arranged for two gold pieces, Vincente said.

Tommy paid the policeman, waited while he signed a receipt with the stub of a pencil, then watched while Ramon's body was carried to the dray. Because Tommy had paid for special treatment, the men from potter's field laid the black boy gently in the bottom of the dray, folded his hands across his chest, and drove off. The soles of his boots as the dray passed from the circle of candlelight into darkness was the last Tommy saw of Ramon.

From somewhere in the night a *volanta* appeared and Vincente hailed it. They rode in silence to the hotel as Tommy examined his thoughts about his dead servant. Too bad Ramon had to die, but at least he had not died in vain. Had it not been for Ramon Tommy himself might have been the one in the bottom of the dray. At least Ramon's last night on earth had been one of the high points of his short life. Tommy had given him something he had wanted badly and he obviously enjoyed it.

He had been fond of Ramon and would miss him briefly. Of course he could easily replace him when he returned to Barataria – if he wanted to. He really didn't need a servant, with Gretchen to take care of him. And he certainly needed no servant to heighten his prestige in Barataria as long as the LaFittes were his sponsors.

No, he would not mourn Ramon. He had a way of easily forgetting people who had played an important part in his life, particularly if they had helped him. Missy Acker was no more than a name to him now, and he supposed he had loved her once. He must have; he had married her. And he never thought of Dovie whose bed he had shared. All she had done was save his life . . .

They were back at the hotel, the driver had been paid and they were climbing the stairs to their room before either spoke. Then:

'Do not feel bad, Señor Tommy.' Vincente was consoling. 'I will take care of you while you are in Havana and I'll do it even better than Ramon.'

Tommy nodded his thanks.

'You know, Señor Tommy, I'm sure it was that damned Jorge.' Vincente took the key from Tommy and opened the door. They went inside. 'Jorge knew that you had money with you. *Ladrón!*'

'But we can't prove it, Vincente.'

'No, we can't prove it, but take my advice, Señor Tommy. Don't go back to see Perla at my house again. I'll take you to Josefina's if you need a woman. It's safe there. It's too dangerous for you to go to my house. The next time Jorge will get some of his friends. It just shows how stupid he is to go after you alone. So, Señor Tommy, promise me that you will forget Perla.'

'I've already forgotten a lot of women in my young life. One more won't make any particular difference. But I really liked your sister.'

'*Si, señor*, I know you did.'

'And a man has to have a woman.'

'Yes.' Vincente nodded in agreement.

'But there is always Josefina's house,' Tommy added.

18

When Vincente roused him early next morning, the last thing in the world Tommy wanted to do was cross the bay to see Hernandez about buying slaves. In fact, he was physically and mentally incapable of any such effort. Tomorrow perhaps, but certainly not this morning. The shock and aftermath of poor Ramon's death had upset him so he had spent a sleepless night.

He did not close his eyes until dawn, and he had no desire to open them now despite Vincente's persistent nudgings.

Vincente was not to be denied, however. He had gone down for coffee, and after propping up Tommy with pillows, insisted on his drinking it. The strong brew made life seem worth living after all. Tommy not only felt more able to face the problems of the day, but even considered going to Regla when he was dressed. He slid out of bed and bawled for Ramon to haul his lazy ass around to help him dress.

When only Vincente responded to his call, the ugly reality of the night before rushed back into his consciousness. Never again would Ramon come to help him dress. Damn! He did miss that dawdling black boy. He wished for a moment that Vincente were a slave and belonged to him so that he could take him to Barataria. No, he didn't either. Vincente would probably be willing, but Tommy did not want the responsibility. Besides, he would not need a bilingual slave in Louisiana. But he'd miss Vincente, too. And Perla. Particularly Perla. Just thinking about her made him horny. But he had a day's work ahead of him so he'd stop thinking about Perla. He'd stop thinking about all women. No women could interfere with the efficiency of doing his job for the LaFittes. To hell with women! – at least until tonight. Tonight he'd go to the House of Josefina and see if these Cuban whores were as professional as they were reputed to be.

His resolution stayed with him all the way to the waterfront and across the harbour. Landing in Regla, however, he did see a girl whose dark eyes and mobile hips intrigued him. Beyond turning to stare at her and receiving a ghost of a smile in return, nothing happened. So, on to the barracoons! When he arrived there, Hernandez had another cup of hot coffee waiting for him. It nearly scalded Tommy's throat but it served to wake him further and dispel the colourful fantasies of women which still plagued him. Now he really was ready for business.

Hernandez escorted them out into the big quadrangle with its floor of hard-packed earth. A table had been set up under a kiosk of thatch which made a comfortable spot of shade in the sun-drenched arena. Noting that there were only two chairs, Tommy asked Hernandez if another might be brought for Vincente. The boy, he told Hernandez, would play an important part in today's negotiations and he wanted him to be as comfortable as possible. Hernandez gave instructions to his two black helpers and the chair was brought. Tommy could almost see Vincente grow in stature as he sat down in it.

With a great deal of shouting, hallooing and pushing, the Hernandez men finally got the slaves lined up in a long straggling black file, awaiting Tommy's inspection. Peering out from under the shade of the palm-leaf shelter Tommy was surprised to see that the men appeared far better looking than the night before. Their skins glistened with rubbed-in oil. They had eaten a substantial breakfast and the excitement of something about to happen had revived their spirits. They were talking and laughing among themselves. Some of them were even doing little jig steps while they lined up in the hot sun. The heat did not seem to bother them as much as the multitude of flies which they were constantly brushing away.

Tommy had Vincente explain his system to Hernandez. Those slaves he would consider buying he would dispatch to the left of the compound where they could rest on the plank beds. Those he would not consider he would send to the right. Hernandez agreed to this and after writing materials had been brought, Tommy started out on his long job. He hoped that he would be able to finish it all in one day.

He beckoned to the man at the head of the line to come up to the table. As the man faced him, Tommy first appraised him with his eyes. He was a formidable brute of a man either in his late teens or early twenties, and stood well over six feet with broad, muscular shoulders, thick smooth neck, a muscle-ribbed belly that narrowed into slender hips, strong legs and feet which were planted firmly on the ground. He was not the shiny prune-black of Africa, rather a mellow chocolate brown. Africa was wont to produce strength but rarely beauty, yet this man had both. His lips were thick and raisin-coloured but not blubbery. His nose was small and straight – not flattened close to his face. One ear supported an earring of crude, carved gold. The eyes, black limpid pools in a field of nacreous white, looked directly at Tommy. Tommy's smile was answered. The fellow needed only a period of good feeding to put on a few extra pounds.

Tommy motioned to him to walk around the table and kneel

at his feet. His fingers ascertained that the man had all his teeth – strong and white which glistened when he smiled again after Tommy removed his fingers. Tommy ran his hands over the thick cap of short, krinkly hair, then down to examine the pillar of the thick, muscular neck and the broad shoulders. Finally the inspection continued along the arms to the hands with their thick, spatulate fingers. The pressure of Tommy's hands under the man's arms caused him to stand.

The fellow was circumcised and Tommy nodded to himself in self-corroboration. He had suspected that this fellow might come from one of the northern Muslim tribes. The fellow's colour, his good looks and his lack of a foreskin all attested to it. Good! These Muslims brought the highest prices. He hoped there were more. Tommy clasped the long smooth penis in one hand and manipulated it slowly. He noted the signs of incipent erection – the heavy purple glans was beginning to swell. He'd be a good breeder, Tommy thought as he cupped the black's testicles, weighing them in his hand. He next slowly appraised the muscular legs, lifted each foot and examined the toes. He turned the man around, made him bend over, and spread his buttocks. No visible haemorrhoids. As far as he could see this man was in perfect condition and he wondered if Hernandez had placed him first because he was such a prime specimen. But no; the next man in line appeared to be equally fine.

Tommy pointed to the left and Hernandez's man led the fellow away, first stopping at a big basket for a joint of sugar-cane which he gave to the slave to chew on. Suddenly Tommy realized that he had forgotten to check one thing – the black's coordination. Although he was quite sure that the man was a splendid athlete, he spoke to Vincente who relayed his demands in Spanish to Hernandez. The ensuing shout caused the fellow to run the length of the compound with an easy, loping stride and return. Tommy nodded his satisfaction. At least he had one fine specimen to take back to Barataria.

And so with the next and the next and the next after him. Tommy congratulated himself with every black he passed. These were Fancies and although they were capable of even the most taxing work in the fields, they were far too good to waste their sweat cutting sugarcane or chopping cotton. These men were studs, destined to sweat in the creaking rope beds of slave cabins, their nights passionately devoted to propagating another generation of handsome, strong-backed slaves for their masters. Tommy was willing to believe Hernandez's opinion, passed on by Vincente, that this was one of the best shipments he had received in a long time. Evidently some petty Arab princeling had raided his neighbours' slave corrals.

Through Vincente Tommy questioned Hernandez. Yes, they were all, or practically all, he assured Tommy, from the caravans of a certain tin-pot Sultan of Sa'aqs who had the reputation along the whole west coast of Africa of having the finest slaves to be obtained on the continent. Sa'aqs had for a long time supported his own slave market in Trinidad. Since the English had outlawed slaves and Haiti, now independent of France, no longer imported slaves, the big Sa'aqs' monopoly in Africa was sending its slave cargoes to Havana, one of the few remaining slave markets in the world.

Tommy went on with his tedious job. There were some exceptions; there had to be in such a large number of men. He found one man with suppurating skin sores which Tommy diagnosed as yaws. Another man had testicles swollen to the size of apples. Another had been born with hammer toes. He rejected yet another whose milky eyes marked him as nearly blind.

Along the way he came upon a most remarkable specimen – a young lad in his teens with ivory skin and dark hair coiling in ringlets to his shoulders. He was as slender as a reed but well formed with a glistening skin that highlighted well-rounded muscles. His mincing walk and the languid movement of his hands and arms set him apart from the rest. He was the only one in the whole courtyard who sported any sort of a personal decoration apart from earrings. He wore a string of red coral beads of which he seemed inordinately proud as he kept twirling them in his fingers. Tommy looked at him and pondered. Here was no burly stud to knock up the plantation's wenches; no field hand to chop cotton all day; no cane cutter, no swashbuckling male to pit against the fighters from other plantations. However – and Tommy nodded to himself – here

183

was the ideal butler or house servant who would delight the owner's wife and daughters and possibly even the plantation owner himself.

The boy was indubitably a Fancy, far removed from the ordinary run of slaves. Hell, they were all Fancies but this was an extra-fancy Fancy. Tommy's examination showed the boy to be well endowed sexually which of course added to his value in a weird and roundabout sort of way. At least he would bring a whopping price in New Orleans. He immediately passed him to the left without having him run. This boy didn't need athletic ability. His good looks were sufficient.

Tommy felt a certain tightening in his groin as he looked at the boy and was immediately alarmed. What could be happening to him? He felt better when he saw Vincente staring with mouth open and eyes slightly glazed. If the boy could have this effect on the two of them here, in this filthy hole, what would he be like when cleaned up and dressed? Tommy visualized black velvet trousers and a white shirt. He pushed the boy towards the left and watched Vincente's eyes follow him to the shade of the sheltered wall, where he was immediately embraced by several of the black huskies who had already run the gauntlet.

The morning was wearing on and Hernandez called a halt for lunch. He would drive them to a café in Regla which was noted even over in Havana for its good food. So, after Tommy had scrubbed himself to get the oil and slave odour off his hands, they departed in Hernandez's carriage to a cool and breezy restaurant where they leisurely ate a delicious meal of the famous *arroz con pollo* washed down with a dry Spanish wine. Hernandez suggested that they skip the usual siesta because he knew that Tommy was anxious to get on with his work.

Vincente, who had been engrossed in the morning's proceedings, begged Tommy to allow him to judge one slave. Well fed, Tommy was ready to humour the boy. So on their return to the barracoons Tommy let Vincente examine the first man in line, a handsome buck. Certainly no slave had a more thorough examination. Vincente had closely observed Tommy all the morning and now went about his task like a professional. He did everything he had seen Tommy do although,

Tommy thought, he was paying considerably more time to the man's genitals than was actually necessary. As a result the man passed over to the left-hand side preceded by a monumental erection which was pointed out by his laughing companions.

Vincente grinned! 'Damn good man, I say. *Verdad?* He make many fine pups.' Tommy had to agree.

By four in the afternoon they had finished their job, including inspection of the local slaves that were also for sale, although only a few of them had satisfied Tommy's requirements. He had Hernandez's man total his choices and found that in all he had 215 good specimens, ready to be transported to Barataria. So far no price had been discussed. The three of them retired to Hernandez's little office where they again sat down at a table covered with foolscap, quills and ink. Tommy was anxious to close the deal.

'Very well, señor, I have examined your blacks and now if we can arrive at a price which is mutually satisfactory, we can conclude our business.'

Vincente was busy translating.

'You must admit, Señor Verder, that the blacks you picked out this morning are all of superior quality.'

'Good, yes, but superior no.' Although Tommy was pleased with the quality, he wasn't going to admit it to Hernandez. 'Shall we speak in dollars, sir? It is easier for me than getting embroiled with the intricacies of gold duros or pesetas or whatever.'

Vincente's head bobbed from one to the other as he tried to keep the conversation flowing.

'Dollars it shall be,' Hernandez conceded.

'Then I would say $150 a head.'

Hernandez waited a long moment. 'I would lose money at that price, señor. Make it $200 a head and I will furnish their food for the voyage to Louisiana.'

Tommy was well aware that prime slaves of this calibre would fetch from $800 to $1,000 and more in New Orleans. Even though $200 was a fair price and would allow a handsome profit, he wanted a better deal. It would do no harm to try.

'I'll pay you $200 a head, Señor Hernandez, but under one condition.' He held up his finger.

'Que quiere mas, señor?'

'I need 300 blacks. I've got 215 now. I'm after a few Fancies but they don't count. So, if you can get me fifty or sixty more slaves equal in quality to these, I'll take the whole lot off your hands at $200 a head and your agreement to provision my ship for Barataria.'

When Vincente had finished, Hernandez sat for several minutes, doodling with his quill. He'd make money on his $200 figure and he'd make money on the fifty or so men he'd have to purchase. Victualling the ship for the slaves would not cost too much. He decided to accept Tommy's offer.

'A gentleman's agreement,' he said, shaking Tommy's hand.

Tommy smiled to himself as he grasped Hernandez's hand. A gentleman? If Hernandez only knew who he really was – Calico, a white nigger with black spots on him – would he still be willing to shake hands with him?

'Agreed, Señor Hernandez. As soon as you are able to find the additional blacks, my bank here in Havana will pay you for everything. My ship is anchored at La Machina.'

'It will be easy to manoeuvre her over to the pier in Regla for the victualling. And in the meantime I'll get in touch with you at the Hotel de Paris.'

'Yes,' Tommy agreed, 'the Hotel de Paris.'

At this moment he was anxious to get back there. It had been a long and strenuous day and the idea of cool white sheets was more inviting than he cared to admit. So, with formal leave takings and expressions of lofty sentiments, Hernandez offered his carriage for the short drive to the Regla pier.

Once back at the hotel, Vincente begged permission to go to his house to see how Perla was. Tommy readily granted it, wanting nothing more than his bed. After the hearty luncheon they had eaten in Regla, he had no desire for dinner.

When Vincente returned to the hotel at eight, Tommy suggested that he send down for a plate of cold meat but Vincente informed him that he had shared black beans and white rice with Perla, and was not hungry. But Señor Tommy? No, he wasn't hungry and he had decided that he would not go out tonight. Vincente said that if Tommy wished it, he could send a carriage later that evening to bring Perla to the hotel, but for once in his life, Tommy was too tired for a woman. He thanked Vincente, and also turned down Vincente's suggestion that he go to Josefina's. He would be content to stay at home for one night.

The dull boom of a cannon startled Tommy. Vincente informed him that it was the nine o'clock curfew. The cannon was fired from El Morro every night. Yes, Tommy said, looking at his watch. They had both better get to bed as they would be up early in the morning. Where were they going? To another slave dealer, Tommy answered, this one called Solano.

'That bastard!' Vincente answered. Didn't Tommy know that he was the most despised man in all Havana? There were stories about him which everyone knew to be true. He was a bad man, *un maricon*, and any slave committed to his house to be sold had the pity of all Havana, particularly if that slave happened to be a young man or boy. Yes – Vincente stuck out his middle finger and curled two others in an obscene gesture – *qué maricon*! He was an old man now but he was still *that way*! If Tommy knew what he meant. Tommy did, but nevertheless, he informed Vincente, they were going to get up early, dress and be ready to leave the hotel at eight. He had important business with this Solano, regardless of his sexual habits. Then, after their visit to Solano, Tommy could wind up his business and go home.

'You really gotta leave?' sniffled Vincente.

'I must. There's a time for everything and my time for buying slaves is nearly over. They're waiting for the blacks in New Orleans. As it is, to feed and condition them will take several weeks, so the sooner I get back, the better.'

'And I go back to shining shoes and pimping for Perla.' Vincente's eyes glistened. He came over to stand beside the bed where Tommy lay, propped up by two pillows.

'Oh, Señor Tommy!' Vincente was so choked up he could hardly speak. 'I can't go shining shoes again. I like clean, decent clothes. I hate rats like Jorge. What happens to me here?'

'Nothing, I guess.' Tommy shook his head and picked at an imaginary hangnail. 'Nothing at all, Vincente, but on the other hand if I took you with me what would you do?'

'I would be with you.'

Tommy smiled at him. 'Would that be important?'

'Yes, Señor Tommy. All I want.'

'What about Perla?'

'Perla big enough now to look out for Perla. She may be go in Josefina's or set up her own house. Alone she can save her money and get some other girls and she won't worry. Girls have it easy, Señor Tommy. Girls got something men want and they sell it. But not me. Oh, Señor Tommy, can't I go with you and learn how to pick out slaves? You saw me today. I learn fast Señor Tommy.'

Tommy motioned to the boy to sit beside the bed. Tommy had a real desire to help him. He had become fond of the boy and he trusted him. He realized the boy's capabilities but he hesitated to take him back to the LaFittes. He did not want the responsibility. Besides Vincente never would be a servant like Ramon. Yet Tommy hated to see him return to shining shoes.

Vincente started to speak but Tommy's lifted finger checked him. He needed to think. He had made his own way in life through lies and subterfuges and he was still living a lie. But his own lie was a matter of life and death to him. To live honestly would mean death or a return to slavery. Vincente faced no such handicap. The boy was white and would never be confronted with Tommy's problem. He could always take his place in society. He was Don Cipriano's son even if he had been born on the wrong side of the blanket. Evidently Don Cipriano liked him or he would not be contributing to his support. Perhaps if Tommy would suggest something to Don Cipriano, he would help Vincente.

Tommy slid over to the edge of the bed and stuck both feet out in front of him. 'Help me off with my boots, Vincente, and then we'll talk.'

Vincente grabbed Tommy's boot with both hands and bent over while Tommy placed his other boot on the boy's backside and pushed while Vincente pulled. The boot slipped off, but Vincente had to tug harder on the other one. Finally he stood both boots side by side at the foot of the bed. Tommy loosened his belt and undid his fly. He next raised himself on both elbows while Vincente pulled off the tight white trousers. He removed his shirt and underpants. Then, clad only in his silk singlet, he stretched out on the bed. He felt the boy's eyes appraising him and for a fleeting moment wondered if the boy might have a special interest in him. He reflected, however, that Vincente's were not the only male eyes which had scrutinized him more with envy and curiosity than with unholy desire.

'You said a while back, Vincente,' Tommy began as he reached down and pulled the sheet up over him, 'that you'd like to go into the slave business; that you'd like to learn how to assay blacks.'

Vincente nodded.

'Well, it's a good business, boy, a damned good business and it's going to be an even better one. The cane plantations here and in Louisiana and the cotton plantations all over the American south are going to need more and more slaves every year. I'd like to see you get some profit out of it.'

'With you in *los Estados Unidos*?' Vincente sat down on the bed beside Tommy.

Tommy shook his head, 'No, boy, with you right here in Cuba. Listen, Vincente, think for a minute of Hernandez. He's an old man. He needs someone whom he can trust to do much of his work for him. I'll speak to him and I'm pretty sure that with Don Cipriano's influence added to my own, we can get him to take you on. He won't pay too much at first but you'll learn and soon you can be one of the best judges of nigger flesh in Havana.'

Vincente listened with attention, but when Tommy had finished he said, 'I rather go with you, Señor Tommy.'

'You wouldn't see much of me when I get back. I'll be pretty busy in one place or another. Besides you'll want to be here to look after Perla.'

Vincente bowed his head and fiddled with his fingers.

'Yes, Señor Tommy, may be if you say so. You think you can get me with Hernandez?'

'I'll try, son. I'll speak to Don Cipriano too.' He looked up at the boy. 'Now all you've got to do is to learn your end of it.'

'I'll learn, Señor Tommy, see.' With a quick motion he

grabbed the sheet which covered Tommy and snatched it away. He picked up one of Tommy's feet, examining it in detail. Tommy pulled his foot away.

'What in hell do you think you're doing?'

'Just starting my first lesson. See, Señor Tommy, you got good feet; you got all your toes and no hammer toes either. Of course I not examine rest of you very good but I say you sure prime.'

'What?' Tommy laughed. 'Only prime? You mean I'm not a Fancy?'

Vincente's eyes swept Tommy's body. 'Yes, may be I call you super Fancy. Anyhow you make one fine breeder, hung like you are.'

Tommy reached over to cuff him but the boy was already halfway across the room.

'You wanta know all about black niggers, ask Vincente,' he boasted. 'That fellow gonna be *Numero Uno* about slaves in Havana.'

'Go to bed.' Tommy threw his pillow at him. 'We've got to get up early in the morning.'

Vincente picked up the pillow and replaced it on Tommy's bed. '*Buenas noches, Señor Tommy.* You good friend.'

Tommy grinned. '*Buenas noches* and go to bed.'

'*A sus ordenes, señor.*' Vincente grabbed Tommy's hand and squeezed it.

19

As he and Vincente waited for a carriage in front of the Hotel de Paris next morning, Tommy, well fed and rested, was momentarily grateful that he had spent the night in his room instead of seeking whatever bizarre amorous contortions Josefina's house might have had to offer. His head was clear, his eyes bright, and his confidence in his own judgment unlimited, yet despite his self-congratulations on his abstinence he was already making plans for this very evening.

This evening he'd take Vincente along to Josefina's and give the lad a treat. The boy's previous sex experiences had almost certainly been confined to his sister and the five-centavo whores of the waterfront, so a visit to what was reputed to be the most elegant brothel in Havana would be indeed an education. It was high time the boy learned what screwing was like in clean beds with white sheets. He would probably amuse Josefina's wenches, too. Nothing like a young boy to bring out inventiveness and the mother instinct in a sex-hardened tart. Tommy had seen it work when he was pimping in New York. Yes, he'd get a lot of fun out of his project, and the thought gave him a fillip of excitement that lasted all through the ride from the hotel to the Solano barracoons.

No, barracoon was hardly the word, Tommy decided after ringing the bell and entering the littered courtyard through the heavy iron gate. The place looked more like a prison than a barracoon. The walls of the courtyard were lined with empty iron-barred cages whose sagging doors testified to long disuse. As Solano had grown older he had let his slave business slip. Now he was specializing only in Fancies and they were evidently kept elsewhere or on an upper floor. None was in sight.

The echoes of the bell were still reverberating inside the building as Tommy and Vincente stepped into the courtyard. A moment later a boy apparently no older than Vincente crossed the weed-grown patio, his mincing steps carefully avoiding the rubbish scattered in the knee-high vegetation. Tommy stopped short, revolted by the boy's languid arm movements, the affected gestures of his hands, and traces of mascara around his eyes. He spoke a soft, sibilant Spanish with the lisping accents of Castile.

'You wish to see Don Policarpo Solano, *señores*?'

He addressed Tommy, who gestured with a thumb over his shoulder to Vincente. A quick appraisal of Vincente apparently convinced the affected one that the lad seemed equally worthy of his special interest and he quickly switched his attention.

'Don Solano is now finishing his breakfast, but he will see you.' The boy smiled at Vincente. 'And also the Americano who comes to look at Señor Solano's wares. If you will just

191

follow me, please.' As he crossed the littered courtyard, Tommy stumbled over broken pieces of furniture which seemed to have been lying there for at least half a century.

It was pleasanter in the little room at the back of the patio where Solano was having breakfast. Some sunshine managed to penetrate the cobwebby slats of the blinds to gather in a luminous pool on the still-handsome mahogany table where Solano sat. Tommy's first impression was that this was by far the most enormous man he had ever seen. Gross rolls of fat padded his body and were it not for the polished bald pate and the small black eyes staring out like raisins in a bun, Tommy would have had trouble orientating himself as to where the slave-dealer's anatomy began and ended.

Don Solano did not arise but greeted his visitors with outstretched arms and curious little beckoning movements of his pudgy fingers, gestures which Tommy interpreted as part welcome and part an apology for not getting to his feet, a manoeuvre which could probably not be accomplished without outside help.

'I am very pleased to meet you, Señor Solano,' Tommy said, not quite truthfully. He could understand the man's sinister reputation in Havana; the slave-dealer was far from prepossessing.

Solano's reply to the words of greeting were delivered at length in a high piping voice that seemed incongruous coming from such a mountain of a man. Vincente translated.

Solano was delighted and honoured to greet the distinguished Americano under his own roof and was consumed with *vergüenza* – great shame – because his physical condition did not allow him to leave his chair for a proper welcome. However, Solano hoped that as a start their relationship would not be encumbered with formalities. Instead of calling him Señor Solano, could not *el Americano* address him by his given name – Policarpo? Because Señor Verder – could he call him Tomás? – was a person *muy simpático*. Would he be seated and share a mouthful of the humble breakfast now on the table?

'Thank you, Señor Solano – I mean Policarpo – but we have already breakfasted.'

Vincente's translation was interrupted by a shrill protest. Tomás will at least have a cup of fragrant Cuban coffee? And some of our delicious Cuban fruits? Has Tomás ever tasted our *anona*? Then he must...

Tommy found himself being forced into an easy chair while the servant with the mascaraed eyelashes was slicing up a small green nobby round fruit and an orange-coloured ovoid as big as a goose-egg. The fruit was presented on a Sèvres porcelain plate while coffee was being drawn from a big silver urn. The green nobby fruit, Vincente explained, was a custard apple; the other was a mango. Inside the thick green rind, Tommy found, the fruit indeed had the consistency of custard, but he almost swallowed the big black seeds. The mango puzzled him. The flame-coloured juicy meat tasted like turpentine at first bite, but was sweet and pleasant at further venture. The single big lozenge-shaped hairy seed, however, was a source of frustration. As he was struggling to suck the juice and the last bit of sweet pulp from the hairs of the oval seed, Solano emitted a high-pitched giggle and said something in Spanish to Vincente.

'Señor Solano asks,' Vincente translated, 'if the hairs on this *gran cuesco peludo* reminds you of something?'

'Tell Policarpo that I have never set teeth in anything like this before,' Tommy replied, wiping his face and fingers with the hot damp towel that the pretty boy had brought him. 'Tell him also that I am anxious to get on with our business. Does he know that Jean LaFitte has commissioned me to purchase a dozen fancy female bright-skins?'

Vincente's two-way translation brought Solano's answer. Of course he knew of the mission of the eminent Tomás. All Havana knew what Jean LaFitte's agent was seeking. But unfortunately the Solano stock of *mestiza* beauties were no longer kept here in Havana. There had been too much vandalism and plain thievery, sometimes romantic, more often crass kidnapping for resale and profit. Solano was now forced to keep his girls on a sequestered beauty farm outside of town. Guadelupe was not far from Havana, but it was necessary to take back roads to throw possible followers off the track. The location of Solano's treasure house of female beauty must be kept secret at all costs. So why does not Tomás and his friend stay the night here and they would all get an early start for Guadelupe in the morning? He would do his best to make them comfortable . . .

Even before he heard the translation, Tommy had a queasy feeling about Solano's Spanish. The wheedling, cajoling tone seemed to convey unpleasant associations. He was quick, therefore, to plead important business in town which would prevent him from accepting Policarpo's kind invitation. If it was not possible to make the round trip to Guadelupe today, perhaps Tommy could come back tomorrow?

Solano heaved a great sigh that seemed to involve the entire mass of his huge body. He spread his hands in a drooping gesture of sadness. *Qué lástima!* He would have enjoyed so much being host to the distinguished and handsome agent of the eminent Jean LaFitte. But of course if it is not possible . . .

Solano ordered the horses hitched to his *calesa*, and when the four-wheeled carriage was brought to the front of the house, it took two servants to hoist him in. He occupied all of the rear seat under the accordion hood, so Tommy took the one facing him. He was glad he was not required to squeeze into the little space adjacent to the fat man, although he was not happy to have Solano's tiny eyes constantly fixed upon his fly with, Tommy thought, a prurient glitter. Luckily Vincente was sitting beside him.

The ride through the steamy countryside was a revelation to the young man from the States. The road ran at first between tall hibiscus hedges ablaze with yellow-tongued scarlet flowers. Behind the hedges Tommy caught an occasional glimpse of an opulent-looking villa. When the *calesa* had rattled past the immediate suburbs and began ducking into side roads, the graceful coconut palms grew fewer and fewer and patches of jungle alternated with cane fields. Brilliant birds swooped, perched, and disappeared amid the tropical foliage.

Solano didn't stop talking for a minute. Tommy made no effort to understand. He was fascinated by the lush unfamiliarity of the ever-changing scenery. Whenever he did look at the man opposite him he found Solano staring at his crotch. He finally crossed his legs.

Suddenly the *calesa* stopped. The pretty boy (whose name was Tobalito) jumped down from his seat beside the coachman and looked in both directions along the straight road. When he was sure there was no other vehicle in sight, he climbed back and the horses turned in the direction they had come. When they had retraced their steps for a hundred yards they turned sharply right into a narrow lane, at the end of which was a great wrought-iron gate. Behind the gate was an astonishing edifice in black and white stone, with a forest of columns supporting Moorish arches, surmounted by a bulbous Saracenic dome.

'*Mi casa*,' said Don Solano proudly, adding surprisingly in English, 'my house.' He lapsed immediately into Spanish which Vincente translated while the gates were being opened and the slave dealer helped out of the carriage.

He had built this house when he first arrived in this tropical paradise from his native Spain. It was something to remind him of his home town, Granada, in Andalusia. It was an imitation of one small corner of the Alhambra. Didn't Tommy admire the Alhambra? Or perhaps he didn't like Moorish architecture?

Not only did Tommy not know where the Alhambra was, but he could not tell Moorish architecture from a hole in the ground. However, the fact that Solano had pronounced two words of English had not escaped him. Where, he asked, had Policarpo learned English?

He had never learned English, Solano replied via Vincente. Oh, he had picked up a few words when he was in New Orleans ten or twelve years ago. He had gone over with a shipload of slaves to try his luck at the St Louis Hotel auctions. That was before he specialized in Fancies and some planter from Alabama had bought most of the lot. Funny, but Solano couldn't seem to remember his name...

They had paused under the arches of the colonnade while Solano handed a huge bunch of heavy keys to his mincing assistant. While pondering the name of the man who had purchased his slaves in New Orleans, he seemed to be staring at Tommy's right hand for a change. Tommy wished he could get rid of that sixth finger if it was going to remind Solano of Tommy's past. Silly, of course, because no one would pursue a fugitive slave to Cuba. Or would anyone...?

'... Falconhurst...'

The one word stood out from the stream of Solano's incomprehensible Spanish.

An icy thumb traced its way down Tommy's spine. He waited nervously for the translation.

No, Solano had completely forgotten the name of the planter, but he remembered the name of the plantation: Falconhurst. Apparently it was quite famous. Had Tomás heard of it?

'Falconhurst? Indeed I have. Everyone knows that Falconhurst blacks are the finest in the country. Bred right there on the plantation.' Tommy thought it was safe enough to boast just a little about his association with such a famous source of slaves. 'In fact,' he said, 'my mother owns a plantation not far from Falconhurst. We were always good friends with the owners.'

Tommy was nevertheless relieved when the iron-bound door swung open and Falconhurst was a thousand miles away. So, too, was the run-down Solano home in Havana compared to this country hide-away. Tommy had never seen anything like the Moorish interior of what amounted to a salesroom of female flesh instead of a rental agency like La Casa Josefina or Mme Alix's Academy of Music in New Orleans.

Two black giants guarded the inner portals, one armed with a Toledo blade, the other with an obsolete-looking weapon which Vincente called a *trabuco* but which Tommy, had he been familiar with ancient weapons, would have called a blunderbuss. Tommy asked: 'Isn't it sort of dangerous having these big bucks loose in a house with all these fancy females?'

When the question was translated, Solano guffawed. No danger, he said, the black giants had been emasculated. 'Cut and nutted,' was the way Vincente rendered the phrase. Tommy nodded.

Just beyond the guards was a room with no windows, lighted by two tall ten-branch candelabras. The fragrance of incense hung on the warm air. The inevitable small boy in the corner hauled on a rope to activate the ceiling sweeps, feebly stirring up tepid currents. Directly in front of him was a spectacle which stopped Tommy in his tracks. He stared wide-eyed at two naked women squatting on a handsome oriental rug, bent over a layout of Tarot cards.

'What – what is this?' asked Tommy.

'A game,' said Vincente, 'called *buenaventura*.'

Solano stopped panting for a moment and said: 'Yes, *buenaventura*. You call it fortune-telling.' The effort of speaking English seemed to have exhausted the fat man, and he lapsed immediately into Spanish. Vincente translated:

'You don't like these Fancies? Maybe too black?'

'They're not bad-looking wenches,' Tommy said, 'even if they are a little dark.' The two women continued to study the Tarot cards as they were turned up. A faint mist of perspiration shimmered on their shoulders and breasts. 'I'd like a closer look at the big one,' he added, 'the big-titted brown gal.'

'Ah, *la princesa*,' said Solano.

'A princess?'

'Well yes, she claims to be a Songhai princess, but everybody calls her Koko. Her people the Songhais used to be the royal family of Timbuctoo but the Fulahs and other tribes have been giving them trouble for centuries, it seems, and she got herself captured by slave-traders. One of Solano's guards was part Mandingo and got her history. She speaks a sort of Mandingo; they all do, the tribes of the western Sudan – the Tschis, the Krus, the Yorubas.'

Tommy was impressed with Solano's knowledge of the African tribes, which matched Ham Maxwell's interest in the ethnic backgrounds of his slaves. It was certainly at odds with his surprisingly gross appearance or the curious sex practices attributed to him.

But Tommy was even more impressed by the physique of the Songhai princess. He repeated his request: 'I'd like to get a closer look at the big brown one – the princess.'

Solano motioned Tommy to a low settee covered with purple silk, and with the aid of his servants lowered himself to adjoining cushions. When he had caught his breath again he piped: 'Koko, *ven acá*.'

The Songhai girl did not look up.

Solano giggled briefly, bowed in mocking deference, and said: '*Alteza, por favor!*'

'He says, "Please, Your Highness"' Vincente translated. The second nude picked up the cards and disappeared.

197

Finally Koko unwound her long legs and stood up. She was tall and statuesque, her straight black hair (not at all kinky or negroid) braided and coiled about her proud head. Her shoulders curved backwards, holding her large breasts firm and high. As she walked towards Tommy with long, slow strides his lower jaw dropped in astonishment. He gasped. Never in his life had he seen such an extensive and luxuriant thicket of pubic hair.

Midnight black against the warm tan of her skin, the curly carpet extended from her navel beyond the pudenda and down the inside of both thighs halfway to her knees. For all its unusually large area, the patch over the heart of the matter stood out as distinctly as if it had been neatly parted with a comb, like a forked beard. And glowing at the very centre was a spot of pink like a rose petal. No, Tommy decided as the girl approached, the floral term was wrong. More like the lips of a pink sweet-pea.

Tommy had previously never thought of the female genitalia as having an existence of their own. Of the dozens he had known during his short young life, he had never considered one as anything but an adjunct to the male, a convenient receptacle for an erect penis in search of pleasure and satisfaction, and of course the proper place to deposit a man's seed if he is breeding for profit. But a vagina with a personality of its own? Unheard of in Tommy's experiences. Whatever character was conveyed through the act of what was known on the plantations of the American South as 'pestering', was a reflection of the personality of the whole woman, by her capacity for deriving pleasure from the male equipment, not through the vagina alone. Yet here was a magnificent furry piece of love mechanism that certainly had its own individuality. He continued to stare in fascination as the big brown girl approached. The labia seemed to stir slightly with each step like the wings of a roseate butterfly caught in a tangle of moss.

When Koko stopped before him, Tommy yearned to reach out and touch the object of his enthralment. He tried quickly to remember if he had ever known a set of standards for judging female Fancies. He had his own scale of values, of course, based on personal sampling, but he remembered no instructions from René Beluche as to a basis for choosing marketable bright-skins. He had watched his former friend Ham Maxwell buy black women for Falconhurst, but Ham was looking for good solid breeders who could produce a sucker every year, women who were comely rather than beautiful, good healthy brood-mares with big tits and broad pelvises. But he was sure that Monsieur Gaspar Cosette of New Orleans, the LaFittes' prime customer for *mestiza* flesh, was looking for something entirely different.

'The princess is a little dark,' Tommy said, 'but I may be able to get rid of an article like her if she's not too expensive. I'll have to finger her first, though, even if she does look sound.'

Solano grunted approval.

Tommy motioned the girl to kneel before him. He ran his hands over the back of her shoulders and down the outside of her upper arms; good solid well-muscled flesh, no doubt about it, but not the flesh he was most interested in. He would try to hold off a little longer. He slipped a hand under each moist armpit and as he moved his fingers downward to feel her pectoral muscles he let his thumbs brush her breasts. He started the routine oral examination and withdrew his fingers just as her jaws snapped shut. She continued to stare at him impassively with just the hint of a sneer on her lips.

So the wench was going to bite him, was she? Well, she'd have to be taught. He was no longer hesitant. Without further ado he thrust a forefinger through the woolly thicket towards the gleaming jewel that had held him hypnotised for the past five minutes.

Instantly something exploded against the left side of his head. His ear rang. Stunned, he still had the presence of mind to grab the brawny right arm of the Songhai girl as she drew it back for a second swing.

'*Ramera!*' Solano's bloated face was scarlet as he screamed imprecations at the girl. The princess screamed back at him. So she spoke Spanish.

Tommy held up one hand, still clinging to the girl's arm with the other. 'Shut up, everybody! What's going on here?'

Vincente translated. 'Señor Solano is furious. He is taking the bitch to the public whipping yard when we return to the city.'

'Whipping yard?'

'Yes.' There was a place in the city, it seemed, where slaves were punished for their misdeeds by being chained to a post and lashed by a professional flagellator until the master decides he (or she) has learned to behave.

'No, no.' Tommy shook his head. He had seen slaves strung up by the heels at Falconhurst and Dove Cote until their backs were cut to a mass of bloody pulp by blacksnake whips. The wounds healed in time but left ugly welts. Nobody would pay top prices for a slave with a welted back and legs. 'Vincente, tell Solano I don't want her whipped.'

'He says she must be punished, Señor Tommy. She hit you.'

'Tell him I can't sell a nigger wench if she's all scarred up. I won't buy damaged goods. What's the matter with Koko anyhow? She acts like a virgin but she's just a slave.'

'She says you can't fool around with her snatch unless you buy her,' Vincente explained.

'Tell Her Highness I won't buy unless I know she's good and healthy. Tell her I don't lay girls in public, and that I got to make sure she's not all poxed up. I can't take her to New Orleans to start an epidemic of clap. Hold her arms, boy, I'm going to finish my examination.'

At last he got down to the business of exorcising the obsession that possessed him. His approach was gentle this time, and instead of a prodding forefinger he used the second and third fingers first to part the hirsute decor, then to separate the glistening pink labia. He felt a quiver run through the girl's body, and her reaction was contagious. Despite his professed strictly-business attitude Tommy couldn't help being naturally horny in the presence of such a stimulating wench. He stood with his back to Solano in the hope that his instinctive response would not be visible in profile to the fat man's lecherous eyes.

Yes, the princess with the bearded underbelly possessed not only sensual but marketable possibilities. He was glad he had been able to restrain his natural urge to retaliate when she had struck him. Now he could probably buy her cheap and sell her for a pretty penny in Louisiana.

'Señor Solano says how can you punish her if you don't whip her?' Vincente asked.

Tommy answered without turning around. 'We will humiliate her,' he said. 'Her Highness is a proud wench and she's worth two or three hundred gold dollars at least. If you sell her for thirty, forty dollars like a cheap whore, she'll feel like dirt.'

Solano protested (through Vincente) that he had paid more than fifty dollars for her in the first place.

'I'll give you sixty,' said Tommy. 'That's as much as you'd get after having her whipped and marked up.'

Solano wailed a little, but finally agreed. After all, a disobedient wench must go.

'Mark it down, Vincente,' said Tommy, knowing full well that the boy could not write, 'and tell our fat friend that I'm ready to look at some mustees for a change. No more princesses.'

Solano waved Koko out of the room and piped instructions.

In a few seconds an old crone in a rusty black dress led two light-skinned *mestizas* into the room.

While Solano was shrilly describing their backgrounds and proclaiming their fine points, Tommy was making his own assessment. They were attractive wenches, both of them, although quite different in everything except the light shade of their tan complexions. They were certainly quadroons, perhaps even octoroons. One girl was petite, small-boned and minx-like. She had eyes too big for her animated pixy face. Her long eyelashes curled. She wore nothing but a scarlet lace mantilla draped over her jet-black hair and brought forward over her shoulders to fall across her bosom. A lively piece in bed, Tommy speculated.

Her companion was a head taller and considerably thicker than she was. Or maybe she looked fatter than she really was. She was wearing what looked like a trailing, short-waisted nightgown with short puffed sleeves and long flowing flounces. Tommy thought the costume rather tawdry – he could not know that it was a soiled and shopworn copy of an Empire gown now the latest thing from stylish Paris – and of course he would have to see what sort of wench was concealed beneath it. He was not totally discouraged, however, for there was a languid air about the woman, a sultry expression around her eyes and a sense of restrained power in her movements that promised a smouldering nature ready to burst into flame at a flick of the tongue.

Solano had finished his harangue in Spanish and Vincente was struggling with the translation.

These two trollops were the last two in the Solano stable who claimed titled lineage. The little vixen – Panchita – liked to call herself Countess because she was once mistress of Conde de Lunablanca, the Vice-Governor of Cuba. The Count had her condemned to the public whips to be beaten to death because in a fit of rage at finding him with another woman she had bitten off one of his balls. However Panchita had screwed her way out of the death sentence, leaving two of the Conde's bodyguards to bear the brunt of his wrath. Panchita was a hot number in more ways than one and Solano would be relieved to get rid of her. But if his friend Tomás found her to his taste, he must be warned to take the utmost precautions in smuggling her aboard ship; otherwise he would never get her out of Cuba.

'Have no fear,' Tommy said. 'I'll sneak her aboard if we have to hide her among the Princess's twat hair.'

Solano was already launched on his selling talk about the Duquesa, showing a surprising (to Tommy) knowledge of contemporary Caribbean politics and history in addition to his ethnic knowledge of African tribes.

The hussy in the fancy nightgown was an octoroon from Haiti, which Tommy assumed was somewhere in Africa. The human blood in her was French. She called herself Antoinette, the Duchess of Limbé, a daughter of His Serene Highness Prince Jules de Limbé, one of the courtiers of King Henri-Christophe of Haiti, by the King's *lingère*, the mistress of the palace linens. After Napoleon sent General Leclerc to Haiti to re-establish slavery, and Christophe was overthrown, the Duchess was forced to flee for her life. Some French officer sold her to a Spaniard who brought her to Cuba with a coffle of niggers from Haiti and Santo Domingo.

'Tell the Duchess to shuck down,' Tommy ordered. 'Let's see how she's built.'

'*Déshabilles-toi*, Antoinette!'

Solano spoke to the Duchess in what Tommy supposed was French; it sounded like the language he had often heard in New Orleans. Did the surprising fat man have any more unexpected learning up his ample sleeve?

Antoinette complied with the order, although she displayed the modest gestures appropriate to a supposed former aristocrat. Her efforts to conceal her most intimate features while undressing did not fool Tommy, however. She betrayed herself – deliberately, he was sure – by the slight smirk that hovered on her full lips, the faintly suggestive movements of her hands, and especially the expression of her eyes as they focused on the growing evidence of Tommy's reaction to his exploration of her contours. Her tongue flickered briefly between her lips as the evidence increased. Well, there were some things beyond his control . . .

Tommy was glad that the Duchess liked what she saw. Showed she appreciated the best things in life, and if he was any judge, she was also a wench of considerable talent. Yes, he was going to bring back a fine variety of mouth-watering goodies for the pleasure of Monsieur Gaspard Cosette and his likes. And he was also getting to be a better and better judge of what he thought the LaFittes were looking for. As Solano's doxies passed in review, Tommy developed a formula for counting up a point score in the rating of female slaves for the love market.

Solano displayed the choicest flowers from his Garden of Venus one by one, and Tommy gave each his close personal attention. Since the Princess Koko had made him aware of the forceful individuality of what he had previously thought of only – if at all – as a twat or a cunt, he now carefully noted the different types. Their variety amused and amazed him, and when he had had a chance to compare them with actual performance, he would have a standard for evaluation. There was the rounded, plump, friendly vagina like Rosita's, for instance. How would that compare in action with Isabel's long, lean, hungry-looking organ? Or a neutral, childlike vagina like

Adelita's? Or a fiercely bewhiskered paraphernalia like Carmen's or Juanita's that from its appearance might very well have teeth? Did the nearly-bald or scantily-feathered appearance that characterized the genitalia of Beatriz and Maria merely illustrate the saying that grass never grows on a busy street? He certainly did not trust the relaxed appearance of Magdalena's baited trap which to him seemed ready to spring shut on the first unwary penis.

Well, all this would require research which Tommy planned to do on the sea voyage to Barataria. He would also have to decide how to award points according to breast shapes. Did pear-shaped tits offer greater passion than the apple models? And what about the conical numbers with long dugs like Adelita's?

He would also have to make his own standards for judging hips. The hips would have a different meaning for LaFitte customers than they had for Ham Maxwell, who was looking for width that would indicate good breeders, whereas buyers like Gaspard Cosette would probably be more interested in plump, well-rounded buttocks. Shapely legs were always exciting, of course, but what about feet? Well, Tommy would have to give pretty feet extra points, particularly if they were equipped with nicely-cushioned heels that would arouse a man ten degrees higher when they dug into his back.

Boy, boy! was Tommy learning to look at women and sex in a new light! René Beluche was still by far the much better judge of black bucks, but Tommy was proud of the skill he had developed in the last few hours in rating light-skinned and light-hearted wenches. He hoped that Jean LaFitte would appreciate the selection of bright-skins he was bringing back. Even the one African wench he was getting for a bargain would turn a nice profit in New Orleans.

After a break for lunch – a huge bowl of spicy shredded beef which Tommy found delicious despite its unappetizing name of *ropa vieja* (old clothes) – they finished the inventory of Solano's stock by early afternoon. Tommy picked eleven *mestizas* and the tan *princesa*. He rejected only three: one was too thin, a second had suspicious-looking warts on her thighs, and the third, Tia Mia, was too old; she must have been thirty-five at least. Solano argued that she was a first-rate cook and would bring a good price, but neither LaFitte nor Beluche had ordered any cooks. Tommy wasn't even sure that Beluche would approve of the Princesa, in which case he was sure he could dispose of her himself. After all, what was $60...?

'Shall we now get down to business?' Tommy suggested.

By all means, said Solano through Vincente. We will adjourn to the *parlatorio* and bargain in a friendly way. He clapped his pudgy hands and the coachman and secretary appeared to hoist him to his feet and help him waddle into the next room. The Louis Quinze furniture had been reduced to a state of dinginess by the heat and damp of the tropical climate, but it seemed elegant to Tommy. The slave dealer was installed behind an elaborate escritoire while he waved Tommy to a spindly-legged gilt chair with mildewed tapestry upholstery.

'I propose,' Tommy began, 'to make an offer for the lot of wenches as a whole, rather than bid on them separately. Except for Koko, of course. We agreed on a price for her.'

Solano grunted agreement. He suggested a lump sum of 85,000 reales.

'No reales,' Tommy countered. 'I can't figure in this foreign money. Let's talk dollars. Gold dollars.'

Solano giggled. He didn't see what was so difficult about counting in Spanish reales which were worth eight to the dollar. Surely the LaFittes must have explained to him about pieces of eight...

Tommy made a mental calculation. At that rate 85,000 reales would make each wench cost almost $1,000. 'Ridiculous,' he said. 'I'll give you $2,000 for the whole shebang.'

Solano threw up his hands and gave a little treble scream of horror. Only 16,000 reales? Had his friend Tomás forgotten that Solano had been in New Orleans and was familiar with U.S. prices? He was no ignorant peon.

'You must consider my expenses in getting these wenches into the States,' Tommy said. 'There is the cost of re-fitting the ship to take care of my slaves, the wages of the crew, the cost of feeding them aboard and in Barataria, to say nothing of the bribes I will have to pay in case we are intercepted by a revenue cutter. I might even have to go to jail.'

As the bargaining proceeded, Solano ordered cold drinks

brought – a mixture of fruit juices and a liquor called *ron*, a spirit of the sugarcane.

'Rum,' Vincente translated.

Tommy, who had taken nothing stronger than wine since his disastrous experience with corn-whiskey toddies on the night of his wedding at the Acker plantation, found the drink pleasant indeed. He sipped it while they argued over who would pay to feed the wenches until Tommy took delivery, the cost of local transport and security guards on the way to the dock, and other incidentals.

'Tell you what,' Tommy said, putting down his empty glass. 'I'll give you $250 apiece for the eleven Fancies, plus the $60 we agreed on for the princess. That's my last offer.'

Solano pondered a moment, shook his head sadly, heaved a mountainous sigh, then nodded and extended his fat hand across the desk.

'*Convenido,*' he said.

When Vincente confirmed that an accord had been reached, Tommy grasped the hand. Solano immediately bawled for fresh drinks and began fussing in his desk for writing materials. He interrupted himself when Rosita arrived bearing the tall glasses.

'*Salud!*' he said, raising his glass to touch rims to Tommy's.

Vincente struggled with a translation of what he said next. The gist of his ceremonial speech upon the conclusion of their agreement was that it was a pleasure to do business with his friend Tomás, and that next time he had especially fine Fancies he thought Tommy would like, he would write him in care of Señor Jean LaFitte. There was one more thing that Solano must insist upon. There must be a clause in the formal agreement to the effect that once the wenches left his house, Tommy must assume full responsibility for their past and future as well as their present behaviour. That was to protect Solano in case the police or Count Lunablanca's henchman should intercept the carnivorous Panchita on her way to the docks.

'My bank will send you the money in the morning,' Tommy said. 'But you'll have to keep the wenches here until I have made sure the *Sainte Claire* is ready to receive them.' Tommy was beginning to feel the effect of the rum. The warmth that had crept from his belly to his arms and had now reached his cheeks was totally superfluous in view of the normal tropical temperature of Cuba, but Tommy did not find it at all disagreeable. In fact, as he took another long pull at the drink which Solano called *leche de tigre* – tiger's milk, according to Vincente – he found that his tongue had been strangely loosened. His formal education was limited to the time he spent in Boston at the school of Dr Jonathan Wainright, the speech expert who was teaching the real Tommy Verder, a deaf-mute, the use of his vocal cords. When the six-fingered original succumbed to the rigours of a New England winter and his six-fingered half-brother had safely (he thought) usurped his identity, he remained at the school as long as the money kept coming from Dove Cote plantation. He had never proved particularly brilliant academically, despite his keen native intelligence. Yet here he was, holding forth glibly on the stupidity of the United States Congress in prohibiting the import of slaves, on the importance of slavery to the American economy, on the essential kindness and paternalism of American planatation owners despite their apparent cruelty at times . . .

Solano could not know, of course, that Tommy's discourse was the second-hand philosophy of Jean LaFitte, René Beluche, and even Hamilton Warren. But he nodded agreement frequently, and occasionally added a few words of approval.

Suddenly Solano clapped his hands for more drinks, got up with great effort, waddled around the desk, and plopped down at Tommy's feet. He had not stopped talking.

'What's he saying?' Tommy asked Vincente.

The boy made a face as though he had bitten into something sour. 'He says you are smart as well as beautiful. He wants you to stay the night here. The guest room is clean and very nice. He says you should try some of the wenches you have bought. He thinks you want to fuck the *princesa*.'

'Well, he's right there,' Tommy said, taking a gulp of his third *leche de tigre*. After all he had spent most of the day poking, stroking, and fingering some pretty exciting specimens of female flesh and he had been in a continuous state of

207

rigidity. He was due – long overdue, in fact – for relief, and either Princess Koko or the carnivorous Panchita would do very well. Maybe both.

'Please don't stay here, Señor Tommy,' Vincente pleaded. 'Please tell me to say no.'

'Boy, don't start telling me what to do!'

'But, Señor Tommy, this big fat fag wants to bugger you.'

Tommy put down his glass with a thump. The lad was right, of course. The rum must be getting the better of him. Despite his apparent erudition, Solano was still repulsive physically, and the very thought of contact of any sort sent a shudder through Tommy. He was instantly sober.

'Tell Don Policarpo Solano,' he said to Vincente, 'that I am sorry I cannot accept his hospitality. Tell him that important business calls me back to Havana and I must be there by sundown.'

While Vincente was translating a curious change came over Solano. His round red face seemed to decompose. His mouth opened but no sound came. Tears welled up in his eyes and rolled down his cheeks. A silent sob shook his huge body which then appeared deflated as his shoulders sagged in disappointment. At last he spoke in a tight child's voice.

Solano was desolate, he said. His friend Tomás was so beautiful. Could he not spare another hour? Was his business in Havana so important?

Indeed it was, Tommy thought. Since he was not able to meet his physical needs here, he must get to the Casa Josefina as promptly as possible.

'Yes, I must see my bankers,' he said, 'so you will get your money tomorrow. I will see you in a day or two to arrange details of delivery. Now if you can call your carriage, Don Policarpo...'

At the mention of money Solano brightened somewhat. He ordered Tobalito to bring the *calesa* to the front entrance.

20

Tommy's night at the Casa Josefina was not exactly the
adventure he expected. It was fun, of course – what big-city
bawdy house is not? – and the lovelies who were there to
indulge him in his favourite pastime were exotically charming
and proficient far beyond merely catering to his pressing
physical needs. Josefina herself had a charm of her own. She
was much more than another Mme Alix with a Spanish
accent, an elaborately embroidered shawl and an enormous
ornate comb gleaming at the back of her raven hair. She was
younger than Alix and although both were daughters of the
Caribbean, Josefina had a charm – genuine or not – that
seemed warmer than Alix's hard-nosed professionalism.

Josefina entered into the spirit of Tommy's desire to initiate
Vincente into the niceties of sex among those who pay in gold
coin instead of small change – a real pleasure for a counterfeit
white man who in a short time had graduated from the slatterns of Fine Points in New York and bed wenches of the
Alabama plantations to the self-styled Southern belles and the
gilded New Orleans parlour houses of the rich.

'Señora Josefina,' said Tommy, pushing Vincente into the
presence of the Mother Mackerel, 'have you got anything
especially nice that will fit this youngster? I'd like to treat him
to something really high class – if it comes in boy sizes.'

Josefina's laugh was as tinkling as the little marble fountain
that spurted and sparkled into a fern-filled basin in the middle
of her reception room. 'Our girls do not deal in boy sizes,
señor,' she said. 'But they have – how do you call it? –
habilidad?'

'Skill,' Vincente volunteered.

'Right. Eskeel. They have the eskeel to make small things
grow beeg.' She clapped her hands, and raised her voice.
'*Pedro! Llama a las chiquitas!*' she called.

Instantly music from some unseen stringed instruments
sounded nearby and half a dozen pretty olive-skinned girls
strolled leisurely into the reception room, fanning themselves
languidly with one hand as the other toyed in mock modesty

209

with the ends of their multi-coloured mantillas – just as Tommy, while still in Barataria, had imagined romantic Havana to be. His spontaneous reaction did not escape Josefina. Her eyes widened as she saw Tommy's breeches change shape.

'The señor *tambien* has problems of size,' she said, 'even more serious maybe than the *mozuelo* here.'

She spoke in Spanish to the girls who had seated themselves on a semicircular red-velvet divan that was set against the wall of bright ceramic tiles. The invisible musicians stopped playing. From her gestures she was calling attention to the dimensions Tommy's distorted fly had assumed. She was apparently offering them a chance to withdraw from a possible ordeal. They all smiled and shook their heads. Josefina also smiled.

'Please choose, señor, the one who pleases you,' she said, 'and also one for the *muchacho*.'

'The *muchacho*,' said Tommy, 'can take his pick of any but the one with the green fan and the breasts like melons.'

'Ah, you like my Lolita? *Bueno*, she is yours for the night if you wish. She is veree beauteous, no? *Muy hermosa!*'

'Look, Señor Tommy, can I take—?'

'Vincente, take your time and take your pick.' Tommy pressed two gold pieces into Josefina's hand. 'But Lolita and I have urgent business upstairs.' He imprisoned the girl's waist. 'And Josefina, please send some wine to wherever we're going. Lead the way, Lolita.'

Tommy was in such a hurry as a result of the day's excitement building up a head of steam beyond his usual high pressure that he forgot all about his plan to watch Vincente's first performance in luxurious surroundings.

*

Lolita was indeed beautiful, Tommy mused as she lay naked beside him, smiling as his rapid breathing returned to normal. She was almost as lovely as Chloe, with the same tea-rose skin and luminous eyes. She was proficient, too, in the arts of love. His own hunger combined with her manifest ardour had brought him quickly to a dizzy, towering climax, much more quickly than was his habit. He noted with satisfaction, nevertheless, that she had fully shared the pleasure of their coupling, so his record of never leaving a woman ungratified was still intact.

The ecstasy that Chloe had given him, however, was missing. Nobody had ever lifted him to such heights as Chloe had. Nobody ever would. Chloe was unique. There could be no doubt that he really loved her. Sleeping with other women was fun. Making love was the greatest pleasure he had found in life, but making love to Chloe was more than pleasure; it was joy.

Lolita was talking to him in Spanish. He understood not a word, but her voice was caressing and the language was musical. And he could guess what she was saying. She was probably asking him if he always wore a shirt while screwing or why he did not take off all his clothes like everyone else. Luckily he didn't understand so he didn't have to go through all the tiresome business of explaining about his idiosyncrasies. Suddenly he thought he caught a familiar word as she pointed at his chest and said: *'Tu es clérigo? Tu es Catolico?'*

Tommy realized that in his haste to get into Lolita he had left Helen's lucky diamond-studded cross hanging around his neck. She probably thought he was a priest or something. He wondered if padres ever came to Josefina's for a little missionary work among the girls. Maybe she had a secret door for them.

'Sure I'm a *Catolico*,' he joked. 'My father was a bishop.'

He laughed but Lolita merely looked puzzled. She kissed him and began trying gently to arouse him again. She reached under the hem of his shirt and stroked his belly. Her fingers were softly exciting as they fondled him. Apparently he was not yet spent, for he rose to the occasion. She opened her thighs to him again. As he rolled her over, mounted her and drove deep, he felt her heels press into the small of his back . . .

Strange, but he was reminded of his thoughts of the afternoon, the plan he had for setting up standards for judging a woman's love-making possibilities in relation to her physical characteristics. Never before had he let extraneous thoughts intrude at moments like this. He must really be getting to be a real slave-trader at heart. Or perhaps not. He was finding it difficult to concentrate on the afternoon's ideas. She really had something, this Lolita. She knew how to drain a man's strength so sweetly, so sweetly . . .

He raised himself on his elbows, and gave a startled gasp.

Perched on the headboard of the bed was some sort of mini-animal – maybe a small lizard? – staring at him with big eyes in which the elliptical pupils ran north and south instead of east and west. As it stared at him, the little beast made small derisive noises in its throat that sounded like *gecko-gecko*, over and over again.

Tommy raised a hand to swat the insect or whatever it was, but Lolita grabbed his arm.

'*No matas al tarentolita!*' she exclaimed excitedly. The torrent of Spanish which followed ended in two English words, probably her entire vocabulary: 'Bad luck.'

Tommy rolled over and swung his legs off the bed. What the hell kind of a whorehouse was this where they had lizards sitting at the head of the bed to stare at you during the high point of the evening? He dressed quickly and went downstairs to pay for the wine (which he had not touched) and to collect Vincente.

On the way back to the hotel he interrupted the boy's glowing account of his first sexual adventure in paradise, a description in detail how it felt to go to bed with an angel.

'Glad you liked it, Vincente,' Tommy said, 'but did you have any animals in your bed?'

'Animals?'

'Some little reptile with big eyes that kept staring at me from the head of the bed. Damned near spoiled my repeat performance. When I went to swat it, Lolita almost killed me. "Bad luck," she said. The damn thing was talking to me. What does *gecko* mean in Spanish?'

'*Gecko?*' Vincente laughed. 'That must be bedroom lizard we call *tarentola*. American sailors call it English-speaking lizard because it say "*fuck you*" not *gecko*.'

'Fuck you? I guess that does sound a little like *gecko*. But what's a lizard doing in a bedroom anyhow?'

'It good luck, Señor Tommy,' the lad replied. '*Tarentola* eat mosquito and other biting bugs. You got one at Hotel de Paris.'

'I have? You sure? I never saw nor heard it.'

'I see him yesterday. He live topside your *guardarropa* – your clothespress, eat all your mosquito,' Vincente said.

'Not all,' said Tommy. 'Anyhow, I'll listen for him tonight and talk back to him.'

Tommy did not hear the *gecko* that night, even though he lay awake for hours. Curious, for he should have fallen asleep immediately. He had had a hard day with Solano and his slave girls, and Lolita had taken care of his pressing physical needs satisfactorily. He had concluded his commissions for the La-Fittes and should have enjoyed the riproaring carefree evening that he had been looking forward to when he had finished his purchase of the 300 black bucks and the dozen fancy floozies that René Beluche had ordered. It must be that he was just realizing the magnitude of the task that still lay before him.

He had joked with René about the problem of getting his human cargo across the Gulf from Havana in such a small barque – 'I'll put corks in their asses and float them across,' he had said; but it was no joke, now that he had to think about it seriously. First thing in the morning, after he'd given instructions to the banks, he'd have to go down to the wharf, look the *Sainte Claire* over, and have a talk with the captain.

He finally fell asleep trying to remember the captain's name – was it Dundee? Or MacTavish? Something Scottish anyhow, and not a particularly pleasant man, as he remembered from his outward journey – a dour sea-going character with a fringe of grey whiskers that fitted under his chin and jowls like a bib. MacFarland, that was his name, Tommy remembered just as he was drifting off . . .

He awoke next morning with a vague feeling of dread at the responsibilities that lay before him in the ensuing days. There was not only the confrontation with Captain MacFarland, and the technical problem of finding room for his slaves aboard the *Sainte Claire*, but the business of transport and security. If he could get the skipper to move the *Sainte Claire* to the pier in Regla he could probably march the coffle of 300 blacks aboard right from Hernandez's barracoon without even manacling them. He'd have to keep them manacled aboard ship, however. If they ever ran riot the 300 of them could surely overpower the crew. He'd have to take that up with the captain . . .

Then there was the business of the fancy females, not only getting them aboard but quartering them there. There was also the extra problem of Panchita, the so-called carnivorous countess, who was wanted by the Vice-Governor's police. Maybe he had made a mistake in including her in his purchase. He had joked with Solano about smuggling her aboard hidden in Princess Koko's luxuriant pubic hairs, but if the Havana police ever grabbed her while Tommy was in the process of exporting her, he'd be in deep trouble. Perhaps he should try to get Solano to keep her, although the fat man was not in a very pleasant mood when Tommy had left him. Luckily Hernandez had offered to furnish food for his *bozals*. Tommy wondered what they ate. Probably the female fancies would not eat the same thing. He'd forgotten to ask Solano. No getting around it, he'd have to see Solano again.

21

Immediately after breakfast Tommy sent Vincente in search of a carriage and set out for La Machina where the *Sainte Claire* was moored. He had considered leaving the lad behind, as he had no need of an interpreter to communicate with her officers, a motley and polyglot gang though they were. However, on second thoughts he took him along; he would need him later in the day for other negotiations.

The steamy morning was already suffocatingly hot when the *volanta* neared the end of the long wharf. Tommy had not seen the *Sainte Claire* for several days and she seemed lifeless today, tied up to the dock. Although he had not been aware of it at the time, he realized now that she had been a living thing under sail, her canvas bellied with the wind, the sea purling under her bows, and the deck lifting gently with the long swells. Motionless in the burning sun, however, she was a dead object. There was no sign of life aboard. A few crewmen were sprawled on the foredeck in the shade of furled sails, probably sleeping off a drunk.

The sight of a gaudily-uniformed customs officer lounging

at the foot of the gangplank reminded Tommy again of a dangerous hazard that still lay ahead of him: getting the Vice-Governor's ex-mistress to the waterfront undetected and then smuggling her aboard. However, the *aduanero* seemed friendly enough. Although he made a desultory search of Vincente's clothing, he let both of them aboard without difficulty.

Tommy found Captain MacFarland in his stifling cabin, stripped to the waist, sweat pearling the grey hair on his chest. The worn uniform cap perched jauntily over one ear bore grimy, almost invisible insignia that Tommy had noted on the outward voyage but had been unable to identify. He wondered if it were possible that the skipper had once been an officer in the Royal British Navy, and wondered what had made him desert King George's ships of the line for Jean LaFitte's free-booting fleet. Had he murdered a fellow officer? Or made off with the wardroom mess fund? Or maybe knocked up his commander's daughter?

The skipper was in earnest conversation with his first mate and bo's'n. Talk ceased when Tommy appeared.

'What's the snot-nose doing here?' demanded the bo's'n, a lean, dark, beetle-browed brigand whose black hair grew down to the middle of his forehead. His name was Cugino, and he was reputed to be a cousin of Vincent Gambi, a tough pirate and an off-and-on lieutenant of Jean LaFitte. Cugino had also sailed with another hard-boiled LaFitte aide named Nez-Coupé-Chighizola.

'Now, now, Coojie, don't be nasty to the big boss' pet,' said the first mate. Tommy had always marvelled at the fact that the mate's face, beard, and bald head were all the same colour – brick red. Not surprisingly his fellow officers called him Red.

The captain spoke last. 'Come in, Verder,' he said. 'What might be ailin' your spirit, lad?'

Tommy sidled in to sit on the edge of the skipper's bunk. Vincente waited outside the bulkhead.

'When will you be ready to head back for Barataria, Captain?' Tommy asked.

'I'll need three or four days to finish loadin' vittles, soberin' up the crew, and fillin' the water casks,' MacFarland answered. 'When can we take yer cargo aboard?'

'Whenever you're ready, Skipper,' Tommy said. 'I can button up the odds and ends while you're finishing up here. Then you must move across the harbour to Regla to embark the slaves.'

'Regla?' Captain MacFarland tore the cap from his head and banged it down on the table before him. '*Must* move to Regla? First of all, nobody says "must" to MacFarland, especially when you're speakin' of an ass-hole port like Regla. I doubt there's enough draught at Regla pier to float a bark the size of the *Sainte Claire*, even at high water and with no cargo. And with a full load—. How many niggers are we takin' on?'

'Three hundred bucks,' Tommy replied, 'and a dozen—'

'Good God almighty and the twelve Apostles!' exclaimed the captain, springing up and raising his arms to heaven. 'Three hundred niggers in the *Sainte Claire* which never carried more than fifty and has no room for more. Good God Almighty!'

'We'll make room,' said Tommy.

'Fifty niggers stunk us out of 'tween-decks,' said the first mate. 'Three hundred will stink us to death.'

'Three hundred will sink us,' said the bo's'n.

'Talk sense, lad.' The captain sat down and tried to speak calmly. 'The *Sainte Claire* was built for cargo. Ye can't just stack three hundred blacks in the hold in layers like kippers.'

'Why not?' asked Tommy. 'We'll build shelves along the walls of the hold and—'

'Ye'll not be boring holes in my hull to anchor bunks for no black bucks!' the captain exclaimed. 'What's more in heavy weather when we batten the hatches they'd be pukin' and crappin' all over one another. I'll not have it. With fifty I could bring 'em up on a leash now and again to shit to leeward and not foul their own nest. But three hundred...! I'm short-handed as it is. I've no third mate. My crew won't have the time to help ye control the bastards. They could take over the craft. They'd outnumber us ten to one.'

'There'll be no problem of control,' Tommy said. 'I'll manacle the lot.'

'Ye'll what?'

'Manacle them. I'm sure the ship chandler I'm seeing today will be able to furnish the necessary iron work before we sail.'

'So ye'd fetter the blacks?' The captain shook his head.

'Exactly. And fasten the shackles to the side of the vessel.'

'There ye go again, makin' holes in my hull. I'll not have it, I tell ye. The whole thing's daft and I'll have none of it.'

'My orders from M'sieur Jean LaFitte, Captain, were to buy and bring back three hundred healthy negro slaves.'

The grey fringe of the captain's beard seemed to bristle. 'I'm commander of the *Sainte Claire*, lad, and what I say goes.'

Tommy suddenly felt the need to assert his importance. After all, he was LaFitte's agent with all the power and financial backing that this represented. He may have thrown out his chest a little as he replied:

'That's true to a certain extent, Captain. You're the boss as long as we're at sea. But with the *Sainte Claire* tied to the dock, as your boss's representative I have the authority to carry out M'sieur LaFitte's orders. Please ask your carpenter to go with us into the hold and see if he thinks my idea is practical for putting up my blacks for the short sail home.'

'The carpenter's ashore,' the captain declared, 'and who said it was a short sail home?'

'It took us only three or four days coming down.'

'Lad, ye know nought of the trade winds or the currents in the Gulf,' said the captain, 'so I counsel ye to lay in enough vittles for your slaves to last at least a week.'

'Very well. I'll put the supplies aboard when you come alongside the pier at Regla.'

'*If* I berth at Regla.'

'I'll be back tomorrow with a ship chandler. Will the carpenter be aboard and sober then?'

'He'll be sober enough to hinder ye from makin' a sieve of my strakes.'

'And another thing, Captain. Since you don't have a third mate, I'll need the third mate's cabin. Furthermore, I'll need the second mate's cabin too. Your two mates will have to double up for the homeward voyage.'

The first mate roared obscenities.

Captain MacFarland clasped and unclasped his fists. 'And what,' he asked sarcastically, 'might be the reason for such nonsense?'

'I've bought a dozen fancy bright-skinned wenches,'

Tommy said. 'And while I can take two or three in my cabin, I'll need some place for the others to sleep.'

Again MacFarland jumped up.

'Holly Willie and St Elmo's fire' he exclaimed. 'Wenches! And in my own bottom! I've sailed from Zanzibar to the North Cape and from Cormorin to Cape Town, but never in my life have I carried a woman or a priest. Ye want bad luck guaranteed? Ship a skirt or a cassock. But not me. Never!'

'You'll start with my wenches then,' Tommy said. 'M'sieur LaFitte ordered them. I'll have to leave you now, Captain, but I'll be back in the morning. Vincente! Where the hell is that boy of mine? Vincente!'

The Cuban lad's head popped out of a companionway. 'Right here, Señor Tommy. I been exploring. Nice ship, I think.'

'We're going ashore,' Tommy said. 'We're heading for the bank. Need any money, Captain?'

*

Tommy felt himself nine feet tall as he climbed into the *volanta* at the end of the dock. Never – he was echoing the Captain's last word – never, he was willing to wager, had a fugitive slave masquerading as white stood up so boldly to a white sea captain (and a buccaneering captain at that) and got away with it. Of course MacFarland was right in being tough; he knew his business. But so did Tommy. And Tommy's business had to be the Captain's business too, for they were both working for the same man: Jean LaFitte. Consequently their business was the same: to get these black bucks back to Barataria. So Tommy was bound to win out in the end. He had a right to feel satisfied with this morning's triumph. He was still congratulating himself when the carriage drew up in front of the Banco Real de España.

The bank official – a tall, thin, distinguished gentleman wearing two commas under his long nose in the guise of a moustache – escorted Tommy and his interpreter into his private office. It was cool in the interior of the bank because small boys stood outside and splashed pails of water on coconut-fibre mats ranging outside the barred open windows. The manager waved to big chairs. Vincente remained standing. As Tommy sat down he noted two *geckos* scurrying across the bright ceramic frieze at the top of the inside wall. They were everywhere, these little English-speaking lizards.

The bank manager spoke English, too, so Vincente was actually superfluous.

'How can we serve you today, Señor Verder?' he asked.

Tommy explained that he had engaged himself to pay $60,000 to Don Emilio Hernandez of Regla, and he assumed that LaFitte credit was good for that amount.

The manager smiled tolerantly. Indeed it was, many times over. Had Señor Verder found the number of good healthy slaves he was seeking?

Yes, he had, thank you. There would also be a few thousand dollars – $2,810 to be exact – to be charged against the LaFitte credit for payment to another slave dealer, a specialist named Solano. Perhaps the manager knew him.

'Indeed I do.' The bank manager's smile became a smirk as he pronounced the name. 'Policarpo Solano. We will pay his bill.'

'I will have a few other bills,' Tommy said, 'although I do not yet know how much they will be. I must first find a ship chandler.'

'Ship chandler?' The manager turned to Vincente with a puzzled frown.

'*Un cabuyero*,' said Vincente, who had done his homework since he had heard Tommy talking about his needs. He explained in Spanish what his employer had in mind.

'Ah, yes.' The manager nodded. 'You may have to go to an ironmonger to get everything you want.'

'Good. Fine.' Here was a chance to make contact with some tradesmen and artisans independently of Captain MacFarland. He didn't fancy dealing with people who might be getting kickbacks from the skipper. 'Could you give me the names of a few men who could do a good, honest job for me?'

The bank manager could, indeed. He wrote down several addresses and handed them to Vincente. Tommy intercepted the paper. He pretended to seek the manager's help in pronouncing the Spanish names and numbers which he read aloud. There was no use exposing the fact that Vincente could not read. The boy had a good memory.

After signing the appropriate papers and shaking hands

with the *banquero*, Tommy was again out in the blazing morning.

'Where first?' asked Vincente, as the *volanta* started rolling again. 'The *cabuyero* or the *ferreteria*?'

'Don't make fun of my Spanish,' Tommy said.

'Oh, no, Señor Tommy. Not me. You have very spry tongue for Spanish words. You can learn Spanish easy.'

'Maybe on my next trip to Cuba. Meanwhile which is the ironmonger?'

'The *ferreteria*.'

'Let's go there. He may have some ideas. We can see the chandler tomorrow when the carpenter's back aboard.'

Then Tommy leaned back in his seat, closed his eyes, and relived the intoxicating moments of his first experience in high finance. He had not been in the least self-conscious in the presence of the *banquero*, had he? he asked himself. He couldn't have been more nonchalant when he tossed off figures like sixty thousand dollars. Sixty thousand! Quite a difference from his first business venture in New York where his stock in trade was a string of two-dollar whores in the Five Points district. And yet the sixty thousand was just small change compared to what the slaves would bring on the New Orleans market. Those three hundred blacks should sell for at least $250,000 and probably as much as $300,000 – 300 or 400 per cent profit. Jean LaFitte should be enchanted with the shrewd dealing of his ten-dollar-a-week apprentice. A quarter of a million dollars? Tommy hoped he would be enchanted enough to pay him a fat bonus. Would five thousand be too much to look for? With five thousand he could go right to Mme Alix's Academy of Music and buy Chloe's freedom. Dear, dear Chloe! Well, at least he could dream...

The *volanta* had stopped.

'Right here the *ferreteria*,' Vincente announced.

The sign over the door read

PEDRO LOPEZ, Ferretero

and the door was like a dark cave-mouth in a mossy cliff of grey stone. Once he had passed through the open door and advanced beyond the glare of the noonday sun, Tommy found the interior cool and damp. Also deserted.

'*Hay alguno?*' Vincente challenged.

After a moment a short, bow-legged, white-haired spectre materialized from the gloom and introduced himself as Pedro Lopez. He led his visitors to a table in a corner surrounded by garlands of chains, kegs of nails, and tools of various kinds.

'*Sientase, señor.*' He waved to chairs adjoining the table, clapped his hands for a servant, and would not allow a word of business to be discussed until cool glasses of coconut milk had been brought.

Lopez had been half expecting his American visitor, he said. He had been sent by Don Hernandez, no?

'No,' said Tommy when Vincente had translated. 'You were recommended by the manager of the Banco de España.'

'*Verdad?*' Lopez was surprised that they had not come on Hernandez's recommendation, for Hernandez warned him that an American named Verder had made an important purchase and would need three hundred *cadenas*. Luckily Lopez had just received a shipment of one thousand *cadenas* directly from Spain. Luckily.

When he came to the word *cadenas* in translating, Vincente seemed stumped. Tommy offered help.

'He must mean manacles,' Tommy said. 'Iron bracelets or leg irons.' He thought, they are all the same, these Cubans. Anything to turn a dollar. Hernandez had tipped off his ironmonger friend in the hopes of getting a rake-off on whatever Tommy bought. Three hundred manacles ought to bring him a nice percentage.

Meanwhile Lopez was singing the praises of his fine Spanish fetters, security guaranteed, keys for each set provided at no extra charge.

'Tell the man our real problem, Vincente,' Tommy broke in. 'Tell him we have to find some way to fasten the fetters to the sides of the ship, because we've got so many blacks we're going to have to have several layers, and the captain is raising hell because he thinks we're going to make holes in his ship.'

Lopez grinned and nodded his white head while Vincente interpreted.

'The señor *ferretero* says no problem,' the lad announced. The Lopez solution involved stretching chains the length of

221

the hold. There would be no bolts or other fasteners set into the skin of the ship. The chains would be fastened to the deck at each end and to the deck at the beams at intervals. Chain loops would attach the fetters to the long chains.

Lopez would go aboard the *Sainte Claire* and take measurements of the hold. He was prepared to install the chains, furnish the loops, and deliver the *cadenas* to wherever Señor Verder wished. Because of the size of the order, Lopez would make a special price to Señor Verder...

Lopez also had ideas for accommodating the slaves in layers in the hold without damaging the ship's hull. He would simply build scaffolding that would hold three or four tiers of planking. Now, he just happened to know a *maderista* who would furnish the planks at reasonable prices...

'Yes, I'm sure you do,' said Tommy. It was the damndest thing how these Cubans tried to cut all their friends in on the pot of gold. Just the slightest smell of money set them off in pursuit like a pack of hounds after a bitch in heat. 'But our ship's carpenter has his own ... ah ... his own—'

'*Maderista*,' said Vincente quickly.

'Send your bill to me at the Hotel de Paris,' Tommy said, 'and I'll see that the Banco Real pays you.'

Tommy thanked the old man, promised to be in touch with him the next day, and took his leave. It was lunchtime and he was hungry.

*

The chef at the Hotel de Paris had made such ambrosia from lobster meat sautéed à la Cataläña that Tommy ate himself into a state of somnolence that required a two-hour siesta to correct. He awoke sweaty and bawling for Vincente to bring bath water.

'Amd you'd better rinse yourself off when I'm through with it,' he said while Vincente was filling the tin tub. 'You're beginning to smell like Hernandez's barracoon.'

'We go again to La Casa Josefina?' The boy's eyes brightened.

'We do not.' Tommy tested the water with one toe. 'I'm afraid we'll have to go and see that Solano again.'

Vincente frowned. 'No, Señor Tommy. Please not. Why you have to see again that fat *Maricón*?'

222

'I'm going to try to call off my deal for that little bitch that calls herself a countess. I've decided she's too dangerous. Hand me the soap.'

'If we get caught, yes. Dangerous. But I think Solano not take her back. He too happy selling her.'

'You think if I tried to cancel the deal, he'd pawn her off anyhow and tip off the police?'

'No,' the boy said. 'He no like you because you don't let him bugger you. But he like American gold.'

'We'll have to think of some way to get her aboard then,' Tommy said. 'Give me that towel.'

'I think of some *juego de manos*— How you say? Trick?'

'It better be a good trick,' Tommy said, 'because I hear your Cuban jails are god-awful.'

'Oh, it will be very good, Señor Tommy, I promise. You will see, I know some very good tricks.'

'We'll see. Hand me a clean shirt.' Vincente opened the *guardarropa* and fumbled for the fresh linen. He helped Tommy thrust his arms into the sleeves, and watched in silence as Tommy tucked Helen's diamond-studded cross into his undergarment before he buttoned the shirt. He frowned thoughtfully.

'You are *Católico*, Señor Tommy?' he asked at last.

'No,' was the reply. 'Why? The wench at Josefina's asked me the same question last night.'

'In Cuba everybody is *Católico*, and you have this cross around your neck like a padre . . .'

'Help me on with my breeches,' Tommy interrupted. 'What difference does that make? The cross happens to be a luck piece given me by a very dear friend.'

'You can maybe play you are *Católico* for one day or two?' The boy smiled broadly.

'What for?' Tommy sat down on the bed and stretched out his legs for Vincente to help him on with his boots.

'For trick to fool *polizia* of Conde de Lunablanca when you put that wench Panchita on ship,' the boy explained.

'For that,' Tommy said, 'I would be a *Católico* for a week.' He stretched out the other leg. 'How would it work?'

'In the Calle Lejana is a little church,' Vincente said. 'I know the padre. He is good man. He will help, I think.'

'I see.' Tommy laughed. 'How much will it cost?'

'Not much. A few *reales* for the *cepillo de pobres* – money for his poor people.'

'I'll give him the money all right,' Tommy said, 'if you'll show me what I have to do to be a *Católico*.'

'Oh, yes, I teach you to kneel, to make a cross with fingers and dip in *agua benedita* when we go inside church.'

'Tell me how it's going to work.' Tommy stood up and flexed his toes further into his boots.

Vincente paced the floor as he recited the details of his scheme. His excitement over his planned intrigue seemed to light up his already expressive face. Failure to recall an English phrase did not interrupt his animated flow of words.

The boy began by telling about his friend Padre Diego, the priest whose church was the Iglesia de la Virgen Triste. No, Vincente had no idea who the Sad Virgin was or what miracle caused the little church to be named after her, but she was probably black. Padre Diego had strange ideas about Negroes. He believed they had souls just like humans, and he was always trying to save them. Vincente first met Padre Diego as a boy when his mother was still alive. His mother had been a pious Catholic – *muy Católica* – and went to Padre Diego for confession. She had taken his sister Perla to Padre Diego's church for her first communion. That was before Perla had become an apprentice *puta*, of course ...

'What the hell has all this got to do with sneaking that little bitch Panchita aboard the *Sainte Claire*?' Tommy interrupted.

'Much,' said Vincente. 'Very much. *Casi todo.* You see Padre Diego also likes saving souls for whores. We tell him you are taking these *mestizas muy claras* to New Orleans to learn sewing or English or maybe go to school. You will say you want the Padre to come to dock to bless the wenches for a *buen viaje.* You will give him money for his *pobres* and he will come. You see.'

Tommy shook his head. 'I don't see how that is going to get Panchita aboard.'

Vincente stopped packing. 'Easy,' he said. 'We dress her like a *monja.*'

'Like a what?'

'A *monja*. How you say? A lady monk?'

'You mean a nun?'

'*Sí*. A nun.'

Tommy made to sit down on the edge of the bed, but collapsed in convulsions of laughter. The idea of the sensuous little minx of a Panchita with her pixy face and wicked eyes, her every curve proclaiming passions just awaiting release – the image of the phony fugitive countess posing as a nun was more than he could bear. He laughed until he had to gasp for breath. Then he started to laugh again until he choked himself into silence.

'How,' he began, the tears wetting his cheeks, 'how do you expect to make a nun out of a red-hot wench like Panchita?'

'Those black dresses and big white nun hats hide everything,' Vincente said. 'And she can wear *anteojos*.'

'What's that?'

'*Anteojos*?' Vincente made circles with the thumb and forefinger of each hand and raised them to his eyes. 'Like so.'

Tommy was no longer laughing. Maybe the boy had something there after all. 'Tell me more,' he said.

'Police not stop girls who have nun for *dueña* and padre to pray for safe sailing, I think. *Aduaneros* also not searching *dueña*, I think.'

Tommy thought for a moment as he scratched one ear. The boy's plan seemed logical. The religious touch was fine for anyone sailing on a ship named after a lady saint, even if he didn't know who Sainte Claire was. Still there were a lot of angles that needed study. Everything had to be worked out in advance and in detail so that nothing could go wrong. He must not risk disaster – but he did want that Panchita wench along. The way she wriggled her little ass would be worth an extra three to four hundred dollars in New Orleans. Besides he had personal reasons: she could do a lot to make the sea voyage less monotonous . . .

'Where are we going to get a nun's habit?' he asked at last. 'From your friend the priest?'

'No, Señor Tommy. For Padre Diego she will be *sordomuda*—*' Vincente pinched his lips together and stuck his fingers in his ears – 'going to your country to see big professor *médico* for learn to speak.'

'Where do we get nun's togs, then? I don't want you to steal them.'

'No, you can buy. If I say where, can I go with you to get them? Please, Señor Tommy.'

Tommy hesitated. What else did this kid have up his sleeve? 'If you'll behave yourself, you can come along. Where do we go?'

'La Casa Josefina.'

'Balls! Don't tell me Josefina has sisters working for her as whores.'

'No, Señor Tommy. But she has good customer with a funny thing like you about fucking. You have to keep shirt on. This fellow Don Antonio, this big rich *hacendado* who owns much plantations, he can't do nothing except with *monja*. So Josefina have nun dresses and nun hats for some girls when he come. She sell you one, I think. You got money and she like you.'

'You've talked me into something,' Tommy said. 'We'll call on Josefina tonight. But this afternoon we'll go see your padre.'

22

The little Church of the Sad Virgin on the Calle Lejana was a masonry structure in the midst of palm-thatched hovels built on stilts to keep them above the swampy ground of Havana's outskirts. Tommy's *volanta* stopped in front of the glorious carpet of purple bougainvillaea growing over the entrance. Tommy remained outside, sweating profusely, while Vincente went in alone to pave the way. After all, Vincente and his sister Perla had been former communicants of Father Diego before they had embarked on their joint venture in the oldest profession. Tommy therefore did not hear the dialogue between priest and pimp. He wouldn't have understood it anyway, as it was in Spanish.

'Well, you young *bribon*, it is years since I have seen you,' the padre greeted the lad. 'I hope you have not come to confess, for I can spare you only half an hour and I am sure your confession would take many hours.'

'No, Father, I have no need to confess, for you have told me that God knows everything that goes on and therefore He does not need me to remind Him of my sins. As for you, I'm sure my sister Perla keeps you up to date on my bad deeds when she comes to confess during Lent.'

'What brings you here then, my son?'

'There is waiting outside a very rich American who wishes to put money in your poor box.'

'I see.' The little priest ran his fingers through his grey hair and shook his head in anticipation of some impossible request. 'And what unholy favour am I supposed to do in return?'

Vincente told how Señor Tomás Verder was taking a dozen wayward Cuban girls to New Orleans to teach them English and give them a chance at a better life. He wanted Padre Diego to bless the start of the voyage and thus make it easier for them to mend their ways in the new land ...

The old priest continued to shake his head. He laughed sadly. 'I don't believe you, my son,' he said. 'And you don't believe this rich American either.'

'I know only what he tells me, Father. He is a very nice gentleman and very generous. Will you see him, Father?'

Still shaking his head, the priest sighed. 'Very well, bring him in. I will wait in the sacristy.'

Tommy performed all the well-rehearsed gestures Vincente had taught him. He genuflexed, dipped his fingertips in the holy-water font, signed himself. In fact, in a reversal of roles he was now imitating Vincente. He followed the boy down the narrow aisle in the gloomy interior. He had never been in a church in his life, Protestant or Catholic, even though Miz Dovie, his former mistress in more ways than one, was once married to an itinerant preacher. When his eyes became accustomed to the half-light he saw nothing unusual in the fact that the rudely-carved Christ hanging on the cross above the altar was dark enough to be of mixed blood; no doubt most of the padre's parishioners were also dark.

Just before they entered the sacristy Vincente made sure

that the heavy jewelled cross which Tommy had earlier tucked inside the bosom of his shirt now gleamed prominently outside.

Padre Diego rose to his full five feet as Tommy and his interpreter came into the room. As Vincente started his introduction, the priest interrupted him by raising one hand.

'I speak English, Señor Verder,' he said, extending the other hand. 'I was Chaplain for the last Spanish troops to leave New Orleans not so many years ago, and I studied—'

He stopped suddenly in mid-sentence, staring at Helen Latimer's cross suspended around Tommy's neck. His lips remained open and his eyes seemed reluctantly fixed in focus, like someone fascinated by a snake coiled to strike.

'That is a very handsome piece of ecclesiastical jewellery you are wearing,' he said at last. 'Do you have some official connection with the church in Louisiana?'

'Not official, no,' Tommy replied nervously.

'Where did you get this cross?'

'From a very dear friend. It was a gift – a talisman. It is supposed to bring me luck – and it has.'

'Would you allow me to look at it more closely, Señor Verder?' The little priest shifted his fascinated gaze to Tommy's eyes, as though seeking some secret there. He smiled slightly.

'Please do, Father.' Tommy met his full-face challenge without flinching. What had he to flinch about?

With a hand on his shoulder Padre Diego gently turned Tommy so that he faced the light from the single window. He lifted the cross in his fingers and examined it intently. His lips moved silently. Was he counting the diamonds? There was a glitter as he turned it over and studied the back for a long moment.

'I thought I had seen this cross before,' he said at last, 'but I may be mistaken. The cross I saw had three words engraved on the back. Of course this cross may be a copy. Or the engraving could well have been effaced. I seem to see faint marks – the traces of some tool...'

'Where did you last see it, Father?'

'In New Orleans. I held it in my hands. If it is the same one, it may indeed being you luck. The man who asked me to

228

hold it was a very pious Catholic who did not want to wear the sacred emblem of universal love while trying to kill another human being in cold blood. He had been challenged to a duel, and before he accepted the pistol from his second, he took the cross from around his neck and handed it to me. A moment later I gave him last rites, for it was he who died in the duel. Had he continued to wear the cross on what he called "the field of honour" perhaps—.' The priest sighed, sat down, and seemed to stare at a little lizard scampering along the top of the frame of a bad copy of El Greco's Pieta. 'I don't suppose you want to part with that cross.'

'I sure don't,' Tommy said. 'What's the name of the man who got killed in the duel?'

'I can't tell you. I am sworn to secrecy.'

'Who did you give it to when the man was killed?'

'His widow, of course. She was left penniless. I suppose it ended up in a *casa de empeños*.' The priest looked for help to Vincente who shook his head. 'Ah. Pawnshop.' Suddenly the padre forced a smile and clapped his hands as if to say he was now ready to talk business.

'We digress, Señor Verder,' he said. 'You must excuse me. But you come with a request, no?'

'I sure do,' said Tommy. He liked this little old man in a brown bathrobe. He felt relaxed in his presence. He looked around for a place to sit down. There was no other chair, but there were several bamboo baskets of vegetables, no doubt contributions from his parishioners in lieu of cash tithes. Tommy sat on a sack of potatoes, and told his well-rehearsed story of the girls he was taking to North America to find a new life and who wanted the benediction of the Church on their departure.

The padre listened without interrupting. He sat in silence for a moment, then fumbled in his desk to find a long, thin, crudely-rolled cigar. He held it out to Tommy.

'Have a *claro*?' he offered.

'Thank you, no,' said Tommy. 'I don't smoke.'

'*Qué lastima!*' said Father Diego. 'It calms the nerves.' He produced a block of friction matches, split off one thick match, and brushed its tip against the stone wall behind him until it sputtered and bubbled into flame. The fumes of sulphur reached Tommy's nostril before the fragrance of the tobacco.

'I'm considering your request,' the priest resumed. 'It is highly unusual. In the first place I don't believe these girls are going to New Orleans voluntarily in search of the finer things in life. They are undoubtedly slaves and prostitutes that you have bought and expect to sell at a profit. Second, I don't believe they have asked for my benediction on their departure. I have no idea why you have chosen to surround their sailing with the odour of sanctity, and I can only hope it is legitimate and will not involve me in trouble.'

The padre paused to contemplate the bluish smoke coiling from the end of his cigar. Vincente was watching him anxiously, trying to guess from his expression what his decision was going to be.

'I am also convinced that you are a rogue,' the priest resumed. 'However, you are a rogue not entirely without compassion. There is something in your face which speaks of suffering. If it were not for the colour of your skin I would say you know from experience what it means to be a slave. So I think these girls have a chance for a happier life with you in your country than they have here. And since you say they are of mixed blood, they are bound to better themselves. I know for a fact that an octoroon can do quite well in New Orleans. If only one of them succeeds in escaping from her bondage, my asking for a blessing will be justified.'

'Thank you, padre,' said Tommy. Vincente beamed.

'Just a moment,' said Father Diego. 'I believe there is a matter of an offering for the poor. That will be payable in advance. And in my hand. I don't mind the more desperate of my flock occasionally filching coppers from the poor box, but this is not a matter of coppers, I take it.'

'No indeed, father. I promise you gold coin. I had in mind one hundred dollars.'

'Two hundred,' said the priest. 'You have twelve wenches. That comes to less than twenty dollars a benediction.' He smiled broadly, put out his cigar, and extended his hand.

Tommy counted out the gold coins. 'I will send a carriage for you on the day we sail,' he said. 'Vincente will come the day before to tell you at what time.'

The sun had been shining brightly when they entered the church. When they left the rain was coming down in torrents. It was only a few steps from the church entrance to the carriage but Tommy was drenched before they reached the shelter of the hood over the back seat of the *volanta*. Vincente apologized for the whimsical behaviour of the Havana weather.

He had reason to apologize. They had not ridden more than five minutes after leaving the church when the horse stopped suddenly and tried to back up, neighing wildly. Frenzied use of the whip by the *cochero* only produced louder equine protests. The driver got out to investigate and found they had stopped at the edge of a swirling freshet. What had been a muddy dip in the road an hour before had become a gurgling brown torrent. And the rain was still drumming and splashing on the hood of the *volanta*. The driver got out and walked to the foaming brim of the new water course. Gingerly he took soundings with his whip. He was shaking his head as he came back.

'*No se puede traversar,*' he said.

'Can't cross,' Vincente translated. 'But rain can stop in five minutes. Rain play funny tricks in Cuba.'

'Suppose it don't stop for an hour. And then another hour for the water to go down. Do we have to sit here all afternoon and evening in the rain?'

'No, Señor Tommy. There is bridge across the arroyo not far from this place.'

'Let's go there,' said Tommy.

A moment later as if on cue the downpour tapered off to a drizzle, then stopped altogether. The sun came out and a rainbow appeared above the glistening leaves of a nearby banana *finca*. The hot ground steamed with the lush, damp redolence of growing things.

Vincente gave directions to the *cochero* then turned to Tommy. The water still dripped from the hair plastered close to his skull, but he launched on a campaign of self-promotion that he had obviously been planning since they left the church.

'I told you Padre Diego would help us,' he said. 'I think Vincente smart boy, no?'

'If the rest of your scheme works out, I'll think you're pretty smart, yes.'

'So smart you must take me to New Orleans, yes?'

Tommy had to laugh at the lad's brashness. The *volanta* crossed a wooden bridge and turned into a cobbled street. Tommy had to raise his voice to be heard above the clatter of the wheels on the stones.

'I thought that was all settled. Don Cipriano is going to arrange for you to learn the slave trade from Hernandez.'

'So you don't think I'm smart, Señor Tommy.'

Tommy made an impatient gesture. 'Of course you're a smart boy, Vincente. But you'd be of no use to me in Louisiana because you can't read or write. Matter of fact, you'd be of more use to me right here if you could read and write. I think I'll have your father pay for you to go to school. I'll pay half myself.'

Vincente sulked. 'You don't like Vincente, Mr Tommy.'

'You know that's not true. You'll learn quickly. Next time I come back I want you to know more than just how to pick slaves. I'll try to persuade the LaFittes to put you on their payroll as soon as you learn your lessons.'

Vincente's disappointment was expressed by his sullen silence.

'Come on, boy, buck up,' Tommy said, 'or we won't go to Josefina's tonight.'

Vincente forced a smile.

*

Josefina was amused but puzzled at Tommy's inquiries about a nun's habit.

'She think you want it for yourself,' Vincente translated. 'She surprised you have funny need like Don Antonio because Lolita tell everybody *muy macho* – don't need no fancy tricks. But I explain.'

Vincente's explanation took liberties with the truth. Tommy had decided that if the Conde de Lunablanca was really determined to arrest and punish the fugitive Panchita, he must have spies everywhere; certainly someone at the Casa de Josefina was in his pay. And the walls had ears. So the yarn Tommy and Vincente had cooked up was that Tommy had taken a liking to the young wife of a rich but impotent old man from some backwoods village and wanted to smuggle her out of the country. However, with a suspicious husband on the alert ... Surely Josefina would understand ...

Josefina not only understood but was delighted at the idea of outwitting a jealous husband in an affair of the heart. Anything she could do to ensure success of the intrigue, Tommy had only to ask. She had religious costumes for several orders and in several sizes because she was never sure which of her girls would be free when Don Antonio arrived in search of his sacrilegious erotic thrills. How big was Tommy's adulterous enamorata?

'She comes up to about here on me,' Tommy said, raising a hand to his chin. 'She's about as big as that Lolita wench I had last night. Is Lolita busy tonight? No? Then dress her up like a good sister for me, will you, Josefina?'

Josefina clapped her hands and gave orders to Pedro. A few minutes later, while Tommy was sipping the glass of sweet ebony-coloured Malaga that the Madame had offered him, Lolita appeared. She was dressed as a Carmelite sister – a long white mantle over a rough drugget robe, with a long black veil covering her head and falling below her shoulders.

'Perfect!' Tommy exclaimed. He was amazed, not only by the demure appearance the habit gave to a wench he had last seen in naked abandon, but by the aphrodisiac effect this saintly garb was having on him. He stood up to give slack to his tight-fitting trousers, then reached into his pocket for gold pieces.

'See that Vincente is taken care of,' he said as he handed the coins to Josefina. 'Lolita and I are going upstairs to find out how I compare with Don Antonio.'

23

It was soon clear to Tommy that the *Sainte Claire* was not going to sail for Barataria in three or four days as Captain MacFarland had predicted. The delay was largely the fault of the skipper's own stubbornness. Tommy had followed through on all his preliminary chores. The Carmelite disguise for the wench Panchita, with the addition of a pair of rectangular iron-rimmed spectacles, was carefully packed away in his room at the Hotel de Paris. Padre Diego's cooperation had been confirmed. The banks had settled with the slave dealers, Hernandez and Solano, and carriages had been arranged to transport the dozen female Fancies. The lumber for building the scaffolding for accommodating three hundred buck Negroes had been delivered to La Machina dock. Pedro Lopez, the *ferretero*, had sent three hundred sets of shackles to the Hernandez barracoon as ordered, and had tried to install the chains aboard the *Sainte Claire* – unsuccessfully. The whole trouble lay there: Captain MacFarland would not let Cuban workmen aboard the *Sainte Claire* to install the chains or build the framework for the slaves' bunks.

The skipper's natural disdain for all landlubbers – particularly an unknown newcomer as young as Tommy – was reinforced by the open hostility of his officers, particularly the first mate and the bo's'n. The second mate – a bow-legged Spaniard named Palo – was apparently neutral. He had been absorbed into Havana and was seen by his shipmates only twice since they had been in port – only when he came aboard to badger the captain for an advance on his pay. The ship's carpenter, a white-mustachioed old seadog named Joe, was perfectly amenable to building Tommy's bunks or anything else – as long as he got his drop of rum at regular intervals.

There was no way for Tommy to force the issue. He knew that in the end the skipper would have to agree to a compromise of some sort. If Jean LaFitte wanted three hundred slaves brought from Havana, no ship's master in the fleet would dare refuse to take them aboard. MacFarland had prepared a channel of escape for himself when it became apparent that he could resist no longer: he told Tommy that he could positively not consider any of his plans – at least until the *Sainte Claire* was provisioned, minor repairs completed, and the fresh water taken on. That moment was now not far off, and Tommy had an idea.

One of the professors at Dr John Wainwright's school in Boston once said something that Tommy had forgotten until now. Tommy had been trying to achieve some goal by threats and bluster when the teacher had intervened to say: 'Be a diplomat, Tommy. Tact will get you further than violence. Honey catches more flies than vinegar.' All right, he would spread the honey for Captain MacFarland. On the pretext of getting the captain to look at the dock in Regla, a perfectly logical request, he would take him to lunch at the little seaside restaurant where he and Hernandez had lunched so well a few days before. When the skipper was full of good food and drink, the two of them could certainly come to some reasonable conclusion.

When MacFarland grudgingly agreed, Tommy said: 'I'll be on the wharf with my carriage at ten tomorrow morning to pick you up, Captain.'

'What for?' MacFarland asked.

'Why, to drive to where we can get a ferry to Regla.'

'You'll do nought of the sort. We'll go all the way by water as befits a seafarin' man. I'll take the *Sainte Claire*'s longboat. These clumsy louts that call themselves *balseros* – I wouldn't even let them handle a dory of mine. I don't trust these foreigners with an oar.'

'Then we'll do it your way, Captain.' This was not the day to argue, Tommy decided.

So at ten next morning Tommy and Vincente sat with Captain MacFarland in the stern sheets of the longboat while four piratical-looking stalwarts rowed them away from the harbour entrance and across to Regla.

MacFarland let the boat drift along the Regla waterfront while he compared the few ships moored there with the draught of his command. He had his crew put him ashore at one landing stage so that he could examine the pilings, then the cleats and bollards on a vacant dock to which the *Sainte Claire* might be moored. Tommy held his breath during the whole tour of inspection. When the skipper had finally agreed that it would be feasible for the *Sainte Claire* to dock here, he nodded – and Tommy breathed with relief. That was one obstacle out of the way.

Tommy suddenly decided to postpone his planned visit to Hernandez – and for good reason. He was going to make his lunch with the captain a convivial affair, a sort of peace conference. The food at the little restaurant was excellent, but there was no sense in spoiling the skipper's appetite, which would be inevitable once they got within smelling distance of the Hernandez barracoons. The monumental stink arising from three hundred sweating Negroes could turn off a starving dog. They would eat first.

Tommy asked MacFarland to have his crew row south towards a little coral reef marking the entrance to the inlet that Hernandez had told him was called Guasabacoa Bay. When he spotted the red-tiled roof and blinding white veranda of the Cantina de los Dos Tecolotes, he made a sign to the skipper. Captain MacFarland barked orders like a true commander and the longboat slid through the mangrove thicket that lined the shore and made fast to a landing stage below the restaurant.

Tommy took Vincente along as far as the veranda to interpret his menu wishes to the proprietor, then sent him back to help the crew of the longboat forage for lunch. The host greeted Tommy effusively; apparently he remembered the lad from his previous visit with Hernandez who was a good customer. At any rate he elaborated on the instructions that Vincente had transmitted from Tommy.

They were first served *cangrejo moro* – succulent crabs with deliciously spiced rice. For the *arroz con pollo*, which Tommy had ordered, the *patrón* took the liberty of making a substitution. He brought to the table an English-speaking waiter to explain. Since the *cangrejo moro* was accompanied by rice, he would not recommend more rice, particularly as today was the day that the Cantino de los Dos Tecolotes regularly barbecued a suckling pig. Therefore if the *caballeros americanos* did not mind, he would suggest the *lechón*.

The *caballeros* did not mind at all. In fact they were in high good humour as a result of the mood-elevating properties of the straw-coloured Manzanilla wine that accompanied the crab. Tommy was beginning to like wine as a tipple. He had first tasted it in Louisiana. His previous drinking had been confined to the rot-gut of New York's Five Points and the corn-whiskey toddies of the Alabama plantations. And more Manzanilla was accompanying the *lechón*.

The dessert – a compote of tropical fruits drenched with an anise-flavoured liqueur from Catalonia – was washed down with Vidonia, a sweetish wine from the Canary Islands. The *patrón* proudly recited the pedigree of the wine.

'Ah, yes, Canary wine, the tipple of the poets,' said Captain MacFarland, whose Scottish burr was thickening with each glass. 'The poet laureate of England is paid off with I dinna ken how many pipes of Canary.'

'What's a poet laureate?' asked Tommy.

'Last I heerd it was Robert Southey,' said the skipper. 'Pity Sir Walter Scott would have none of it. Dinna care for Canary, no doubt. An infeerior talent, Southey. But he did write two lines I well remember. "Thou hast been called, O sleep! the friend of woe. But 'tis the happy who have called thee so." A most infeerior talent. Now Bobbie Burrrns—'

'Who's Bobby Burns?' interrupted Tommy, who had been listening in open-mouthed incomprehension.

'No matter,' said MacFarland, draining his glass. 'We're not here concerned with mice nor men, now are we, laddie? We're here to put our heads together and come up with an answer to the impossible problems of transportin' I've forgotten how many black assholes home to that French pirate in Barataria. Aye, lad?'

'Aye,' Tommy echoed dutifully. Looked like he was going to have to learn still another language on this job, even if he couldn't tell whether it was Scotch or just sailor talk.

What a lot there was to learn in the world besides judging slaves, Tommy mused. Especially about people. It was not surprising that an old queer of a slave dealer like the fat and odious Solano should know all about tribal distinctions in Africa, but his knowledge of the history and politics of the neighbouring islands amazed Tommy. And now this buccaneering sea captain with his talk of poets and poetry...

'I take it,' said Tommy, 'that we may now go ahead and build those plank bunks in the hold.'

'No,' said the skipper. 'No "we". That deceesion is mine alone. I'm still givin' it thought.'

MacFarland was getting redder and redder in the face but the stone wall of his command mentality was still intact. He was at least getting more approachable, however. His iron-grey fringe of beard no longer seemed to bristle.

'Would you like to take a look at the coffle that's going to be our cargo, captain? The barracoon's just a mile or so from here. Just to give you an idea—'

'I've no need of black ideas,' said the skipper. 'As you may have infurred, I've no love for niggers, neither their sight nor their smell. I'll see and smell more than a suffeeciency before we get them ashore in Barataria.'

'But you wouldn't mind bedding a well-washed light-skinned wench, would you now, skipper?'

'A clean, lively, and comely lass has sometimes come favourably to my attention, if she's not too dark. And a bit of hooghmagandie never did anyone harm. What's on your mind lad?' The skipper was beginning to seem a little more congenial. His heavy eyebrows lifted and he almost smiled.

'I thought it might help solve our space problem on the *Sainte Claire*,' Tommy suggested, 'if one or two of those octoroons that LaFitte ordered were to sleep in your cabin. They might give you a little fun when you're off watch...'

'Aye, off watch.' MacFarland chuckled mirthlessly. 'Yer an innocent, lad. These Carib seas can keep a man on watch for days on end and if a *vendaval* blows far enough east he may have to lash himself to the binnacle to keep from goin' overside. However, I thank ye for the thought, and if we have a calm passage...'

'Oh, I'm sure we will,' said Tommy. He was going to say that they were bound to have good luck because the voyage was to have the special blessing of a Cuban Catholic priest, but caught himself just in time. He suddenly remembered Captain MacFarland's belief that nothing brought misfortune like a priest or a woman aboard ship.

He was on the point of explaining to the skipper that the nun who would be coming aboard with the octoroon Fancies was not really a nun but a high-class whore and was not to be considered an evil omen, but he changed his mind. The fewer people who knew that he was smuggling the former mistress of the Vice-Governor aboard the *Sainte Claire* the better, to avoid getting into trouble with the Cuban authorities. Mac-Farland might very well refuse to be a party to Tommy's scheme, and turn the wench over to the police.

No, Tommy was not going to jeopardize his project by getting MacFarland's back up. Not only was Panchita going to bring a good price in New Orleans, but Tommy was looking forward to sampling her talents with more and more breathless anticipation. In fact, just thinking about the hot little wench made him as horny as a schoolboy in a harem, even in the forbiddingly anaphrodisiac presence of Captain MacFarland.

'How about another touch of that Canary wine, Captain?' Tommy said.

'A much more attractive proposal than a visit to your nigger vendor's salesrooms,' said MacFarland. 'Just a wee drop.'

Tommy signalled the waiter. Keeping the skipper in a good mood was much more important to his project than visiting the barracoons today. He would see Hernandez in the morning.

Next morning, however, found him aboard the *Sainte Claire* – at the skipper's suggestion. He sent Vincente with messages to Lopez the *ferretero* and the *maderista* to get their hardware and planks aboard the barque before the captain changed his mind. He also bought a demijohn of rum for the white-haired ship's carpenter, who would supervise the installation.

The captain's change of heart did not cause an outbreak of brotherly love among his officers, however. They watched in glum silence as Cuban workmen carried the planks, the kegs of nails, and the other impedimenta across the gangplank. All but Cugino, the beetle-browed bo's'n, who was neither glum nor silent; he was furious and voluble.

'Gardammit, skipper, how can you let this snot-nose bastard turn this vessel into a stinking nigger pigsty!' he shouted. 'He oughta be keelhauled.'

'Save your breath, Coogie,' said the skipper. 'He's just carryin' out LaFitte's orders.'

'Why in hell can't LaFitte let us snatch our niggers on the high seas like we always done? Why all this damfoolishness about letters of marque if we gotta act like frigging merchantmen? Next thing he'll have us carrying passengers.'

'Big boss's orders, Coogie,' the skipper said. 'If ye don't like 'em ye'd better jump ship before we sail.'

'Big boss, big shit.' The bo's'n spat in Tommy's direction. Then he turned around, bent over slightly, aimed his lean buttocks at Tommy and emitted a resounding fart.

Tommy's first impulse was to launch a swift kick at the offending posterior, but he was able to restrain his natural reaction. With the skipper on his side, however half-heartedly, and the LaFitte authority behind him, he opted for the better part of valour. He would not make the captain's task more difficult, even if it meant ignoring the insult. He would not, however, ignore the hostility expressed by the bo's'n's gesture. Cugino would be his enemy at least until they returned to Barataria and would not hesitate to express his enmity in more violent ways than breaking wind. Tommy would have to protect himself. He made a mental note to have Vincente buy a gun for him. Or better yet, take him to a gunsmith where he could choose his own. It would not be the first time in his life that he had had to kill a man to save himself.

The incident caused Tommy to give up his visit to the Hernandez barracoon for another day. He would make sure the construction of the bunks got off to a good start and that there would be no malicious interference with the stringing of the first chains. He persuaded the captain to accompany him into the hold on several tours of inspection in the hope that the skipper's presence would discourage any acts of disruption. There were none.

As the work seemed to be progressing without interference next morning, Tommy spent the following days completing final arrangements ashore, returning to the dock only to make an act of presence and to satisfy himself that all was normal.

He made his twice-postponed trip to Regla to confer with Hernandez. Captain MacFarland had convinced him that feeding three hundred men in addition to the crew would be too much for his cook to handle, so in the interests of peace aboard ship Tommy had Vincente explain the situation to Hernandez. He was to persuade the slave dealer that in addition to providing food for the coffle, he should put aboard at least two or three overseers familiar with the care and feeding of blacks to handle their problems at sea. Tommy would pay these men and see that they were repatriated by the next LaFitte ship leaving Barataria for Cuba.

Hernandez received Tommy with his customary formal politeness and the ritual glass of sherry. The wine did little to dispel the barracoon smell which had fortunately been absent from Tommy's nostrils for the past few days. While Vincente interpreted, the slave dealer's cold blue eyes peered at Tommy through rectangular spectacles, his hands clasped on the head of his mahogany cane.

Yes, Hernandez replied in Spanish when Vincente had finished, he quite understood the situation, and was prepared to let Señor Verder have two men who were expert slave handlers and would be just right for his needs. They were very good men. One of them spoke Ashanti which was more or less understood by most Gold Coast blacks, and they were both well versed in African customs.

Of course, Hernandez continued, Señor Verder must understand that he would have to replace these men during their absence and men of their calibre and experience commanded good pay. He must count on being deprived of their services for at least a month, probably more. Would Señor Verder be prepared to pay $200 for the use of these experts?

'Yes,' said Tommy when Vincente had translated. 'I am prepared to guarantee payment up to $200. However, I will pay you now only $100. If for any reason the men are not back inside one month, my bank will pay you another hundred. Agreed?'

Hernandez ran his fingers through his thinning white hair during the translation. Then he smiled.

'*Convenido*,' he said, extending his hand. When Tommy shook it, he added: '*Tomaremos una copita mas*.' And he poured more sherry.

His usual squeaky voice became grave as he continued speaking in Spanish. His face fell as though he had just learned that his best friend had died.

'He got bad news,' Vincente announced.

The bad news turned out to concern one of the Fancies Tommy had chosen, the young boy with the ivory skin and long dark ringlets. The lad was ill and would probably have to be withdrawn from the shipment.

'That's bad news indeed.' Tommy remembered the youngster well – a slender boy with a mincing walk and a necklace of red coral of which he seemed so proud. 'How sick is he?'

Too sick to travel, was the answer. Hernandez hoped he did not have *la plaga*, but he had separated the lad from the other slaves just in case. *La plaga* was very catching, but he was sure he had taken precautions in time.

'Damn!' said Tommy. 'That boy is a valuable property. He's worth at least a thousand dollars as a butler or houseboy. Vincente, do you think this old bird got a better offer for him and is holding out on us?'

After a brief exchange in Spanish Vincente reported that Hernandez would be glad to show Señor Verder the place where the boy was lying sick, but would not go himself, because after all it just *might* be *la plaga* . . .

'We better trust him, I think,' Vincente added.

Hernandez understood that Señor Verder was particularly taken by the boy with the red beads and he would replace him with a specimen of equal quality. He would offer several for Tommy's choice whenever he desired.

'Tell him to have the replacement here when the *Sainte Claire* docks in Regla to pick up the other 299 bucks,' Tommy said.

When would that be? Within the next two or three days . . .

*

Before tying up any more loose ends, Tommy took care of his anti-Cugino defensive measures. Vincente accompanied him to an *armeria* – the best gunsmith shop in all Cuba, the lad said – to buy sidearms. He came out with a brand-new type of flint-lock – a pistol said to have been invented by an American living in England – which fired a number of shots separately and consecutively. The bullets were contained in a sort of cylinder which was rotated by hand after each shot was fired and the pistol cocked again. It was an ingenious weapon and quite expensive. As the shop also specialized in Toledo steel blades, Tommy bought (on Vincente's suggestion) a short dagger which was easily concealed and more readily available should he be jumped from behind and unable to get his complicated pistol into action in time. Vincente shared Tommy's distrust of the bo's'n as a sinister character.

A more pleasant last-minute errand was a courtesy visit to Don Cipriano to thank him for his many favours and to discuss the future of his illegitimate son Vincente. There was more ceremonial sherry, more toasts to the loyal friendship with Jean LaFitte, and pledges of further aid on Señor Verder's next trip to Cuba – all faithfully translated by Vincente whose new clothes looked less out of place in the mausoleum-like grandeur of the Olivarez mansion than had the rags of his first visit.

When the time came to discuss Vincente's future, the boy seemed not at all embarrassed in translating Tommy's words of praise.

'I have been very pleased with his services to me as interpreter and general guide,' said Tommy. 'In fact, he has been indispensable to me. He is a very bright lad.'

The dignified old Cuban made a slight bow as though the praise was for himself. He was not surprised, he said through Vincente. After all, the boy was of his own blood.

'I would like your help in developing his intelligence,' Tommy went on. 'If you will get him accepted in a good school I will pay the tuition. He must learn to read and write, at least in Spanish. Otherwise half his intelligence is wasted. Will you attend to the education of your bastard son, Don Cipriano?'

Indeed he would. He would give him a letter. Don Cipriano pleaded guilty to negligence, but excused himself on the grounds that it was the custom of his class and his country to show little concern for the offspring of casual matings. He was glad that Vincente showed promise.

Yes, he would arrange for Vincente's apprenticeship at the barracoons of the ageing Hernandez. What a great thing if this boy, even though born on the wrong side of the blanket, could find a place in the important LaFitte organization...

When he had finished translating Vincente engaged Don Cipriano in a long and spirited dialogue, obviously on his own behalf.

'Hey, what is this?' Tommy cut in. 'What's going on?'

Vincente stopped suddenly and looked sullenly at his shoes.

'I tell Don Cipriano I rather go with you on ship, Señor Tommy,' he said. 'He say no.'

'Of course he says no, just like I do,' Tommy replied. 'You'll first have to learn to read and write, and I predict it won't take you long. Now will you tell your father how much I appreciate his help and courtesies, and that I look forward to seeing him and his brother on my next trip to Cuba?'

Vincente obliged.

Don Cipriano bowed and shook hands. '*Vaya usted con Dios*,' he said.

*

Once begun in earnest, the re-fitting of the *Sainte Claire*'s hold for human cargo proceeded quickly. Tommy spaced his visits of inspection to no more than one or two a day in order not to inflame the bo's'n and his fellow potential mutineers unduly. On the fourth day he found the ship's carpenter directing the sweeping up of sawdust, shavings, and metal filings.

'We sail in the morning,' Captain MacFarland announced. 'We'll cross to Regla and pick up your niggers and supplies at the second change of watch. I'll want your wenches aboard by ten o'clock.'

Despite all his impatience to get under way, the captain's announcement came as something of a shock to Tommy. Here his dream of romantic Havana was ending almost before it had even begun. There had been nothing romantic about the slave barracoons or the curious negotiations with Solano for the dozen Fancies. Vincente's sister Perla was a sweet young thing and his couplings with her had been exciting despite the sordid surroundings and their tragic ending with the murder of poor Ramon. His squabbling with the crew of the *Saint Claire* had been downright disagreeable with every prospect that it would be even more so. The only really exotic episodes of his brief tropical dream were his nights at Josefina's, and they too had much that was familiar routine once the outer trappings were stripped from the wenches. Of course he had to admit that he had never before engaged in erotic gymnastics with an English-speaking lizard looking on.

Well, he'd better bestir himself and get all his last-minute errands done. He made final visits to both banks to assure himself that the slave dealer and the various merchants and artisans had been paid. He also drew enough money to pay his hotel bill and take care of whatever eleventh-hour expenses might have to be liquidated.

He bought more gifts to take back with him – brilliantly-embroidered mantillas for his beloved Chloe and for her mother Helen, as well as a bottle of French scent for Mme Alix. On second thoughts he bought another bottle of scent for

Perla. He even toyed with the idea of spending his last night in Havana with the teenage Perla, but vetoed it when he thought of her squalid lodgings. He'd have Vincente take it to her, and then move on to Josefina's for a final fling. To leave Havana without making some woman happy would be a crime against nature – his own horny nature. Of course the voyage home would not be marked by the painful continence he had suffered on the way down, but he was definitely in need of some emergency treatment tonight.

When he charged Vincente with the mission, however, the lad made a counter-proposition. Señor Tommy would present the scent to Perla himself. No, not at their home. Right here in the hotel.

'She desires much to wear that fine mantilla you gave her,' Vincente said, 'and I bought her a new dress to go with it; you can repay me if you like. So she will not disgrace you if she comes here. *Le gusta a usted?* You like?'

Tommy hesitated. He had visions of that murdering pimp Jorge following Perla and raising unholy hell – if not bloody murder – right there in the Hotel de Paris. Still he needed a woman and Perla was very much to his taste. Having Perla for a farewell romp between clean sheets would be a fine windup.

'You sure that bastard Jorge won't make trouble?' he said at last.

'No chance,' Vincente replied. 'Outside our own *vecindario* Jorge is small mouse.'

'Good.' Tommy looked forward to having Perla without an audience. 'And just to make sure he keeps away, you'll stand sentry outside in the hall.'

'But Señor Tommy, you do not know the Spanish. How will you—?'

'I don't have to talk to Perla, Vincente. She understands perfectly what I want. Go and get Perla.'

Perla indeed knew what Tommy wanted. Moreover she had the native skills to provide it to perfection. Tommy thought he had sampled the wares of enough wenches, both amateur and professional, so that there was nothing new between the sheets, nothing that could surprise him. Perla was to prove him wrong.

She arrived after dinner with her new mantilla over her new

245

dress, a simple dimity sheath. She slipped them both off while Tommy was giving instructions to her brother.

'I don't want to see hide nor hair of you for at least an hour,' Tommy said. 'In an hour you can bring a tub of warm water. When you knock on the door I'll tell you if I need anything else. Now disappear.'

When he locked the door and turned around, the girl stood naked before him. Her dark eyes burned with desire such as he would have thought impossible in a girl for whom passion was an article of trade. Her virginal pink nipples were hard and distended as she pressed herself against him. She threw her arms around his neck and kissed him. As she felt his rigidity growing against her bare abdomen, she reached down to undo the buttons of his fly. Instantly his swollen phallus sprang out at her. He disengaged his lips to say:

'Hey, not so fast. Let me get some clothes off!'

For reply she pushed him a few steps towards the bed, clasped both hands behind his neck, stood on tiptoe, gave a little leap, swung her legs apart and planted her little heels against his buttocks. Almost without realizing it he slid into her. He was her prisoner.

He was scarcely aware of her subtle undulating movements. He was aware only that his whole being was flowing towards his loins, concentrating in a brimming reservoir of sweetness. He tried to hold off the climax but he was helpless against the tenderly relentless demands of her body. She was the eternal and inevitable female, not to be denied. The strength flowed from his body and poured into the girl in ecstatic surges. His knees buckled and he staggered backward against the edge of the bed. He toppled over on his back, gasping for breath. He lay motionless on the bed.

Still astride his hips, the girl moved her body in tiny, gentle circles to drain the last drop of his manhood. Then she extricated her feet to kneel beside him. She nuzzled the hollow under his chin.

'Perla, Perla, Perla!' he murmured when he got his breath.

She laid a finger across his lips and started to undress him. She had a little trouble getting his boots off, but succeeded when he regained consciousness sufficiently to flex his instep.

The trousers, tight as they were, posed no problem. Neither did his shirt. When she tried to remove his undershirt, however, he sat up to resist.

Wasn't he being silly? After all, he'd probably never see this girl again, and who in Cuba cared whether he had Negro blood in his veins? Still, he must cling to his habit of secrecy for his own protection. Carelessness had almost cost him his life in Alabama, and he must never be careless again. When Perla started to pull up on the hem of his undershirt, he seized her wrists. He smiled and kissed her. She smiled back. Obviously her brother had explained his idiosyncrasy.

She stretched out next to him on the bed for a while, speaking softly in his ear. He didn't understand a word she said, but he liked the sound of her voice, the intonations, the lilting syllables. Spanish was indeed a musical language, he decided, especially when spoken by a sexy young girl. Just listening to her mellifluous phrases made him randy all over again. And when she started sketching circles around his navel with the gentle forefingers of both hands, he was erect again. When the expanding circles began running through his pubic hair, he was rampant. He rolled her on her back and instantly was into her again.

This time he was in command – or so he thought. This was routine copulation, the response to a physical need, his partner was of no importance personally. The rhythm was to be his, the usual long strokes to excite the girl under him, the tempo to increase as she reacted. However, he had scarcely reached his deepest intromission when he became aware of something strange happening. Each time he plunged and was about to draw back, the tip of his penis was caught in a gentle squeeze. The girl must have muscles far inside her genitalia that she could contract at will. It was driving him mad. Impossible to hold back. He increased his speed involuntarily. At the end of each stroke there was still this exquisite little nip. Then he lost all control. Banging away madly he had no thought but to achieve the ultimate ecstasy as quickly as possible.

The girl's gentle moans reached a crescendo just as an involuntary cry escaped his throat. Perla dug her heels into his back. They had achieved climax simultaneously.

This time she had exhausted him. There could be no repeat performance. Even when he had caught his breath it was long minutes before he could move. This girl was something. She was no Chloe, true, but then he was in love with Chloe. But her techniques – they seemed really too instinctive to be called by the self-conscious formalized term 'technique' – were more exciting even than those of an old pro like Helen. She would be a sensation in New Orleans. For a moment he toyed with the idea of taking her with him, but that didn't seem practical. She was not a slave, even though she was in a way in bondage to Vincente for the moment, so she could not be put up for sale like the dozen wenches he was bringing back. He couldn't very well sell her to Mme Alix, even though she would surely get star billing at the Academy of Music. Maybe Alix would give him a bonus – or at least give him credit towards the release of Chloe – if he could smuggle Perla in as his personal import. But there he would have to give Vincente his percentage and that would involve complications with Vincente still in Havana. He had better forget the whole business . . .

'Hey, what are you doing to me Perla?'

While Tommy was lying prone, musing upon Perla's impressive talents and wondering how he could turn them into his own profit, the girl had been busy with a project of her own. He had scarcely noticed when she turned him gently on his back. He was vaguely aware of the feathery touch of her fingers caressing his scrotum. He thought: she's an optimist; she'll never get a dead horse to jump the fence. When her fingers danced lightly over the limpness that had very recently been his pride and joy, he felt definite stirrings. And when her tiny pink tongue flickered along the growing length of it, he knew she had won again.

Tommy started to sit up but she pushed him back almost before his shoulders had left the bed. She bent over for a final encircling kiss, then she was quickly astride his loins and he was into her again. Or rather she had absorbed him with her hot, quivering lubricity.

By shifting her weight from one knee to the other she managed to rotate her body through half circles, slowly at first, then faster and faster, her torso erect, her hands clasped behind her head. As the tempo increased she added another dimension to her frenzied movements. She bent forward and back, raising her buttocks with each half-turn, lowering them with the next.

The fierce paroxysm was upon Tommy with pulsating, terrifying suddenness. He cried out, clasped Perla to him, rolled from side to side, lay still, panting.

There was a knock at the door. Perla squirmed off the bed.

The knock was repeated. 'Señor Tommy, it's me, Vincente.'

Tommy swung his feet to the floor. 'Go get the bath water,' he said.

'I got the buckets already here.'

'Then get me some clean towels.'

'But Señor Tommy—'

'Go for the towels. I'll let you in when you come back.'

Tommy waited a few seconds, then unlocked the door and yanked it open. He half expected to find a peeping Vincente lingering at the keyhole, but the boy was gone. He quickly closed the door, went to his clothes and drew out a gold coin. He handed it to Perla.

'I want you to keep this for yourself,' he said. 'Don't share it with Jorge. Not even Vincente.' He pointed and gestured, shaking his head as he indicated the door through which her brother would enter, and nodding vehemently when he pointed at her. 'Can you hide it?'

She apparently understood. She smiled broadly and said something in Spanish as she took the money. Then she turned her back and squatted. When she stood up and faced Tommy the coin had disappeared.

At this point Vincente returned. While he was pouring water into the tin tub, he queried Tommy.

'Perla do good this time?'

'Wonderful,' Tommy answered. He tested the water with one toe. 'Couldn't be better.' He stepped into the tub.

'Good enough for New Orleans, you think so?'

Tommy hesitated before sitting in the water. Curious that Vincente and he should have the same idea. He wondered if the boy had coached his sister to put on a special performance – a sort of sample of goods suitable for export. If so he had been a good tutor or Perla had been an apt pupil or both. But

249

he still thought her intuitive feelings, an instinct that could pass for sincerity, would alone make her very popular in a house like Mme Alix's.

'What did you have in mind, Vincente?' Tommy asked. He sat. Immediately Perla was ministering to him with a cake of Castile soap.

'You think Perla too good for *ladrones* like this fella Jorge, no?' Vincente said.

'That I sure do. But—'

'Then why you don't take her with you tomorrow, Señor Tommy?'

'Impossible, Vincente. Perla's not a slave. I couldn't sell her like we will be selling Solano's wenches.'

'She could make believe she is *mestiza*, no?'

Tommy laughed briefly, bitterly. Or perhaps it was Calico, the Negro slave, who laughed ironically at the idea of a white girl posing as a mulatto. He said: 'You don't know what you're trying to do to your sister, Vincente. In Louisiana, all over the American South really, a *mestiza* is a Negro and a Negro is not even human. Here she is free and white.'

'Why can't she be a free white *puta* in New Orleans? I go along and be her *alcahuete*. Padre Diego say many Spanish still in New Orleans. And for Americans who want Cuban whore I translate.'

Tommy stepped out of the tub and let Perla towel him. She was listening intently, trying to understand.

'Look,' said Tommy. 'It's not as simple as all that. I might be able to get her into a good house through Captain Dominique You, who is one of LaFitte's top men and a good friend of Mme Alix. But I must have permission from LaFitte to take her aboard, something I don't have for this trip. I'll speak to Captain You and if he says yes, I'll take her next trip.'

'And Vincente too?'

'Only if you learn your lessons, boy. You'll stay in Havana until my next trip. That's settled.'

'*Qué lástima!*' Vincente shook his head sadly, made a drooping gesture, and turned a mournful face to Perla. 'Too bad! Because I think Perla loves you. She'll help you dress.'

Tommy took his trousers from her outstretched hands and fumbled in his pocket.

250

'This is your commission,' he told Vincente, 'and carriage fare to take Perla home. I don't want her molested by Jorge. Myself I'm going to bed because we have to get up at the crack of dawn. I want you here at seven o'clock with the carriages to pick up Solano's wenches. We'll also have to pick up the padre, and I can't take a chance on the bridge being washed out again. We have to get the wenches aboard by ten. Good night, Vincente. *Buenas noches*, Perla, and *adiós*.'

The girl put her arms around his neck and kissed him. Then she turned to her brother and said something in Spanish.

'She say,' Vincente translated, 'you don't give her that French scent you promise.'

Tommy laughed. He opened the armoire and produced the bottle of perfume.

Perla kissed him again.

24

Morning was just exhaling its first warm and humid contribution to the burning tropical day when Tommy's caravan arrived to pick up the flower of Solano's Fancies. There were three closed *carrozas* which would hold four wenches each, and a *volanta* for Tommy and Padre Diego (who would join them later) with Vincente sitting on the seat beside the driver. Perhaps Panchita would join them on the jump seat after they had changed her costume – a surprise of which she was not yet aware – to complete the religious touch. Tommy did not want to unveil the Carmelite nun disguise until after they had left Don Policarpo Solano behind. Tommy did not trust Solano. The erudite paederast was just the sort of bird who would tip off the police to intercept the iniquitous Panchita before they reached La Machina wharf. There would be plenty of time for a little treachery while they detoured to the little church on the Calle Lejana.

Solano had transferred the dozen wenches from his spurious

Alhambra in the outskirts to his dilapidated premises in Havana proper. Solano himself, the enormous fat man with the little voice, came out to greet the caravan with a fawning welcome. He waddled through the courtyard, supported on one side by Tobalito, the effeminate secretary, and on the other by his part-Mandingo boy. As Tommy stepped from the *volanta* he saw Solano struggling to free his arms from his servitors and he hurried to shake one hand in order to forestall any more intimate embrace.

Solano made an effusive speech of farewell with gestures. He had enjoyed their relationship and hoped next time he came to Cuba they would get to know each other better – much better.

After Vincente had translated, Tommy made a businesslike reply, as courteous as he thought necessary, and told Solano that they must start immediately as they were behind schedule. Solano's huge face contorted into a desolate moue, and he clapped his puffy hands. The sound was almost inaudible, but his shout brought out the wenches in a colourful procession.

The women were dressed in their Sunday best – a variety of costumes that spanned the Caribbean and reached across the Atlantic. There were brilliant mantillas, Haitian imitations of Parisian styles, the latest from Madrid in copies by Havana *modistas*. There were bangles, earrings, a few necklaces. The trollops all carried cloth-wrapped bundles except Antoinette, who had a scuffed leather bag.

Leading the group was Koko, the Songhai princess, whose proud bearing and stately stride gave no hint of the magnificent bearded underbelly beneath the bright African scarves with which she was draped. Close behind her were the other pseudo-peeresses. Antoinette, the so-called Duchess de Limbé, with her full lips and suggestive walk, trying to be very French in her imitation Empire gown; and Countess Panchita, the big-eyed little minx who did not yet know that she was on the verge of becoming a Carmelite nun for the day.

Tommy tried to remember how he had rated the other girls when he had examined them intimately a week ago. As they stepped into the carriages at his indication, he called the names that stuck in his mind and made an effort to fit the appropriate bodily attributes that went with each. There was Rosita, who had the plump, friendly vagina, and Magdalena whose genitalia reminded him of a baited trap. There was Carmen, Juanita, Beatriz – which one had the pear-shaped tits? – Maria, Adelita – who had the apples, who the melons? Well, there would be plenty of time on the way to Barataria to refresh his memory . . .

Tommy climbed into the waiting *volanta*, turned and waved to Solano.

'*Vaya con Dios!*' Solano waved back.

'*Hasta luego*,' said Tommy, showing off one of the dozen Spanish phrases he had learned.

The caravan rolled down the avenue of ceiba trees for half a kilometre until the Solano house was out of sight, then turned off into a side road and stopped. While Vincente kept watch at the junction, Tommy opened the door of the first *carroza*. He shooed out three of the girls, then stepped inside with the bundle of Carmelite apparel.

Panchita's shrill staccato protests when Tommy began to undress her became squeals of laughter when she saw the drugget robe, the white mantle and the long black veil and realized what they were for. She fumbled in her effects for a fragment of mirror to adjust the veil and to fit her square-framed eyeglasses on her nose. She giggled as Tommy rolled her lay clothes into a wad and stuffed it into a sugar sack he had taken from the galley of the *Sainte Claire*. He then got out and shooed the other three wenches back in.

'*Adelante!*' he cried proudly. Another week or so he would be speaking Spanish fluently, he had boasted to Vincente.

*

The purple bougainvillaea growing across the façade of the little Church of the Sad Virgin was resplendent in the hot, dazzling sunlight as Tommy's caravan of female Fancies was braked to a halt. Vincente jumped down, ran up the few steps, and entered the church. Tommy followed him, but more slowly. When he reached the top step he stopped. He felt that there was something wrong – he had no idea what it was or why this curious feeling had come over him. Perhaps it was some subtly unrecognizable smell or a barely perceptible sound

253

that he could not identify. Vincente had disappeared from view so Tommy advanced a few paces more, past the holy-water font, into the gloom of the nave. Suddenly he saw two candles burning in the half light at the end of the nave. As his eyes became used to the dimness he could make out a bier and several old women with shawls over their heads crouching before the altar. Then the drone of prayers punctuated by sobs came clearly to his ears. He stopped short, a cold spot forming at the nape of his neck. He was in the presence of death.

The cold spot trickled down his spine. He wanted to turn and run but his feet were frozen to the floor. He was not afraid of death but he had a superstitious fear of the dead. He hated death because it was a cessation of life, which he loved, and he was awed by the mystery of death. He felt he must do something to show his respect for the unknown corpse, so he awkwardly made the sign of the cross as Vincente had shown him when they were plotting to make Father Diego a party to their fraud. Then he back-pedalled into the little vestibule, turned around and ran down the steps into the sunlight. He breathed deeply, listening to the stupid beating of his heart.

'Bad news,' said Vincente when he emerged from the church. 'Padre Diego can't come with us. You want he give back your money, Señor Tommy?'

'Why can't he come?' asked Tommy, although he knew the answer.

'One of his *parroquianos* is dead. He must say the mass and bury him.'

'Why can't he just duck down to the wharf with us now like we planned? He could come right back and bury his pal later,' Tommy pleaded.

'No, Señor Tommy. The padre is very busy and very sad. One more *parroquiano* is dying, he think, and two *parroquianos* also very sick. The padre must pray for them, pray very hard because he think there is *epidémio*. Is *la plaga* I think.'

'*La Plaga?*' That was what Hernandez had said was the matter with that tall, handsome young slave with the red coral beads. Very catching, Hernandez had said. Three long, leaping strides and Tommy was in the *volanta*. 'Let's get the hell out of here.'

'You don't want the padre give you back your money, Señor Tommy?'

'Come on, boy, jump in quick or you'll get left behind,' Tommy yelled. '*Adelante!*'

Vincente jumped in. The coachman cracked his whip.

Damn, thought Tommy as the horses clop-clopped their way into Havana proper, everything seemed to be going wrong! He wasn't worried about this disease they called *la plaga*. It must be something like what was known as 'The Fever' in New Orleans – a good thing to keep away from. But after all he hadn't gone near the light-coloured young slave who was sick at Hernandez's barracoon, and he sure as hell hadn't snuggled up to the dead man in Padre Diego's church. But *la plaga* had certainly smeared up their carefully-drawn plan for smuggling Panchita aboard. What the hell was the matter with that stupid priest anyway, that he couldn't take off an hour or so for two hundred gold dollars? His pious corpse would not be any deader when he got back and his burial would be just as holy an hour later. His silly prayers weren't going to help the other three sick people anyhow. Maybe he should have taken his money back, as Vincente seemed to be insisting.

But money was not the thing he was worried about. Without the ecclesiastical blessing of Padre Diego on the whole group of wenches, would Panchita's seraphic disguise pass muster with the police or customs or whatever uniformed service tried to stop her? He'd better ask Vincente's advice. As the wheels of the *volanta* were rattling noisily over the cobbled streets leading to the Havana waterfront, Tommy leaned forward to slap Vincente on the rump.

'Hey, big thinker,' he said, 'what do we do now that your smart scheme collapsed?'

'I get your money next time in Havana,' Vincente said without turning around.

'It's not the money. Do you think we can pass Panchita without the padre?'

'Sure, Señor Tommy, sure. Don't worry.' Vincente turned and grinned. 'Vincente always think up tricks, no?'

Tommy shook his head and grunted, far from reassured. At the end of the street he could already see a thicket of masts and spars that marked the dock area. He would soon know if Vincente's nonchalance was justified. He could not bear the thought of anything happening to a successful mission just as the last stage was beginning. If the padre were along Tommy would ask him to start praying. Damn the padre! Damn *la plaga*!

The horse was slowing up. Tommy leaned out to one side to peer ahead. There was a tangle of stalled vehicles of all sorts at the entrance to the wharf. A score of nondescript soldiers were making some sort of inspection. Tommy's horse stopped. A barefooted soldier reached up and grabbed the bridle.

The coachman shouted at the soldier and raised his whip. Vincente grabbed the coachman's arm and joined in the shouting match. Two other ragged soldiers came loping up and started pulling open the doors of the carriages in which the dozen wenches were riding. A fourth soldier who seemed to be a noncom of some kind ordered the women to get out and line up. At this point Vincente jumped down from his seat beside the driver and started running.

'Vincente!' Tommy shouted after him. 'Where the hell—?' But the lad had disappeared in the crowd.

All four soldiers were now engaged in searching the wenches. Tommy gesticulated and protested loudly. They ignored him. The noncom seemed especially interested in Panchita, not the least impressed by her religious garb. She was screaming at him.

'See here,' Tommy shouted. 'You've got to show respect for this nun.'

No reaction.

Tommy swore. Serves him right for being so stubborn about getting the little bitch aboard. He should start thinking with his head instead of with his balls.

The noncom parted the white mantle with his dirty hands and pawed the drugget robe. Panchita swung and landed a resounding smack on the side of his head. He drew back one foot to kick her when an officer in a smart white uniform approached, a letter in his hand. The noncom came to attention and saluted.

One pace behind the officer's dangling sword came Vincente.

'*Mi capitán,*' said Vincente, '*quiero presentar el caballero americano* Don Tomás Verder.'

'*Muy alegre,*' said the captain, handing the letter back to Vincente. He gave an order and the search was abandoned. The angry wenches got back into their carriages, Tommy and Vincente resumed their places, and the officer waved the caravan through the barricade.

'Boy, that was a close one,' said Tommy, mopping his brow. They were now moving down the long wharf. 'What the hell was going on? Was there a tip-off about Panchita?'

'No, Señor Tommy. They did not want Panchita.' Vincente looked very smug. 'Some *puta* stole the archbishop's gold chalice, so they search all women on every dock. They don't want she take it from Cuba.'

'And what was that letter the officer gave to you?' Tommy couldn't help admiring the boy's enterprise.

'That was from my father Don Cipriano.' Vincente made a nonchalant gesture. 'He gave it to me when you ask him to help me to school. It say: "Show my son Vincente every courtesies and give him all help he needs and oblige Cipriano Olivarez." Capitán is impressed, no? Cipriano Olivarez very important name.'

'But why didn't you show the letter to the soldiers, Vincente, instead of running off like a bat out of hell and leaving me here alone scared pissless?'

'Because, Señor Tommy—' Vincente was pontificating, '– I must find officer. These soldiers can't read.'

'Neither can you read, Vincente.'

'True,' was the reply. 'But I know what letter says. I tell my father what to write.'

*

As the trollop caravan drew alongside the *Sainte Claire,* a kaleidoscope of bright hats and headclothes appeared in the carriage windows. Two of them were pushed aside to make way for the fanciful headdress of Princess Koko. As the Songhai woman twisted her head and craned her neck to look up at the masts and rigging of the barque still moored to the wharf, Tommy could not help marvel at the intricate way a thousand little black braids were interwoven to form what resembled a birdcage. Probably took her all day to fix it. He wondered what happened when she washed it – then decided she probably never did. The warm breeze brought the smell of coconut oil to his nostrils . . .

Captain MacFarland stood at the rail shouting at him through cupped hands.

'Good God almighty and the Twelve Apostles!' he cried. 'I said the second watch, and we're still waitin' for you and LaFitte's goddam constellation of cunts. You get those waggletails aboard pronto because in three minutes there'll be no gangplank, and those that can't fly will be left behind.'

There was a cackle of approval from the officers at the rail and a few supplementary obscenities from the bo's'n. Tommy tried to ignore the hostile chorus and organize his Fancies. Vincente interrupted to say: 'I'll take your bags aboard, Señor Tommy. Then I'll go. I won't say good-bye, because I might cry, Señor Tommy. I don't want to get all choked in my throat. So I'll just say *hasta luego, amigo*. Come back soon.'

'*Hasta luego*, Vincente. Take care of Perla.'

Vincente grabbed Tommy's two bags and scurried up the gangplank – one bag Tommy had brought from Barataria, the other one he had bought in Havana to contain his new acquisitions, his gifts, his Cuban shirts, and the few poor garments of which the late Ramon had been so proud. Poor Ramon! Well, there was no use in letting his few clothes go to waste. Someone in Barataria could find use for them . . . Ramon belonged to the past.

Vincente too was out of mind once he had reached the deck and disappeared with the bags. Tommy was too busy herding his Solano Fancies up the gangplank, trying to ignore the obscene bellowing from the rail. As the wenches climbed the incline, ignorant of the meaning of what might have been cheers, Tommy became aware of shouts from above. For the first time he noted that there were men in the rigging and astride the yards. The square sails were reefed on the foremast and mainmast, but the fore-and-aft triangle was flapping at the mizzen for reasons beyond him. He supposed it had something to do with the fact that the *Sainte Claire* was being towed across the harbour to Regla and would not really get under way until the 300 blacks were aboard.

A roar from the skipper brought him back to realities.

Tommy was climbing the gangplank with the last of the wenches, one hand firmly gripping the arm of the pseudo-Carmelite.

'Hell's bells and Paul's balls!' the captain bellowed. 'What are ye doin' to me laddie? I'm stretchin' a point for yer quail tail, but ye know full well I canna take an eccleesiastic aboard.' He stretched a hairy arm across the head of the gangway.

'Now look, Captain, I know your rules,' Tommy said. 'But this trollop is not really a nun. She's not even a virgin as I'm sure you'll find out before we get back to Barataria. Skipper, I was planning for her to share your cabin, remember?'

'But why in holy hell——?'

'The masquerade? Simple Captain. She's a runaway.' Tommy hesitated. Should he tell MacFarland the truth? Better not. The skipper would want no trouble with the police. He might not even want to sleep with a bitch who had the temper and the emasculating tricks of Panchita. 'She's running away from a bastard who beats her.'

'You mean she's a runner?' The captain's expressive eyebrows went up.

'No, no, no, skipper. The bastard who beat her was not her legal owner. He lured her away with a lot of lying promises he never kept. He never had a bill of sale——'

'All right then. Strip those sanctimonious duds off her before I have a mutiny on my hands. Lock her up with the rest of the cunts and let's get under way to pick up the other cargo.' MacFarland handed Tommy four heavy iron keys. To one of them was attached a damascene plaque inlaid with a gilt thistle; this one he held back an instant. 'Ye'll returrrn this one to me before we cast off from Regla,' he said.

The key with the plaque attached fitted the captain's own cabin door. The others locked the doors to the cabins of the first and third mates and Tommy's own.

Tommy was leading the wenches to their allotted sleeping space when he heard the loud thump of the gangplank being dropped to the dock. Immediately afterwards he heard the skipper shout, 'Cast off aft.' A pause. Then, 'Cast off forward.'

After turning a key in the fourth lock, Tommy made his way to the helmsman's station to hand the captain his own key, and to remain on deck to watch the sweating, straining backs of the Negroes bending to the oars of the two longboats towing the *Sainte Claire* across the harbour.

Docking at Regla was accomplished quickly and routinely. Tommy was mildly surprised to see the white-haired Hernandez standing on the pier, his hands clasped on the head of his mahogany stick. Next to him stood a handsome young Negro, more than a head taller than the slave dealer.

Tommy shouted a '*buenos dias*' to Hernandez – and suddenly felt naked without Vincente at his side. Silly how much he had been dependent on that boy as an interpreter. He was wondering how without a knowledge of Spanish he was going to carry on last-minute negotiations when the Negro shouted up at him. His voice had a marked British accent.

'Mr Verder, Señor Hernandez regrets to inform you that the young slave you liked so much died yesterday. He is offering me to take his place. My name is Trafalgar.'

'That's fine, Trafalgar, but you understand I'll have to finger you first and decide if you pass muster,' Tommy yelled. 'Ask Señor Hernandez to come aboard for a glass of sherry and to bring you along.'

'No sherry,' said Captain MacFarland, who had been listening with interest to the exchange. 'Give him a tot of rum.'

Hernandez climbed the gangplank with the help of the muscular black. He refused the proffered drink but took a seat in the captain's mess, speaking constantly in Spanish during Tommy's examination. That Trafalgar was a perfect physical specimen was evident to the eye but Tommy went through the routine of poking, feeling, hefting the testicles and peeling back the foreskin anyhow. Without being prompted the Negro bent over for Tommy to part his buttocks in a check for haemorrhoids. After straightening up, he took Tommy's silence for approval and asked permission to resume his only garment, a pair of duck trousers. Any other garments, Tommy supposed, would be in the goatskin sack on the deck beside him. He nodded permission.

'You a Fanti?' Tommy asked.

'Yes, Mr Verder, sir.'

'Where'd you learn to speak English?'

'As a boy I was body servant to an officer of the Royal

British Navy, sir. He was killed in the battle of Trafalgar and I was captured by a Spanish naval officer.'

'Who consequently changed your name to Trafalgar?'

'Yes, Mr Verder, sir. And brought me here to Cuba where he sold me at auction. That was some years ago – long enough for me to learn Spanish.'

'Hernandez has been speaking Spanish for the last fifteen minutes without stop. What did he say?'

'He wanted you to know, Mr Verder, sir, that he had been obliged to pay considerably more for me than the average price of the slaves he sold you. However, he does not regret the extra expense because he knows how your heart was set on the unfortunate youngster who died. He hopes you will be pleased.'

'Tell him you'll do nicely.' He would indeed. This was not a plantation hand or a breeder of field hands. Trafalgar would bring a handsome price. He'd like to own him himself. 'You still speak Fanti?'

'Yes, Mr Verder, sir.'

'Then I'm not going to spancel you. You can sort of help out in managing the coffle coming aboard. I hope you got no ideas about running?'

'None, Mr Verder, sir. I'm looking forward to this voyage. I've never been in the American colonies before.'

'They're not colonies any more, not for over 30 years, in case you haven't heard, Trafalgar. Anyhow I'm going to test you. I want you to help Old Man Hernandez ashore. Take him to the end of the pier. I'll be watching you, and I warn you I'm a pretty good shot.'

Trafalgar grinned – showing a wide white octave of teeth. 'You won't have to prove your marksmanship, Mr Verder, sir.'

Tommy liked this big Fanti. He was ingratiating, he was intelligent, and best of all he was respectful. He made Tommy feel he was really a white man just as the bullying of the ship's officers was beginning to make him feel he would never escape the haunting dread that he would always be Calico, the white Negro slave.

25

Tommy stood in the bow of the *Sainte Claire*, relishing the wind in his face, watching the sun sink into the sea. He breathed deeply – the first time in days, it seemed now, that he had really breathed freely. The hurdles of language and doing business in a foreign land had been cleared, his self-created problem of smuggling a fugitive from the country had been successfully solved, and the cargo of blacks and fancy trollops was safely aboard and bound for delivery to Barataria. He hoped the LaFittes would be properly appreciative of his efforts.

The afternoon was well advanced before the *Sainte Claire* had been able to sail. Loading the three hundred slaves and their provender had taken longer than Tommy had calculated and was more trying. The sacks of beans, maize and whatever were carried aboard the sweating backs of shackled blacks themselves. And after surveying the throng of the Africans as they swarmed from the barracoons, Captain MacFarland decided he needed to load more casks of fresh-water – a time-consuming operation, as it turned out.

The actual embarkation of the Negroes had given Tommy a queer uneasy feeling. As they marched aboard in clanking groups of ten he could detect an undercurrent of potential rebellion in their mood, in their bearing, and their incomprehensible talk among themselves. This was going to be his first prolonged contact with *bozals* just off the boat from Africa, and he found the contrast with American-born and domesticated blacks startling. Plantation hands, even when they chafed under the yoke, were good humoured in their resignation. These blacks were surly, resentful at their recent loss of freedom. Even their unfamiliar lingo seemed to have overtones of menace compared to the friendly if highly idiomatic talk of the tame slaves of Alabama.

Tommy sensed the hostility of his charges when, as each group came to the foot of the gangplank, the captain bellowed from the deck: 'Verder, have your niggers pee off the end of the dock before they come aboard. Make them crap, too, if they can. That will delay the stink in the hold for a day or so.'

Tommy transmitted the order to Trafalgar (was he glad to have Trafalgar!), who passed it on to the two overseers Hernandez had sent along. That the message came third-hand did nothing to soften the obvious resentment of the slaves.

He made trips to the hold with the first few groups to oversee the assignment of sleeping space and the attachment of the shackles to the side chains. Keys to the shackles were to be held by Cugino, the flatulent bo's'n, whom the captain had charged with discipline and security. The hold was hot and stifling, and as Tommy watched the sweat dripping from the black bodies, he said to Trafalgar: 'Tell them it won't be so hot when we get to sea.' Was he getting soft?

Trafalgar rendered Tommy's reassurance into Fanti in an expressionless tone. The faces of the blacks were just as expressionless.

Then there had been the unhappy wenches. The birds of the Solano paradise were all very unhappy about being locked in the airless ovenlike cabins during the long process of getting to Regla, loading the blacks, and preparing for sea. They were not bashful about expressing their unhappiness, plaintively at first, then forcefully and finally with violence. The timid knocks and polite requests through the locked doors were followed by pounding and loud demands. Then came kicking, banging, and shouted protests that showed a surprising vocabulary of profanity in several languages, including the English. Tommy wondered which one of his brightskins was threatening, among other things, to 'esheet onda ceiling' if she wasn't let out instantly – and where she had learned her English.

While the sails were being set and the *Sainte Claire* was being towed out to the entrance of the harbour to catch the wind, Tommy began taking the wenches for a walk around the deck, two by two. Perhaps he was being overcautious while the crew was occupied with the business of seamanship, but he felt he might be overextending himself if he exposed more than a pair at a time.

The *Sainte Claire* had cleared the Morro Castle and was headed in a westerly direction on a starboard tack when Tommy had got all the females back under lock and key and given them a sketchy meal. In his own cabin he had billeted the three supposed peeresses. He did not dare hope he could service all three of them this night, but he'd try. At least he wanted to give 'Countess' Panchita a good hump before passing her on to Captain MacFarland as promised. After all the trouble and risks he'd taken to get her out of danger and out of Cuba, he felt he was entitled to the first crack. Then of course he'd have to exorcise himself of his obsession for Princess Koko, she of the splendid pubic shrubbery. Duchess Antoinette might have to wait until morning if the first two exhausted him. They'd have to take turns sharing his bunk. He'd spread a blanket on the floor for the odd peeress...

When he'd finally got all his dozen settled, he made his way forward to stand in the bow and relax. The beauty of the sunset and the quiet of the evening soothed his taut nerves. The clouds that had been piling up along the horizon as the sun went down seemed to catch fire. He had never seen such flaming colours – scarlet, crimson and blood-red streamers that filled the western sky and were reflected in the long oily swells of the Gulf of Mexico. The gulls that had been following them since they left Havana grew golden wings as they swooped and dived after flotsam dumped from the galley.

After a few moments a raucous voice rose above the muted swish of the sea as it was cleft by the prow. Tommy turned. At first he saw only the bellied canvas of the foresails, now dyed pink by the sunset. Then he made out the figure of the first mate, shouting orders at crewmen in the rigging. The mate's beard and polished pate appeared redder than ever in the sunset glow.

When the manoeuvre aloft had been accomplished, the mate came a few steps forward to stand beside Tommy, peering ahead. Tommy felt impelled to make conversation, for Red had been the least objectionable of the officers.

'I was admiring the sunset,' he said. 'Beautiful, isn't it?'

'Not to me it ain't.' The mate did not turn his head.

'Oh? What's wrong?' Tommy hadn't expected an argument.

'Everything. Too damn red, to start with. And I don't like the way them clouds are piling up.'

'Bad sign, is it?' Tommy wished he hadn't started this dialogue.

'Maybe.' The mate shrugged. 'Can't tell. But I don't like it.'

'Of course I don't know much about the sea, Mr First Mate,' Tommy said. 'Before this I made only one sea voyage – from New Orleans to Boston – when I was just a boy. But I've always wondered—'

But the mate was gone. Without a word he had disappeared into the gathering dusk.

The sunset had been fading rapidly for the past few minutes, but now the colours seemed to wink out with a suddenness characteristic of the tropics. The thunderheads billowing above the horizon turned to lead. The first stars pricked through the pale afterglow above. Tommy walked aft.

As he passed an open hatch he paused a moment to listen to snatches of a chant in a minor key that drifted up from the hold. It was a mournful sound and he was sure that if he could understand the words they would be even less cheerful. After all, there was nothing in the immediate future that held much promise for the singers. Tommy toyed with the idea of going down into the hold for a moment to see how the slaves were faring, but abandoned it almost immediately. If there was anything wrong, either one of Hernandez's men or Trafalgar (whom he had left unfettered) would report to him. He had more enjoyable plans for the evening . . .

*

'Hey now, hold on, Countess or Duchess or whatever you claim to be, wait a minute. Stop that, Panchita, don't pull on that. Wait till I get some clothes off.'

As soon as Tommy had entered his cabin he had been set upon by the naked little minx he had saved from being whipped to death. Panchita began undressing him with more enthusiasm than method, pulling and unbuttoning at random. When she had managed to get his trousers down as far as his knees, Tommy took over. Now fully aroused, he pushed her against the edge of the bunk and parted her thighs.

The fact that the bunk was already largely occupied made no difference. Princess Koko was lying there naked, stretched full length, and she languidly raised herself on one elbow to watch. The so-called duchess from Haiti was curled up on the deck in a corner of the cabin. She opened one eye sleepily but apparently found little of interest for she closed it again.

Panchita devoted herself wholeheartedly to her task with great zeal and considerable native talent. While he was enjoying her, he could not help being aware of the teeth that had got her into her near-fatal difficulties. Maybe knowing her history kept him from finding the frenzied piece that he had expected. Perhaps she was merely showing her gratitude – combined of course with natural homage to his superior endowment. Despite his preoccupation with prosaic thoughts, her antics brought him quickly to the glorious heights of sensation. He cried out as his vitality peaked and surged into Panchita.

An instant later he cried out again – in pain.

Princess Koko had bit him on the left buttock!

'Hey!' Tommy had been too engrossed to be aware of Koko's manoeuvring herself into a position where she could dominate his bare bottom.

'Ow!'

She bit him again – on the right buttock.

Damn! Do all these wenches have cannibalistic tendencies?

Tommy remembered she had tried to bite his hand while he was fingering her at Solano's. There was no controlling her now, but he had no time to be alarmed. Inflamed by watching Tommy copulate with Panchita, the Songhai girl moved quickly. She pulled Tommy off Panchita even before he had lost his rigidity. Holding him securely by one arm, she brushed Panchita rudely off the bunk with an elbow. The fugitive countess yelped as her bottom thumped on the deck, but the princess was regally unconcerned.

Koko's eyes were bright with admiration as she clasped Tommy's massive equipment in both hands. She hefted the heavy scrotum like a slave dealer judging the procreative powers of his purchase. Her long fingers tested the rigidity of his erection, then added a few deft strokes to ensure its firmness.

During all this time Tommy was standing immobilized beside the bunk. His pants were still half-masted at his knees leaving him hobbled.

With a little moan Koko fell back on the bunk, clasping Tommy to her full firm breasts, dragging him on top of her. She swung her legs around his bare hips. Tommy felt himself

266

absorbed – that was the only word to describe it – absorbed into the mysterious thicket he had so admired. It was like plunging deep into the heat and humidity of a tropical forest. He drove deeper and deeper...

The next few minutes were indescribable. To Tommy they were more like a wrestling match than anything he had encountered before. The princess rolled her hips and shoulders like a soul in pain. She reared and bucked like a wild mare being broken to the saddle, but her arms and legs tightened around Tommy to keep him close. Her quickening breath came in harmonic gasps, tonal syllables that seemed to link into a plaintive chant. Tommy wondered if this could be some sort of ritual liturgy when the tempo increased and the notes ran together in a thin wail that increased in volume until it became an animal howl. Her body trembled violently like someone in the throes of a high fever. Tommy's whole system vibrated in tempo until he achieved a biological response – and an involuntary shout escaped his lips.

He lay inert and exhausted for a moment when he was aroused by a timid knock on the door. Only when the knock was repeated did he summon the energy to reply: 'Who's there?'

'Petty officer of the watch, sir,' came the answer. 'Need any help, Mr Verder?'

'No, no, no help, thank you,' said Tommy. He really could use a little help but nothing the petty officer of the watch could provide.

'You're sure you're all right, Mr Verder?'

'Yes, sure. Fine. I'm all right.'

'You're not in any trouble, sure? I thought I heard—'

'Oh that,' said Tommy, trying to sound reassuring. 'Well I guess we were having a sort of heated argument in here. Sorry we disturbed you. Everything's fine. Good night now.'

'Good night, Mr Verder.'

Nice young fellow, that, Tommy mused. Must speak to captain in the morning. Put in a good word for him. Put in a – Tommy fell fast asleep regretting he had not been able to service the young Frenchified wench from Haiti ... must apologize ... must take care of her ... morning...

The banging on the door would have wakened anyone three

days dead. Tommy sat up suddenly, every nerve a-quiver from being roused from a profound slumber.

The banging – it was not the timid knock of the petty officer of the watch – was repeated noisily.

'Who is it?' Tommy asked. It was pitch dark. The one candle had gone out.

'Nevva mind who,' said a grating voice, that Tommy recognized as belonging to Cugino, the bo's'n. 'It's the skipper wants to see you, not me sure as hell. Better haul your ass up to the wheelhouse and pronto.'

'What's the skipper want?' Tommy asked. No answer. Cugino had delivered the message and left.

When Tommy tried to swing his legs off the bunk he realized he was still hobbled. His legs were still entangled in his lowered trousers. He managed to hoist the pants waist high and, fumbling in the dark, found the buttons. He could not find his shirt but since his undergarment was in place he was more or less respectable. He opened the door slowly and looked out. A lantern burned dimly in the empty passageway. He started forward towards the wheelhouse.

Only Captain MacFarland's face was visible in the glow from the binnacle lamp as Tommy entered.

'So ye've come, Verder,' the skipper said. 'As ye probably know, we've a stowaway aboard.'

'A stowaway?'

'Aye. Cook caught 'im stealin' vittles in the galley.'

'But why should I know about it?'

'Ye sneaked 'im aboard. He's your lad. Stand up, scum!'

His eyes accustomed now to the gloom, Tommy made out a figure cowering in a corner, untangling his legs to stand up.

'Vincente!' Tommy was astounded. 'How ... why ...?'

'Just couldn't stand your going away, Señor Tommy.' If the lad was contrite it didn't show in his voice.

'You disobeyed me!' Tommy was indignant and it did show. 'You promised to take care of Perla, and here you are miles away from Havana. You promised to learn to read, and—'

'Enough talk,' the skipper interrupted. 'Verder, I'm assumin' this brat did not come aboard with your connivance.'

'He sure didn't!' Tommy shook his head emphatically.

'Then he's a downright stowaway,' the captain declared. 'I could put 'im in the brig, but I'll put 'im to work instead. He can earn his passage in the hold, helpin' tend the niggers.' He cupped his hand and shouted: 'Bo's'n!'

'Señor Tommy, help me.'

'He can't help you. I'm master of this barque. Bo's'n!'

'Señor Tommy, you won't let them send me back to Cuba? Please! Vincente help you fool police with that Panchita wench, no? Please don't send me back, Señor Tommy!' Vincente was on his knees.

'Once we dock what happens to 'im is up to Jean LaFitte,' the captain said. 'Bo's'n...! Ah, yer here at last. Bo's'n, take this stowaway and lock 'im up till morning. Then set 'im to emptyin' slop buckets and moppin' the hold. And between times he can holystone the afterdeck.'

'Aye, sir,' Cugino grabbed Vincente's arm and yanked him to his feet. 'Come along, spick.' He pushed him from the wheelhouse with a raised knee.

Captain MacFarland was silent for a long moment. Only the upper part of his body was illuminated by the binnacle lantern, making him look like the sculptured bust of a Roman emperor. The light emphasized the bib-like fringe of his grey beard, transforming it into a jawbone of pewter. He was staring straight ahead as he announced:

'That's all, Verder. Ye can now go back to yer friggin'.'

26

Tommy was not sure what had awakened him. At first he thought it was the motion of the ship which during the night had developed a side-to side roll in addition to her slow rise and fall as she slid over the long swells. Then he became aware of a pleasurable sensation in the vicinity of his groin. He opened his eyes.

Lying prone at the foot of the bunk he saw the so-called

duchess from Haiti, her full bosom bulging against his knees as she watched the growing effect of her busy hands. Her eyes were wide with surprise and admiration as the dimensions expanded. Her head moved forward, her lips parted.

Tommy sat up suddenly, torn between desire and alarm. He had to be wary of these tropical wenches. Impossible to tell whether they were going to kiss or bite. He'd take no chances. Reaching out he seized the Haitian girl under the arms and turned her on her back. Then he crawled over to begin the orthodox papa-mama routine, always a pleasant if unimaginative way to start the day. He was warming up to his task and quietly approaching a climax when there was a knock on the door.

In full crescendo Tommy couldn't possibly stop what he was doing. His breath was coming in short gasps so he couldn't even ask who was there.

The knock was repeated. Tommy was not only breathless and speechless but was floating somewhere in space.

'*Quién es?*' It was Panchita who awoke to challenge the intruder.

'Mr Verder there?'

Panchita looked around the cabin. '*El señor esta muy ocupado,*' she said. 'Veree beezy.'

'I gotta see Mr Verder,' the voice insisted.

Tommy returned to earth. He managed to collect his faculties and summon enough strength to call out, 'Who is it?'

'It's me – Pops.' Pops was the ship's cook, a venerable Greek from Malta whose full name was Something-populos. 'I got coffee for you.'

'Just a second.' Tommy disengaged himself from the Haitian duchess and got off the bunk. He opened the door just wide enough to take the steaming mug Pops handed him.

'I gotta talk to you, Mr Verder.' The cook tried to open the door wider but Tommy pushed it shut.

'Later,' Tommy said. 'I'll be in for breakfast in ten or fifteen minutes.'

He looked around for means of making a rudimentary toilet. There wasn't even a bucket of water. He surely missed the services of poor Ramon. Maybe he could get the captain to let Vincente serve him, now that the boy was on board. Or

Trafalgar? That was the answer, Trafalgar. The big black had once been a naval officer's servant...

When Tommy sat down at the bare table used by the ship's officers, he was clad in his seagoing togs – old denim pants and a torn shirt. He was alone in the mess; the officers had breakfasted much earlier. The cook came in with more coffee.

'Morning,' said Pops. The ends of his long white handle-bar moustache turned down, giving his rugged face a mournful expression. 'You want me to cook some of your eggs now?'

'My eggs?' Tommy was puzzled.

'Yoh, must be yours. I didn't believe him when he said he brought 'em, but—'

'Who didn't you believe?' Tommy interrupted.

'That Cuban kid been hanging around you all week. I catch him in galley with sack of eggs. He say he bring eggs for you, but I think he stole 'em, so I take him to skipper. Guess I done him wrong, because this morning when I count eggs I find fifteen extra. I go to skipper again and say my mistake, but skipper say no difference, he stowaway. You want now eggs? How you want I fry? Upside down?'

'Upside down is fine,' Tommy replied absently. He was thinking about Vincente. What a tricky little bastard! But not all bad. He had been considerate and useful and often kind in helping him. Of course there was no doubt that he was trying to make himself indispensable, so that Tommy would take him along to Louisiana. He wondered now if Vincente might even have engineered the murder of poor Ramon, just to clear the way for his own employment as body servant as well as interpreter. He had certainly brought those eggs as a sort of counter-irritant to Tommy's wrath at finding him aboard against orders. He had doubtless remembered hearing Tommy complain of the lack of eggs on the menu during the outward voyage of the *Sainte Claire*. He had probably planned to make his first official appearance this morning, serving Tommy a plate of eggs – a double surprise.

Well, he could certainly use a flunkey as able and willing as Vincente. Maybe Tommy would talk to the captain about him after all, despite his resentment over the boy's flouting of his wishes. And his leaving Perla. Funny he should be disturbed about Perla. He wasn't worried about her getting along without Vincente. It was just that he hated to see her youth and talents wasted when they might have brought profit to the three of them.

After breakfast Tommy went on deck for a breath of air and a limited walk. The weather seemed to have deteriorated overnight. The wind had risen to set up an eerie humming in the rigging. The land birds were no longer following the ship. Scraps of low cloud scudded rapidly beneath the high dome of the dark overcast. The motion of the ship had changed again. Instead of the stately waltz-time to which she had glided over the long swells, she now danced to a quicker, nervous tempo. Tommy didn't like it; he had a restless feeling in his stomach. He stepped to the rail. He had never known seasickness and had no intention of learning about it now. He had every intention of keeping possession of his breakfast eggs. He looked over the side and noticed for the first time that the surface of the sea seemed strewn with some sort of orange vegetation, like a field of marigolds. He strolled towards the wheelhouse.

The first mate stood outside, his legs apart, his red beard parted by the wind as he lifted his head to study the set of sails. Tommy waited until his observation was apparently completed before approaching him.

'Morning, Mr First Mate,' he said. 'Quite a strong breeze blowing today.'

'Yes,' said the mate.

'Think it will help speed up our trip home?'

'No.'

Red Reddy was evidently not in a talkative mood. Tommy decided not to ask him about good or bad signs. He would generalize the one-sided conversation.

'What's all that yellow-brown stuff floating out there?' Tommy pointed.

'Gulfweed.' The mate shook his head. 'Don't know why they call it gulfweed. Don't grow mostly in the Gulf here. Books call it sargassum 'cause it grows in the Sargasso Sea.' He frowned. 'Never see this much of it this far west at this time of year.'

Tommy didn't ask for an explanation. He was sure it would not be favourable. He asked: 'Captain MacFarland in the wheelhouse?'

The mate shook his head. 'Skipper's gone below to get some sleep in advance,' he said. 'Expects to be on watch all or most of the next twenty-four or forty-eight hours.'

'Oh,' said Tommy. 'Why?'

'Glass is way down,' was the reply, 'and still dropping.'

'Oh,' Tommy said again. He didn't understand what glass was down or what was in it, or what it could possibly have to do with the captain's sleep. He'd rather not know. From the ominous expression on the mate's ruddy face he judged there was bad news in the offing.

'You ain't asked my advice,' said the mate, suddenly speaking without a question to prime him, 'but if I was you I'd start bringing your niggers up out a that hold in tens and twenties, so they empty their guts and pee to windward. My guess is that we'll have to batten down the hatches afore nightfall.'

'I appreciate the tip.' Tommy felt a twinge of guilt. He had been avoiding the hold, telling himself that his mission was accomplished once he got the slaves aboard. He knew better, of course. Until every one of the three hundred was delivered to Barataria, his job was not yet done. 'I'll see the bo's'n at once. He's got the keys.'

'You still ain't asked my advice,' the mate said, staring up at the bulging foresail, 'but if I was you I'd take a look at those niggers yourself. They're your responsibility.' And he walked away.

As Tommy climbed down the ladder into the hold, clinging tightly to each rung to avoid being swung off by the motion of the ship, he realized he hadn't seen Trafalgar since the previous evening. He remembered he had purposely left the big fellow unfettered so that he could make periodic reports on the state of the cargo. What with the excitement of Vincente's unexpected appearance and his own eagerness to sample his purchases from Solano, he had been neglecting the business at hand. Still he could not understand why Trafalgar had failed to report, and thus remind him that he was still working for the LaFittes.

The further Tommy descended into the hold, the more fetid became the atmosphere. Despite the fact that the hatches were open, the warm effluvia from three hundred sweating Negro bodies was almost overpowering. Even in the open air of the barracoons black flesh in the mass was redolent with a special funkiness, and here within the confines of a ship's hold in the tropics the stench was an active threat to the stability of Tommy's queasy stomach. He swallowed hard as he stepped off the bottom rung and started walking into the half-light. He became aware of a strange dissonance, the chorus of a hundred alien tongues blending in an ugly buzz.

'Trafalgar!' Tommy shouted. He peered into the gloom. The angry buzz – Tommy couldn't tell why he thought it was angry, but that was his conviction – stopped suddenly. The silence was eloquent. Tommy had to shift his feet to keep his balance on the slanting deck reacting to a deep roll of the ship. The changed angle allowed a broad beam of sunlight to flash across the hold, striking sparks from the chains that stretched alongside the rude bunks.

'Trafalgar!' Tommy called again. 'Trafalgar, where are you?'

A small, halting voice pierced the silence. 'I'm here, sir.'

Ten quick strides brought Tommy to the point where the voice originated. Trafalgar was lying on a mid-tier bunk completely naked, shackled hand and foot, the foot-shackles attached to the running chain. There were dark stains on his rumpled white duck trousers which lay on the deck nearby. He did not look at Tommy.

'Trafalgar, what's going on here?' Tommy was shocked. 'I gave instructions you were not to be spancelled. Why are you shackled like this?'

'Because I resisted,' said the big Fanti, eyes still averted.

'Resisted who?'

'The man with no forehead. A white man whose black hair grows down to meet his eyebrows.'

Damn! The description fitted Cugino. What right had the bo's'n to chain up this man? He'd have to get the keys back.

'I'll get the keys and unlock you right away,' he said.

'Mr Verder, sir, am I *your* slave?' Trafalgar turned his head so that he looked squarely at Tommy with anguished eyes. 'Do I belong to you?'

'Well, in a way, yes. Temporarily. But I bought you on behalf of Jean and Pierre LaFitte.'

Trafalgar sighed. 'Mr Verder, sir,' he said, 'I quite understand that as a slave I have no rights. I am a piece of property. You as my master can do with me as you will. But my previous masters have always respected my rights to my own person. I mean except for being lent to a friend occasionally to impregnate a female slave, my body is at the sole disposition of my master. Mr Verder, sir, have you authorized anyone—? I mean, sir, am I expected to submit to—?'

'Good God!' Tommy interrupted. 'Did that son-of-a-bitch of a bo's'n chain you up so he could—? Why damn his eyes!'

Trafalgar nodded sadly. 'It was a painful experience, Mr Verder, sir,' he said, 'and believe it or not, my first – in spite of my years in His Majesty's Navy.'

'Damn his eyes!' Tommy repeated. He was truly outraged, not so much by the painful violation of Trafalgar's person, but by the bo's'n's consummate gall in chaining up a slave that Tommy wanted left free to serve him.

He was suddenly conscious of dozens of eyes in addition to Trafalgar's staring at him. Every slave within earshot seemed to be trying to understand their conversation. Some were listening propped up on an elbow, others were sitting up as best they could. One man was standing up on his third-tier bunk to see better. The occasional clank and rattle of chains sounded very loud in the silence.

'I'm going to complain to the captain,' said Tommy.

Trafalgar translated into Fanti, and a murmur ran through the nearby bunks, spreading through the hold. Tommy couldn't tell if it was approval or indignation. 'I'll be back soon,' he said, patting the Fanti on the shoulder.

'Mr Verder, sir, could you tarry another moment, sir?' Trafalgar pleaded with his eyes. 'If you are seeing the captain, sir, you might tell him we are ill fed here. Señor Hernandez's men are now engaged in the morning feeding. Perhaps you should observe them, Mr Verder, sir. They are coming down this aisle now. It will just take a minute, sir.'

The Fanti gestured with his head and Tommy's gaze shifted to the direction indicated. Hernandez's men were only four or five bunks away now. Each carried two buckets and a gourd dipper. The first man would set down the buckets in front of the tier and ladle out a dipperful of some viscous pottage.

Each slave would hold up two cupped hands close to his face while the slumgullion was poured into them. When some of the sticky stuff could drip through his fingers the slave would carefully lick his hands front and back after he had swallowed the double handful. Then the second man would pass a gourdful of water.

Tommy turned his head away. His gorge rose. His queasy stomach wouldn't let him watch any longer. He swallowed repeatedly.

'What . . . what's in that stuff?' he asked.

'Heaven only knows, Mr Verder, sir. Beans, I suppose. Stale bread possibly. Scraps of inferior meat. Wormy maize probably. Rather nasty on the whole, Mr Verder, sir, and definitely scanty. Last night it ran out before they reached the end of the aisle. Tell the captain, sir, that we're grown men and should be fed full rations.'

'I'll tell him, Trafalgar. But now—'

'Another thing, Mr Verder, sir. Is there a doctor aboard?'

'Afraid not, Trafalgar.' Tommy swallowed harder. The stench, plus the sight of the feeding system which reminded him of the way they slopped the pigs at Dove Cote and Falconhurst, were doing things to his stomach. He'd have to reach fresh air soon. 'The captain has the key to the medicine chest and the carpenter sets broken bones, makes bandages, and gives out purges. Did that bastard really hurt you?'

'It's not me, Mr Verder, sir. It's the man just below me. He has an awful bellyache, sir. He was moaning before he fell asleep.'

'Probably just seasickness,' Tommy said. 'Well, I've got to see the captain.'

Tommy's hand-over-hand ascent up the ladder was so rapid that he was not even aware of the roll of the ship. He fairly leaped up the last two rungs and sprawled on the deck. He lay for a moment breathing deeply. When he stumbled to his feet he had trouble keeping his balance. A lash of salt spray stung his face.

He found the skipper standing outside the wheelhouse, scanning the horizon through a spyglass. The first mate was standing beside him, facing in the opposite direction, head bent back, shouting orders to crewmen aloft.

'Captain MacFarland,' said Tommy, 'I'd like to lodge a complaint against your bo's'n. He's spancelled a man I wanted for a body servant. What's more, he took advantage of his helplessness to sodomize the poor fellow. I demand that Cugino turn over to me the keys that unlock the spancels.'

The captain did not answer at once. He was still peering through his spyglass. When he lowered the long glass he said:

'Ye come at a bad moment, Verder. I've no time to supervise the sexual behaviour of my officers or men. The slaves are your responsibility entirely. Ye want the keys, find the bo's'n and take them. Meanwhile, look there.' He pointed.

Against the darkness of the lowering clouds Tommy could make out the darker outlines of two monstrous funnel-shaped spectres. The broad ends of the funnels reached up into the sky while the tapering stems twisted downward to meet the sea near the horizon.

'What's that?' he asked.

'Water spouts,' the captain replied. 'Sea-goin' tornadoes. That's just the start.'

27

The hatches had been battened down for two days. The nightmare had begun within an hour after the captain had pointed out the water spouts to Tommy. The wind had risen almost to gale force before the afternoon was well advanced. Before nightfall the seas were running high and the waves had assumed what had seemed to Tommy to be mountainous proportions. Driving rain swept the decks. The *Sainte Claire* would lift sickeningly as it climbed the near side of a wave, then plunge dizzily into the trough of the next. Green water poured over the bow to run along the deck in a boiling white torrent. Cries of surprised anguish arose from the hold as the flood streamed into the open hatches.

Sailors appeared from nowhere to drag the hatch covers into place and haul tarpaulins over them. Tommy had protested to the captain.

'They'll smother to death in there, skipper.'

'Can't be helped, Verder. You can see for yourself, the sea pourin' in. They'll not only all be drowned, but the *Sainte Claire* will founder with the rest of us.'

'You'll destroy a valuable cargo, skipper.'

'Maybe half will survive.' MacFarland had to shout to be heard above the howl of the wind and the rush of water in the scuppers. 'They won't all suffocate in their own stink.'

The captain had walked away to bellow at half a dozen sailors inching their way up the shrouds, holding onto the ratlines for dear life. The skipper was reducing sail. The barque was barely answering her helm.

That night had been a harrowing experience. The captain's last words had been 'fer Godsake, Verder, stay inside, but if you have to come on deck keep to leeward if you can find the lee, and hang on like a leech to whatever you can find that's tied down'. Tommy managed to reach his cabin after nearly knocking himself out banging his head against the bulkheads on the way, trying to keep his balance. There was complete silence when he entered. The cook had left a tray of bread and dried beef, but it had been untouched. The three wenches were sitting stiffly side by side on the edge of the bunk, obviously terrified. When he had opened the door the candle flickered and went out.

There was plenty to be frightened about, Tommy reflected as he shed enough of his spray-dampened clothing to be comfortable. The creaking of the timbers as the ship seemed to soar on the crest of a wave, and the shuddering crash as she ploughed into the trough; the rush of water along the deck and the gurgling in the scuppers; the shriek of the wind in the shrouds, and the thunderclap of canvas as the sails caught a change of helm or sudden shift in the erratic blasts ... No wonder the trollops were cowed.

He pushed his way between two wenches to stretch out full length on the bunk behind the row of them. He lay with his eyes open, listening to the ominous ship noises. He had no thought of sleep or love-making. The wenches were equally uninterested in sex; they were too sure that this night would be their last. Tommy could feel one of them trembling as she inched backward against him.

Suddenly a crash more violent than anything that had come before shook the ship. The *Sainte Claire* shuddered and stood on her beam ends. Tommy and the trio of Fancies were thrown off the bunk and dumped brusquely to the deck. There was one scream, then all lay in a silent heap.

What seemed like minutes passed, and the deck still slanted precariously, keeping Tommy and the three women, now a tangle of arms and legs, pressed tightly against the bulkhead. Pots and pans clanked to the galley deck and there was the crash and clatter of breaking crockery somewhere in the offing. Tommy was still entwined with female flesh. Would the ship never right itself?

At last by a series of little lurches the craft gradually had gained an even keel, only to heel over the other way. One of the wenches – he could not tell which one in the darkness – whispered. Someone else reached out and touched him; he thought it was Panchita. The warmth of her fingers aroused him, and he lifted an arm to clasp her to him. Still not sure who she was, he quietly, almost imperceptibly, entered her.

It was an embrace without passion – a gesture of fear seeking security, of near-panic finding calm reassurance. Another hand reached out to hold his. He felt a cheek pressing against the cheeks of his buttocks. He fell asleep.

*

There had been no abatement of the storm by next morning. The *Sainte Claire* was certainly proving she was seaworthy, with all the violent battering she had been undergoing. The galley was a mess, however. There was no hot breakfast. One particularly big wave cascading the length of the craft had extinguished the fire in the cook stove and ruined half the comestibles in the food locker. Tommy hoped his live cargo was not deteriorating too much under storm conditions. He had better do what he could to keep them in the best shape possible. He'd see the skipper.

Making his precarious way along the careening, slippery deck, he was drenched before he reached the wheelhouse. He envied the captain his yellow oilskins, but not his worried frown or his bloodshot eyes. The man had obviously not slept.

'Captain MacFarland,' Tommy began, 'we got to do something about those slaves.'

'They're your niggers,' the captain said. 'You bought 'em.'

'But since you battened the hatches, they're without food and water, captain.'

'They can go without vittles for a few days. They'd only puke it up anyhow in this weather. And there's a dozen barrels of drinkin' water in the hold.'

'They can't get to it, captain. They're shackled.'

MacFarland turned away from Tommy to shout orders to the helmsman. The wheel had spun violently from his grasp.

'What the hell happened to those two nigger-tamers we shipped at Regla?' MacFarland asked at last.

'They were caught up here on deck when the hatch covers went on, skipper. You can't let LaFitte's niggers rot down there.' Tommy had pleaded in earnest. He had not become a humanitarian overnight, but he was determined that the slaves should be delivered in as good condition as possible. That was his job.

'All right, lad. Then go below yourself. There's a small ventilatin' hatch aft that's big enough to accommodate a man your size. I'll have it opened and lower you down with a rope.'

Tommy was taken aback. The very thought of the foul-smelling, revolting mess that must be in the hold by now – the stink of urine, faeces, and vomit – brought him to the verge of vomiting himself. He'd have to think quickly.

'I have a better idea,' he said. 'Turn my boy Vincente loose until we get to Barataria and we'll lower him into the hold to take things in hand and report. I agree with you that a stowaway must be punished. But let him work for me until we reach port. Where has the bo's'n got him locked up? Where is that bastard of a bo's'n?'

'Leave the bo's'n be, Verder,' shouted the captain to be heard above the wind. The *Sainte Claire* sloped sharply to starboard. 'For once he's earnin' his screw. He's aloft with the men, reefin' sail. We're about to heave to. In another hour our canvas'll be whipped to shreds.'

'But the boy, captain.'

'If I know the bo's'n, ye'll find the boy locked in Cugino's cabin. Here's a master key. Now busy yourself with land-lubbers' business and let the rest of us deal with the sea.'

As the captain had predicted, Tommy found Vincente locked in Cugino's cabin. The lad was lying prone on the deck when the door swung open. He sprang up, cringing, until he recognized Tommy. Then he dropped to his knees, clasping Tommy's legs.

'Oh Señor Tommy, what joy!' he exclaimed. 'Get me out of here.'

'You've no right being aboard in the first place,' Tommy said. 'You're getting only what's coming to you. Where the hell are your pants?'

'I do not know, Señor Tommy. That fella hid them. *Qué animal*, Señor Tommy. *Qué bruto*. He almost hung heavy like you. I hurt when I sit down. Please, Señor Tommy.'

'Stand up, Vincente. Don't snivel. You asked for whatever you're getting. I don't know what will happen when we get to Barataria, but I'm going to let you out of here on one con-dition. You'll go down into the hold and do what you can for those niggers I bought. See that they get water and whatever food you can find. I don't want to have to carry them off feet first when we get to port. All right?' Tommy stuck his lower jaw out to emphasize he meant what he said.

'I not like to be *ama de cria* for no niggers.' Vincente sulked. 'Do I got to be nurse maid to those *bozals*?'

'Yes. Unless you want to stay locked in here.'

'All right then, if you say so, Señor Tommy.'

So Vincente had been lowered by rope through the ventila-tion hatch – alone. Tommy had found Hernandez's men so seasick they were useless. The lad had been hauled up again at nightfall, pale and shaken. He had staggered to the rail to throw up for five minutes without stopping.

'*Qué zahurda!*' he exclaimed when he could speak. A pigsty would be like the Hotel de Paris in comparison. He had given water to the slaves. They were miserable. Those who weren't too seasick were furious. That big Fanti fellow was double furious. 'No food, no water, and he got sore ass-hole too,' Vincente had said. 'Then that fella in next bunk gonna die. He got *la plaga*, I think.'

281

'Just seasick probably.' Tommy had to keep trying to convince himself that his diagnosis was correct. The opposite was too dreadful to contemplate.

'I think no.' Vincente shook his head. 'He don't crap crap. He crap like bath water. He puke water too. *La plaga*, I think. When you gonna unlock the shackles, Señor Tommy?'

'When the storm's over Vincente. The captain won't let me bother the bo's'n for the keys while he's working to keep us afloat.'

'Do I have to go back in that filthy stinking place again, Señor Tommy? Please no. I'll die, Señor Tommy.'

'You'll go back tomorrow morning. That's part of your punishment. You can sleep in the passageway in front of my cabin tonight. But when the hatches are opened, you'll help clean up the mess.' Tommy himself gagged at the thought of the process. 'The captain says we'll have to get the slaves on deck and pump water into the hold to sluice the shit into the bilges.'

Vincente stumbled to the leeward rail and threw up again.

*

During the third night after the hatches were closed the wind dropped to moderate gale force, according to the captain, and by next morning the sea had begun to flatten out. When Tommy came on deck, the crew was already at work repairing the damage. The staysails had been blown away. The fore topsail had been ripped to shreds before it could be reefed, and the yard split. The tarpaulin covering one of the hatches had been torn to tatters. But at last MacFarland ordered the hatches opened.

Tommy stood by while the tarpaulins were dragged away, the battens knocked off, and the covers lifted. He imagined he could actually see the effluvia rising; he could certainly smell it from a distance. He waited five minutes before he sent Vincente and the two Hernandez men down to test the noxious fumes like canaries in a coal mine. When they had gone down the ladder he listened for cries or other sounds indicating trouble. There were none. At last he summoned the courage to go down the ladder into the nauseous atmosphere himself. The stench was unbelievable. He retched three times before he felt strong enough to push his way to the bunk occupied by Trafalgar.

'Trafalgar!' The Big Fanti was lying with his back to Tommy. He did not turn around.

'You all right, Trafalgar?'

'By the grace of God,' said Trafalgar. He still didn't turn around. 'You were in no hurry to come back to see us, Mister Verder, sir.'

'Oh but I was, Trafalgar. But there was trouble with the weather, as you may have guessed.'

'We guessed.' Trafalgar gestured over his shoulder with his two manacled hands. 'If it's of any interest to you, Mr Verder, sir, the man in the next bunk is dead.'

'Dead?' Tommy took a step backward. 'What...? How ...?'

'Cholera,' said Trafalgar.

'Then it's not what the Cubans call *la plaga*?'

'That's one of the maladies the Cubans call *la plaga*,' Trafalgar replied. 'But in India where I served a year with my master, Lieutenant-commander Smith, they call it cholera. I've seen much of it. The symptoms are unmistakable. The pains, the high fever, the vomiting and diarrhoea like skimmed milk ... You'd better report it to the captain, Mr Verder, sir.'

'Yes. Yes, of course.' With scarcely a glance at the man in the next bunk who was obviously dead, Tommy fled. He went up the ladder to the upper deck.

Captain MacFarland was not exactly overjoyed by the news. He located the bo's'n on a yard arm and ordered him to go below and release the dead man for tossing overside.

Ten minutes later Cugino was in the hold with his keys. He prodded the corpse with the toe of his boot and asked Trafalgar: 'When did he die?'

'Last night.' Trafalgar turned around at last. He tried to sit up. 'It was cholera.'

'Nobody ast you what it was.' The bo's'n drew out a set of keys, inserted one on the dead man's manacles, unlocked them and yanked the corpse to the deck.

At that moment Trafalgar sat erect, raised his arms high

above his head and brought them down viciously. The steel fetters crashed against the back of Cugino's head. The bo's'n collapsed against Trafalgar.

Trafalgar once more raised his arms and swung the manacles again and again until the back of the bo's'n's head was a bloody pulp. Blood ran from Cugino's eyes, gushed from his nose and mouth, dripping off Trafalgar's knees to form an expanding puddle on the deck.

When Trafalgar was convinced that he was dead, he pushed him off to slide to the deck. He took the keys from Cugino's dead fingers and unlocked his own fetters, one by one. Then, with a savage cry he whirled the manacles about his head and brought them down again to slash the dead man's face.

'You bastard, you bastard, you dirty bastard!' he screamed. Then, to make sure the spirit of the late bo's'n understood, he repeated the insult in half a dozen other languages. *'Puerco maldito! Suwar-ka-bacha! Sale con!'*

His voice rose in tone and in volume. The suave British veneer of speech, the product of his youth as a body servant in His Britannic Majesty's Navy, suddenly evaporated. His savage scream came from deep in the jungles of Africa. The elemental values of his ancestors came shrieking back through the centuries with all their naked cruelty. He stopped to pluck a knife from the belt of the dead bo's'n. Brandishing the blade above his head, he leapt along the tiers of bunks, howling in Fanti or some dialect of Ashanti, stopping before each black who had the strength to raise himself, and unlocking the fetters. His yells were echoed as more and more Negroes jumped up on release from their irons, swinging the manacles as weapons in imitation of Trafalgar.

Vincente, who had been tempted to follow Tommy up the ladder when he left to report the death of the cholera victim, was shocked into immobility by the brutal murder of Cugino. As much as he hated the bo's'n, he was stunned by the emergence of stark savagery from the apparent urbanity of Trafalgar. And when the significance of Trafalgar's release of the slaves finally dawned on him and he started for the ladder to warn Tommy, he was caught in the beginning of the stampede. Yelling blacks, swinging their unlocked fetters above them, were already blocking the approach to the ladder.

Vincente reversed his course. As he ran aft, he was bucking the stream of released slaves and was knocked down twice by blindly rushing black giants. He was heading for a patch of daylight he had spotted towards the last tier of bunks. He hoped there was a ladder there leading to the upper deck, and that he would find Tommy in time to alert him before the potential mutiny had gained momentum.

28

'What the bloody hell is *la plaga*?' demanded Captain Mac-Farland.

'I'm not sure, skipper,' Tommy replied, still shaken. 'But that big Fanti, the ex-flunkey to a British naval officer, says it's what in India they call the cholera.'

'Cholera!' The captain's eloquent eyebrows rose in alarm. 'Hell's bells and Paul's balls! If we got cholera aboard, we're sunk. We'll be lucky if we don't lose all your niggers and half my crew. Get the hell below and make sure the bo's'n jettisons the dead nigger overside first thing.'

'Right away, skipper. I sure don't enjoy cruising with a dead man.'

'Another thing, Verder.' The captain grabbed Tommy's arm. 'Find Joe the carpenter. If he's sober enough tell him I want him to go with you and see if he recognizes any more cholera cases among your niggers. If he finds any symptoms at all, we have to get rid of the poor bastards before we all get it.'

'Right away, skipper.'

Tommy had scarcely left the wheelhouse when he saw the first of the Negroes come swarming up out of the hold. He was puzzled at first. He wondered what the hell had got into that bastard of a bo's'n that he had unshackled the slaves and let them come on deck in such numbers without their usual escort. There must be thirty or forty and they were still coming. It was only when a chorus of yells arose from the blacks and they began to move away from the hatch, the pallid sun flashing on the manacles which they twirled above their heads, that his puzzlement gave way to alarm. At the same moment he heard a voice behind him shouting: 'Señor Tommy, Señor Tommy! Your keys! quick your keys!'

Tommy turned to face a harried Vincente. 'What's up, boy?' he demanded. 'Where's the bo's'n?'

'That *maricon* is dead. Killed. Your keys, Señor Tommy. Quick. I must get your pistol. I know where it's packed.'

'We don't want any gun play, Vincente. Why—?'

'You must have pistol, Señor Tommy. We have *motin*, I think. There is riot.'

'All right, get the gun.' Tommy produced the key to his cabin. 'But don't shoot. I don't want to lose any more of my slaves. And Vincente – don't feel with the wenches.'

Vincente ran.

The naked blacks were now advancing towards the wheel-house nearly a hundred strong. At their head Tommy saw Trafalgar, knife in hand. Tommy walked to meet him.

Behind him he heard the captain bawling for the first mate. The significance of what was happening was immediately clear to MacFarland.

'You will muster the starboard watch immediately, Mr Reddy!' he ordered.

Tommy planted himself in the path of the big Fanti slave. 'Look here, Trafalgar,' he said, trying to sound calm. 'Where do you think you're going with those men?'

'Out of the way, Mr Verder, sir. We are going to confront the captain.'

'Ye'll do nought of the sort,' bellowed the captain. 'Take yer bloody blackamoors below where they belong.'

'Stand aside, Verder.' No more *Mr Verder, sir*. The dead bo's'n's knife flashed in Trafalgar's hand.

A dozen sailors of the starboard watch came trotting around the wheelhouse carrying capstan bars and brandishing rope ends. Trafalgar shouted something in Fanti, and the Negroes yelled in unison. They advanced slowly, swinging their fetters in overhead circles.

'Have your men charge, Mr Reddy!' ordered the captain.

Before the sailors could move twenty Negroes released their

286

spinning shackles like missiles. A cloud of metal flew glittering through the air. Two sailors went down. The line of capstan bars and thrashing rope ends moved forward.

'Here, Señor Tommy.' Vincente breathlessly handed Tommy his new-fangled gun. 'Bullets already in.'

A length of chain struck Tommy on the cheek bone. He went over backward, one hand raised to his bleeding face. Trafalgar stooped to snatch the pistol from Tommy's fingers. Vincente tried to grab it back. The Fanti kicked him in the groin. Vincente howled, released the gun, and clasped his lower abdomen.

The swinging fetters were giving way before the longer capstan bars. The battle was still joined, however, and there were bloodied heads on both sides.

While Trafalgar was fumbling with the unfamiliar mechanism of Tommy's pistol, Captain MacFarland was again bawling orders.

'Mr Reddy,' he shouted, 'I want these bloody niggers back in the hold immediately!'

'One moment, Captain.' Trafalgar had resumed some of his former dignity. He threw back his shoulders. 'We are slaves, sir, but we are also men, not animals. Before we return to the filth and muck—'

'Ye'll go at once!' the captain roared. 'I'm still master here!'

'No longer.' Trafalgar raised his right arm. Tommy's pistol in his hand was aimed at MacFarland.

The first mate shouted.

A shriek rose from a hundred black throats.

Trafalgar pulled the trigger. The hammer clicked down. The charge did not ignite.

Captain MacFarland calmly drew a duelling pistol from his waistband, pointed the long barrel at Trafalgar, and fired.

The big Fanti's torso jerked backward, then straightened up. He seemed to be making an effort to keep his arm outstretched, but inch by inch it went down. The gun dropped from his fingers, and his knees buckled. He collapsed to the deck in slow motion. Blood oozed from his head to make a crimson halo. Or was it a setting sun? The Trafalgar mutiny was over.

The whirling manacles stopped whirling and fell limply.

The rebellious chorus was silent. The black phalanx retreated step by step.

Vincente retrieved the pistol which had failed Trafalgar. Then he put his arms around Tommy and lifted him to a sitting position on the deck. He tore strips from the shirt-tail of his long Cuban shirt and tried to wipe the blood off Tommy's face. The wound was merely seeping blood now.

'Mr Reddy,' the captain called to his first mate. He had quickly put away the duelling pistol. 'Please select whatever men you will need from the starboard watch to carry out the following duties. One, I'll want a guard to ensure that the nigger mutineers remain in their present position on deck. Two, you will immediately dispose of the corpse of the mutinous nigger I had to kill to maintain discipline. Three, you will take a detail to the hold to reclaim the bodies of Bo's'n Cugino and the slave who died of cholera, taking precautions, naturally, to protect yourselves against infection. Four, you will dispose of the nigger cholera victim as quickly as possible. If we can find anyone who can read the prayers for a Christian funeral, we'll give Cugino a proper burial at sea, even though I doubt he was ever a Christian. Five, I want you to take over the disciplinary and security duties of our late bo's'n. I want you to organize the able-bodied slaves into work details to help you flush the shit and corruption out of the hold. That dead nigger may have had a point there.'

The captain paused and looked wistfully at the body of the dead Trafalgar lying on deck.

'Six, after the carpenter has bandaged up our friend Verder,' the captain went on, 'I want him to make sure we have no more cholera aboard. And last, I'll want you to resume your regular duties and get us the hell under full canvas again. We've been blown at least forty miles off our course, and we're behind schedule. Got that all clear, Mr Reddy?'

'Aye, sir,' the first mate replied.

'Good. Fine, Red.' The skipper grinned and relaxed his formal command manner. 'When you have somethin' to report, come and tell me about it.' The skipper disappeared into the wheelhouse.

*

While Joe the carpenter was smearing Tommy's battered face with nards and ointments, prior to putting on the bandage, two sailors were dragging the body of the slave called Trafalgar to the side of the ship. He had been a heavy man, and they had trouble lifting him high enough to clear the rail. Tommy closed his eyes to shut out the sight of the honourable Fanti being consigned to the deep. He could not, however, shut his ears to the dread sound of the splash that spelled the end. He opened his eyes and stood up to see the turbulent spot of boiling foam drifting past to mark the slave's disappearance in the clean vastness of the sea. He tried not to notice the sinister black triangles that streaked the surface of the water and began circling the spot before it was lost to sight.

Fascinated, Tommy remained on deck while the macabre proceedings continued. He had expected to feel no regret when the body of the bo's'n was hoisted from the hold, but when he saw the pitiful bloody mass of what had once been Cugino's sneering face, he could not repress a few qualms of compassion on behalf of humanity in general. Nobody could be found to read a prayer for the hard-boiled shipmate of Nez-Coupé-Chizighola, but because he was a member of the complement of the *Sainte Claire,* his body was lashed in sail cloth before being slid into the sea.

No such niceties were accorded the body of the nameless slave dead of cholera. Not only was he swung into the sea with the same rope that had hoisted him from the hold, but the rope itself was jettisoned. The sailors who had touched the cadaver decontaminated themselves by rubbing their hands with crushed tobacco and potato peelings.

Tommy forced himself to go below with Joe the carpenter on his medical inspection of those two hundred slaves still fettered in their bunks. To his dismay they found another dead man and two more slaves dying, according to Joe, of cholera.

'Gotta gettem outa here right away,' said Joe.

'All three?' Tommy dreaded the answer.

'All three.'

'What will you do with the two who aren't dead?'

'Overboard,' said Joe.

'What?' Why was Tommy shocked? Was the one-eighth

Negro blood showing through? Was the compassion of a runaway slave fighting the white man's mentality he had tried so hard to develop? Of course not. He deplored the waste, that's all. He had already lost three of his slave cargo. 'How can you toss a nigger overboard while he's still alive?'

'They sick.' Joe twisted one end of his long white mustachios. 'Captain's orders.'

'But they might get well, Joe. You can't just dump a thousand dollars in the sea. Let's give them a chance to get well.'

'Captain's orders,' said the carpenter, attacking the other end of his moustache. 'They got the cholera. Captain don't want nobody else catching the cholera.'

'I can't believe the skipper is so anxious to throw away La-Fitte money,' Tommy said. 'I'm going to speak to him.' And he climbed the ladder.

But Captain MacFarland was deaf to arguments.

'Can't risk it,' he said. 'They'll probably die anyhow. And I'll not have a cholera epidemic in my fo'c's'le.'

'The LaFittes'll be mad as hornets at all that money gone to the bottom.' Tommy shook his head at the thought of the angry reproaches he was bound to get for losing part of his cargo.

'Come, come, lad.' The captain tried to smile paternally. 'The LaFittes are rich men because they like to squeeze a dollar, but they're businessmen. They expect normal losses. What's yer debit count so far?'

'Five,' said Tommy, 'including the one you shot.'

'A piddlin' pittance. Less than two per cent of three hundred,' said the captain with a gesture that could have been intended to wave away an imaginary gnat. 'In this trade, Verder, a ten per cent loss is always expected. Remember, yer dealin' in a perishable commodity, and a twenty per cent shrinkage is acceptable. Yer doin' fine, lad. Why not go aft and diddle one o' yer fancy wenches. Just leave it to MacFarland to get the rest o' yer cargo safe to port.'

Despite the captain's half-facetious disposal of the matter, Tommy worried over how his maiden performance as a slave trader would look in the eyes of men like Jean LaFitte and René Beluche. If he lost many more of his blacks he could say good-bye to his expectations of a fat bonus, fat enough to ransom Chloe. He did not 'go aft and diddle'. He steeled himself to the ordeal of watching the execution of the captain's sanitary measures. He was not alone – a fact that added to the solemnity of the occasion. The hundred rebel Negroes who had been disarmed – if manacles could be called arms – and herded together under armed guard near the forward hatch, were interested spectators also.

The casual watery discard of the mortal remains of the second anonymous cholera victim was witnessed in silence by both Tommy and the slaves. The second burial – that of the living patient – was also accomplished without much emotion because the victim was comatose and so far gone he did not struggle when he went over the rail. The third, however, was something else again.

The third was a big black Ashanti from the Gold Coast. He knew very well what was happening to him, and although he had been so dehydrated and debilitated by the diarrhoea and vomiting caused by the disease that he was unable to put up effective resistance, he was certainly determined to cling to life. He fought with the seamen who hauled him out of the hold. His lack of strength was almost compensated by the reluctance of his executioners to come into physical contact with a sufferer from a deadly disease. Even though he was overpowered, however, he could not be silenced. Although his shrill screams were incomprehensible to Tommy, their meaning was quite clear. He did not want to die. His screams became howls and his howls swelled to shrieks as his captors overcame his feeble struggles and dragged him across the deck. Tommy was sure that as long as he lived he would never forget that final wail which ended in a splash and a horrid gurgling.

He turned his back so he would not have to watch the sinister black fins streaking towards the spot for the *coup de grâce* ...

It was not until the quarrelling sharks had drifted far behind the *Sainte Claire* that Tommy realized he had missed the chance for a little target practice with his new-fangled multiple-shot pistol. He certainly needed to learn how to use it if it were not to fail him in an emergency the way it had failed the late Trafalgar. What better targets were there to practise on than cruising sharks?

Tommy retrieved the gun from Vincente, who, he found, had been put to work in the hold. Vincente had hidden the pistol in one of the many pockets in the voluminous folds of his Cuban shirt. Vincente had already discovered why the pistol had not fired for Trafalgar. He explained to Tommy that Trafalgar had not released the safety catch – 'See. Right here.' – which locked the trigger and prevented the gun from going off.

Back on deck Tommy practised shooting at brightly-coloured jellyfish that floated past. He quickly mastered the mechanism that allowed him to fire consecutive shots in fairly quick succession. Rotating the cylinder by hand to bring fresh bullets to the barrel was a little awkward at first but it was certainly faster and more convenient than reloading separately after each shot...

Curious, the strange turns fate took. He had bought the gun for protection against his enemy Cugino, and now the bo's'n was dead by another's hand. Tommy had not had to use the pistol. Still, he would not let it out of his possession in the future. With the atmosphere aboard still heavy with the threat of violence, he would keep it always loaded and always on his person. It was very smart of Vincente to think of the gun when the mutiny had started. That reminded him: he must call the captain's attention to Vincente's exemplary behaviour during the crisis. Perhaps the skipper would give the boy a reprieve...

Tommy intercepted Captain MacFarland on his way back to the wheelhouse after taking a much-needed half-hour nap. He had noticed Vincente in action during the trouble, the skipper said, and agreed that the boy should be rewarded. After he had finished helping out with the sanitizing of the hold, he would allow him his freedom to serve as body servant to Tommy.

'Bright lad,' said the skipper. 'Incidentally, Verder, I have a message for ye from one of the wenches ye drydocked in my cabin. Remember a sprightly trollop named Rosita?'

'Indeed I do.' Tommy certainly did remember Rosita – she with the plump, friendly vagina.

'Well, Rosita sends word that she'd like to see ye at yer earliest convenience. I gather it's a private matter.' The captain winked broadly. 'By the bye, Verder, do I recall correctly that ye mentioned smuggling aboard that counterfeit nun for my personal inspection and possible approval?'

'Aye, that I did.' No doubt about it, Tommy was getting to talk like MacFarland.

'Then lad, now that the sea has calmed somewhat and we are on course again,' the skipper said, 'I think the time may not be far off when I might give serious consideration to your offer.'

29

The first shore birds had appeared that morning and were now riding a following wind as they hovered hopefully over the *Sainte Claire*. The breeze carried new smells – the scent of damp foliage with just a hint of wood smoke.

'We'll make a landfall by sunset,' said Captain MacFarland. 'If the wind holds, we'll be in Grand Terre before the sun's over the yardarm tomorrow.'

Tommy heard the announcement with mixed feelings. He was happy to return to Barataria because that meant he would be close to New Orleans and his beloved Chloe. Still he felt trepidation over the thought that the LaFitte judgment on his mission was now imminent.

The last days of the voyage from Havana were comparatively uneventful. He had lost two more slaves – an insignificant figure, according to MacFarland. He supposed he should consider himself lucky that the captain's Draconian measures had prevented the cholera outbreak from assuming epidemic proportions.

First mate Reddy had taken command of the slaves and their quarters and proved himself an efficient manager. He had brought the whole coffle up out of the hold and made them live on deck for twenty-four hours of cold tropical night, warm tropical rain and burning tropical sun while he had the hold flushed out. He then fumigated the space by burning brimstone and tobacco leaves.

The tobacco leaves were the mate's idea. Personally, he said, he found the stink of brimstone as bad as the stink of niggers, but since that foul odour could kill rats and roaches it ought to be foul enough to exterminate whatever evil humours brought on the cholera. But he bought the tobacco leaves in Cuba because he thought the pleasant smell when they burned would tame the brimstone. He didn't share the popular idea that tobacco leaves alone were a cure-all.

They were certainly a failure as far as counteracting the odour of brimstone. The *Sainte Claire* reeked of sulphur for days and still smelled faintly sulphurous as they approached Barataria. The smell of course offended the three putative peeresses. The other nine female Fancies also wrinkled their noses prettily at the pervading reek, but their loudest protests were against the quality and quantity of the food. Since the storm had played havoc with the galley and the galley stores, everybody had been on short rations.

The wenches also complained that Tommy had been rationing himself too closely. Since his responsibility for the final transport and welfare of the slaves had been impressed upon him by the events of the first days of the homeward voyage, he had been neglecting his planned classification of his female purchases according to their physical characteristics. He had been spending a good deal of his time practising with his patented rotary-feed pistol. He also spent considerable time in the hold, making sure that his live cargo would arrive in the best of shape. As a consequence some of the wenches had been deprived of his favours. He had by no means spent a monastic ten days, but he had not functioned as he had anticipated.

All grousing among the trollops stopped, however, as soon as word was passed that landing was imminent. Primping and prettification became a full-time occupation.

At daybreak the *Sainte Claire* had passed the long fingers of muddy water that marked the protrusion of the Mississippi delta into the Gulf. By midmorning they were approaching the islands guarding the entrance to Barataria Bay, but Captain MacFarland cautiously kept his course more than three miles off shore, outside the territorial limits of the United States. A lookout in the crow's-nest kept his spyglass on a constant 360-degree watch around the horizon. When he shouted the word that there were no U.S. revenue cutters in sight, Captain MacFarland came about sharply, and the *Sainte Claire,* the colours of the Republic of Cartagena (whose letters of marque she carried) flying from the mainmast, headed for Grand Pass. Tommy had to admire the Captain's seamanship as the barque slid neatly between Grand Isle and Grand Terre and shortened sail. It was shortly before noon when the last of the torn and patched canvas fluttered down and the lines were made fast to the dock at Grand Terre.

The *Sainte Claire* had apparently been spotted by a land-based lookout before she came through the pass, for there was a small crowd already waiting on the dock. As Tommy stood on deck waiting for the gangplank to be raised, he spotted the figure of a husky man in a scarlet broadcloth coat and skin-tight white trousers. So René Beluche had come personally to greet them.

René was the first man aboard. After shaking hands with Captain MacFarland he threw his arms around Tommy's shoulders as though welcoming a long-lost friend.

'Good to see you, Tommy boy,' he said. 'We were half expecting you last week. From the looks of your ragged canvas and the cock-eyed yardarm you must have hit some dirty weather.'

'On the contrary,' Captain MacFarland interposed. 'The dirty weather hit us.'

'I've got a lot to tell you, René, as soon as we wind up our business at hand,' Tommy said.

Beluche was staring at Vincente who stood by the gang-plank with Tommy's bags. 'I see you got yourself a new boy,' he said. 'What happened to that black youngster you had? What was his name? Ramon?'

'He got himself killed in Havana,' Tommy answered. 'Stabbed to death. This kid here is really a stowaway. Sneaked aboard without my leave. What happens to him here is up to Monsieur LaFitte.'

'Jean is in New Orleans this week,' Beluche said. 'I'll make the decision for him. Do you want to keep the boy?'

'Yes, I do. Vincente has been very useful to me both in Havana and aboard ship.'

'Far as I'm concerned he's earned his passage,' the captain said.

'Keep him then,' Beluche said. 'Take him up to your house and introduce him to Gretchen. She's waiting for you impatiently. I'll take a quick look at your *bozals* while you're gone.'

As he stepped off the gangplank, Tommy felt like kissing the solid ground. Grand Terre was no Garden of Eden, God knows, but after the long nightmare of the return voyage any corner of terra firma would resemble paradise. Hurrying home, he found that even the shabby huts he passed on his way to the third house from the corner on River Street had a pleasant homey look.

Vincente was straggling behind, setting down the heavy bags now and then to pant and look around him. He was obviously puzzled by the mixture of neat cottages and neglected hovels, and he was impressed by the big brick LaFitte mansion at the end of the tree-lined street.

'That big red house up ahead, Señor Tommy, that where we gonna live?' he asked.

Tommy shook his head.

'I should say not,' he said. 'That's where the big chief lives. That's the Jean LaFitte's house. My place is that cottage just beyond the corner.'

The news of the *Sainte Claire*'s arrival had apparently preceded him by word of mouth, for the Junoesque Gretchen was standing outside the front door waiting. Even her plain blonde wholesomeness looked good to Tommy, although he could certainly not complain of any lack of feminine companionship during his absence. She opened her arms and clasped him to her pneumatic bosom.

'Welcome, welcome, Mr Tommy,' she gushed. '*Ich bin so glüklich!* I was lonely here.'

'Glad to be back, Gretchen. I missed you, too,' he lied. 'I brought you a little present from Cuba. But first meet Vincente. He's going to work here a while.'

'So?' Gretchen stared at the curly-haired boy with surprise

tinged with hostility. She wasn't sure she was going to like the idea of a stranger in the house. 'Where's that black boy you had? Where's Ramon?'

'Ramon is dead. Got himself killed down there in Havana.'

'Ach, schade! What a shame!' Gretchen seemed genuinely touched by the news of Ramon's death, although she had certainly yelled at him and browbeat him unmercifully when he was alive. 'Did you buy this fellow in Havana, Tommy?'

Tommy worked himself free of Gretchen's embrace.

'Vincente's not my property, Gretchen,' he said, 'but he'll be my servant for the time being and help out around the house. Monsieur LaFitte will have to decide what he wants done with him when he gets back from New Orleans.' He looked sternly at Vincente. 'We may send him back to Havana.'

'Oh no, please no, Señor Tommy. I wanna stay with you, Señor Tommy.' The lad seemed about to burst into tears.

'I told you we'd have to wait and see,' Tommy said. 'But right now you can unpack my bags. Gretchen will show you where to put my stuff. And you do whatever she tells you, you hear, Vincente?'

'I hear, Señor Tommy.'

'And no Señor Tommy while you're in the United States. It's Mr Tommy here.' He turned to Gretchen. 'Box his ears if he doesn't behave, Gretchen. I'll see you for dinner.'

He started for the docks at a fast lope, but soon dropped to a walk. Funny he should forget so quickly that in Louisiana, too, perspiration lies close beneath the skin.

Tommy found René Beluche in the captain's cabin, having a drink with MacFarland and the first mate.

'Nice work, Tommy,' was Beluche's greeting. 'You picked a fairly good assortment of bucks. You've developed a pretty shrewd eye on your first buying trip.'

'You think M'sieur LaFitte will be pleased?' asked Tommy eagerly. 'He won't be too unhappy about our losing seven niggers on the way up?'

'He always expects to lose a few.' Beluche drained the glass before him. 'And the survivors ain't in what you'd call the peak of condition after the trip. Fact is, some of 'em are downright seedy. But we'll fatten 'em up some and have 'em rested and oiled and in good shape by the time Jean gets back.'

'Did you get a look at the wenches I bought from Solano?' Tommy was still thirsty for praise.

'I got a quick look.' Beluche put down his glass. 'On the whole you brought back a good marketable product. Some of 'em are real elegant – ought to make old man Gaspard Cossette piss his britches for wanting to get into all of them at once. There's one, though, that's a little on the dark side. The one with the bird-cage hair.'

'That's the princess,' Tommy explained. 'I got her cheap – only sixty dollars. Solano was glad to get rid of her. Wanted to have her whipped for acting up sassy. If you don't want her, I'll buy her back. I think I can make a good deal for her. She's damned good. And you never saw such twat hair. Reaches from her bellybutton nearly to her knees.'

Beluche reached over to poke Tommy playfully in the stomach. 'Guess you can guarantee them all personally, hey, Tommy?' he said. 'Tested and found up to sample, yes?'

Tommy laughed with mock bashfulness. 'They've all got what it takes,' he said. 'I picked the best the old fart had on hand. What happens to them next?'

'Jean wants to put 'em up in one of the guest houses till he gets back. We got a couple of fat black mammas to feed 'em and get 'em back in shape.' Beluche winked broadly. 'And keep the doors locked against horny trespassers looking for a free piece.'

'These wenches can protect themselves,' Tommy said. 'They bite. One cute little bitch bit off one of the balls of the Vice-Governor of Cuba. I had to smuggle her past the Havana police to get her aboard.'

'But she didn't make a soprano out of *you*, apparently.' Beluche laughed. 'Or doesn't she like white meat?'

'I kept my chastity belt on,' Tommy said. 'By the way, if you're going to keep the wenches locked up, do I get a pass-key?'

'You?' Beluche's laughter became a guffaw. When he had caught his breath, he said: 'Tommy boy, you won't need a pass-key. If I'm any judge of what you've been shoving into these wenches – and don't forget I've seen you at work – as

298

soon as they find out where you live, they'll be jumping out the windows and racing each other to get to your place.'

'The lad's probably hung like the bells of St Swithin's,' Captain MacFarland volunteered. 'His sea-goin' wenches speak highly of him.' He seemed to notice for the first time that Tommy was still standing. 'If yer goin' to yarn much longer with this blackbirder here, ye'd better sit down, lad. Ye might even drip yersel' a drap of the elixir here.'

The captain's burr indicated that he had personally been dripping the elixir for some time already.

Tommy sat down but did not avail himself of the elixir. 'Seriously, René,' he said, 'what's my next step in seeing this Cuban deal of mine through to a conclusion?'

'Your part?' Beluche was pouring himself another drink. 'Just sit tight, Tommy boy. If you want the honour of escorting your wenches to the guest house, fine. But the business of the *bozals* is all a matter of routine. Mosho and his strong-arms will be down this afternoon to get them up to the stockade. From then on, it's all in the hands of Jean LaFitte.'

Tommy squirmed uneasily in his chair.

'You think maybe he might want me to take the coffle up to New Orleans to auction off on the vendue table – at the Hotel St Louis, maybe?'

'Maybe,' Beluche replied. 'But sometimes he holds an auction down here. The planters like to come to Barataria because they have a real carnival here. All they can eat and drink, and real choice bed wenches. Jean gets better prices here, too.'

'I sure would like to take at least a hundred to New Orleans, René. I really would.'

Beluche frowned. 'What's so special about—? That's right,' he said. 'I forgot. You got a special itch for Helen's daughter up there in Alix's parlour house. What's her name now?'

'Chloe,' said Tommy seriously. 'And it's more than an itch. I'm in love with her. I want her all to myself. I'd like to ransom her from the Academy of Music. Do you think M'sieur LaFitte will give me a bonus for my Havana job – at least enough to make a down payment on Chloe?'

'Maybe.' Beluche nodded. 'How much does Alix want to release the gal?'

'Five thousand dollars.'

'Five thousand?' Beluche whistled. 'That's quite a hunk of dough.'

'I know,' Tommy said. 'But he'll make at least a quarter-million dollars out of my trip to Havana. Surely that's worth more to him than the ten dollars a week he's paying me.'

'True,' said Beluche. 'Quite true. And Jean is usually very generous with his men. He may come through. In the meantime why don't you relax? Be irresponsible and have fun until Jean gets back. Go home and make love to Gretchen and pretend all is right with the world. Yes?'

'I'll try,' said Tommy.

And he did. He didn't realize how tired he was until he got home. He was so nearly exhausted that he didn't really appreciate the homecoming dinner Gretchen had prepared. She had *Kasseler ripchen* – she had no idea how the commissary came to have pork chops, smoked German style; one of La-Fitte's corsairs had undoubtedly captured a German ship, because there was good Bavarian beer, too – and sauerkraut cooked with caraway seeds in it. However, he told her how delicious everything was and went right to bed.

When Gretchen came to bed after overseeing the cleaning up of the kitchen, he woke up and made love to her perfunctorily. Then he went to sleep again and dreamed of Chloe.

30

Mme Alix, Mother Mackerel of the Academy of Music, New Orleans' most elegant whorehouse, had nearly finished her morning chocolate and brioche. Although she wore a frilly pink négligée as she reclined in her gilded chaise longue, she was already heavily made up. Every hair of her brassy dyed coiffure was in place, and her fabulous jewels flashed at her ears and on her wrinkled hands. There was a knock at her door.

'Yes, what is it, Drum?' she called.

'That young man from Falconhurst still here, Madame,' came the reply through the closed door.

'Then show him up in five minutes, Drum.'

Madame Alix spent the interval in verifying the cosmetics of her face in a small gold-rimmed pocket mirror and in making sure the feathery lace of the throat of her négligée fitted snugly enough to conceal the wrinkles in her neck. She was proud of the innate charm which had survived both her years and the brazen professionalism of her calling.

Drum ushered in a well-built dark young man who carried himself with the confidence of success despite an awkward walk that marked the social unsophistication of an up-country planter. Madame Alix extended her bejewelled fingers, and the young man clumsily kissed them.

'Mayhap yo' don' 'member me, ma'am,' he said, 'but I'm Hamilton Maxwell o' Falconhurst Plantation.'

'Indeed I do remember you, Monsieur Maxwell,' Madame Alix said. 'I even recall the first time your father brought you here as a boy. I remember his name, too. Monsieur Warren Maxwell.' Madame Alix's faint French accent was having a little trouble with the Ws. The name came out Varrenn Maxwell. 'How is the old gentleman?'

'Right poorly, ma'am. He so cripped with rheumatiz he cain' hardly walk. He bin dreanin' some o' that rheumatiz outa his laigs to a little nigger boy, but it don't he'p much.'

'Sorry to hear that,' said Madame Alix. She motioned to a spindly gilt chair and Ham Maxwell sat down. 'What was it you came to see me about?'

'Two things, ma'am. First off, guess yo' kin figger I come to N'Orleans to sell a herd of niggers. I cain' decide if I auction 'em or sell 'em at private sale. 'Course Falconhurst niggers git high prices either way, but since that damfool law makin' it criminal to ship in *bozals*, nigger market's way up.' Maxwell leaned forward in his chair. 'I bin thinkin', ma'am, that since all the riches' planters get to Madame Alix's sooner or later, mayhap yo' know some big visitin' plantation owner jes' desprit to buy some high-class Falconhurst bucks at private sale. Mayhap—'

'No, Monsieur Maxwell.' Madame Alix held up her hand to

stop him. 'I'm surprised your father has never told you that any man from out of town is anonymous at the Academy of Music. All the local aristocracy, even the local *haute bourgeoisie*, come here as to their club. I know only their first names – officially. But the planter from New Iberia or Alabama or Mississippi – for me he has *no* name. I don't want to know it. I'm sure if you go to the St George Hotel or one of the big vendue houses, they will give you names galore. But that's not really why you came to see me, is it? Confess.'

Ham Maxwell coloured slightly. 'That right smart thinkin', Miz Alix,' he said. 'Papa always says yo' right smart. He the one say yo' shore to have news 'bout who in town with pockets stuffed with cotton money, lookin' to buy Falconhurst niggers.'

'And the other thing you came to see me about, Monsieur Maxwell? Don't tell me. Let me guess.' Madame Alix placed two jewelled fingers against her temples and closed her eyes as if in deep thought. '*Ah, j'y suis!*' The eyelids popped open and she smiled. 'It's about Chloe.'

Ham Maxwell's jaw dropped. 'Yo' shore a mindreader, Miz Alix. How—?'

'Pooh,' said Madame Alix, picking up her fan and snapping it open. 'No trick at all. Every young man falls in love with Chloe at first sight. She's the most beautiful of my girls, perhaps the most talented. And you spent the night with her.'

'Never had anyone like her,' said Maxwell, shaking his head as though he still didn't believe his experience was real. 'Like to take her home with me.'

'I'm afraid that's impossible,' Madame Alix said.

'Ain't nothin' impossible,' said Maxwell cockily, 'if'n yo' got the money. 'N' the Maxwells has.' The Maxwells certainly had – pots of it, literally dozens of iron pots buried around the big boulder behind the barn. Papa Maxwell didn't believe in putting money in banks or in mortgages where he couldn't count it whenever he felt like it. Actually neither he nor Ham knew exactly how much was buried on the Falconhurst Plantation. A conservative estimate would come to more than half a million. 'How much it take to git title to Chloe?' he added.

'Monsieur Maxwell – or may I address you as Hamilton?'

'Call me Ham. Ever'body does.'

'*Bien.* Ham it is. Ham, this is not entirely a matter of money. I have promised Chloe to someone else.'

'Oh?' Ham made a gesture with his left hand which seemed to say, *So what?* He actually asked. 'How much this lucky gent gonna pay yo'?'

'Five thousand dollars.' Alix closed her fan with a snap.

'Five thousand?' The figure shocked even Ham Maxwell. Despite the hundreds of thousands of dollars buried on the Falconhurst Plantation, the Maxwells were not accustomed to handing out that kind of money, even for a prime stud with other talents to boot. And for a wench, never. Papa Maxwell would die of heart failure at the very thought. Still, there were ways of presenting accounts – a thousand here, a thousand there – when the total take was added up after the blacks were sold. 'Ain' that a penny high for a unproductive wench?'

Alix snapped her fan open again. 'That's the going rate for an octoroon a lot less beautiful than Chloe,' she said. 'There's no use trying to bargain, because Chloe is not available. I can offer other girls of almost equal beauty who are.'

'Nobody like Chloe,' Maxwell said. 'Nobody. Who this rich bastard who think he kin take what I want?'

'Why do you ask, Ham?' Alix was suddenly cautious. She didn't like the note of arrogance that had suddenly crept into Ham's voice. She put down her fan and sat up straight. 'What do you intend to do?'

'Buy him off,' said Maxwell. 'Lik'n offerin' yo' six thousand 'stead o' five, then a-temptin' this rich cocksman with another thousand ... Who is he?'

'I don't think you'd interest him.' Alix shook her head. 'He has an important job with Jean LaFitte. Chloe is more than a matter of money to him.'

'Where kin I find him?'

'You can't.' Alix was being just as stubborn. 'He's somewhere in Cuba on vital business.'

'When he comin' back?'

'I don't know.'

'I kin fin' out,' Ham said, ''n' I kin wait till he come back. I shore hanker for that Chloe, so I'll be comin' back here ever' day 'n' ever' night till I sell all my niggers. Thank yo' kindly, Miz Alix. Good-bye.'

303

He stalked out with angry strides, one arm moving in quick short arcs as though he were brandishing a blacksnake whip.

Alix did not see him again for two days. She did not miss him, but she was uneasy about the way he had left. As it turned out, she had reason to be. When he burst into her ground-floor office in mid-afternoon, his face was flushed, his eyes blazing, and his lower jaw thrust out.

'I bin askin' aroun',' he announced angrily, ''n' from what I hear yo' promised to sell that Chloe to a nigger.'

'Don't be ridiculous, Monsieur Maxwell,' Alix said. 'Please sit down and calm yourself, or I'll have Drum put you out. The man to whom I've promised Chloe is as white as you are.'

'White?' Ham laughed bitterly. 'He fool yo', too. He preten' his name Tommy Verder?'

Alix's uneasiness increased sharply. 'What difference would a name make?' she demanded. Why quote Shakespeare to this lout?

'Plenny,' Maxwell declared. 'Ain' he got six fingers on one hand?'

Alix opened her mouth to reply but said nothing. She was stunned. She could not deny that strange sixth finger which she had of course noticed.

'That nigger he purentee polecat,' Ham pursued without giving her a chance to reply. 'Yo' ain' believin' he mustee, yo' jes' take off his shirt. That stinker got nigger skin down his spine from neck to ass-hole.'

Madame Alix bristled. Gentlemen didn't use coarse language in the Academy of Music, even if it was a whorehouse.

'Suppose he should be a mustee,' she said. 'He's a very handsome one and he certainly deserves a beautiful mate like Chloe. You forget that Chloe too is an octoroon. There's nothing to stop their getting married, in fact.'

'Ain't there?' Ham Maxwell sneered. 'Since when kin a runaway nigger slave git married?'

'What is all this nonsense? Are you trying to tell me that Tommy Verder is an escaped slave?'

'Yes, ma'am. I bin tellin' yo' that this mustee call hisself Tommy Verder ain' Tommy Verder 'tall. Tommy Verder bin long daid. This polecat callin' hisself Tommy Verder ain' got no real last name. His ma call him Calico on account those black spots on his back. Next time he come here, ma'am, yo' je' look at his backside.'

Madame Alix picked up her fan and worked it furiously to hide her confusion. She didn't want to believe him, because she was fond of Tommy and detested this young Maxwell. Yet he seemed sure of his facts.

'I still don't believe you,' she said at last.

'Then I bes' tell yo' the whole story from the beginnin',' Maxwell said. 'Yo' ain' ask me to, Miz Alix, but kin I set down? It a long story.'

'You may take a chair, Monsieur Maxwell.' The fan was still waving nervously.

Maxwell sat.

'Reason I know,' he began, 'is that goddam Calico who call hisself Tommy Verder once belong to me. My papa bought him for me when I was 'bout fourteen. He was goin' to be my playboy. He'd bin playboy for the real Tommy at Dove Cote Plantation. He the real Tommy's half-brother I guess, 'cause his papa bin studdin' around quite some afore he disappear. Anyhow all three of 'em got six fingers on the right hand. The real Tommy, tho', he purentee white. His mother Miz Dovie Verder of Dove Cote. But that real Tommy cain' talk nor hear. He born a dummy, 'n' can only yell 'n' make noises. But he yell so much when my papa buy his playboy that Miz Dovie come over to Falconhurst 'n' buy him back.'

Maxwell mopped his perspiring brow with a blue polka-dot bandana he drew from a pocket of his tight-fitting fawn-coloured pantaloons.

''Bout five years ago Miz Dovie she send The Dummy – that the real Tommy Verder – up no'th where some doctor perfessor goin' to learn him to talk,' he continued, ''n' she send Calico along 'cause Calico could talk. I don't know how they got the names mixed up there, but I 'spect Calico told 'em he was Tommy. Po' Tommy cain' talk so he cain' tell 'em who he was. Calico don' look like a nigger with his trogs on. Anyhow them damn no'theners so dumb they cain' tell a nigger from a white man even if'n he got stripes all over him like a zebra.'

Maxwell leaned forward, gnashing his teeth as he began to

305

relive the impact of what he considered a momumental betrayal.

'Come winter,' he went on, 'the real Tommy died o' cold up no'th. Las' year this Calico mustee come back south. When I meet up with him in Natchez that lyin' bastard tell me he Tommy 'n' I fool enough to believe him, even if'n he talkin' that highfalutin' no'thern talk 'stead of plantation lingo like the rest of us. Never did learn to talk like us, he say, 'cause he cain' talk at all till he went no'th to that school where they teach no'thern talk. Miz Dovie believe him, too. She think he her son Tommy.'

Maxwell clenched his fist as he raised his voice to declare: 'That bastard my bes' friend till I fin' out he a nigger. I can' stand no mustee shammin' to be white. Cain' stand it!'

Maxwell's indignation at his former best friend's deceit was so violent his face turned slowly red and he almost choked. While he was swallowing his hate, Madame Alix recovered her own composure. She put down her fan and asked:

'When did you discover that he was not worthy of being your best friend?'

'When that dirty bastard had the goddam nerve to marry up with Missie Acker,' Maxwell replied, practically spitting out the words. 'Her papa own Twenny Oaks plantation. She mighty pretty girl 'n' she almos' die when she fin' she marry up with a nigger. Mister Acker he like to whop Calico to death. Would 'of, too, if'n Calico'd ever got his dirty mustee pecker in Missie.'

'You mean the marriage was never consummated?' Madame Alix was genuinely surprised. This did not sound like the Tommy she knew, the charming randy rogue she admired. 'What happened?'

'Drank too much corn,' Maxwell said. 'Passed out cold after the weddin'. Couldn't of got it up even if'n he hadn't conked out. We had to put him to bed. Missie took his trogs off 'n' found all them nigger spots on his back. She hollered 'n' yelled so we drug him out to the barn and manacled him on his weddin' night. Miz Dovie Verder she stop us from stringin' him up. Calico her personal property, she say, even if'n he ain' Tommy her son. She only one got the right to punish her own slave, so she take him back to Dove Cote. But the bastard stole a horse and runned. I shore glad to know where he's at now. When he comin' back from Cuba, Miz Alix?'

'I told you I didn't know, Monsieur Maxwell,' Alix replied. Her lips scarcely moved as she spoke, and the icy stare with which she wordlessly dismissed him seemed to freeze his smug expression.

'I'll fin' him.' Ham Maxwell stood up and put on his wide-brimmed hat. 'I warnin' yo', ma'am, yo' keep that mustee away from Chloe. Yo' goin' to sell her to me. 'N' when I fin' that Calico, I goin' to whop him good afore I manacle him and take him back to Dove Cote where he belong. I warnin' yo', ma'am. Jes' don' tangle yo'self up with the law for harbourin' a runaway slave.'

He left without a formal good-bye.

Madame Alix sat motionless for several minutes after he had left. She needed to think. At last she reached for the bell-pull.

'Drum,' she said when the handsome young Negro appeared, 'I want you to send a boy to the LaFitte blacksmith shop on St Philippe Street and tell Captain Dominique You he must come here as soon as possible. Say it is urgent.'

Twenty minutes later the corpulent white-haired Captain You was sitting in the office of Madame Alix's Academy of Music, mopping his round florid face.

'And what, *ma chère amie,* can possibly be of such urgence at this time of day?' he asked.

'Dominique, I think you may be in trouble,' Alix announced.

'Trouble? I, at my age? You must be mistaken, *chérie.*'

'Not you personally, perhaps. But the organization. When does that young rascal Tommy Verder get back from Havana?'

'I got word just today,' said Captain You, 'that the *Sainte Claire* reached Barataria Wednesday noon. Jean is quite pleased with the lad's work. You should be seeing him in a few days I hear.'

'He should not come here,' Alix said.

'Ah?' Captain You held his breath. 'Why not? He's still in love with Chloe, I understand.'

'That's just the point. The young man's in trouble.'

'What kind of trouble?'

'First of all, his name is not Tommy Verder. He's really an octoroon, a runaway slave called Calico. That's why he might mean trouble for the organization.'

'Why should that mean trouble?'

'Does Jean want to be charged with giving shelter to an escaped slave?'

'*Mon Dieu, mon Dieu!*' Captain You's bulging belly shook with laughter. 'My poor Alix, have you forgotten that Barataria today gives shelter to murderers, thieves, rapists, and fugitive brigands of every shape and colour? What do we care if Verder is a mustee and a runaway slave as long as he does his work well.'

'*Tout de même,*' said Alix trying to hide her pique, 'don't you think you should get a word of warning to Tommy? He should be told that a man named Maxwell from Falconhurst, formerly his best friend and more recently his deadly enemy, is looking for him with blood in his eye. He should know that Maxwell has identified him as a slave called Calico because he has six fingers on his right hand. Furthermore he should be alerted to the fact that I have told Maxwell that I had promised Chloe to Tommy as soon as he can raise five thousand dollars. I have told Maxwell that I will not go back on my word, despite the fact that Maxwell will pay more. Tommy – and Jean LaFitte and René Beluche too – should know that this Maxwell will kill Tommy without hesitation, not only to have Chloe, but just to punish Tommy for being a mustee who pretends to be white. *Tu es d'accord, n'est-ce-pas?*'

'*Écoute, ma petite,*' said Captain You. 'How many times have I told you, *maintes fois,* that Jean LaFitte takes care of his people black or white, French or English or American or Spanish – felons and pirates and cutthroats and garrotters – as long as they are loyal to him. Isn't that enough?'

'No.' Alix's jaw was set. 'You haven't said that you will get word of warning to Tommy before he leaves Barataria.'

'*Enfin!*' Captain You flopped his arms like wings. 'All I can do is send word. It must go overland and by canoe through the bayous to get ahead of river communication. Tommy may have left already. I know he is anxious to see Chloe. I can hope. I cannot pray because I have forgotten how. That's the best I can do. I want to help that boy. Will that be enough, *mon amie?*'

'Yes, if you say so, *mon vieux pote*. As for the prayers, I will ask the Abbé Bontemps to act for us. He comes here every Friday.'

31

Jean LaFitte returned to Barataria from New Orleans by the most direct route – overland by horse, through the creeks and bayous by canoe, and the last lap across Barataria Bay by sloop. It cut off the long roundabout journey by sailing ship which entailed travelling the final length of the Mississippi to the outmost tongue of the delta and heading back northwest to his island base. He arrived at Grand Terre during the night while Tommy Verder was ensconced in the comfortable embrace of his placid Gretchen.

After the bizarre exciting amours of the Caribbean wenches and the harrowing emotional experience of the *Sainte Claire*'s homeward journey, Tommy welcomed the homely, *gemütlich* caresses of his blonde housekeeper. They aroused him without overstimulating him, satisfied him without exhausting his vitality, and actually left him soothed and relaxed. He was able to sleep long and soundly, for René Beluche had decreed that until Jean LaFitte returned, their usual routine should be slackened somewhat. Consequently Tommy had been sleeping late and not joining Beluche at the barracoons until midmorning. He had just awakened to the aroma of fresh coffee which Gretchen was bringing him in bed when Vincente burst into the room with the excited announcement:

'Wake up, Señor Tommy – I mean Mister Tommy! – The *jefe* is back!'

Tommy sat up in bed so suddenly he almost upset the coffee. 'You mean Monsieur LaFitte?' he asked.

'Right,' said Vincente. 'Monsieur Beluche's black man

Mosho just now come to our door. He say you must come to Big House in half hour to meet with Monsieur LaFitte and Monsieur Beluche. You want I get your clothes ready, Mr Tommy?'

'I sure do,' said Tommy, scalding his lips with the hot coffee. 'Pronto.' He couldn't refrain from using one of the dozen words of his Spanish vocabulary. He got up.

Vincente lingered in the doorway. 'I told that Mosho you be right on time,' he said. He hesitated. Then, 'Mr Tommy, can I ask you something?'

'After you've brought my clothes,' said Tommy. 'What is it you want?'

'When you see the *jefe*,' the lad said, 'promise me you'll ask him if I can stay here with you. Tell him you need me, Mr Tommy. Don't let him send me back to Havana.'

'I'll do my best, Vincente.'

*

As soon as he reached the door of the red-brick mansion, Tommy was ushered into the big boss's presence by Lionel, the mulatto with the violet tail-coat. Jean LaFitte got up from behind his desk, came around and greeted him warmly with a friendly slap on the shoulder.

'Congratulations,' he said. 'René here tells me your maiden voyage was quite a success.' He nodded to Beluche sitting beside the desk. 'I've already made the rounds this morning to check up on your work, and I think I agree with René. You've made a good beginning – for an amateur. Of course you must realize that you've still got a lot to learn.'

'Thank you, sir.' Tommy was glad that at least LaFitte didn't seem too upset by the slaves he had lost en-route. 'What did I do wrong, sir?'

LaFitte sat down again and riffled through some papers on his desk. 'Of course I can't blame you for the bad weather and the damage to the *Sainte Claire*,' he said, 'but I wonder—' He paused.

'You're not blaming me for the cholera aboard, are you, sir?'

'No, not exactly. But I was wondering if there were any cases among Hernandez's blacks before you shipped them. Did Hernandez try to hide anything from you?'

'No, sir. There was one case of sickness – a fine specimen, a real Fancy – that ended in his death. I had no idea it might have been cholera. Hernandez was quite open about it, and assured me the sick man had been isolated from the rest.'

LaFitte ran his fingers through his curly black hair. 'In a case like that,' he said, 'I think I would have taken better precautions. You've always got to watch out for disease in the tropics. After learning of one man's illness and death, I would have delayed loading of the coffle for four or five days to see if an epidemic was in the making.'

'Captain MacFarland was very anxious to get under way, sir.'

'You'll have to learn to deal with sea captains, boy.'

'You can hardly blame me for the bo's'n getting murdered, can you, Monsieur LaFitte?' Tommy was hoping for a little praise at this point.

'No, certainly not. Cugino was a mean, scurrilous bastard, but he was a good fighter and a first-rate sailor. He'll be hard to replace.' LaFitte brought the flat of his hand down hard on the pile of papers. 'There's one criticism I'd like to make about your mission, though, Tommy. I think you spent too much money refitting the *Sainte Claire* to accommodate the slaves.'

Tommy flushed.

'I didn't build those tiers of bunks because I thought the niggers had to be treated like humans,' he protested. 'The shackles and the chains prove that. Only I wanted to deliver your cargo in the best possible shape. The *Sainte Claire* is such a small ship that if I tried to pack the niggers in a single layer, I could have lost—'

'Yes, yes, I understand that, and I certainly approve your intentions,' LaFitte interrupted. 'But by making a capital investment of that size you condemn the *Sainte Claire* to the slave trade exclusively.'

'You told me, sir, that the slave traffic had become an important part of the LaFitte enterprises.' Tommy was surprised to find himself arguing with his boss. He must watch himself.

'True,' said LaFitte. 'But Captain MacFarland and his crew resent being restricted to blackbirding. The *Sainte Claire* carries letters of marque from the government of Cartagena, and the skipper likes to be free to seize any Spanish cargo he finds. So we may have to charge the cost of re-fitting to this single voyage, and that would make a dent in the profits.'

'Which will still be considerable, you will admit,' said Tommy. Thinking of those profits in the hundreds of thousands of dollars always made him bold.

'True again.' LaFitte smiled as he nodded agreement. 'But if you are going to grow in importance to the LaFitte organization – and I am sure you are – I want you to be cost conscious. People in New Orleans like to speak of me as "LaFitte the Pirate", but it would be more accurate to call me "LaFitte the Trader". I am really a merchant at heart.'

Tommy chuckled to himself. Merchant indeed! With a sales staff of cutthroats and ruffians!

'Speaking of costs,' he said, 'I have a personal problem, sir. René may have told you that my black boy Ramon was killed by a hoodlum in Havana, and I employed a Cuban lad as body servant and interpreter. His name is Vincente and I found him very useful. He boarded the *Sainte Claire* without my permission and Captain MacFarland considered him a stowaway. However he did work his passage, and René has authorized him to stay on Grand Terre. Do you agree?'

'You say he's a bright lad?'

'Very. He's a woods colt of your good friend and agent in Havana, Don Cipriano.'

'Well, well! Don Cipriano!' LaFitte leaned back in his chair and smiled wistfully, obviously remembering some common experience. 'He's got good blood in him, then. Of course he can stay.'

'The only thing is,' Tommy pursued, 'I'm paying him two dollars a week and his keep, until he can make a place for himself in the organization. That takes quite a chunk out of my salary of ten dollars a week.'

LaFitte and Beluche threw back their heads and guffawed in unison.

'Tommy, you have a delicate way of asking for a raise,' said LaFitte when he had stopped laughing. 'First of all, we'll take care of Vincente and depend on you to work him into a job he can handle. Then we'll obviously have to make new financial arrangements with you.'

312

'Thank you, sir,' Tommy grinned.

'From now on,' said LaFitte with an expansive gesture of both hands, 'we'll pay you one hundred dollars a month and free food and lodging.'

Tommy's grin disappeared. A hundred a month was only a little more than double ten a week. His heart sank. Good-bye to his dream of a bonus big enough to ransom Chloe. 'I sort of hoped,' he said, 'that you'd be pleased enough with my purchases to offer me a little lagniappe...'

'Lagniappe?' Again LaFitte and Beluche guffawed in unison. 'Do you expect lagniappe,' LaFitte demanded, 'in addition to your shares?'

'Shares?' Tommy's heart started to beat again but he didn't dare feel elated. Not yet. 'What shares?'

'All members of the *Sainte Claire*'s crew share in the profits of the voyage,' LaFitte said. 'And while I don't think you should have a captain's share on your first trip, we might let you have a first mate's shares.'

Tommy felt weak with relief. Nobody had told him about shares. He asked: 'About how much do you think that will be?'

'Can't tell,' Beluche answered, ''till after we sell the cargo. Then Dominique You figures out the costs and the net profits. Finally we get together with Captain MacFarland and I allot the shares.'

'Think it might come to as much as five thousand?' Tommy held his breath.

'Might,' said LaFitte. 'What do you need the five thousand for?'

'He wants to buy himself a wench in New Orleans,' Beluche volunteered. 'He picks out a dozen beautiful Fancies from Havana, but no, they're not good enough for him. He's got to have Chloe, Helen Latimer's daughter who's one of Madame Alix's prettiest. And Alix has to have her drop of blood.'

'I'm in love with Chloe,' Tommy said. 'I want to see her soon. When can I take the coffle to New Orleans, Monsieur LaFitte?'

'You can't,' was the reply. 'The niggers aren't yet in shape to be sold. Besides I'm not sure I want to put them all on the vendue table. I let the word get around in New Orleans that a big shipment of *bozals* had just arrived from Havana and I'm sure that by now a good many tongues are hanging out. I think I can load up the brigantine *Jena*, now lying in the curve of the river at New Orleans, with about twenty rich planters. They love to come to Barataria because we have good Cuban rum and Spanish wines here *à volonté*. And they eat well here, and *à l'œil*. What's more, they have money and they know black flesh. Any blacks left over I can auction off in New Orleans. *D'accord*, René?'

'*Oui, tout à fait*,' said Beluche. 'Quite. Sorry, Tommy. But love springs eternal. Or is it hope?'

'Whatever it is, I have to see Chloe or I'll go batty.' Tommy pointed his two forefingers at his temples as though about to blow his brains out. 'What about the Fancies, Monsieur La-Fitte? Are they fit to be shown? Can't I take them to New Orleans soon?'

'Ah yes. Monsieur Cosette's order. I think they are in condition for the market. They seem to have been well taken care of.' LaFitte winked broadly at Beluche. 'René, do we have that ketch ready to move up the river tomorrow or the next day? The *Jerome*? She'll accommodate the dainty dozen, yes? Good. We'll ship them on the *Jerome*.'

'And me?' Tommy was sitting on the edge of the Napoleon chair. 'Do I go along with the wenches to New Orleans? I picked them. Can't I deliver them?'

'Of course, Tommy boy.' LaFitte stood up and held out his hand across the desk. 'You picked a lubricious lot and the customers are already panting for them. Right after I got word that the *Sainte Claire* had docked, I ran into Gaspard Cosette at the bar of the St George Hotel. I told him that you'd just brought the finest bevy of bright-skinned wenches that Havana had produced in ages. I thought old man Cosette would go off in his pants. Some of the other plantation bigwigs at the bar seemed equally interested. One young fellow was quite excited. He made the old man promise to let him know the minute you arrived with the wenches.'

'Where do I make delivery?' Tommy asked.

LaFitte came around the desk to put his hand on Tommy's shoulder. 'I've set up this procedure,' he said. 'As soon as the

314

Jerome docks, Dominique You will come aboard. He will have carriages waiting to drive you and the trollops to Madame Alix's Academy of Music. Then he'll get word to Gaspard Cosette who will get first pick. I've promised him that. Then you can auction the rest right at Alix's or whatever Dominique decides. Once your business is concluded you can rush into the arms of your Chloe. When will the *Jerome* sail, René?'

'At dawn tomorrow,' Beluche answered, 'to catch the flood tide at the mouth of the river.'

Tommy rushed home to tell Vincente to pack his bag.

'Where we going, Mr Tommy? Not Havana, I hope. New Orleans? Do I go too? *Gracias a Dios*, Señor Tommy. I mean Mr Tommy. You are finest *caballero* in whole world.'

Gretchen, on the other hand, was desolate. 'Oh, Mr Tommy, you have just come home and again already you are leaving. I have such a fine dinner prepared.'

'Don't worry, Gretchen, I'll eat it. And see if you can find a bottle of good wine in the commissary to go with it. I won't be gone long this time. You won't even have time to miss me. And don't forget – we have the whole night before us.' He wrapped his arms around her plump yielding torso and gave her a brotherly kiss.

32

A light rain had fallen through the night and the decks of the *Jerome* were wet as she sailed close to the wind along a westerly course on the approach to New Orleans. Dawn mists shrouded the Mississippi as the ketch tacked to enter the southerly reach of the great elbow that cuddled the city. Suddenly a flare blazed on the bank, painting an irised halo on the haze. A voice called faintly, '*Jerome*, ahoy!'

A dark craft pushed off from the bank, a single figure in the stern paddling furiously towards the ketch.

'*Jerome*, ahoy!' The shout came again, and the occupant of

what appeared to be a pirogue gestured with his paddle between strokes.

'Ahoy, *Jerome*! I have a message from Captain Dominique You,' cried the paddler.

'Come alongside then,' called the mate on watch. A sailor threw the messenger a line which he made fast to his canoe. A rope ladder was lowered and the man clambered aboard.

Tommy Verder slept through the commotion on deck. He had spent a busy night saying good-bye to his dozen wenches, and he was exhausted, despite the fact that his farewells were restricted in scope, not only by the time limitations, but by female reluctance to have coiffures spoilt just before going ashore. He was fast asleep when Vincente pounded on his cabin door shouting: 'Wake up, Mister Tommy, please. Captain wants you on deck pronto. But get dressed first, I think.'

Rubbing his eyes, Tommy stumbled into his clothes and sleepily made his unsteady way on deck. He was surprised to see an odd-looking stranger standing beside the captain, clad only in a loin cloth. His wet naked torso glistened faintly in the half-light of dawn. His straight black hair fell to his shoulders.

'This man here,' the captain said to Tommy, 'brings a message from Captain Dominique You. Your plans have been changed. You are to accompany the messenger.'

'Where to?' Tommy squinted suspiciously at the strenger.

'He does not say. He was told it was a secret,' said the captain.

'Monsieur LaFitte instructed me to accompany the wenches to an address in Dumaine Street.'

'Yes, I know. But plans have been changed. Captain Dominique himself will meet the wenches and take them to Dumaine Street personally. You are to go with the messenger.'

'Who is this character?' Tommy asked warily.

'I don't know exactly. We call him Pancho. He's a Houma Indian and he's been working for the LaFittes on the river for the last few years.'

'Very well, since you vouch for him.' Tommy turned to Vincente. 'Get my bags.'

'Sorry, Verder,' said the captain, 'but there'll be no room for your bags in the pirogue. Or for your boy either. He's got to stay with the wenches.'

'Damn!' Tommy shook his head. 'But there's one thing I've got to have. Vincente, go get—'

'I already got it, Mr Tommy.' Vincente beamed, proud of his own prescience. 'I knew you'd want that pistol. It's all loaded up with bullets, too.' He handed Tommy the unwieldy weapon.

'Better push off now, Verder, so we can get under way,' the captain said.

Tommy followed the young Indian down the rope ladder. He narrowly missed going into the water as the pirogue slid away from the side of the ketch. Pancho grabbed his arm and pushed him into the bow of the little craft. Tommy teetered, sat down abruptly and waved nonchalantly to the skipper and Vincente while the Indian cast off the line and began paddling strenuously.

For half an hour Pancho paddled in silence. There was now sufficient daylight for Tommy to watch the play of supple muscles under the Houma brave's shoulders as he dug his paddle into the brown surface of the Mississippi. Tommy was increasingly uneasy about the mysterious change of plans. Despite the captain's assurance, he did not quite trust the man called Pancho. Was he really acting under Captain Dominique You's orders? What could possibly have prompted the removal of the Cuban wenches from his hands before delivery? What had gone wrong? Or was this Pancho acting on behalf of some enemy of his?

This didn't seem possible. What enemies did he have? Tommy asked himself. There was of course always Ham Maxwell, his bosom friend as Tommy Verder and his deadly enemy as Calico, the white Negro slave. But how could Ham have found out that he was aboard this particular ketch from Barataria? ... The only other possibility might be Old Man Acker of Twenty Oaks plantation, father of Melissa Acker, the Missie that Tommy had married a few hours before his secret had been discovered. If Acker ever found out that Tommy had prematurely seduced his Missie .. Hell, who had seduced whom? Missie had practically raped him. She had unbuttoned his trousers to get at him. True, he had helped her with his belt buckle, that moonlit night under the big oaktree. But it was an undeniable fact that he had slept with her before their marriage (ostensibly unconsummated), and it was possible that as a consequence Missie could give birth to a Negro baby. If that had happened Acker would certainly seek him out to the ends of the earth to make sure he was appropriately beaten to death or burned alive...!

Tommy squirmed restlessly in his seat and the pirogue mimicked his movement, shipping water from each side in turn.

'Sit still!' ordered the Indian behind him.

'Well, so you can talk after all!' Tommy exclaimed. 'Tell me, Pancho, where the hell are you taking me?'

'You find out pretty quick,' said Pancho.

'Have we got far to go?' Tommy asked.

Pancho again lapsed into silence as he continued to paddle.

Tommy's uneasiness suddenly took a big leap towards panic. With a start he realized he was without his good-luck talisman. The night before he had taken off Helen Latimer's diamond-studded cross while saying good-bye to his prize wenches and in his hurry to dress this morning he had neglected to put it around his neck again. Oh well, he wasn't superstitious anyhow. As long as he had his trick pistol, he wouldn't have to worry. Good boy, that Vincente, to remember the gun...!

With a few quick strokes Pancho swung the pirogue around at right angles and nosed the craft against the sloping bank with such abruptness that Tommy was thrown backward. Pancho jumped out, pushed his boat further up the bank and motioned to Tommy.

'Out,' he said.

Tommy climbed out. Pancho dragged the pirogue through the bushes and over an expanse of mud to what apparently was a bayou. As he nosed the pirogue into the water an alligator rose to the surface before him and streaked away.

'In,' said Pancho.

Tommy obeyed. Pancho gave the craft a final push and got in himself. He resumed paddling with long, slow strokes. After a moment Tommy got the impression that they were travelling across a green meadow studded with blue flowers; the bow of the boat slid through a floating mass of water hyacinths. After a few moments Pancho beached the boat again.

'Out,' he said. He led Tommy for perhaps a quarter mile through a grove of tall bearded swamp cypress until they came to a little clearing. In the middle of the clearing stood a small log cabin. At the door of the cabin Pancho produced a big key from the folds of his loin cloth and handed it to Tommy.

'Inside you lock,' he said. 'Don't open for nobody. Bime-by man may come, but you don't unlock. Man have own key.'

And the Indian disappeared into the trees.

Tommy stood staring at the cabin door for a long moment, fingering the heavy key, listening to the crescendo of his own heart beat, wondering what kind of a trap he was being pushed into. Who was the man with the other key, the man who would come 'bime-by'? If he were a LaFitte associate, why all this devious secrecy? Why was Tommy not allowed to proceed to Dumaine Street with his wenches as previously ordered – Dumaine Street where his Chloe would be waiting?

He tried looking through the single window that flanked the door, but could see nothing. For an instant he thought he glimpsed the flicker of a candle flame far in the back of the cabin, but it was probably an optical illusion. The first rays of the sun were filtering through the cypresses and making points of light on window panes.

Well, Tommy, he asked himself, are you going to stand here all day?

He shifted the key to his left hand. His right lifted his pistol tucked inside his belt. The feel of his grip on the butt of the gun restored his composure. After all, if he had to shoot to kill, it would not be the first time. The instinct of survival had never failed him yet. He had felt no compunction in killing Moe the Magimp, King of the Pimps in New York, when Moe had declared that Five Points was getting too small for the two of them. And later he had not hesitated to use the same gun in shooting Ransome Lightfoot, when Dovie Verder's second husband uncovered his piebald torso. He had calmly gone to bed with Dovie, his putative mother, that same night.*

Tommy turned the key in the lock, put his foot against the

* See *Flight from Falconhurst* by Lance Horner.

door and pushed. When the door swung inward he jumped to one side – stupidly, he decided on second thoughts. Anyone waiting for him inside would certainly let him walk into an ambush. He cocked his pistol, stepped boldly through the door – and stopped.

No doubt about it. There was certainly a candle or some sort of flickering oil lamp in a back room. He advanced cautiously, step by step, his finger on the trigger of his gun. At the threshold he paused.

The small room was carpeted with mattresses. On a mattress in one corner a pile of blankets appeared to be roughly moulded in human form. For an instant he thought he detected movement, but decided it was another illusion caused by the conflict of the brightening daylight with the wavering glow of the guttering candle. To be sure he raised his pistol as he moved to the edge of the blanket mound. He held his breath.

'Who's there?' he challenged.

Instantly the blanket fell away and a head and torso popped up.

Tommy gasped. There was no mistaking the long black hair streaming over the full breasts to the waist. Nowhere in the world could there be luminous eyes and silken lashes like those, nothing to match the rose-petal pink and ivory of the cheeks, the dazzling teeth between the parted red lips. He could not believe his eyes.

'Chloe!' He dropped his pistol and fell to his knees. 'Chloe, Chloe, Chloe, my darling!' He gathered her in his arms. 'I must be dreaming. Don't let me wake up.'

'Oh, Tommy dearest,' she said when she could free her lips. 'I've been waiting for you all night. I must have just fallen asleep.'

'Chloe, my love.' Never had Tommy been so expansive with a woman. 'I've been waiting for months. Let's wait no longer.' He was unbuttoning his fly when she stopped him with a frantic gesture.

'Tommy, sweet, the door is open. You must go quickly and lock it. We are in real danger.'

'We?'

'Yes.' There was fear in her dark eyes. 'Go quickly.'

Tommy ran to the door, retrieved the key from the outside lock, and fastened the door from inside. He hurried back to the girl, a thousand questions churning in his head. They would have to wait. Wordlessly he dropped to the pile of blankets. She was ready for him, clothes and all.

His clothes. She herself was naked except for a flimsy négligée which he easily whisked away. His clothing bothered him more than the unknown danger of which she had warned him. His whole consciousness, his entire being was focused on his fusion with his dream, the object of his months of yearning, the only woman, he was now certain, he had ever loved.

Chloe was the ultimate, the pinnacle of aphrodisia. The dozens of women he had made love to, the exotic wenches of Havana, were all fun and games. He had never really known true ecstasy except with Chloe. The emotion was so strong that he was whirling to a soaring climax before he was fairly buried in her warmth. He cried out. She echoed him. Strangely his desire did not abate with the exquisite acme of his rapture. Neither did his male rigidity. He drove deeper with each stroke. He felt he could go on forever, having orgasm after orgasm, exploding like a string of firecrackers. She kept pace with him, moaning as she clasped him to her bosom.

Suddenly she pushed him off and sat up, listening.

'We're mad,' she said. 'Here we go on as though there was nobody in the world but you and I. And the world may end at any minute. Our world.'

'But our world has just begun, my Chloe.'

'Maybe. We can hope.' She shook her head sadly. 'But you must believe we may both be in terrible danger.' The tone of her voice, the dread which had come into her eyes brought him back to cold reality. He rose to his knees.

'I believe you,' he said. 'But there is so much I don't know. Where does the danger lie? What is it? How did you get here? What made Alix let you go? Why—?'

Chloe laid a finger across his lips. 'Not so fast, my darling,' she said. 'One question at a time. How did I get here? In a fiacre.'

'But that's impossible. I came by pirogue. How—?'

'There's a road runs only a hundred metres behind this

cabin,' she interrupted. 'We're not far outside the city. Drum drove me here in a closed carriage with shades drawn.'

'Drum?' Tommy's eyebrows went up. 'Mme Alix's Drum? What made Alix let you out of the house in the first place?'

'Alix likes you. She detests the man who wanted to buy my way out of the Academy of Music. And she wants to keep you alive so you can go on working for Captain Dominique and the LaFittes. It's as simple as that. Alix is really a very kind woman.'

'But not that kind. She knows how to squeeze a dollar. Somebody must have put up the five thousand.'

'Six thousand.'

'She promised me I could have your freedom for five thousand. That's what men usually pay at the Octoroon Ball,' Tommy said.

'But this other man offered her six.'

'And who paid Alix the six thousand?'

'Nobody paid.'

'I don't believe that.' Tommy shook his head. 'Alix didn't let you go just out of the goodness of her heart, any more than she'd send me her right hand wrapped in tissue paper. You're one of her most valuable assets. Who paid?'

'Nobody paid. But Alix had Captain Dominique send word to a rich widow they both knew. They thought she should know that you were in trouble, partly because of me, and she promised to put up the money.'

'I see.' He did see, and a warm feeling of gratitude suddenly came over him. He was touched. 'Was this rich widow Helen Latimer by chance?'

Chloe nodded and coloured slightly. 'I think my mother is in love with you,' she said. 'I don't blame her. I understand, but I've been terribly jealous of her. I suppose I can't be jealous of her any more, can I, darling? She's given me to you, and with me out of the way, she may have saved your life.'

Tommy leaned over to put his arms around Chloe. He kissed her. 'What's this nonsense about saving my life?' He laughed. 'What's the danger? Who wants to kill me?'

'The man who offered Alix six thousand.'

'And who the hell is he?'

'A client of Mme Alix's.'

'She has dozens of customers. Why does this one in particular want to kill me?'

'Because he wants to take me away with him, and Alix won't let him because she promised me to you.' Chloe did not look at Tommy as she spoke. Her voice was scarcely more than a whisper.

'That's not the real reason.' Tommy was insistent. Was this long-dreamed-of reunion going to deteriorate into a quarrel? Well, let it. He had to know. 'Why does he want to kill me?' he continued.

'Because he hates you.' She was still avoiding his eyes.

Tommy stood up. It was an aggressive gesture. If someone hated him he could not just remain defensive. Still a cold finger of apprehension touched his heart.

'But why?' he demanded. 'Why does he hate me?'

Chloe, too, got to her feet. At last she looked him square in the eyes. Then she reached up to draw his head down so she could press her cheek against his.

'Because, darling,' she said, 'he says he hates all mustees who try to pass as white. He says you are not Tommy Verder at all, but a mustee called Calico.'

The cold finger of apprehension became an icy, clutching hand. His knees dissolved. He threw his arms around Chloe to steady himself.

'Ham!' The syllable was a shout. 'Hamilton Maxwell! Is that his name?'

'Yes, I think so.'

'The bastard!' After all his precautions, despite his trust in the anonymity of the city, that son-of-a-bitch Ham Maxwell had run Tommy to earth.

'Is it true, darling? Are you really Calico, the mustee?'

'Yes, I'm a mustee. But I'll never be Calico again. Never! As long as I live I'll fight to be Tommy Verder. I *am* a Verder.' He held up his right hand. 'See? My birthright. We Verders have all had six fingers on the right hand.'

'All right, I'll call you Tommy.' Chloe kissed him. 'But if you really are a mustee, we can get married, can't we?'

'No.'

The brusque monosyllable affected Chloe like a slap. She winced. 'Don't you want to?'

'Wanting has nothing to do with it. Calico is a runaway slave and you know perfectly well that a runaway slave not only can't get married but has to keep running to stay free. And now that Ham Maxwell has established the link between Calico and Tommy Verder...'

'It doesn't make any difference, darling, whether we're married or not.' Chloe managed a smile. 'As long as we can stay together.'

'I apologise to you for laughing, Chloe dear, when you said we were in danger. We are. Ham Maxwell wanted to kill me long ago.'

'I hate him!' Chloe's white teeth gleamed in a fierce grimace. 'When he came to see me last he had a coiled black snake whip in his pocket. He lashed out with it to knock over a vase across the room to show how accurate he was. He said he could decapitate a man with it.' She shuddered.

'And would gladly.' Tommy gently disentangled his arms from Chloe and walked into the front room. He looked out the window a moment, then, noting there were no shades or shutters, returned to the back room.

'We're sort of exposed here, in spite of being rather isolated,' he said to Chloe.

'Nobody knows where we are,' she replied reassuringly, 'except Mme Alix, Captain Dominique, and Drum.'

'There's also a Houma Indian named Pancho,' Tommy said. He still had misgivings about Pancho. 'He brought me here.'

'I don't know about him. He must be one of Captain Dominique's men.'

'The captain seems to have plotted this thing down to the last detail.' Tommy appeared surprised at the efficient staff work of the jovial captain. He did not know that Captain Dominique You had been an artillery officer with Napoleon from Marengo to Austerlitz. 'What's the next step? Where's he taking us from here? And when?'

'As soon as feasible, the captain said, he will have us picked up. Probably not until dark, but you never can tell. Stop pacing, darling. Don't be so nervous. There's nothing we can do to hurry matters. Don't you trust the captain?'

'I guess I'll have to.' Tommy was on his knees again, groping in the mussed blankets for his pistol which he had dropped when he first saw Chloe. He found it and stuck it under his belt. He got to his feet again. 'Did he say where he planned to take us? Barataria?'

'No.' She shook her head. 'If you're hungry there's a ham hanging in that closet there, and a jug of wine and a loaf of bread.'

'I'm not hungry – for food.' His eyes were caressing her again from head to foot. What an entrancing female she was! His breeches stirred.

'We could always eat to pass the time,' she said. 'Anyhow I'd better get dressed in case the captain's schedule is advanced.'

'Before you put any clothes on,' Tommy said, dropping to his knees again, 'I'll try to think of a better way to pass the time.'

33

Hamilton Maxwell turned off St Louis Street and walked into Pierre Maspero's Exchange through the Charles Street entrance. As he strode across the sanded floor, his gaze swept the extent of the block-long bar. Just beyond the noisy journalists' table, he spotted the man he was looking for.

Gaspard Cosette stood at the bar dripping water into a spoon that held the tiny tip of a sugar loaf. The sweetened water overflowed the spoon to drip into a glass of greenish absinthe. He was a dandified old Frenchman. His long hair and his close-cropped beard were obviously dyed black, and the pale lavender stock was wrapped tightly to hide his wrinkled neck. His écru linen coat, his tight, fawn-coloured trousers, his many-buttoned waistcoat of the same colour and his shiny high boots made an appropriate costume for a wealthy sugar planter and rum distiller, even if it was not exactly the thing for the New Orleans climate. He was so intent on watching the absinthe gradually turn opalescent as the water dripped into the glass that he was unaware of

Maxwell's presence until the young man spoke.

'Monsieur Cosette, I gotta thank yo' fer sendin' word 'bout that boat from Barataria,' Ham said.

'Ah, Monsieur Maxwell.' Cosette put down the water jug but continued to hold the spoon over the glass of absinthe. 'I'm sorry I could not get to the dock myself. Did she arrive on schedule?'

'Jes' a little late,' Ham said.

'Allow me to offer you something to drink.' Cosette slid the sugar bit into his glass and stirred. 'Some absinthe, perhaps? Or a Sazerac?'

'Don' cotton much to these fancy tipples,' Maxwell said. 'Could use a toddy, though.'

'Of course. Jules' – Cosette addressed the mustachioed barman – 'can you make a toddy for this gentleman?'

'If I can get some hot water from the kitchen.' The bartender's eyebrows rose at the idea of a hot toddy in the noonday heat.

'Don't fuss none,' Maxwell said. 'Jes' pour me a slub o' corn 'n' splash in some spring water.'

'Did you see the wenches?' Cosette asked.

'They purty secretive 'bout gettin' 'em ashore,' Maxwell said, 'but I got a look while they loadin' 'em in carriages. Mighty fine lot o' cunt, I'd say.'

'Then you got the first look. You are lucky. *A votre santé*, monsieur. To your very good health.' Cosette raised his opalescent drink.

'Same to yo', m'sieur.' Ham Maxwell downed his whisky in two gulps. 'But yo' get first pick so yore luckier'n me. Hope yo' don' take all the hottes' pieces.'

'There will be plenty to go around, I'm sure, Monsieur Maxwell. Plenty.'

'Got a frien' who'd like a little new quiff too, ifn any's left,' Maxwell said. 'Mayhap yo' know him. He own Twenny Oaks plantation up in Alabama. Name o' Acker. Came to N'Orleans along with me to buy some buck niggers, but he'll look at yore Fancies, too.'

'I don't believe I know him,' Cosette said.

'Yo'll meet him here,' Maxwell said. 'He due soon to have a toddy 'th me.'

'I'd like to meet your friend, monsieur, but—' Cosette tugged at a gold chain across the front of his vest and produced a thick gold repeater watch. He pressed a small spring on the rim and the watch gave off two slow-spaced pings and two quick ones. 'Unless he arrives very shortly, I shall miss him. I have promised Captain You that I will call at Dumaine Street to examine the imported beauties at three o'clock.' He pocketed the watch.

'I'll be there myse'f at three-thirty,' said Maxwell. 'Mayhap yo' still be there an' meet Mr Acker.'

'I hope so, Monsieur Maxwell.' Cosette drained his glass.

'Yo' don' be too greedy, yo' hear,' said Maxwell. He winked. 'Be sure yo' leave a couple o' wenches for us.'

'Don't worry, monsieur.' Cossette paid for the drinks, shook hands with Maxwell, and departed.

Maxwell ordered another drink of corn while he waited for Acker. It was not true that Acker had come to New Orleans to buy slaves. His plantation, Twenty Oaks, was not very prosperous. He was still trying to make a living planting cotton, and the soil was about played out. Acker had even tried to get money from Dovie Verder when the man everyone thought was Tommy Verder was going to marry Missie Acker. It was on account of Missie that Acker was in New Orleans.

When the so-called Tommy got drunk and passed out on his wedding night, everybody thought the wedding had not been consummated. Then Tommy was revealed as Calico and had disappeared. But two weeks ago Mrs Acker had packed her three daughters (including Missie, of course) into a carriage and driven off on a visit to her sister in Natchez. Inasmuch as Mrs Acker had never been particularly friendly with her sister whom she hadn't seen in years, Acker couldn't get rid of the awful suspicion that Missie could be pregnant.

Missie and her mother denied it vehemently, of course, but Tommy-Calico had been such a handsome devil and Missie had been so crazy about him before she found out that he was a mustee, that it wouldn't surprise Acker if the skunk had seduced her before their invalid marriage. The idea that Melissa, one of the real belles of Alabama and the daughter of a highly respectable plantation family, might give birth to a black baby was too horrible to contemplate. Acker would never be able to hold his head up again. The family would be disgraced. He would have to sell Twenty Oaks and move away. But where? It would be hard to pull up roots. Acker had ridden down to Falconhurst plantation to seek advice from the Maxwells.

Ham Maxwell, who had never forgiven Calico for impersonating Tommy and daring to become a friend just as if he were white, had wanted to beat the mustee to death in the first place. He was delighted to join Acker in trying to run down the varmint. He had heard from Bannion, the storekeeper at the crossroads, that the so-called Tommy had been last seen riding off in the direction of New Orleans. So as long as Ham was taking a coffle of niggers to New Orleans that week, he invited Acker to come along. Together they would find Calico and avenge the honour of the Acker family – if it had really been dishonoured.

Acker was a grey little man, an eminently respectable and unprepossessing person, who looked out of place among the flamboyant characters lining the bar at Maspero's Exchange, but he downed the corn whiskey with great gusto as he joined Ham Maxwell. He looked a little less harassed as he set his glass down on the bar.

'Well.' He looked hopefully at Maxwell. 'Have you found him?'

'Not yet,' said Maxwell. 'But—'

'I was afraid of that.' Acker shook his head sadly and pushed his empty glass towards the expectant barman.

'But I ain' lost him,' Maxwell continued. 'I talk to the crew. He's on the boat leavin' Barataria. They sneak him off somewheres last night.'

'So I've come all the way here for nothing.' Acker was the picture of dejection.

'Don' believe it.' Maxwell also signalled the barman. 'Yo' don' know Ham Maxwell, Mista Acker. Ham he git what he start out after.'

'How are you going to find him?'

'Easy.' Maxwell looked about him to make sure none of his fellow drinkers seemed to be listening. 'I spot this Cuban kid on the dock. Cain' hardly talk English but he herdin' these fancy cunts to they carriages. Damn, they fine lookin' wenches! Got to hand it to the mustee bastard, he kin shore pick 'em. Great cocksman. Shoulda known he a nigger the way he hung. Never saw the like, black or white. No wonner gals spread they legs fr'im. Prob'ly even screwin' that Miz Dovie Verder who s'posed to be his mama.'

'About this Cuban boy,' Acker interrupted.

'Oh, yes. I ast aroun' 'n' he come up from Havana with the mustee. Name of Vincente. He go right to Mme Alix's with the wenches, 'n' I folla. I figger soon'r or late he gonna join up with Calico. Then we got Calico by the balls.'

'How so?' Acker was sceptical.

'Jes' trus' Ham Maxwell.' Ham winked with the whole left side of his face. 'I tol' yo' Ham know how to git what he want. When I go to Dumaine Street's mornin' I go roun' to Miz Alix's stable. She got a groom used to be Falconhurst nigger name o' Neptune. Neptune he like me 'n' he like my money even better. When this Cuba kid go fin' Calico, Neptune he gonna folla so he kin tell me whereat he hidin'.'

Maxwell didn't mention the fact that he also hoped to find Chloe where Calico-Tommy was. He had called at Mme Alix's the night before and had tried unsuccessfully to spend the night with the beautiful octoroon. Mme Alix had said that Chloe was occupied with an all-night customer, but Maxwell was sure she was lying. Just wait, he said to himself, Ham gets what Ham wants...

'I swear I'll kill that impostor,' Acker was saying. 'I should have killed him the night we discovered his masquerade, as I wanted to.'

'Shootin's too good for that polecat,' Maxwell said. 'Don' go shootin' him 'fore I whop some meat off his back.' He patted his hip pocket. 'Don' forget my blacksnake here.'

'If I can keep my finger off the trigger long enough.' The hate that had grown out of the fear of his daughter's possible pregnancy put a bitter edge on Acker's words.

'Le's drink on it,' said Maxwell, signalling the barman. 'Le's have two more toddies afore we call on Miz Alix ... 'n' her groom name o' Neptune.'

34

Tommy had no idea how long he had been dozing. First thing he noticed after opening his eyes was that the daylight was fading. When he finally realized where he was, and that he was naked, he sat up abruptly and looked around. Chloe was propped up on one elbow, adoring him with those luminous eyes of hers.

'Now are you hungry for food, darling?' she asked. 'I told you there was a ham in the closet, remember?'

'I remember.' Tommy nodded. 'But right now I have a more important question: Is there also a chamber pot in that closet?'

Chloe laughed. 'No such modern conveniences,' she said. 'And the windows don't open either. You'll have to use the great outdoors, love. I suggest the bayou side – the way you came – for greater privacy.'

'Maybe a few clothes would help my privacy, too,' Tommy said. It was the first time that he had made love to a woman by daylight without wearing an undershirt. It was a good feeling.

When he had relieved himself and returned to the cabin, locking the door behind him, Chloe was dressing.

'Do you know what I was just thinking?' she said as he came in.

'No.' He buttoned his fly. 'Maybe about when we are going to get out of this place?'

'Not at all,' she said, with an annoyed toss of her head. 'I was thinking about how I knew from the first time I saw you that you were one of us.'

'One of us?'

'We're both octoroons,' she went on.

'And you knew I was a mustee when you first saw me?'

'Perhaps not when I first saw you,' she admitted, 'but when I first felt you.'

'Oh come now, Chloe dear. I know that I'm better endowed than most men, but that has nothing to do with the fact that one of my distant ancestors came from Africa. There are plenty of thoroughbred whites just as well hung. And in my experience as a slave buyer I've seen puny blacks, too.'

'Tommy darling.' She put her arms around his neck. 'You know that I've been working for Alix ever since I've had things growing between my legs and on my chest. But all my men have been white – every one of them – until you came along. That made it quite simple for me, because I could watch myself as an objective observer. I did my job well – after all, I know my business – without participating. Oh, sometimes I enjoyed it physically. But rarely. Too often it was physically inadequate, even repulsive, like with your former friend Maxwell. But the moment you touched me, I felt something I had never felt before, somthing new and different and wonderful.'

'That's because we loved each other from the start,' Tommy said. 'It has nothing to do with whatever Negro blood we may have in our veins. I never felt that sleeping with a black wench was any different than humping a white woman.'

'What we have together is more than just love,' Chloe said. She unwound her arms, took his hand and drew him down to sit beside her on the mattress. 'A professor who used to come to Madame Alix's occasionally, a Frenchman, had a name for it. He called it *négritude*. You say you are a slave dealer – yet I'm sure you have compassion. You are not cruel to your brothers. You would not kill.'

'I've killed two men,' Tommy interrupted.

'They were white, I'm sure. You killed to save yourself, didn't you?'

Tommy did not reply at once. It had not occurred to him that he might have shown more compassion for blacks than for whites like Moe the Magimp or Ransome Lightfoot. No, it was nonsense. He felt badly when Ramon had been killed, but he did not eat his heart out. And it was too bad about Trafalgar, too, but he himself might have killed Trafalgar – in self-defence, true, but it would have made no difference that he was black.

'That's all nonsense,' he said at last. 'No use trying to turn me back into Calico after I've decided that I'm going to be Tommy Verder, white. And Ham Maxwell notwithstanding, I'm going to stay Tommy Verder, the man who loves you.'

He kissed Chloe. 'Let's stop this silly argument. Maybe I'm hungry after all. And how about some light?'

The candle that glowed when Tommy had arrived had long since burned itself out, but they found some tallow stubs in the closet and the dark was pushed away.

They ate bread and ham and drank wine out of the jug. They talked of the future – if there was going to be a future for them – after Captain Dominque You had taken them away from immediate danger. He supposed they would be going to Barataria, at least as a first step. Tommy remembered what Jean LaFitte had said before the start of the Havana venture – that the fast schooner *Seraphine* was being readied to rescue Napoleon from Saint Helena and that Tommy might be assigned to accompany Captain You on the expedition.

'Of course,' he said, 'I'll probably have to go abroad now and then, but I have good friends at Grand Terre and they'll look after you while I'm away . . .'

But Chloe had not heard him. She was sitting very straight, listening to some sounds outside. She had paled slightly. Suddenly she leaned forward and extinguished the candle.

'What's the matter?' Tommy asked.

Chloe laid a finger across his lips. 'Horses,' she whispered. 'Or at least a horse. I'm sure I heard a carriage stop.'

Tommy listened in his turn. The darkness appeared to grow more opaque. He could hear nothing except his own breathing for what seemed like many minutes but was probably only a few seconds. Then he detected the faint rhythm of footsteps. He groped for his pistol, found it, and got to his knees to look out the window.

He saw a tiny point of blue light that expanded into a yellow flame then went out – probably a defective sulphur match. He cocked his pistol.

The footsteps grew louder and more distinct as they approached the rear of the cabin. Tommy felt the cold sweat forming on his forehead and in the palm of his hands. His grip on his pistol butt tightened.

There was a knock on the back door.

Chloe's fingers again covered Tommy's lips.

The knock came again, louder.

Silence. Tommy held his breath.

332

The knock now became a tattoo, and above it came a voice crying, 'Let me in, Señor Tommy. I know you're there. It's me, Vincente.'

Tommy breathed again. 'I know him,' Tommy said to Chloe. 'He's my friend.'

'Don't open,' Chloe whispered. 'He may not be alone.'

'Who's with you, Vincente?'

'Nobody, Señor – I mean Mister Tommy. I alone. I bring things for you. Very important, I think.'

'Do I know your family, Vincente?' Chloe was right in being suspicious.

'Please not joke, Mister Tommy. Sure you know my family. You mean you forget my sister Perla so soon?'

'Who's your father, Vincente?'

'Don Cipriano, Mister Tommy, you know very well. He live at 128 San Felipe. Why can't I come in, Mister Tommy?'

'He's authentic,' Tommy said aloud to Chloe. 'Light the candle. I'm going to open for him.'

'You're taking a chance,' Chloe said, 'but it's your neck.'

A friction match sputtered into flame and the candle flared. Tommy unlocked the door but held his foot against it as he opened it a crack wide enough for the muzzle of his pistol. When he was convinced that Vincente was alone he let the lad in, closed and locked the door after him.

Vincente immediately filled the cabin with his voluble presence. He was glad that he was able to bring Mister Tommy his good-luck piece, his golden *cruz talismánica* which he always wore. How come he had left it behind when he quit the ship that morning? He must have missed it at once, no?

'It is important I bring it to you, I think,' he said. 'Or you will have bad luck.'

The gold and diamonds glittered in the candlelight as Vincente produced Helen Latimer's cross. Chloe stared as if she had seen a ghost. Her jaw dropped as Tommy took it from the Cuban lad's fingers and hung it around his own neck.

'Isn't that my mother's cross?' she asked almost reverently.

'It was,' said Tommy. 'She gave it to me. Said it would bring me luck if I always wore it.'

Chloe shook her head as if she didn't understand, but said nothing further.

Vincente then brought forth a jewel case and handed it to Tommy. 'You buy these in Havana for this señorita, I think,' he said. 'This your *novia*, Miss Chloe, no? You are very beautiful, señorita, *muy linda*. Mister Tommy speak of you often.'

Chloe's features relaxed into a smile for the first time since Vincente had entered. 'What did you bring me from Cuba, Tommy darling?'

Tommy remembered buying something for Chloe, but he couldn't quite remember what it was. Havana seemed too far away now ... He snapped open the case and presented it to Chloe with a bow.

Her eyes reflected her pleasure when she saw the golden earrings set with pearls and diamonds.

'How lovely!' She kissed Tommy. 'So you did think of me down there.'

Suddenly her expression changed. She frowned. 'I still think you'd better find out how this boy knew where you were,' she said to Tommy.

'You're right,' Tommy agreed. 'Looks mighty curious, boy, your turning up here like this. Have you an explanation?'

'Sure.' Vincente made a gesture with upturned palms as if to say *What's so mysterious?* Actually he said: '*El Capitán Domingo*, he fix everything.'

'How?' Tommy demanded.

Well, it was a long and complicated story, Vincente said. First of all, he was so busy getting the wenches settled and taking care of the baggage Tommy had left aboard the *Jerome*, that he hadn't had a chance to approach Captain Dominique about the problem of locating Tommy. But when the obese old Napoleonic artillery-man had finished licking his lips over the goodies Tommy had brought from Cuba, he told Vincente that there was no way of communicating with Mr Verder. However, when Vincente explained how important it was to reunite Tommy and his lucky charm and had shown Captain Dominique the diamond-studded cross, his whole attitude had changed.

'He take me pronto to see boss lady, Señora Alix,' said Vincente. 'He tell me, show her that cross. I did, and she get *muy agitada* – very excited.'

Alix had taken the cross into her own hands to examine it more closely, and then agreed that Vincente should indeed take it to Tommy as soon as possible.

'So I am here,' Vincente concluded.

'Who brought you?' Tommy asked. 'Not Captain Dominique, surely?'

'No, no,' said Vincente. 'One of Señora Alix's *estableros*.'

'Her what?' Chloe asked.

'*Establero*. He take care of horses. He drive me. A black man but very nice. Name is Neptune.'

'Is Neptune waiting to take you back to Dumaine Street?' Tommy wanted to know.

'No, Mister Tommy. He already gone back. El Capitán say I stay here with you till he come to move us tonight. You glad I bring your lucky cross, Mister Tommy, no?'

'Indeed I am. Thanks, Vincente.'

'I thank you, too, for thinking of the earrings,' added Chloe, smiling. She was beginning to relax.

'I also bring,' said Vincente, patting one of the capacious pockets of his voluminous Cuban shirt, 'some more bullets for your pistol, Mister Tommy.'

Chloe stopped smiling.

35

'Are you sure we're on the right road, Mr Hamilton Maxwell?' said George Acker as the carriage rattled through the outskirts of New Orleans. His exaggerated formality as well as his slurred speech were due to his consumption of more than his usual quota of alcoholic stimulants. After the few early afternoon corn whiskeys at Prospero's Exchange they had enjoyed Mme Alix's hospitality while they were making their token appearance at the first showing of the new girls from Cuba. They had then dined at the St George Hotel and Acker had gone on to French wines and brandy (Maxwell had begun to ration his intake of corn) while they were awaiting the closed carriage whose driver had been briefed by Neptune.

'Shore am,' Maxwell replied after reassessing Acker's sobriety. 'Trust Neptune, I do,' he added. ''cause I not payin' him that other dollar till we get back.'

'I can hardly wait to get my hands on that ... skunk, that despoiler of Southern womanhood,' said Acker.

'Been athinkin' 'bout that Calico,' said Maxwell. 'Been athinkin' we better not kill him right off. Yo' ain' right sure yet Missie gonna have a sucker.'

'Don't argue with me, Mr Maxwell,' Acker said. 'Just the idea that the impostor wanted to impregnate my daughter is enough to drive me mad. I can't sleep nights, Maxwell.'

'I been athinkin',' Maxwell pursued, 'this Calico still Miz Dovie Verder's proppity. Yo' heard her turn down my offer of $2,500 for him jes' after we find he a nigger. She not gonna thank yo' ifn yo' destroy $2,500 o' her proppity.'

'Do you imply, Maxwell,' said Acker indignantly, 'that my family honour is not worth more than $2,500?'

'Course not, Mr Acker.' Maxwell saw that he would have to humour Acker's drunken indignation. He had been having second thoughts. On reflection he had decided that he would get much more satisfaction if he could return Calico to Dove Cote, then buy him. He could think of many delightful ways to humiliate and torture him for the rest of his life – such as forcing him to watch him in bed with Chloe. In the end, Ham was sure, he would get Chloe. 'I jes' think yo' better let me whop him good, then we take him back to Dove Cote like any other runner. Better gimme yore pistol, Mr Acker.'

'No, sir, Maxwell. I flatly refuse to let you disarm me. It is my constitutional right to bear arms, Mr Maxwell.'

The carriage had stopped and the coachman was opening the door. ''Scuse me for interruptin', Masta suh,' he said, 'but this yere's far's we go. You gotta walk down that there path to Mista Cap'n Dominique's cabin, Masta suh.'

'Wait for us here, driver,' Maxwell said as he steadied Acker getting out. 'We be right back – with two more fares.'

Maxwell patted his hip pocket to make sure he still carried his curled blacksnake whip.

*

Tommy had been pacing the floor nervously.

'What time did Captain Dominique say he would come for us?' he asked Vincente.

'Didn't say exactly, Mister Tommy,' Vincente replied. 'But coming very soon now, I think.'

'Wonder what's holding him up,' said Tommy.

'Don't be impatient, darling,' was Chloe's comment. 'You don't even know where you'll be going next.'

'Maybe Havana,' said Vincente.

Tommy snorted. 'You were so anxious to get away from Havana you stowed away on the *Sainte Claire*,' he said. 'Now you talk about going back. What's got into you?'

'This afternoon,' said Vincente, 'I have good look at whore-house of Mme Alix. I got good ideas. Maybe we open new place in Havana to steal customers from la Casa Josefina. My sister Perla—'

'Forget it!' Tommy was brusque. 'You'll go wherever you're told – and be thankful for it. Captain MacFarland could have thrown you overboard. He does that, you know.'

Chloe clapped her hands in mock applause. She said: 'Tommy darling, since you have now taken over as strict schoolmaster, tell your boy Vincente that Captain Dominique will not need a light in the window to guide him to his secret lair, and that it might be a good idea to move that candle into the other room or put it out.'

'You heard her, Vincente,' Tommy said. 'Do what she says – always, from now on. Take the candle into the next room.'

'Sure, Mister Tommy.' Vincente's response was not exactly enthusiastic. He was obviously reluctant to accept orders from a woman, but he did not dare dispute Tommy. He picked up the candle and walked with leaden feet into the front room of the cabin. The faint shadows of Tommy and Chloe projected on the back wall made giant silhouettes that grew gradually smaller as the light source moved away. Tommy reached out to put his arm around Chloe's shoulders.

She suddenly stiffened. 'Listen,' she murmured.

Tommy listened. He heard confused sounds and turned to face the back entrance. 'Must be Captain Dominique,' he said.

At the same moment there was a crash and tinkle of broken glass. Tommy saw a black streak like the tail of a serpent flick through the jagged hole and disappear. He heard a torrent of indistinct profanity of which he could recognize only a few phrases: ... 'son-of-a-bitch of a mustee ... goddam filthy nigger ...'

He snatched his pistol from his waistband.

Simultaneously the ugly black hole of a gun muzzle poked through the broken window, spewing flame and thunder.

Something struck Tommy in the chest and the impact knocked him down. He dropped his pistol as he fell backwards.

The bullet ricocheted off the golden cross at his breast and ripped across the throat of the girl beside him. With a little cry she fell next to him. Her cry diminished to a whimper which became a horrid gurgle. Her blood spurted over him in ebbing jets.

Vincente dropped the candle, rushed from the front room, picked up Tommy's pistol, and began firing through the broken window. The first shot made a frightening roar. He turned the cylinder and fired again. And again. And again ...

*

'Get down, you fool!' cried Ham Maxwell to Acker. He gave him a sharp shove. Acker was trying to reload his pistol while sprawled on the ground. 'Can't you see he's got a bodyguard in there?'

'Horse shit, Mr Maxwell,' said Acker. 'He's all alone. I think I got him. I saw him go down. I got to finish him off.'

Two more shots blasted through the broken window.

'Get up!' Maxwell grabbed Acker's arm and pulled him to his feet. 'No man kin reload 'n' start a-shootin' ag'in that fast. We gotta git back to the buggy afore that coachman hear the shootin' 'n' run off 'thout us.'

'But I must be sure I got that nigger bastard,' Acker protested as Maxwell elbowed him into the path leading to the New Orleans road.

Another shot rang out.

'Cain' do nothin' more tonight ifn they gang up on us liken this,' Maxwell insisted. 'Need help, we do. But ifn he still alive tomorra we git a legal paper 'n' take 'im back to Dove Cote.'

*

When Vincente had reloaded Tommy's revolving pistol with

the bullets in his pocket, he crept out the back door to carry on his one-man battle. The unknown enemy had disappeared but Vincente fired two more shots just to make his presence known. When he heard the sound of retreating hoof beats on the New Orleans road, he returned to the Cabin.

The candle had gone out. Vincente found and relighted it.

The yellow glow revealed Tommy, his clothing covered with blood, kneeling beside Chloe, trying to coax her to speak to him. Vincente shook his head.

'She stop bleeding,' the lad said. '*Qué lástima!* She dead, I think.'

'She can't be dead! We've just begun to live!' Tommy's was a child's voice, pleading, protesting against what he knew to be true but refused to accept. 'She can't be dead.'

'*Pobrecita,*' said Vincente softly. He set the candle gently on the floor beside Chloe's head. '*Lo siento mucho.* I am very sorry.'

Tommy did not hear him. He was staring in continuing disbelief at the dead girl who seemed to stare back at him with eyes wide open in a fixed expression of sad bewilderment. Despite the ugly gaping wound at the base of her neck, she was still beautiful. Even the waxen pallor now spreading across her face gave her profile the classic lines of a fine carving.

'Chloe, Chloe, Chloe,' Tommy murmured – and was surprised to feel tears on his cheek. He jumped to his feet, annoyed with himself. He had never wept since he was a small boy and even then the tears were tears of rage when the real Tommy Verder, the deaf-mute, used to ride him like a pony and beat him when he didn't run fast enough. And now...

Well, it served him right for letting himself get so emotionally attached to a woman. He gritted his teeth. Never again would he commit himself to love anyone so much that he could be hurt. Once was enough. He could still gladly kill Maxwell for trying to kill him – who else would have tried? – but he was ready to write off Chloe's death as an accident. Which it was.

'Hey, Mister Tommy!' Vincente was approaching to lift the candle. He held it close to the cross which still hung around

Tommy's neck. There was a dent in the centre of the cross and a furrow that bent one of the arms. 'This lucky *cruz talismánica* sure save your life, I think. The bullet bounce right off.'

'And killed Chloe.' Tommy seemed to be blaming himself despite his resolution to keep himself above sentimentality.

'You rather be killed instead?' Vincente pursued. He set the candle down again. 'No, Mr Tommy. I think you can say thank you to that lucky cross and also to Vincente who bring it to you. No?'

'Yes, Vincente. You're right.' Tommy couldn't keep his eyes from Chloe's dead face, now more and more assuming the impersonal beauty of a piece of sculpture. He was fascinated still, even though he was aware that as a person, as an embodiment of not only the ultimate in sensual delight but of that imaginary state of mind called love, Chloe was rapidly fading into the past. And the temporarily deranged Tommy, the soft-hearted romantic Tommy, was as dead as she was.

He was suddenly aware that Vincente was speaking again. 'Sorry, Vincente. But what were you saying?'

'I saying, Mr Tommy,' was the reply, 'Vincente do good shooting with your new self-load turn-round gun, no? Quick shooting make *ladrones* run away, I think.'

'I think there was only one *ladrón*, Vincente, and he will certainly be back – unless Captain Dominique shows up pretty soon,' Tommy said.

As if he had been waiting in the wings for his cue, Captain You pushed open the back door which Vincente had left ajar when he came back after the shooting.

'*Nom de Dieu!*' he roared, standing in the doorway bareheaded, the candlelight gleaming faintly on his fringe of white hair. His round face was flushed with anger as he kicked the door shut behind him. 'Who leaves the door unlocked when I say lock it always? What fool—?' He stopped with his mouth open. He had just noticed the lighted candle and the dead girl on the floor. 'What happened?' he asked.

'We were attacked,' Tommy answered. 'Ham Maxwell.'

Dominique stared at the blood on Tommy's clothes. 'You hurt?' he asked. He glanced at the corpse and crossed himself.

'No.' Tommy shook his head. 'There was just one shot fired. The ricochet killed Chloe.'

'But I heard half a dozen shots as we came along the road.'

'That was Vincente with my new-fangled pistol.'

'A fiacre rushed past me on the road back to New Orleans going like mad. They almost forced me off the road. You think that was Maxwell? Why was he giving up?'

'He thought he was out-gunned. He took Vincente's one-man fusillade for a squad of LaFitte corsairs.'

'Come on, Verder.' Captain Dominique grabbed Tommy's arm. 'You've got to get out of here quick. Maxwell has already got the sheriff of the parish looking for a runaway slave named Calico. There's a fiacre outside to take you on the road to Chalmette. Jean Desfarge will see you to the waiting pirogue. You've got to travel to Barataria through the bayous and the marshes. *Allez! Vite!*'

'But I can't go off and leave Chloe like this,' Tommy began. 'She—'

'You can't do a thing for the poor girl now. She's dead. Leave everything to me. Alix will see that she is properly remembered. Come, Verder.'

Tommy held back. He was getting sentimental again; he couldn't help it. He knelt beside Chloe again, took her mother's cross from around his neck and placed it on her breast. Then he was instantly the cynical realist once more.

'All right, captain,' he said as he got to his feet. 'Let's go.'

'Leave the candle,' Captain Dominique said. 'I'll be back when I have made sure you are in the carriage.'

As soon as he was outside the cabin Tommy realized that Vincente was not with him. He turned and called: 'Vincente, where the hell are you?'

'Coming pronto,' answered the Cuban boy. He had paused to pick up the golden cross Tommy had left on Chloe's breast and dropped it into one of his voluminous pockets. He was now groping over the floor for the jewel case Chloe had dropped when she fell.

'Vincente, dammit, I'm going off without you.'

'Right there, Mister Tommy,' said Vincente, as he added Chloe's earrings to the salvage in his pocket.

36

René Beluche sat across the desk from Jean LaFitte and made a helpless gesture with both hands.

'That man from New Orleans insists on seeing you personally,' he said. 'I'm afraid I can't put him off much longer. He talks of sending the militia to Grand Terre to burn the place down.'

LaFitte touched the ends of his black cavalryman's moustache with two fingers of his right hand. After a pensive moment he asked:

'Is there any danger of Tommy Verder walking in on us while the man is here?'

'Hardly,' Beluche replied. 'From all reports he has a hard time walking at all, the shape he's in.'

'How long is Tommy overdue?'

'About a week.'

'And you think he can't get here before tomorrow?'

'At the earliest,' Beluche said.

'Make sure that he doesn't.' LaFitte slapped his desk. 'See that Verder's intercepted in the bay before he reaches Grand Terre. Have him put directly aboard the schooner *Marengo*. I want to be able to say truthfully that we have nobody with his name or description on the island.'

'And the man outside?'

'Let him wait another five minutes, then send him in.'

When Beluche had left, LaFitte arose, came out from behind his desk and crossed to the opposite wall to look at himself in an ornate gilt-frame Louis Fifteenth mirror. He had been warned that a man of the law would be down from New Orleans and he wanted to be dressed in a manner befitting the Lord of Barataria when the man arrived. He ran his fingers through his dark curly hair and nodded his strong pointed chin in approval of his favourite costume – a blue cutaway jacket with wide lapels and brass buttons. He adjusted the embossed leather sword belt and drew his sabre an inch from the scabbard before clicking it back. He was standing in front of his desk when the man from New Orleans was ushered in.

The newcomer was a husky six-footer in civilian clothes.

'Monsieur LaFitte, my name is Petit,' he announced. 'I have a warrant signed by Governor Claiborne of the State of Louisiana calling for the arrest of a fugitive slave by the name of Calico, alias Tommy Verder. Where is he?'

'I don't know, Mr Petit,' said LaFitte, giving the name the French pronunciation while reflecting that it was a misnomer for a man of such burly proportions. 'But if I did know I am not sure I would tell you. We in Barataria do not recognize the authority of the state of Louisiana. Many of us have lived here under French rule and some of us since the land belonged to Spain. We have our own laws here.'

'Ah?' Mr Petit started unrolling an official-looking document. 'Do they tolerate murder, Monsieu' LaFitte?'

'In certain circumstances.' LaFitte smiled, remembering the time he had shot one of Vincent Gambi's lieutenants for questioning his authority. 'Is your runaway slave – what's his name? – a murderer?'

'The so-called Thomas Verder killed a prostitute,' Mr Petit said.

'In what brothel was this?' LaFitte was still smiling.

'No brothel.' Petit was grim. 'In a cabin belonging to the Brothers LaFitte on the outskirts of New Orleans.'

'Well! That brings the matter to my doorstep, *n'est-ce pas*? There are witnesses of course?'

'Of course. Two gentlemen from Alabama. One of them formerly owned this so-called Verder. They were looking for him to return him to his plantation when they saw the killing. They had to flee for their own lives when he and four of his accomplices opened fire on them. I have information that he and his accomplices are here in Grand Terre.'

'Please sit down, Mr Petit.' LaFitte waved to a chair and resumed his own seat behind the desk. He stopped smiling. 'I give you my word, Mr Petit, that your man Verder is not on this island or Grand Isle either. I know that you and your people call me LaFitte the Pirate and therefore regard my solemn word as worth no more than ... than ... *une crotte de chien*. A dog turd. Therefore, Mr Petit, we want you to assure yourself that your man is not here. Monsieur Beluche will go with you to show you around and to open any door that is locked. Or, if you had rather, go alone. Satisfy yourself. Take several days, if you like. Be our guest. We rather pride ourselves on our food here, and we have recently received some vintage wines from France. And I want you to stay as long as you like. I will furnish transportation whenever you are sure that I am not harbouring a criminal.'

'Thank you, Monsieur LaFitte, you are very kind,' said Petit, looking very glum. 'I accept your invitation. But I think I should like to look around by myself for a while.'

*

When Tommy Verder's pirogue slid into the upper end of Barataria Bay near Pointe à la Hache he should have felt elated, but he did not have the strength. He was still some twenty miles from the end of his journey, but the final end would be smooth paddling for only a few hours. He didn't care. He was exhausted physically and listless mentally. He lay back on the boughs with which Vincente had lined the canoe and tried to remember all that had happened during the past ... how many days had it been?

The phantasmagoria had begun shortly after he had said goodbye to Captain Dominique. The first thirty-six hours had been nasty but bearable – a constant change from waterborne transport to portage across knee-deep mud and slush, through clouds of fierce mosquitoes, down creeks a-squirm with water snakes. He slept only in snatches while the pirogue was crossing the comparative quiet of alligator-infested bayous.

The fever began rising at the end of the first day. The second morning he was burning up. His face and arms were so flushed that Vincente commented:

'You don't feel good, Mister Tommy?'

Tommy, who had never had a sick day in his life, had to admit that something might be wrong: he wasn't quite up to snuff. But he kept up with the progress of his relentless guides – until the pain struck his joints. The shoulders and elbows were not so bad, as he was carrying nothing. But when the agony seemed to cut off his legs at the knees, he could go no farther. Walking was excruciating torture. He sank down in the mud and wept from sheer anguish.

Vincente and one of the guides carried him across the swamp to a trapper's cabin where they left him with some hard-tack, a slab of sowbelly, a canteen of drinking water – and Vincente. The guides would proceed to Barataria, report the situation, and return when they had new instructions. Vincente shouldn't worry about the trapper if he came back. He was a friend of the LaFittes.

Tommy lay on a stinking pile of untanned muskrat hides and drifted into delirious sleep. He dreamed of the first wench he had ever had – a mulatto that Ham Maxwell had brought him when he was Calico, Ham's slave playboy at Falconhurst. Then the wench had turned into Missie Acker and Ham had killed her because she had borne a black baby who turned into Jean LaFitte who refused to give Tommy five thousand dollars to buy Chloe from Madame Alix. So he got his self-loading pistol and killed Chloe and LaFitte and Madame Alix and Trafalgar and Cugino, the bo's'n of the *Sainte Claire*. But he couldn't kill Ham Maxwell because there were no bullets left. He woke up screaming.

'You still hurt, Mister Tommy?' Vincente was kneeling beside him, wiping the sweat from his face.

'I'm going to die, Vincente.'

'No you ain't, Mister Tommy. You still got your lucky piece. I brought it along. See?' The lad produced the dented golden cross and slipped it over Tommy's head. 'You get well now.'

Tommy stared at the cross. It looked double. He couldn't remember where he had lost it. It didn't matter now.

'I've got the *plaga*, haven't I, Vincente?'

'No, Mister Tommy. You don't shit right for *la plaga*. You don't even shit at all, so you don't got it.'

'But, Vincente, I've never had such pain.' Tommy closed his eyes. 'In my head, in my legs, my back, all over.'

'Sure. You got the dengue.' Vincente nodded wisely. He was proud of his diagnosis. There were epidemics of dengue in Cuba sometimes. It was very painful – *muy doloroso* – with high fever but people didn't usually die of *el dengue*. After a few days they felt better and got red spots on their hands and arms and sometimes on chest and back...

The spots had already started to appear on Tommy's hands by the time the boatsmen came back for them. As Vincente had predicted, he was in full bloom with the dengue rash by the time his pirogue was approaching Grand Terre. Good thing he wasn't planning a new feminine conquest. He wouldn't be up to much anyhow, the way he felt completely washed out. He must be a rare sight with his spots and a week's growth of beard. Well, he was sure Gretchen wouldn't mind. He hoped that LaFitte or René or whoever got word of his imminent arrival would tell Gretchen so she could have a hot bath waiting for him.

*

Gretchen opened the door to the knock and stared at the tall stranger standing there.

'Is this Mr Thomas Verder's house?' the stranger asked.

'Yes, it is,' Gretchen replied.

'Could I speak to him, please? I'm a friend of his from New Orleans.'

'Mr Verder is not home just now. Didn't you see him in New Orleans? He is there now.'

'I must have missed him,' said the stranger. 'I understand he is due back today, though.'

'Oh, I hope so.' Gretchen clasped her hands in front of her apron. 'He has been away in Cuba for such a long time.'

'But when he comes back, you would see him before he left again, wouldn't you, miss?'

'Oh sure, sure. He would have to come here for clean linen. He didn't take much with him.' Gretchen's face clouded. 'But he wouldn't leave again so soon, I hope. Or have you heard something I don't know. Tell me, sir. Why do you say he is leaving again?'

'I merely wanted to be sure I didn't miss him,' said the tall stranger. 'I understand there's a ship sailing today, and I was afraid he might be on it.'

'Today? You mean maybe the schooner *Wagram*. She sails tomorrow only.'

'Then I'll have time in case Mr Verder should show up.' The stranger turned to go. 'I'll be here for several days. Monsieur LaFitte has invited me. So I'll see you again.'

'Won't you come in and have a cup of coffee, sir?'

'No, thank you.'

'Could you tell me your name, sir, so I can let Mr Verder know who has been looking for him?'

'I'd rather surprise him,' said the stranger. 'He doesn't know I'm here.'

Gretchen watched him go down the few steps from the stoop. Mr Tommy has such distinguished-looking friends, she mused.

37

Mr Petit had a big night on the town. Everything was '*aux frais de la princesse*', according to Jean LaFitte, who added: 'or as you Americans say, on the house.' Jean and René Beluche were determined to get him drunk. With the quail on toast and with the *pâté de foie gras au porto* Petit drank Napoleon's favourite red Burgundy, Chambertin. With the breast of pheasant he drank champagne. And all during the evening he drank Napoleon's favourite brandy while he played *trente-et-quarante* – and won, not being confused by the cognac or the six packs of cards. When he said good night in the small hours of the morning, he had done very well in keeping his feet – and his head.

He was up at dawn to make sure the schooner *Wagram* had not sailed. He had seen preliminary preparations the day before that she was being fitted for sea. He haunted the docks all morning, and when he saw the water casks and sacks of flour being taken aboard, he made his move. He walked up the gangplank to board the schooner, but was stopped before he could step on deck. The watchman summoned the bo's'n, a French half-caste from Martinique named LeMay.

'You cannot come aboard,' said the bo's'n. '*C'est défendu.*'

Petit showed his papers and explained that Jean LaFitte had promised him free access to everything on the island. The bo's'n sent a messenger to get advice from René Beluche. Beluche came aboard himself and confirmed the statement.

'Show him everything,' he said.

And when Petit had disappeared into a companionway, he

added: 'Go with him. Keep him below at all costs for at least half an hour.'

Before the half hour was up a long pirogue came alongside the *Wagram* from the offshore direction. One of the boatmen shipped his paddle and helped Vincente disentangle Tommy Verder from his bed of boughs. They seized a line dangling over the side of the schooner. They propped him up and looped the end of the rope under his arms and around his shoulders. Then they lifted him from the pirogue and lowered him into the water. He sank up to his chin.

'Hey!' he protested. 'How long—?'

Vincente put one hand over Tommy's mouth, then removed it and reached above Tommy's head to grasp the rope firmly with both hands.

Tommy was too weak to struggle. The water was warm enough not to be disagreeable, but he looked around anxiously for sharks. One of the boatmen passed his paddle behind the rope, holding the little craft close to the ship's side. Tommy heard sounds of running feet out of sight on the deck above him. There were shouts of men in the rigging, and the creak of tackle as sails were being hoisted ...

*

'You must go ashore now,' said the bo's'n at the head of the gangway.

'Who says so?' demanded Mr Petit, wiping the sweat from his forehead.

'Monsieur Beluche say so before 'e leave ship,' said the bo's'n. 'We are sailing now.'

'And if I refuse to go?' Mr Petit was defiant.

'Overboard.' The bo's'n made a throwing motion with both arms. 'I 'ope you can swim.'

Mr Petit looked at the two bruisers standing behind the bo's'n and opted for the better part of valour.

The gangplank dropped.

Several minutes after the schooner got under way, the pirogue pushed away at a signal from above, and Tommy and Vincente were hauled aboard.

The minute his feet touched the deck Tommy collapsed from sheer physical weakness and pent-up emotions of the past week. He fell asleep before he could pick himself up.

Vincente and a sailor carried him into a cabin that had been set aside for him. He snored while Vincente pulled off his wet clothes and rubbed his naked body with some coconut oil he had found in the galley.

By the time he woke up the schooner had cleared the Grand Pass and was well into the Gulf. He sat up and yawned.

Vincente tossed him a pair of denim trousers and asked: 'Think you can walk now, Mister Tommy? The captain wants to see you.'

Tommy frowned at the trousers. 'These aren't mine,' he said. 'Where are my trogs? Why didn't somebody have Gretchen bring my own stuff aboard?'

'Sure don't know, Mister Tommy. Can you walk?'

'I can try.' Tommy slipped into the trousers and stood up. He took a few barefoot steps and nodded. 'Lead the way,' he said.

As soon as he stepped through the wheelhouse door he recognized the faded uniform cap and the bib-like grey beard.

'Captain MacFarland!' he exclaimed. 'Am I going to spend the rest of my life in your lap?'

'Ye'll be doin' me no favour, that I'll tell ye,' MacFarland scowled. 'Ye look a bloody mess with all that seaweed on yer face and the wrath of God tattooed on yer arms and belly like a murderin' red Indian. What's been happenin' to ye, lad?'

'I've been through hell, skipper!' Tommy shook his head.

'This time ye'll not be makin' holes in my hull to build bunks fer yer niggers,' the captain said. 'This schooner is big enough to hold a king's phalanx o' blacks without yer fancy contraptions.'

'What happened to the *Sainte Claire*?' Tommy asked.

'The barque's been careened on the beach for repairs. That storm opened up a few seams and she's bein' recaulked. And since I've always been a schooner man, they've given me the *Wagram*.'

'But why am I being rushed away like this without even being allowed to go home for clean clothes?' A worried frown creased Tommy's brow. 'Am I being exiled? Don't I get any bonus pay? Wasn't Monsieur LaFitte pleased with my Havana job?'

'Aye, that he was, lad,' said the skipper, 'and ye'll get yer shares of the *Sainte Claire* profits when we return. The boss has left instructions with me, together with letters of credit and some petty cash for fun and sundries. He wants you to bring back another two or three hundred niggers.'

'Really?' The frown disappeared. 'From Cuba?'

'Aye, from Havana eventually. But first we're bound for Saint Domingue to pick up some of our men. One of our ships foundered and the crew's marooned there.'

'Where's San Domang?'

'An island in the Caribbean, lad. Some call it Haiti, but on my charts it's marked Saint Domingue.'

Haiti! That was where one of his octoroon fancies came from. What was her name now? Antoinette? Yes, that was it, Antoinette, so-called Duchess of Limbé. Not a bad little trick, as he recalled. In fact, he remembered she was damned good. She was the one with the big tits and very busy little hands ... Haiti might very well merit further exploration.

Things began to look up. Life could turn out to be worth living after all, even without Chloe. Funny how rapidly her image was fading. Oh, he felt a little stab whenever he thought of her, and he remembered their last hours together with pleasure and gratitude. Yes, he had really loved her – the only woman he had ever felt that way about. But she was gone now, and life was continuing. Life was a little like the sea, he mused as he felt the deck rise to the easy swell of the Gulf – unpredictable, beckoning to adventure, and teeming with fish just waiting to be caught.

'It's sort of nice to be sailing with you again after all, skipper,' said Tommy to Captain MacFarland.

Kyle Onstott & Lance Horner
The popular Falconhurst Series

Mandingo 80p

Mandingo blood – the finest slave strain you could buy. The
Maxwells of Falconhurst treasured it, bet on it, bred from it . . . and
in the end it wrecked them; tore the plantation apart, with death
and unforgettable dishonour. A shattering novel of slavery as it
really was in the Old South.

Drum 60p

The great bestseller – now a major film.

A sweeping novel, ranging from the jungles of Africa to high life in
New Orleans and the slave-breeding plantations of Falconhurst.
An electrifying story that unmasks the emotional conflicts of
black–white relationships.

Master of Falconhurst 95p

The Civil War strikes the rich Alabama plantation where slaves
are stripped bare in the market-place and sold like fertile cattle.
This is the exciting story of Drummage, the proud and powerful
ex-slave who becomes master of Falconhurst – and of the selfish,
sensual woman who rules it.

Also available in the Falconhurst Series

Falconhurst Fancy	80p
The Mustee	80p
Heir to Falconhurst	80p
The Mahound	80p
Flight to Falconhurst	80p
Mistress of Falconhurst	80p

Selected bestsellers

- ☐ **The Eagle Has Landed** Jack Higgins 80p
- ☐ **The Moneychangers** Arthur Hailey 95p
- ☐ **Marathon Man** William Goldman 70p
- ☐ **Nightwork** Irwin Shaw 75p
- ☐ **Tropic of Ruislip** Leslie Thomas 75p
- ☐ **One Flew Over The Cuckoo's Nest** Ken Kesey 75p
- ☐ **Collision** Spencer Dunmore 70p
- ☐ **Perdita's Prince** Jean Plaidy 70p
- ☐ **The Eye of the Tiger** Wilbur Smith 80p
- ☐ **The Shootist** Glendon Swarthout 60p
- ☐ **Of Human Bondage** Somerset Maugham 95p
- ☐ **Rebecca** Daphne du Maurier 80p
- ☐ **Slay Ride** Dick Francis 60p
- ☐ **Jaws** Peter Benchley 70p
- ☐ **Let Sleeping Vets Lie** James Herriot 60p
- ☐ **If Only They Could Talk** James Herriot 60p
- ☐ **It Shouldn't Happen to a Vet** James Herriot 60p
- ☐ **Vet In Harness** James Herriot 60p
- ☐ **Tinker Tailor Soldier Spy** John le Carré 75p
- ☐ **Gone with the Wind** Margaret Mitchell £1.75
- ☐ **Cashelmara** Susan Howatch £1.25
- ☐ **The Nonesuch** Georgette Heyer 60p
- ☐ **The Grapes of Wrath** John Steinbeck 95p
- ☐ **Drum** Kyle Onstott 60p

All these books are available at your bookshop or newsagent;
or can be obtained direct from the publisher
Pan Books, Cavaye Place, London SW10 9PG
Just tick the titles you want and fill in the form below
Prices quoted are applicable in UK
Send purchase price plus 15p for the first book and 5p for each
additional book, to allow for postage and packing

Name _____

(block letters please)

Address _____

_____

While every effort is made to keep prices low, it is sometimes
necessary to increase prices at short notice. Pan Books reserve the
right to show on covers new retail prices which may differ from
those advertised in the text or elsewhere